A NOTE ON THE AUTHOR

Ros Huxley lives on Dorset's Jurassic Coast and recently graduated from Exeter University with an MA in Creative Writing. After the Covid pandemic she left her job as a charity fundraiser to write, snack and play pickleball.

Kendal Acts Up is her first novel.

Kendal Acts Up

Ros Huxley

write side left

2025

ISBN: Trade paperback 978-1-0685188-2-9
ISBN:eBook: 978-1-0685188-3-6

Compilation & Cover Design by S A Harrison
Published by WriteSideLeft UK
https://www.writesideleft.com

Kendal Acts Up

Ros Huxley

1

This was a whole-day hangover. She'd have to do her fake-flu voice. Kendal foraged for her phone. In the next room, Mad-Maxine slammed cupboards and cursed the empty fridge. Outside, the street was feverish with traffic and overly cheerful builders. Kendal's mouth was dry and her face damp. An outstanding night though; she'd owned the dance floor, snogged the fit DJ, and hadn't paid for a single drink or line. Not bad for a forty-four-year-old.

The phone rang as she found it. Her finger accidentally hit accept.

"Ms Tudge?"

"Who wants her?"

"Gary Vaughan here, warden of Jurassic Court. It's your uncle. Our files say you're Clem's closest relative."

"Yeah, I am. Is he OK?" She couldn't remember a warden. Only shuffling old people, endless soup, and Clem's gold drinks trolley. Kendal pulled the duvet close.

"I'm afraid he's left us." His voice was strong and deep but very slow. Probably went with the job. Talking to zombies in hearing aids.

"But he likes it there. I got a Christmas card."

"Your uncle passed away two weeks ago. I've left a lot of messages."

"I don't answer unknown numbers."

"It happened quickly, his heart." Not cancer then, like Mum and Dad.

"Could you get to Dorset today, Ms Tudge? The funeral's this afternoon at three."

She hadn't left London for months. Too expensive.

"I think I am entitled to, um, what's it called? Bereavement leave? I'll have to stay over though."

"We have a guest room."

"I'm broke."

"It's free for family of residents." The warden cleared his throat. "And the wake is pre-paid. Clem was superbly organised."

An ice cream van jingled and Kendal recalled the cherry ice sticks Clem used to buy. She should have visited him more. Too late now.

"OK, what time and where?"

"Three o'clock. St Michael's and All Angels."

"Right, text me the link."

"I'm not sure I can. Just ask when you get into town." Kendal sighed. Ealing's boomers were bad enough, causing queues at checkouts and fussing on buses, but straw-chewers were worse.

The warden was still talking. "Do you think you might like to say a few words about your uncle, Ms Tudge? We can fit you into the service."

Kendal snorted. "My boss says my presentation skills suck." The warden was silent. Kendal winced as Mad-Maxine slammed the front door. "What's the dress code?"

"It's a traditional funeral. We'll be in black."

"I don't do black. So ageing."

"It's your choice, Ms Tudge. I'm so glad to have got hold of you at last. Please accept my condolences. Have a safe journey."

"OK, but don't call me Ms Tudge. Kendal is fine."

In the kitchen Maxine had stuck a giant Post-it on the cafetière:

K – you owe three month's rent and two month's bills. It's getting ridiculous.
Do not eat the cupcakes in fridge. Josh and his mum are coming round!!!
Leave the bathroom clean!

Kendal stepped into Mad-Maxine's room. She'd told the truth about never wearing black, but her flatmate wore little else. She selected a satin jumpsuit, a black boxy jacket, lacy gloves and a vampy black veil fascinator. Kendal sniffed the shiny material. A hint of cigarette but otherwise clean.

Kendal seized the Post-it pack and scrawled a note:

M – family emergency. Got to go. Will sort out rent soon, I promise.

She opened her phone and emailed her manager at THRUm.

Apologies Deirdre but it's my uncle's funeral today in Dorset. Only just found out. Will have to stay the night.

Kendal stuffed week-end clothes into her pull-along, threw two bananas and a cupcake into her backpack, and hurried to the tube station.

The train from Waterloo had rubbish Wi-Fi, no trolley service and infuriating announcements making it impossible to sleep. It was at least three years since she'd visited her uncle. The tricky summer when she tried polyamory and lost her job at Pret. The train stopped endlessly at places with stupid names and no Costas. At last, they reached Bloscombe. Literally the end of the line. It was almost three. She'd be late for her only relative's funeral. Uber hadn't discovered dead-end Dorset. Kendal wheeled her case to the only taxi.

"To the church, as fast as you can."

"I don't take Goths."

"I'm going to a funeral, for God's sake."

The taxi driver shrugged. "Ten-minutes. Down the high street. Up the hill."

Bloscombe didn't do recognisable shops selling normal stuff. Just hand-painted signs, expensive price tags, and silly names.

Three o'clock, but the shops were shut. Kendal peered into Mines-A-Double off-licence. Heaving shelves of artisan gin and a flimsy sign on the door: "Early closing – Thursday".

Bloscombe was in a time warp. Probably still had rationing and dried egg.

A beige poodle sniffed the wheels of Kendal's case. Its owner twitched the retractable lead. "She won't hurt you. Lettie, leave the lady alone."

"Do you know where St Michael's and His Angels is?"

The dog owner beamed. "In heaven, with Letitia's parents, of course."

Kendal frowned. Religious nuts weren't confined to London, then.

"I mean the church. I'm late for a funeral."

"So sorry. Next turning left, then up the hill. Closer to God."

The church was gloomy with the pathetically small congregation squeezed together at the front. A bent-over official thrust a card at Kendal as a voice began to speak through a crackly P.A. system. She slipped into the closest pew and watched a tall, besuited man stride from the front row to stand beside the wicker coffin containing poor Uncle Clem. Even viewed through the fascinator mesh, he was something to behold. Chiselled chin, chestnut hair, wide shoulders and, apart from her, the only person under a hundred. Tall-man coughed and began to speak. A strong, deep, slow voice.

"It has been my honour to have known Clem for five years. What a privilege to spend time with such a kind, erudite and funny man. We mourn his passing at seventy-five, when he had so many more years to give to our community, but we celebrate that his death was easy and peaceful."

The warden was hot! She would have visited more if she'd known there was such an attraction to bump into. In the pink and blue light from the stained-glass windows he looked positively angelic. Kendal watched from under her veil as he described her uncle's naval career and the many roles he'd played in Bloscombe in retirement: chair of the croquet club, president of Rotary, treasurer to the literary festival and fundraiser for the lifeboats, blah blah blah. Clem had achieved a lot. But then, he was seventy-five and didn't have Netflix.

Kendal examined the order of service card. A grinning Clem on a red mobility buggy waved a flag on the cover whilst a young naval officer in shorts saluted in front of a palm tree on the back. He looked serious, with a sense of purpose. No caption, saying where the picture was taken. Might have been somewhere Kendal had visited. Not Ibiza, obviously, but maybe Singapore or Thailand. Too late now to find out.

After a thin elderly lady in a black turban had sniffed through a poem, and an organ grumbled through a hymn which only the vicar seemed to know, four undertakers lifted the coffin and executed a nine-point turn to face the door. Turban-lady laid a hand on the back of the coffin and sobbed noisily. The warden took her arm and together they accompanied the coffin down the aisle, followed by the small group of ancient mourners. Kendal tugged her veil low and slunk into the seat.

"Ms Tudge, I mean Kendal, I am so glad you made it in time." He turned to the old lady. "Audrey, you go on with the others. I'll see you later."

Kendal stared at the warden's white teeth and healthy tan. She offered a black-gloved hand. "You made a lovely speech. I learned so much about my uncle. Wish I'd spent more time with him."

The warden smiled. "Don't blame yourself. We were all surprised. Seventy-five is young for someone as fit as Clem."

Seventy-five was far older than Kendal's parents when they died. Clem had lived longer than anyone she knew. She folded the service card into the pocket of the jumpsuit.

The warden cleared his throat. "I'm accompanying your uncle on the final leg of his journey. Would you like to join me?"

"Um, where to?"

"The crematorium. There's room in the hearse. The residents are going back to Jurassic Court to rest before the wake."

Exciting to go for a ride with the hot warden. But not to a crematorium.

"I'm not used to illness. Or old people. It's been a long day. I could do with a rest too."

The warden nodded. "Fine, settle yourself into the guest room and join us in the day room later for the wake."

He took Kendal's case and they walked into the bright light. The warden swept his arm in the direction of Jurassic Court. "Turn right, towards the sea. Left along the prom, and you will spot us by a small park. Big gates and a white building." He handed Kendal her case. "See you later. I'm so glad you came."

It was good to be out of the dark church and all those old people but the hangover was persistent. Maybe she was too old for midweek raving? Kendal reached the prom, breathed salty, seaweed air and remembered a game her parents played when they visited Uncle Clem long ago: First to see the sea rules the holiday!

She'd always won.

Without the case, Kendal could've walked the whole prom. Maybe found an ice cream van and commemorated Clem with a cherry ice stick. She turned inland, passed a small park, and reached the gates of the sheltered housing complex. Her lip gloss cracked as she smirked at the sign:

Jurassic Court retirement village.
Rear entrance for deliveries.

Kendal hovered over the bell panel. Should she ring Clem's bell or the warden's?

"The code is 1945. A date the residents remember." A woman in a grubby black raincoat, with wild eyebrows and a blotchy complexion, leaned across Kendal to punch in the code. "Hello, you must be? No, I can't remember."

"Kendal, Clem Tudge's niece. Gary, the warden, invited me. For the, um, final journey."

"Right, I'm Nicola, from the community nursing team. Sorry for your loss. Clem had a good passing and a lovely funeral. It's all we can hope for in life."

Kendal followed the nurse up the gravel drive, passing a manicured lawn dotted with white croquet hoops. A fountain trickled in the centre of a fishpond. The nurse bent to straighten a bird feeder.

"The residents love the birds. Especially Clem."

Kendal nodded, as though this was something she knew.

At the top of the drive was the main part of Jurassic Court housing the communal facilities. Single-storey arms spread east to west containing individual apartments with small patios. There were benches and tables surrounding the building, and wide gravel paths criss-crossed the lawns. It was clean and very white. It reminded Kendal of the Club 18-30 resort she'd sneaked into on a school trip to Brittany. Minus swimming pools and hot French boys, of course.

The nurse led Kendal through automatic doors into a bright lobby decorated with giant wooden letters: FRIENDS HOME WELCOME.

"Do you know where I check in for the guest room?" Kendal asked.

"First room on the east wing. You don't need a key here. Only Londoners lock doors. See you later when what's-his-name is back from the crem."

"Gary?"

"Yes, him. Does so much for the residents. Easy on the eye for us nurses too."

Kendal winced. The woman must be at least sixty. Gross to be still lusting. She should act her age.

The guest room was overheated, and the window overlooked the car park not the beach, but the sheets were clean, and the pillow perfectly plumped. Kendal's hangover was tenacious. A nap was wholly appropriate. Mustn't miss the free food and hot warden at the wake. She unsilenced her phone to set an alarm. Two messages from Dogbreath-Deirdre, her controlling boss.

"Kendal, your behaviour is ridiculous and is impacting the team. Do you take me for an idiot? You've claimed three funerals already this year."

Kendal sighed. She should be more imaginative or keep a list of her lies. She played the second message. Dogbreath-Deirdre was in jargon overdrive.

"Be aware you have exceeded compassionate leave allocation. Any further absence MUST be logged as holiday. Additionally, you have failed to register on the dashboard for a digital resilience workshop and are, therefore, incompliant. I will be actioning this omission."

Kendal threw the phone on the bed and opened her case. She was too angry to sleep. She needed a drink. Time to check out the free wine at Uncle Clem's after-party. Fresh lip, a straightened fascinator and a swig of mouthwash. Kendal Tudge was wake-ready. And warden-ready too, hopefully.

Clem must have paid a sum for his pre-paid funeral plan. The buffet table was crammed, and the wine came in bottles with corks. Old biddies thrust ancient mobiles at her and Kendal peered through the veil at their photos. Clem smiled in all of them. Each old bat wanted to shake her hand and waffle on about Clem. Without the veil some would've lunged in for a disgusting hug. Old people were gross.

She'd almost finished a bottle when the warden entered. He steered Kendal to a sofa and handed her a plate of soft egg sandwiches. "Your uncle was a hugely popular resident as I am sure you can tell."

Kendal raised her hands in the praying gesture Mad-Maxine loved to use. He really was a drink-on-a-stick.

"You organised it so well. I wouldn't have known what to do."

"I'm well versed in mortality," smiled the warden.

Kendal touched his knee. "Have you lost your family too?"

The warden shifted. "I mean working here keeps you familiar with um, the circle of life."

Was the hot warden woo-woo, or did he just like The Lion King, which was a bit childish for a straight man, surely? Kendal reached for the bottle, her hand wobbling. Gary steadied it and poured. Strong arm muscles, lovely eyes. She was glad he couldn't see hers. Still bloodshot from the excesses of the night before.

The party was breaking up, the residents shuffling away. Gary walked Kendal to the guest room as *EastEnders* leaked through the apartment doors into the corridor. Kendal swayed at the guest room door and touched his arm.

"Funerals are an aphrodisiac apparently."

"Not when you go to as many as me. Always upsetting. The residents are my friends. Well, most of them. Clem certainly was."

"I've only been to two," whispered Kendal. "Three now." She straightened the fascinator which was digging into her scalp. "Don't you miss normal people?"

"The residents are normal," said Gary. "But I'm careful about protecting myself and keeping boundaries."

"How?"

"On my days off I like to unwind on Dartmoor." His deep voice had dropped to almost a whisper. Was unwind code for something?

It was tempting to lure the warden into the guest room but Kendal, in her haste to get to Waterloo, was in rubbish underwear with unwashed hair. She nodded. "See you in the morning, Gary. Thank you for being so kind."

Kendal stared at her reflection in the guest room's tiny mirror, glad she didn't have to wear black at work like women in law firms or posh restaurants. Being a sales executive at a pointless charity was boring and badly paid but, at least, she could wear anything. The lick-arse millennials she worked beside wore tame, neutral shades but she loved to turn heads with leopard prints and hi-vis glam. She knew how to keep looking fit and young.

It was a relief to remove the tight fascinator but the sight of her hair made Kendal wince. Wolf cuts were great for the rock-chick-look she'd sported for years but only if you could afford constant salon highlights and she'd not been inside a salon for months. The shadow roots which were allegedly now cool, simply made Kendal look rough and old. Tomorrow was Friday. She would stay and enjoy a free mini break by the sea, buy hair colour, dress in proper clothes, with improper underwear, and then the angelic warden would be easy meat.

Soft sandwiches were insufficient for someone with Kendal's appetite and persistent hangover. She grabbed a hoodie, slipped on trainers and followed her nose to a chip shop where she feasted on hot, salty, thick chips and surveyed the empty beach. To the east, the cliffs rose in zigzags of red rock and on the horizon was Portland where her parents once took her camping in an orange tent. She'd slept between them. It was cosy. It was long ago.

Jurassic Court's gates were shut and Kendal couldn't remember what the ugly nurse had said about the code. A pensioner in a blazer and beret appeared and punched in the correct numbers.

"Welcome to wonderland. I hope you'll enjoy your life here. We all do."

"I'm not staying," barked Kendal. "I'm visiting. I'm Clem Tudge's niece."

"Miss Tudge, do forgive me. You are far too young, of course. And beautiful."

"Please call me Kendal. I don't like Tudge."

The old man attempted a bow. "Your wish is my command, my dear Kendal."

Kendal hurried away from the creepy old man. Eight-thirty and the place was dead. No sign of the warden, or anyone. She peeked into the day room. The bottle by the sofa was still there.

In the guest room, Kendal poured wine into a plastic toothbrush mug and slumped onto the bed. She hadn't unpacked her vibrator but something was already digging into her hip. Her gravel drive and the big gates. Behind them was the prom and then the sea. Clem had a brilliant view. Kendal's head began to throb. Either it was a new hangover, or the old one was super resistant. Maybe it was the sun streaming through the French windows? Kendal opened her bag and retrieved her wraparound sunglasses. Good to hide behind their huge lenses and channel a film star vibe.

The arms of the reclining chair were greasy, but the tartan blanket looked clean. Kendal climbed in, pulled the rug around her feet, sipped the gin and closed her eyes. Add a walking frame and she'd look like a resident!

Kendal woke to the sound of knocking again. Firmer this time.

"Yep, who is it?"

"Gary, the warden. Could I have a word?"

Kendal pulled her hood tight and dragged the rug to her chin. She'd not done her make-up or hair. At least the sunglasses covered most of her face.

Gary shouldered the door, carrying a tray with two mugs of coffee, a plate of buttered crumpets, and a large brown envelope.

"How are you feeling, Kendal?"

"Better now the funeral's over. Sorry for getting pissed."

"No problem. Funerals are hard, even when someone has had a long life."

Gary passed a mug and the plate and sat at the table.

"I suppose I should start sorting Clem's stuff?"

"No rush."

"Won't you need to get a new tenant?"

"It's not rented. Clem owned this flat." Gary blew on his mug. "Take as long as you like."

"I've been sacked so I've got to get back to London and find a new job. I owe tons of money to my flatmate Maxine, and my credit card is maxed out." Kendal felt her eyes prick. She hadn't cried for years. She reached for a crumpet.

"Did you enjoy your job?"

out a cash machine to buy hair colour for making a move on the warden, but the old lady was up and tugging Kendal's wrist with a surprisingly strong grip.

Apart from a new flat screen and reclining chair, Clem's flat was as she remembered it; two doors off a living space with French windows opening onto a patio. There was the galley kitchen, highly polished dining table, stuffed bookcases, and the familiar gold drinks trolley.

Kendal opened the first door and winced. A spattered razor and toothbrush hung above the sink, and beige rubber mats lined the shower. The toilet lid was mercifully down. In front of the towel rack was a red mobility buggy. A Christmas copy of the *Radio Times* lay in the front basket and fairy lights dangled from the handlebars.

The other door was the bedroom. Kendal left it closed and scanned Clem's display of photographs in the living room instead. She smiled at a large black and white portrait of her parents in shorts and sun hats on a beach. She could slip it into her bag. She didn't have anything in London of her parents. On the back of the picture was a handwritten message:

To Uncle Clem, thanks for the cheque. Here we are celebrating twenty-five years. Our first holiday alone. Kendal's on a school trip to France.

Kendal did the maths. Her parents had married when they were twenty so they were forty-five in the photo. Only one year older than she was now. They looked healthy, happy and grown-up but three years later they'd both be dead. She picked up a kitchen roll to polish the photo and reviewed the drinks trolley. No tonics for the gin, sherry was an old person cliché, Noilly Prat sounded weird and it was too early for a whisky. Even for someone freshly sacked and almost homeless.

Kendal poured a small gin, added some tap water and gazed at the view. She could see the croquet lawn, fountain, sloping

2

Someone was tapping at the guest room door. Kendal groaned. Double-day hangovers were the worst. The turban-lady stood in the corridor in a pink fluffy sweater with matching lipstick and orange foundation. Her eyebrows were well defined but, unfortunately, on different levels.

"Morning dear, letting you know breakfast finishes soon." She held out her hand. "I'm Audrey, by the way. Your uncle's neighbour. Well, I was. So sorry for your loss."

Kendal looked at the wall-clock. She'd slept for twelve hours. Must be the sea air. She pulled her hoodie tight to cover her hair, licked her fingers to rub away any mascara-eyes, and followed Audrey to the dining room where more old people murmured and chewed. Audrey pointed at an empty seat opposite a crone in enormous, thick glasses.

"Take Clem's place," said Audrey. "With Pam. She's got glaucoma, poor thing, but she can hear you."

Pam kept her cloudy eyes on the food. Kendal concentrated on the perfectly boiled eggs, soft buttered toast and cafetière of delicious coffee. The dining room had large windows onto the gardens and she studied the warden in the garden, filling bird feeders in delicious aquamarine shorts. He stretched to reach a high branch and she spotted a line of dark hair travelling from the waistband of his jeans to his abs. Kendal loved the dip by the hip slim men had. Such a perfect place for inquisitive fingers

Audrey was on the next table cackling with the old man who'd let Kendal into the gate. Kendal drank another coffee, pocketed a banana from the fruit bowl and stood.

"Would you like me to take you to Clem's flat, dearie?" called Audrey. "It's next door to mine." Kendal had intended to seek phone! With another voicemail from Dogbreath-Deirdre and a text from Mad-Maxine. Kendal sighed. She was at a funeral, for God's sake.

> K – sorry about your uncle but a tiny bit annoyed you've raided the fridge, AND my wardrobe AND left the bathroom in a state. Josh says your rent arrears are beyond reasonableness. He's talking of moving in, so you must pay up!

PoshJosh was an absolute prick. Kendal drained the glass and pressed play.

"Kendal, your failure to follow due processes means I have no choice but to instigate the disciplinary process and sever your employment contract. HR will be in touch with dashboard links for resilience opportunities and your P45 form. Be aware, I am unable to provide references under the charity-wide redeployment protocol. Thank you for your contribution to THRUm's vital success in bringing bold and human communities together."

Kendal swore. No bloody job and almost no home. On the day she buried (well, technically the warden had cremated) her only bloody relative!

Kendal threw the phone at the wall. It made a satisfying cracking noise. She poured a fresh glass and tried to imagine what might be read at her funeral.

Easier to think about Gary unwinding on Dartmoor, whatever, or whoever that was.

"Not really. THRUm is a charity but they're not charitable to me. Their ridiculous targets and all that key-performance-indicator shit is mental. I do it for the money, to be honest. I have to, there's no one else to look after me. I've got nothing and no one."

Gary tapped the envelope on the table. "You obviously aren't aware then?"

"Of what?"

Gary handed Kendal the envelope. "You're the main beneficiary of Clem's estate."

"What do you mean? I don't get you."

"Clem left you almost everything. Small sums to the lifeboats and cancer research, and the rest to you."

Kendal gasped. "Why didn't he tell me?"

"I don't know. He made me the executor. He loved you very much, Kendal."

The crumpet was impossible to swallow and her eyes burned. Gary passed the kitchen roll. "You'll sell this flat easily. There's a massive demand for sheltered housing on this coast. And then there's his adapted car and mobility buggy. He hardly ever used them because he was so fit. Walked brilliantly, most of the time. His paintings are probably worth something too and I'm pretty sure the ornaments are rare Royal Doulton."

"So, I'm, like, an heiress?"

"Indeed, but you'll have to wait till probate clears. I'll get it in motion with the solicitor. I need you to vacate the guest room, but you can stay in this flat while you sort through his stuff. It's being deep cleaned this afternoon. Clem paid the service charge in advance, so the meals and activities are free and some of them are genuinely entertaining."

The people at work were always banging on about how expensive it was to buy property. Maxine had only managed it because her posh parents paid the deposit. Maybe Kendal could buy a flat? Be a proper grown-up. Was it rude to ask the warden how much Flat 4 was worth?

"Um, Gary, what kind of price do these retirement properties go for?"

"Well, last Christmas one went for £140,000."

Even a bedsit-land girl knew £140,000 wouldn't buy a flat in London. Probably not even a shed. Then there were those things like solicitors, and stamp duty, and she already had a huge overdraft. Gary placed the envelope on the table and lifted the tray. He turned at the door.

"Movie Night tonight. *Mamma Mia!* Singalong version. Followed by something tougher for those who can stand the pace."

Twenty crones sipped ouzo and sucked olives as Kendal entered the day room. They waved and smiled as she squeezed between walking frames to perch on a padded stool.

"So glad you can join us," said Audrey. "Gary loves Movie Night." She attempted a wink. Her eyebrows were more even now. "He adores Mandy Streep."

Gary, in faded jeans, was busy with the projector. Kendal was glad she'd hidden her hair in a Harris tweed cap she'd found in Clem's wardrobe.

"Hello, Kendal. Have a drink."

"I've avoided ouzo ever since a messy weekend on Lesbos."

"Plenty of wine left from the wake. It's technically yours. Help yourself."

Kendal poured a large glass and watched the warden close the blinds. He had large hands, straight and clean nails, and an unadorned, long ring finger. What did the length signify? Was it penis size or sense of humour? Both would be nice.

Mad-Maxine was obsessed with *Mamma Mia!* and Kendal had always considered it a lame way to spend an evening but singing along with uninhibited oldies and good-time Gary was surprisingly entertaining. Most of the residents wore hearing aids and didn't care how she sang. Better than the karaoke team-building trips at THRUm where the know-it-all drones hit perfect notes and never fell over.

When the movie ended, the residents clapped, thanked Gary, and shuffled or wheeled back to their flats.

"They go to bed so early," observed Kendal.

"Older people's body clocks revert to those of children," nodded Gary. "I'm going to watch *The Irishman* now. Want to join me? Scorsese is one of my favourite directors."

Kendal nodded. Buff-looking and a film-buff. Result! She opened another bottle of the wake wine as Gary pulled two reclining chairs into the centre of the room. Kendal climbed onto the comfortable leather. She pressed the seat controller to raise the footrest up and down.

"Jurassic Court is awesome. I could get used to this."

"No you couldn't. Bloscombe would bore you senseless," said Gary. "It's the opposite of London."

"Apart from the funeral, I'm having a lot of fun. I could live here."

"You wouldn't be allowed," said Gary, pointing the controller at the projector.

Kendal frowned "Why? I'm the owner now, aren't I?"

"Yes, but you're too young to live here."

"So, how come you do?"

"I don't. I stay in staff accommodation if I need to be here. The apartments are well-designed, and in a great location, but I'm not old enough to own one. Residents must be sixty or over."

"No offence, but they look way older."

"They are," said Gary. "When the Quakers opened this place, sixty was old. People live longer now but sixty is still the youngest anyone can be to live here. It is in the terms and conditions. It's the rule."

"That's crazy. Like apartheid or something," scoffed Kendal. "Or men-only drinking clubs."

Gary filled their glasses. "Like I said, you can stay in Flat 4 while you sort stuff out. But you can't be a resident."

Kendal hated "can't" even more than Tudge.

Gary lifted the controller. "Ready for the second movie?" Kendal nodded. This was fun. Macho gangster movies were erotic, weren't they?

After ten minutes she sat upright. "I can't understand what's going on."

Gary pressed pause. "Their accents are difficult. I'll turn on subtitles."

"It's not the voices. They look weird."

Gary nodded. "The director used CGI to make them look young so he could tell their back stories, but he only altered faces, not bodies. They're moving like the elderly people the actors actually are. They can't act young."

Gary crossed the room to the wine bottle. He turned, smiled at Kendal, and returned carefully with a slight sway at each step, grunting as he sat and groaning as he bent over to fill her glass.

Kendal laughed. "You've nailed it. You've aged twenty years."

"There's not much I don't know about old people."

"They should've hired you."

It was agreeable sitting with the warden in the dark. Fun to attempt a seduction but the old people vibe in the day room was a turn-off and Kendal still hadn't bleached her roots. There would be other opportunities. She faked a yawn and grasped the bottle.

"Thanks for a lovely evening. Most educational."

Gary waved. His long fingers caressed the controller.

Kendal opened the curtains in Flat 4. More stars than in London and no sirens or alarms. She poured a glass of wine and slipped into Clem's reclining chair. Her reclining chair in her flat!

She smiled at the photo of her parents. They'd loved the beach, like Clem. They might have retired to somewhere like Jurassic Court if they'd lived longer. Tragic they'd died so young though it hadn't seemed that way when it happened. They were her parents, so they were simply old. Now she was nearly their age.

Kendal undressed and brushed her teeth. The bathroom was spotless. The cleaners had done an excellent job. She walked into the bedroom, opened the wardrobe and ran her fingers over tweed, linen and well-pressed cotton. Clem had been a classy dresser. Nothing cheap about her uncle. Everything in the flat was top quality.

The linen sheets smelled of citrus and the pillows supported her head perfectly. The best bed she'd slept in for years. A bit weird as it was where poor Uncle Clem had died but, then again, far worse things could've happened in the many beds she'd slept in. This was the best accommodation ever. Space, views, comfortable furniture, big television and no noise (apart from Audrey-next-door's television). The lay-out was perfect, probably because it was designed for a single person instead being carved out of a big house like the rubbish flats and bedsits she'd rented in London. And it was all hers. With free meals and a hot warden too.

An owl hooted. Kendal remembered dad's favourite joke.

"What kind of owl does the washing up? A tea towel!"

She wished she could share the joke with someone.

The bed was divine, she'd had loads to drink, but Kendal could not sleep. Her mind was fizzing. She walked into the living room and gazed at the stars. She slid open the French windows and listened. No owl hoots, just waves on shingle.

"Thank you, Uncle Clem," she whispered.

Summer was coming. The worst time to be in oppressive London. Especially trying to find a new job and a new place to live. She had nothing to go back to. Kendal closed the French windows and placed the wine bottle in the fridge. She wiped the shiny galley kitchen and straightened the photo of her parents. They were a good-looking couple. She touched her mother's face and then her father's.

"I'm going to stay by the sea," she whispered. "Live the life you should have had."

3

Gary was filling the bird feeders again. He wore snug jeans and a white T-shirt revealing well-defined biceps. Behind him, two old men played croquet; the creep who'd told Kendal the pass code for the gates and the one holding hands with Audrey at *Mamma Mia!*

"Thanks for encouraging me to come to Movie Night. It really cheered me up."

"You're welcome, Kendal," smiled the warden. "And you made the right decision to call it a day. It was the latest I've been up for ages. Had to go for a run this morning to get a clear head."

Kendal imagined the warden on the prom, the sea breeze ruffling his hair and sweat trickling down his pecs.

"You go the extra mile for the residents, Gary. Everyone is so well looked after."

"I have a lot of help. It's not me on my own."

"But you're the responsible person who makes it special."

One of the old men tied a croquet mallet to his walking frame and was attempting to swing it against the ball.

"That's a broken knee about to happen," sighed Gary. "Philip and Brian are so competitive." He turned to Kendal. "We could have another session before you go back to London. You can choose the film."

Kendal pushed her sunglasses tight. "Lovely, Gary." She ran her tongue across her teeth. "But I'll take a nana-nap next time. It's hard to stay up late at my age."

Gary snorted. "You're sounding like a resident. This place must be rubbing off on you."

"It is rubbing off on me and no wonder. Communal living has huge benefits for people with no family."

Gary shook his head. "But you're not elderly."

Kendal picked at a peanut poking from the bird feeder. It fell on the grass and a sparrow swooped, pursued by a seagull.

Gary clapped and both birds scurried across the lawn.

Kendal took a deep breath. This was the moment.

"Actually, I am elderly, Gary. Though I prefer to think of sixty as mature."

The warden frowned; dark eyebrows framing brown eyes. He stepped away. "You're sixty? Really? You don't look it."

Kendal pulled Clem's tweed hat over her ears, turned to the side, and lifted her hip in her favourite Insta pose. "Thanks. I like to keep trim, and I've had a bit of work."

The seagull attempted a second peanut raid. Gary lunged towards it. Kendal took advantage and spoke to his back.

"So, as I am sixty, it means I comply with Jurassic Court's terms and conditions and can live in Uncle Clem's flat for as long as I like, doesn't it? I love living here. By the sea."

Gary fiddled with the bird feeder. Kendal held her breath. The mallet hit the ball loudly and, at last, the warden turned to look at her.

"Don't you want to sell your flat? There's a huge demand for retirement properties around here. You'll go back to London with a tidy sum."

The croquet ball rolled towards Kendal.

"Jurassic Court is my forever home."

"What about your career, your family, your friends?"

Kendal blocked the ball and bent to bowl it back to the old men. Remembering the lie, she affected a wince and pushed her hand into her back.

"I'll get a job here and wait for my pension to come. Uncle Clem was the only family I had. London is a big place and it's hard to keep in touch with friends. This place is perfect for people like me. Single, with no kids or masses of possessions. Simple, restful, cheap."

Gary took another step back. He was nearly in the pond.

"Um, I hope I wasn't, um, inappropriate watching the movie? I was explaining the film, not mocking older actors. I respect senior citizens. I thought you were my age, or even younger."

Kendal smiled. "It's fine, Gary. I'm flattered."

The warden frowned, then nodded.

The lie was embedding.

Kendal concentrated as the warden explained how the service fees and dining charges worked. Clem had paid a year in advance. It wouldn't cost anything for Kendal to live and eat at Jurassic Court until after Christmas. No problem, she would have found a normal place to live by then.

The two old men limped to the final croquet hoop. Gary cupped his hands and shouted. "Don't forget the manhole cover at the end. It's a trip hazard." The walking frame man gave a thumbs up sign.

"They are so lucky to have you, Gary."

Gary shrugged. "Well, if you're going to be a resident, not a visitor, you'll have me too."

Kendal kept her face in neutral. Since she'd arrived she'd thought of little else.

"Come to my office later. We can do the paperwork and get you formally registered as a resident." He splashed the water to scare the gulls and shook his head. "Though it seems impossible to believe."

Kendal's heart raced like the rush of shoplifting, or a first line of coke. Gary had believed her lie.

"Thank you, Gary, I'll look forward to it."

She turned towards Flat 4, forcing herself to walk instead of running and fist-pumping. He'd believed her, she'd nailed it! Because what woman would lie upwards about her age?

Safe inside Clem's flat, her flat, Kendal stood in front of the mirror and removed the tweed cap and sunglasses. She was forty-four. No one ever told Kendal Tudge to act her age but now she must tell herself. What was the dumb mantra Maxine chanted before she went to work?

"I am. Here now."

Kendal grinned. "I am. Six Oh. Sixty."

She gazed out of the French windows. Her view. A tiny sailing boat drifted over the sea and children on scooters zigzagged along the prom. She re-ran the croquet-watching scene.

Gary had stepped away after the shock announcement. Good in terms of him not having a close view of skin, hair or teeth, but bad if it meant he no longer wanted to be near her since she was well-up for being a cougar, or a MILF or whatever the new term was for sexy, mature women. Disappointing if Gary now felt Kendal was inappropriate shag material. No problem, she would find a way to get him; play the long game, defer gratification. Something she appreciated in men, even if she never practised it. Kendal giggled. Wham bam, thank you mam, or sir was her approach to sex. It would be an interesting challenge to take her time. Quite grown-up!

Kendal opened the French windows. The patio was perfectly positioned to catch the sun. It was strong for April. Sun was ageing. She giggled again. Bring it on, UV bastards. Do your worst. I need to look sixty.

Kendal brushed cobwebs off a deckchair, slumped into its striped canvas and tried to think of a sixty-year-old she could model her new persona on for ways to dress or behave. At THRUm only directors were old and they didn't mix with bottom feeders like her. Nicola, the district nurse could be sixty. She looked ancient. Those awful shoes and hairy face. Kendal rubbed her hand over her chin and prodded a suspicious protrusion. Perhaps she should stop plucking and let the buggers do their worst? Another issue could be her tramp-stamp. Did old people, other than sailors, have tattoos? She couldn't afford to have it removed.

The big change to get her head round was, of course, the change itself. The menopause. As a sixty-year-old, she'd have had it, surely? Kendal ran through what she knew about post-menopausal symptoms: mood swings, extra weight, hair in the wrong places, memory loss, grumpiness and, according to the few articles she could recall reading, a loss of libido.

The loss of libido thing was going to be tricky when the warden was so hot. Maybe she could pretend to be on HRT? Supposed to keep middle-aged ladies aroused, wasn't it?

Thinking about hormone replacement therapy led Kendal to contraception. When she'd arrived in Bloscombe she'd not planned to stay long. The pack of pills would finish soon and a local GP might question a request for contraception from someone who was sixty.

She needed to look, think, dress, talk, breathe like someone who was sixty. Maybe even smell like one? There were a lot of issues to tackle to make the ageing fraud work. The warden had swallowed her being sixty story, but he hadn't been up-close yet. Veils, sunglasses, hoods, and tweed hats had kept her covered so far. She needed an invincible back story and identity and be sure of key dates in her new life. So much to think about. What was it Dogbreath-Deirdre at THRUm said when Kendal moaned about an overwhelming workload? "Prioritise your priorities."

The punishing cow had a point.

The most important priority was to adopt a convincing disguise before she saw Gary again and he had a chance to examine her closely. Kendal grabbed her bag, stepped over the patio wall and walked towards the drive.

The croquet players were recovering on a bench.

"Fancy a game, Kendal?" asked Philip, the creepy Gate-man. "I need a better opponent. Brian's too old."

"I'm only eighty-six," said Brian, Audrey-next-door's boyfriend. "How old are you, Philip?"

Gate-man beamed. "Seventy-one. A mere spring chicken. Don't you agree, Kendal?"

Kendal didn't care. They both looked primeval. "I'd love to learn croquet," she lied. "But I'm going shopping. To get summer clothes."

Brian leaned against his frame. "Going to Marks and Sparks in Exeter? Could I trouble you with a list? I'm running through my boxers."

These coffin dodgers were disgusting. Kendal reminded herself to be polite. It was Dorset, not Dalston.

"Sorry, I'm just doing the charity shops. To get some new-old-clothes."

In London, Kendal eye-balled men or attractive young women but walking towards the high street she studied the many older women. In ten minutes, she'd counted twelve waterproofs, eight tweed jackets, four oversize cardigans, three kilts, ten black stretchy trousers, one pair of jeans and a hideous mother-of-the-bride-waterfall disaster. No leopard skin or animal prints. Not one pair of palazzos.

Kendal chose the Cancer Research shop as the place to source her disguise because it smelled better than the other charity shops and, since cancer got her parents, she'd prefer they got her money than the stupid donkey sanctuary or dogs' kennels.

The cancer research shop grouped clothes in colour. Kendal started at pink-purple and selected a lilac Cotton Traders anorak, a coral gilet, and a floral scarf. At the beige rail she chose a baggy cardigan, cream polyester trousers and a striped polo neck. At blue, she reluctantly ignored a bargain Hollister mini-dress, and picked a calf-length navy skirt, paisley blouse, jeans with an elasticated waist, and a denim fisherman's smock. There were no kilts.

"We have a changing room if you want to try anything?" said a sales assistant, with Delphine on her badge.

"I'm fine," said Kendal.

"I hope you don't mind me saying, but they look somewhat large." Lipstick had spread into the cracks around Delphine's lips. "And we're not keen on returns."

"I won't be returning them."

"Just visiting? We get a lot of day-trippers. From the caravan park."

Kendal pursed her lips. Old bags were nosy. "I live here. In my uncle's house. He's died. I'll probably be bringing his suits and stuff here, if you play nicely."

Delphine stopped smiling. "So sorry for your loss. Let me take these to the cash desk. My colleague Brenda will hold them till you're ready."

Kendal moved to the shoe shelf. Gross to wear second-hand shoes, but she'd spotted a pair of rubber-soled, black flats that were perfect for the disguise. She checked the price label. Fifteen pounds? Ten items of clothing had only cost twenty-nine.

"Excuse me, is this right?"

"Yes dear, bargain, aren't they? Orthopaedic, size six and plenty of room for bunions. Only just put them on display. They'll walk out of the shop, I assure you."

As the biddy brigade helped each other at the till, Kendal perused the glass cabinet by them. Second-hand jewellery was almost as offensive as previously worn shoes, but imitation pearls and boring silver studs would be excellent substitutions for her hoops, snake chain bracelet and moonstone choker. Farewell, ghetto gold which flattered pert breasts and fresh nails. Hello, authentically oldie, insipid silver.

"Delphine, can you add two pairs of studs, those pink plastic beads, the diamanté brooch and..." Kendal turned to the queue behind her, "the pearl necklace?"

She waited for the laugh. No response to an excellent joke.

Kendal shrugged. The old ladies processed her purchases in slow motion. Beside them was a display of leaflets featuring scientists in white coats and nurses holding fruit baskets.

Change your lifestyle to live longer

What the cancer researchers didn't know, what no one knew, was she, Kendal Tudge, was altering her style to change her life. Her secret, hidden from the warden, the residents of Jurassic Court, the batty old volunteers and every Dorset dullard-boomer in the queue behind.

"Contactless is playing up. You'll have to use your number," mumbled Brenda.

"No problem," replied Kendal, tapping the keyboard.

"Marvellous!" piped Delphine. "No awkward forgetting-my-code scene. We've had quite a few of those senior moments today."

Laughter erupted behind Kendal; the queue united in their enjoyment of this remark. Pearl necklace unfunny, dementia jest hilarious. Weird.

Leaving the shop, laden with bags, Kendal bumped against a shopping trolley whose owner was distracted by discounted Christmas cards and scented pillows. Nothing signalled old person more than a pull-along-trolley. She was tempted to grab the handle, but the dog pattern was unusual and might be recognised in a small place like Bloscombe. No point jeopardising a big fraud with a small theft.

Next priority was hair. Kendal couldn't cover it with Clem's hats forever; it shouldn't be blonde if she was supposed to be old.

Excluding barbers, Kendal counted ten hair salons in Bloscombe. She was tempted by punning names: Illegally Blonde and Anita Haircut but plumped for Hair By Barry due to its authentic old-person-vibe; net curtains, unfashionable model photos, vintage hood dryers and a lone customer asleep with walking sticks between her legs.

Kendal opened the jangly door, and a sweet smell greeted her evoking the salon her mother used to attend. Kendal had loved going there in school holidays; the manager gave her rainbow drops and mum was always happy with fresh hair and scarlet nails. Perhaps, she'd inherited her style?

The hairdresser sat at the back of the shop eating a doughnut.

Kendal put her bags on a chair. "Can I book a consultation?"

"No, but I can cut your hair." The hairdresser chortled, wiped her hands on pink leggings, and spun a styling chair round. "Sit down. Aggie's cooking nicely under the dryer. Plenty of time for a chat. Fancy a cup of tea?"

"I'm a bit time-limited actually," said Kendal. "But I know what I want. It's quite unusual."

The hairdresser raised her eyebrows and turned up the old lady's dryer dial. "I don't do head shaves. Against my religion."

"No," said Kendal, lowering her voice. "I want to go grey."

The hairdresser beamed and thrust a pile of magazines at Kendal before running into the back of the salon. As a kettle boiled, she shouted. "Barry will be gutted to miss this; he's been desperate for someone to transition. Check out *Modern Salon*. February edition. I'm Cheryl, by the way. Sugar?"

Kendal sat in the styling chair and stared at her reflection. Transition? She never said no to girl-on-girl action but she didn't look like a man. She reached for the magazine pile. *Hello*, *Woman's Weekly* and the *TV Times* were sticky. *Modern Salon* was untouched. The front page featured a montage of grey heads:

"Fifty Shades of Grey: Silver, Grey, Steel, Slate!
Your choice for the top trend."

Ten shiny pages followed with young women sporting hairstyles in every iteration of grey, alongside boxes explaining the instructions for the techniques and products to turn normal hair silver. How had Kendal managed to not know grey hair was on trend? Was she losing her touch?

Cheryl passed a mug and smiled at Kendal's reflection. "With your colouring, I'd recommend slate. Stunning. Oh, look at me, only gone and done a consultation, haven't I?" She giggled. "I could do it now if you want. Aggie will sleep on, bless her."

"How much?" asked Kendal.

"No one's asked yet even though we've had the products for ages. I'd do it for nothing, but Barry wouldn't be pleased. Let's say forty."

Cheryl mixed her potions and Kendal returned to the magazine: "Own your grey, be powerful!"

Kendal had dyed her hair for so long she didn't know if she had any grey to own. It was years since she'd ventured into a salon, preferring to save money and self-esteem with a DIY job, administered on hungover Sundays. Cheryl didn't care if Kendal's hair was steeped in supermarket colour. Nice, not to be judged.

Kendal closed her eyes and re-ran the scene at the charity shop to analyse why her pearl necklace joke had failed. The banter at work had been hard enough with the twenty-something drones sending stupid gifs and emojis instead of speaking. Those snowflakes were always staring at screens, giggling at nothing and sharing posts. None of them talked properly and puns, Kendal's favourite form of funny, were habitually misunderstood. Once, an intern had even lodged an official complaint, alleging Kendal's jokes were borderline assaults. Yet here in Bloscombe it seemed jokes about senior moments were perfectly acceptable. Like Jews joking about Jewishness, she supposed. She'd have to learn pensioner-friendly jokes. Hag humour.

"Want a trim, or a restyle?" asked Cheryl. "I'll throw it in with the price."

Kendal smiled. "Thanks. Something mature."

Cheryl snipped and Kendal sipped a second cup of tea and tried not to look at her hair which now silver and tidily bobbed, was straight and neat. Tousled-rock-chick turned boring-pigeon.

"Can I ask something?" asked Kendal swiping her bank card.

"Only if you let me take some pics," answered Cheryl.

Kendal frowned. "OK, from the back. Not my face. What are the ways older women let themselves go, show their age?"

"Eyebrows, blackheads, and powder. They can't see proper and don't buy magnifying mirrors." Cheryl nodded at Aggie whose legs had opened letting her sticks fall. "Pelvic floor goes too. Proper shame. Don't worry, love. You look great. Perfect eyebrows, good skin, great hair. Two consultations! And all for free."

Kendal seized her shopping and marched to the chemist. Boots in Bloscombe was nothing like Ealing's. Only one small shelf for condoms, lubricants and tampons, but a complete aisle for incontinence pads and vitamins. She browsed the make-up shelves and picked a cheap powder compact, grey eyebrow pencil, and Warm Nude pale lipstick. Tempting to pocket the purchases – store detectives seemed as rare as contraceptives in Bloscombe – but she was buzzing enough. Time to watch your blood pressure, Kendal. Now you're old.

4

A banging gong announced lunch as Kendal returned to Jurassic Court. She hurried to her apartment, pulled on the elastic-waisted baggy jeans, dusted powder over her face and replaced her giant hoops with silver studs. She joined a table with Philip, Brian and Pam.

"Successful shopping mission?" asked Philip. "Town busy?"

"Yes. I got lots of stuff," answered Kendal. "Managed to get my hair cut too. What do you think?" Pam kept her eyes on the beige vegetable pâté. Brian and Philip stared at Kendal.

"You look a little below par," said Brian. "Probably the funeral catching up."

"Need to be in peak form this afternoon, my dear," said Philip. "Gary's kicking off Well-being Walks again. Marks the start of spring."

They ate quietly and Kendal attempted to guess if the pudding was lemon posset again or egg custard. Tiny portion, whichever.

"Cheeky monkey," said Brian pointing at a squirrel climbing the bird feeder outside the dining room.

"It's always hungry," said Philip. The two men folded their napkins, helped Pam fold hers, and ambled away. Kendal slid into the kitchen next door. Carla and Emma, the well-padded kitchen staff, were smoking outside. She slipped her hand into the biscuit tin and grabbed two Kit Kats.

"You and me, monkey-squirrel," she whispered, and crept to her flat.

Gary, in a tight hi-vis vest, stood in the foyer trying to corral the residents and their mobility buggies, wheelchairs and walking frames. No sign of the confusion of the morning.

He smiled at Kendal. "Good to see you, Kendal, thanks for joining in." He pointed at her backpack, "You might be a tad over-equipped. It's a gentle stroll. To the park and back."

"Gentle stroll is perfect," smiled Kendal. "I'm taking it easy."

The warden waved at the automatic doors and raised his voice over the excited pensioners. "Right, best foot forward. Jacob, Jim and Jennifer, put your mobility buggy speed regulators onto Tortoise, not Hare."

The drivers obediently switched their controls and glided graciously towards the gates. Audrey and Philip followed on foot, concentrating on their posture, and refusing to look at the ground. Next was Brian with his walking frame, his arm held carefully by Pam. Carla-from-the-kitchen came last pushing a wheelchair with Albert, Jurassic Court's largest resident.

Kendal tried her best to keep pace but walking so slowly was surprisingly difficult and she reached the buggy drivers first.

"Hello Kendal, I'm Jacob. Your uncle had the best buggy," said a ginger-haired, freckled man. "Top of the range Rascal."

"Don't speak ill of the dead," snapped the second driver who wore a large lanyard reading "Jim".

"Rascal is the model," said the third driver, a woman sporting a red, white and blue headscarf over a stiff perm. She prodded Kendal. "Ridiculous name. Concocted by dreadful marketing types. I'm Jennifer, by the way."

"He went miles once," said Jacob "Had to get a breakdown truck." He tapped his nose. "I hope you've kept it plugged in. They've got to be kept on charge."

"First dibs, when you sell," said Jennifer. "The Rascal saddle is to die for."

Brian, who had finally reached Kendal, leaned on his frame, and wheezed into Kendal's face. "Whatever she offers, I'll give you fifty quid more."

When the group had negotiated the gates, Gary stood in the road and waved the crocodile to the park entrance. A five hundred metre journey had taken twenty minutes. Inside the park, the group split: the buggy riders, who had dialled up to Hare, did circuits, whilst stick- and frame-walkers made straight for the benches. Carla-from-the-kitchen parked Albert and got out her phone. Only Audrey, Philip, Gary, and Kendal were left walking. The path was lined with poo bins and trees decorated with white and pink flowers.

"Beautiful blossom," said Philip. "Cherry, I declare."

"Plum, actually," said Gary. "The cherry trees are on the south side and their blossom comes out late April. Remember, we came last year and took photos? It was like Japanese Hanami."

"Clem did a lovely painting of it," said Philip.

"And Pam had a turn," added Audrey. She grabbed Kendal's arm. "Her father was a prisoner of war in Japan. Carla had to take rice off the menu."

Kendal wondered whether park plum trees had fruit you could eat. She should learn about fruit on trees. Save money, and curry favour with the nature-loving warden.

"First trees of spring, Gary?" she offered.

"Not really," he replied. "The blackthorn and hawthorn are already out. But you've got to see them in the wild. Like the garlic and the bluebells. There's lots of those in Almonds Wood. They're early this year."

"Sounds lovely. Will you have a Well-being Walk there?"

"Too far for most of the residents. We'll go in the minibus."

Kendal nodded. "I'd like to go if there's room. Pick a few flowers for my flat."

"That's illegal, actually," said Gary. "Native bluebells are protected. You're welcome to pick the Spanish ones in the gardens at Jurassic Court. They're immigrants. They need controlling."

They were back at the entrance. Audrey and Philip sat on a bench and Gary left to untangle Jim and Jennifer who'd locked shopping baskets at a tight corner.

Kendal wondered if the warden didn't like Spaniards or

immigrants. He was super pleasant to old people but it didn't guarantee he wasn't prejudiced. Bloscombe was weirdly white, and she'd noticed some dodgy-sounding events on the Jurassic Coast activities board: African Evening, Exeter Chiefs Live and Race Night. Kendal imagined telling the millennials at work. It would blow their woke minds.

She turned to Audrey and Philip. "I'm going to walk a bit further. Get some fresh air. Can you tell the warden?"

Audrey smiled. "You do what you like, Kendal. We're free and easy here."

When she was out of sight Kendal reverted to her normal walking speed. The insipid make-up made her appear pale, but the early nights were doing her the world of good. She wanted to walk fast and feel a stretch. The prom was smooth and clean. No dog turds, litter, and hardly any chewing gum marks.

When Kendal returned to Jurassic Court Gary was updating the activities board. She hoped there wouldn't be any offensive words. Hard to lust after a racist, even a hot one.

Gary smiled. "Did you enjoy your extended walk? You've got some colour now. I hope you don't mind me saying but you looked a bit off-kilter before." He stared at Kendal. This was awkward. She had to divert him. Kendal scanned the white board:

Monday – Well-being Walk
Tuesday – Visit from the Donkey Sanctuary
Wednesday – Bluebell Minibus Magic Tour
Thursday – Visit from Hair By Barry. Gary's day off
Friday morning – Well-being Walk
Friday afternoon – Boscombe Handbell Ringers + PUke Club
Friday evening – Beetle Drive

Kendal pointed at the board. "Not sure I like the sound of Puke Club."

Gary laughed and rubbed the letter P out "Uke Club. It's going to be a turn-your-hearing-aid-down day."

"What's a Uke Club?"

"Come on, everyone's into ukuleles."

"Not me," said Kendal. "But I like hiking. And I am keen to see the bluebells."

"Sorry, the minibus is full. It's Albert's wheelchair. Takes too much room."

Kendal mimed a disappointed face. Gary laughed and Kendal smiled. They were back to normal. Doing banter and connecting, weren't they?

"Tell you what. I'm going to do a bluebell recce tomorrow, after supper. Up Almonds Hill. Better way to see them than from the bus. It's a bit of a climb but I could lend you some poles."

Kendal had a pleasant flashback to three builders from Kraków she'd encountered on Ealing Common. Best not to use that pun for banter. Not when you were supposed to be sixty.

"Thanks, Gary, I'll think about it."

Kendal walked along the corridor, feeling the warden's gaze. She slowed her pace and realigned her backpack, emitting a distinct groan.

"You OK?" he called.

"Feeling my age," shouted Kendal over her shoulder. She walked into her flat and collapsed on the bed. She smiled at the photo of her parents.

"Should have sent me to stage school," she whispered. "Seems I've a talent for acting."

Sunday morning without a hangover felt odd. It would be nice to go for a walk on the prom, celebrate her inheritance with chips, ice-cream, or a cheeky burger but she needed to work. Hair, clothes, and make-up were sorted (even though people thought she was ill); now she needed to firm up Fake-Kendal, create a watertight back story and get to grips with the world of oldies. She must inhabit the part, learn her lines, and make her lie fool-proof.

Kendal set the table with a full cafetière, a plate of Kit Kats, a notebook she'd found with a lifeboat on the cover, and Clem's vintage Casio calculator. In large letters she wrote *The Tudge*

Transformation Toolkit on the cover and Kendal's CV on the first page. Google would help her create Fake-Kendal's life.

Kendal decided she would have passed the eleven plus and gone to a grammar, taken lots of O-Levels and three A-Levels.

University was harder. Tempting to choose bonkers-sounding American Studies at Brighton, but it meant knowing about books not just movies. Peace Studies was pleasingly nebulous but taught in unappealing places she'd never even visited like Warwick or Bradford. Eventually, she selected Media Studies at the Polytechnic of Central London. A cinch to bluff about and next to the big Hennes in Oxford Circus.

Fake-Kendal should have better jobs than real Kendal but if she fabricated a television or radio career, someone might check online. Journalism was an easier lie. She'd read loads of magazines!

Travel was simple; think of all the places she'd ever visited; check they still had the same name and then use the calculator to take away sixteen years from the date she had actually visited. Turned out Ibiza was already buzzing in the early seventies.

Love life was awkward. No point in inventing husbands or children but she wasn't going to use the term spinster. Nothing wrong with being free and single at sixty, surely?

By the time the gong rang for supper Kendal was immersed in her new, older persona. She knew how many shillings in an old pound, why Windscale became Sellafield, what the three-day week was and why Vietnam wasn't always a tourist destination. Her earliest memory was the moon landing in 1969 and her favourite group, T Rex. Her phone, however, was almost dead. The crack where she'd thrown it against the wall was getting wider and a day of typing had made the keyboard jam.

If only her manager could have witnessed her efforts. Dogbreath-Deirdre was always criticising Kendal for lacking focus but then the tasks she was given at work were nothing like *The Tudge Transformation Toolkit*. If her job had been more inspiring, or she'd been allocated interesting projects, she might have progressed in a career and had a genuinely impressive CV, instead of a made-up one.

Kendal rummaged in the wardrobe and found a box file labelled ADMIN. Alongside Uncle Clem's certificates and bank statements was a folder entitled Living in Jurassic Court. Kendal opened it and skimmed the Terms and Conditions leaflet. She shook her head at the stupid "must-be sixty or over" rule. A box file was the perfect deterrent for nosy cleaners. Kendal had done a stint as a chambermaid and knew how hoovering could be enlivened by snooping. She added her vibrator, contraceptives, and a box of tampons and slipped the box under the bed.

After supper (corned beef hash and mashed potato), Kendal put on the coral gilet and cream polyester trousers and walked to Gary's office. Odd to be wearing such loose clothes, but it hid her stomach which was bloating – probably the endless carbs?

"Does your offer of a bluebell walk still stand?"

Gary closed his laptop and scrutinised her. "Are you fit enough? You don't look yourself."

Kendal hunched her shoulders. "Clem's passing, the funeral, leaving work. It's catching up."

Gary stood. Today's shorts were aquamarine. "OK, meet you at the gate in twenty minutes. You want me to bring the poles?"

"No, let them have the evening off."

Gary laughed. Kendal clenched her fist. Boomer banter nailed!

5

Almonds Wood perched on Bloscombe's western cliffs. It was a steep climb and Kendal was relieved when Gary stopped to point out landmarks. His face crinkled as he explained why the Jurassic Coast was a world heritage site and the difference between Triassic, Jurassic, and late Cretaceous geology. He looked like Sam Neill in *Jurassic Park*. Kendal could almost see dinosaurs racing across the grass.

The view from the top was exhilarating, stretching from a distant Portland in the east to shadowy cliffs in the west. Kendal would have liked to stop and watch the sunset, perhaps with a chilled rosé. Instead, Gary romped into a dense, dark wood. The temperature dropped and there was a strong smell of cat piss. Gary mounted a tree stump and spread his arms like Jesus.

"We've arrived at exactly the right moment," he announced. Kendal stared. Was this some woo woo rubbish? Gary pointed at the ground and Kendal lowered her eyes grudgingly. Every space between the knotted trees and rotting stumps burst with bluebells. Green, blue, and white.

"Amazing," cried Kendal. "So many flowers, it's almost tropical."

"They're my second favourite flower."

"What's your first?" Kendal didn't care but wanted to keep the conversation going.

"Hyacinths."

Kendal had a sudden memory of a glass vase with a papery hyacinth bulb her mother used to place on Kendal's bedroom windowsill every Autumn. She'd not thought about it for decades. She remembered watching the white roots grow down and the green shoots move up. Could bluebells trigger hallucinations like the Amazonian ayahuasca? Her stomach was still bloated. Awful to vomit like she'd done in Mexico when she'd confused ayahuasca with mezcal.

"They're related to asparagus too," added Gary, kneeling to caress the tiny flower heads. "Bluebells take five years to grow from seed and they've been here since the ice age."

Her mother used to measure the hyacinth's growth every week and somehow it always peaked on Christmas Day. The blowsy pink flower matched her favourite Quality Street sweet wrapper.

Gary was an expert but, unlike mansplainers she'd met at work or in city bars, he regularly stopped his explanations to check she was still interested. When she smiled or nodded, he'd resume in a gentle tone. Was he naturally unassuming, like an enthusiastic geography teacher, or was it a technique he'd adopted to deal with old people? Either way, it was hugely attractive, and she found herself absorbed by his words as well as his body.

She needed to calm down; she was losing control. Three weeks since she'd had sex with anyone other than herself. Kendal bent to examine the bluebells, remembering to emit a pensioner's groan. She grasped some sticky stems.

"Don't pick them, Kendal. They're protected." Gary put his hand on hers. Kendal tried not to gasp. Gary stood quickly and held out his hand to help Kendal. The air was heady, the trees were full of noisy bird song. The bloating had disappeared but now her breasts ached and her back felt stiff. Of course, her period was due, always the horniest time.

"Almonds Wood is as good as you promised," said Kendal, turning her head to take in the expanse of flowers. She pointed at a tree bursting with blossom. "An almond?"

Gary smiled. "It's a hawthorn. There are no almond trees here. It's called Almonds Wood because it belongs to Sir Anthony Almond. His family owns everything around here. Always have."

Gary pressed his finger to his lips. Kendal tensed, expecting to see an angry farmer pointing a gun.

"A cuckoo. Fantastic!" Gary beamed. "The first of the year. The first for several years."

"Cuckoo, it's an onomatopoeic word, isn't it?" said Kendal. Bit of a lame remark, but it was the best she could come up with. She knew about words, not nature. But she was happy to learn if Gary was the tutor.

Gary shrugged. "I'm not sure, but the arrival of the cuckoo shows spring has sprung."

Gary was as excited about a bird as most men were about football.

At the flat, Kendal rushed to the box file and was gutted to discover her vibrator was flat. She'd left the charger at Mad-Maxine's along with the Kindle plug. She took out *The Tudge Transformation Toolkit*. She would record the intel she'd gathered for Fake-Kendal to exploit at appropriate moments. Two new sections:

Boomer Banter (for insights into humour and small talk)
Nature Notes (for impressing Gary)

By the time she had recorded her successful joshing with Gary plus all the notes about cliff formation, spring blossoms and indigenous flower species, the theme tune for the news was seeping through Audrey-next-door's wall. Kendal stowed away the notebook and took out the box of tampons. Only five. She hoped there would be enough. Recently her periods had been crazily irregular and huge. She couldn't afford blood on the sheets. The cleaners might tell Gary.

At breakfast, Brian made a beeline for Kendal. His walking frame moved faster in the morning, but it still took an age to cross the room.

"Is breakfast too early?" he asked.

"It's the same every day, Brian," answered Kendal. No response. Boomer banter failure.

"To jump in Clem's grave, as it were."

Audrey, piling marmalade and jam onto toast, leaned forward. "He wants to try Clem's mobility buggy. He's jealous of Jim and Jacob."

Brian grinned, dislodging bran flakes from his teeth. "Unless you're using it yourself?"

Kendal laughed. "I may be sixty, Brian, but my feet function fine. You're welcome to try the Rascal. It's in the storage shed. I'll check the battery and drive it to your flat."

Clem's scooter was parked by a pile of commodes, plugged in to a wall socket. Kendal inserted the tiny key. It worked! The seat was comfortable, the rubber grips on the handles clean. As she wound the power lead, Kendal spotted a scuffed, pull-along shopping trolley. The tartan design was just right for elderly ladies. The perfect accessory for Fake-Kendal and super handy for smuggling stuff.

Holding the shopping trolley between her legs Kendal turned the regulator to Tortoise and sedately motored to her patio to drop off the shopping trolley, then switched to Hare, and accelerated to Brian's apartment. Jennifer was wrong. Rascal was the perfect name for the nippy, naughty vehicle.

Kendal beeped the horn. Brian and Audrey wobbled at the French windows. Audrey appeared to have lost her blouse and her morning turban had unravelled.

"I'll leave the key in the ignition," shouted Kendal. "Any damages must be paid for." Brian gave a thumbs up and Audrey blew a kiss.

From her flat, Kendal watched the Well-being Walkers navigate the drive. Brian was recklessly overtaking Jennifer, Jacob, and Jim. She smiled.

When they were out of sight, she selected six ornaments from Clem's shelves and stowed them in the shopping trolley with the empty wine bottles she'd amassed. She stood in front of the mirror and practised oldie-trolley moves; stop, sigh, stare blankly from side to side. Grasp the handle, rest, resume.

She grabbed the keys of Clem's adapted car and wheeled the shopping trolley to the car park, nodding at Carla and Emma having a smoke behind the kitchen. The Renault Kangoo looked like something Postman Pat might use but old-people-cars were ideal for people who hadn't been in a driving seat for years; the controls were simple and large, and the wheelchair space was perfect for the shopping trolley. Kendal grinned as she drove easily out of Bloscombe. Sometimes sensible was easier than cool.

Dorset's roads were emptier than those in London and rural motorists more polite. No one gave her the finger as she nipped across the rare roundabouts or forgot to indicate. The car parks in Exeter were full so Kendal slipped into in a disabled spot behind the main street, placed Clem's blue driver permit in the window, and affected a limp as she climbed out.

It felt familiar being in a city, even one as small as Exeter: normal shops advertising recognisable brands, people of every colour and age, plenty of homeless people and chuggers to avoid. Kendal reverted to city-walking. No need to smile, nod hello or make the oinking sound which everyone in Bloscombe said instead of "Good Morning".

Gary was correct about the ornaments being rare Royal Doulton. The guide prices suggested by the double-barrelled staff in the auction house sounded fantastic. Who knew there was such a healthy demand for ugly ornaments? Kendal handed over Clem's sailors and simpering shepherdesses and celebrated the imminent arrival of new funds with a bowl of noodles at Wagamama, a trawl of the wine aisle at Marks & Spencer and a visit to Ann Summers to take advantage of their two-for-one offer on vibrators. She tried to buy a new phone but her card was refused. She had no idea how long it would take for the country bumpkin solicitors to get off their horses and process her probate stuff. No more money until the auction or her final salary came through. Brian, better buy the Rascal.

As Kendal towed her laden shopping trolley back to the

Kangoo, she spotted a traffic warden. Her disability would have to be an invisible one in order to reach the car in time. It felt good to run and even better to wave at the traffic warden as she drove away.

Edging through the traffic, Kendal observed groups of teenagers drifting home from school, clutching ice creams and phones. She thought about the classmates she'd known in suburban Sussex; girls to bunk off with, borrow essays from, drop for boys with cars. A few had made contact when her mum, and then dad died, but their sympathy was oppressive and Kendal ignored them, saying she could cope. She was fine. Sixteen with an empty house and money. She'd been popular, especially with guys, until the money ran out, the house repossessed, and the car failed its MOT. By then, most school friends had moved to college or jobs in cities and any that stayed were soon bogged down with babies.

Kendal wondered what it would be like to have a best friend, someone to discuss her new life with. London was lonely, but Bloscombe was lonelier. The only person who had touched her deliberately in the last few weeks was Cheryl at Hair By Barry.

She left the city and was back on the winding, country roads. She switched on the radio. The pre-sets were for Classic FM and Radio 3. The metal interiors of the Kangoo amplified the sound and swirling orchestral music filled the air. She let the waves of sound sweep around her. Big build-ups followed by soulful drops. Almost as absorbing as the deepest grooves at her favourite Hackney bar.

When the sea came into sight, Kendal pulled into a gorse-bordered parking spot, opened the door, and breathed the earthy scent. There was a crescent of sails on the water, and she could see Bloscombe's tennis courts and bowling green; a tiny train was pulling out of the station to go back to London.

The car filled with a long round of applause. "Britten's *Sea Interludes* performed by the Bournemouth Symphony Orchestra last summer in…."

Kendal switched off the radio and lifted the disabled parking card. She touched Clem's photo.

"Thank you, Uncle Clem. For the flat, the car, the ornaments, and, it seems, a thing for classical music."

The gates at Jurassic Court opened before Kendal could tap in the code. Brian, astride the red Rascal, steamed past. "My dear, it's delightful. I'm off to the bank. I presume you want cash?"

"But Brian, we haven't discussed a price."

"I've been on eBay. These are going for £750 so I'll give you £800?"

"Bought as seen then, Brian?"

Brian lifted his hand for a feeble hi-five. "Deal!"

Kendal was pleased with her day out. More fun than a regular Monday at THRUm. She plugged in the vibrator charger, picked a hardback from Clem's bookshelves and examined the bottles she'd bought. She selected a Mateus Rosé. Mum's favourite.

Spring had arrived and she would celebrate her retirement.

At forty-four.

6

The next morning, every resident gathered in the day room for the visit from the Donkey Sanctuary. If Gary had been there Kendal might have attended, despite the unpleasant smell; since he was nowhere to be seen, she decided to explore her new home. Nurse Nicola was correct when she said no one locked their flats and while everyone else cooed over the donkey, Kendal made a comprehensive assessment of the whole complex.

Each apartment had the same basic layout with different decorations and furniture. It reminded Kendal of rooms in a student tower block (minus Blu-Tacked walls and hot rock carpet burns). Some had dining tables, minibars, or desks squeezed against walls. Others abandoned attempts to recreate a normal home and had no chairs or sociable sofas, only enormous recliners, flanked by grab-and-grip sticks; magnifying glasses; giant shoehorns, oversize telephones; sticky remotes, boxes of tissues and bags of mints.

She fetched the Lifeboat notebook from her box file to make notes:

Resident Insights
Flat 1: Philip. Purple walls, fake fur cushions.
Flat 2: Jim. Leather world and girlie pictures.
Flat 6: Prue. Rocks and stones plus hippy-shit posters.
Flat 8: Wendy. Six wigs on stands — creepy.
Flat 9: Jacob. Dumbbells and exercise bike.
Flat 10: Sam (who is s/he?) Victorian brothel style.
Flat 11: Albert. Biscuit boxes and crisp packets.
Flat 12: Brian. Lots of mirrors.
Flat 13: There isn't one.
Flat 14: Shirley (the sleepy one?) Black and white décor.
Flat 15: Jennifer. Locked.
Flat 17: Pam. Dusty, cramped.

It was hard writing by hand. Kendal needed a keypad but her laptop was in London and she'd ruined the mobile. London was full of handy places off-loading electrical stuff and fixing phones but Bloscombe shops seemed only to sell candles, plant pots and expensive things to cook with. Perhaps Emma and Carla from the kitchen would know where she could get a second-hand phone. They were local and under forty.

The donkey sanctuary visit was still going on. Emma and Carla had abandoned lunch preparation and joined the residents in the day room. There were no chairs. Kendal had to stand in the door. The donkey, sporting plastic socks and a sash that said Sonja, stood patiently as the residents stroked and talked to her. A pale teenage girl, in a hi-vis vest, held the donkey's bridle and a giant dustpan and brush. Her boss, a middle-aged woman with balayage hair, mocha foundation, and statement specs, was handing out clipboards and leaflets to the residents. She wore a large, gold lanyard, reading: "Sheila Gunny – CEO No More Tears Donkey Sanctuary".

"Good to have some new blood at Jurassic Court," snarled boss lady, offering a leaflet. Her sledgehammer scent was stronger than the donkey's. Kendal skimmed the flimsy paper:

"A gift in your Will can stop suffering for Sonja and her friends. Do it for donkeys (and mules)."

"Do complete this helpful survey," murmured Sheila Gunny. Kendal glanced at the clipboard:

Wessex Wealthwise Attitude To Risk Survey
How do you feel about an 8% return on your investment?

Kendal wasn't the only person fooling the residents. No More Tears CEO was Suspicious-Sheila in her eyes.

"Does the warden know what you are doing?" asked Kendal.

"He is aware of my services."

"And are you aware group activities are supposed to help the physical, mental, and emotional well-being of residents? Things to make them, I mean, make us, happy?" Kendal paused, remembering the activities board. "Bluebells and ukuleles and stuff."

"Everyone's happy making their money work."

"Not everyone has money to play with."

The donkey chose this moment to deliver a big load. The residents roared with laughter as the teenager swept the dung.

"My clients are extremely satisfied with our services. But we're done here, for today."

Suspicious-Sheila circled the day room retrieving clipboards and slipping business cards into handbags. Kendal rolled her leaflet into a tight ball and aimed it at the giant dustpan. It stuck on the donkey poo.

"Excellent shot," shouted Philip. "You really must join our croquet game, my dear."

Kendal smiled. "Thanks, but no thanks, Philip." She glared at Suspicious-Sheila. "I'm going to get some fresh air. It's not just the donkey that stinks here."

Kendal turned on her heels and walked as quickly as she thought viable for an older person to the foyer. She had to get a new phone. She would ask Cheryl at Hair By Barry.

The salon was packed with pensioners.

"Tuesday's two-for-one hairdo day," explained Cheryl.

"For people with two heads?" quipped Kendal. No one laughed. Banter failure again.

"For two pensioners at the same time," said Cheryl slowly.

"Right, I'll bear it in mind," said Kendal.

"What can I do you for, love? I'm chocca today."

"I wondered if you knew anywhere selling cheap laptops. Or if there was an internet café in town."

"This is Bloscombe, not London. But the library has computers anyone can go on. Use it or lose it!" said Cheryl. "Said the actress to the bishop."

The salon exploded with laughter. Definitely one for the Boomer Banter section in *The Tudge Transformation Toolkit*.

Bloscombe library was a brick building with steep steps and a long walkway in a quiet road off the top of the high street. Kendal could have climbed the steps in two seconds but remembered her role and took the oldie sloping path. The automatic door opened painfully slowly but, at last, she was inside. There were four computer terminals. All occupied by one-finger typists.

Kendal approached the issue desk. The librarian wore a blue badge: Clare – loving libraries, living well.

"Hi there, how can I help?" West Country, but posh.

"I need to use a computer. I'm not local. I'm visiting. Staying at Jurassic Court."

"I'll book you in for an hour. Write your name and contact number on the list. Do you need silver surfer training?"

"I know how to use a computer."

"Of course. Sorry."

While she waited for a free terminal Kendal perused the crammed noticeboard. Bloscombe was rammed with rubbish activities to fill dull people's lives: Art (water, acrylic, charcoal, life drawing); Anger management, Bowling (crown green, short mat, indoor, ten-pin, men, women, mixed); Beach clean; Blood pressure testing; Boarding school surviving; Croquet; cricket; computer skills, creative writing…

At last, a tattooed homeless man vacated a terminal and Kendal stepped forward. The seat was damp, the keyboard sticky. She logged in and frowned at the dozens of emails, many with maddening flags attached. She jammed her finger on Delete All.

Sadly, there didn't seem to be any computer or phone shops in Bloscombe. Even if she'd had enough money. It was good to be using a keyboard and getting instant answers. Kendal created a new document entitled Ageing Insights and filled four pages with information about elderly illnesses and symptoms, ranging from arthritis, cancer and dementia to hair loss, dental implants and a scary foot condition called plantar fasciitis. There were so many horrible conditions that could afflict older people. Fortunate, then, that she was wasn't really one of them.

A sweet, sickly smell wafted over Kendal's shoulders. The tattooed man was lurking behind Kendal's chair clutching a vape. He prodded her arm and pointed at the library clock.

"Everything OK?" said the librarian as Kendal passed her desk.

Kendal ignored her. She needed a personal computer. And hand sanitizer.

The next morning, Brian handed Kendal the money for the mobility scooter. She hid most of the cash in the box file under her bed, spent a few pounds on hand-sanitiser, snacks and proper coffee and spent the rest of the morning sorting through Clem's possessions. It was enjoyable to try on his cashmere sweaters and interesting hats. Some of the shirts and waistcoats could be repurposed, creating a kind of coastal grandmother ensemble, but the trousers, jackets and shoes had to be given away.

Delphine and Brenda at the cancer research shop couldn't believe their luck.

"Do you pay tax?" asked Delphine, thrusting a clipboard towards Kendal. Her breath smelled of onions.

Kendal frowned. "What's it to you?"

"It's for gift aid purposes. If you pay tax then we can claim money from the government." The cracks in Delphine's lips were orange today.

"I'm not working at the moment. But I was paying tax."

Delphine waved the clipboard. "So can I take your details? Name, address, age?"

Why was it so hard to give to charity? Kendal turned and walked out of the shop. "I don't do forms," she shouted, over her shoulder.

Kendal was getting used to not having Google maps and found the marina easily. Fresh air was essential after handling Clem's clothes. It was actually more enjoyable to keep your head high and follow your nose than hold a phone. Most of the boats were still wrapped in winter tarpaulins; with seagull mess covering the cabins and rubbish bobbing in the water. On the slipway an oversized canoe made of wood was being lovingly caressed by a gang of men and women drinking beer. A large banner hung from a trestle table. Someone had a thing for exclamation marks:

Gig Club Taster Session!
Free! Friendly! Fun!!
Get Fit on the Sea!!!

A tanned, muscled man greeted Kendal as she walked past. "Can I interest you in a taster? Gig rowing is easy."

"I'm not sporty."

"No worries, we have all ages and abilities here. I'm Graham, club secretary, and this is Judy, the ladies' team cox."

"Women's team, not ladies'." A wiry, thirty-something with a nose stud, stood in front of Kendal. "We're always looking for fresh blood. What's your name?" Apart from the staff at Jurassic Court this was the first youngish woman Kendal had spoken to in Bloscombe.

"Kendal. I've moved here."

"Cool name, unisex."

"My parents met in the Lake District. In Kendal. It's a place."

"I know," said Judy, moving closer. The pupils in her eyes were huge. "Where the mint cake comes from. So sweet. Hits the spot when you've worked up a sweat."

Kendal winced. These two were as pushy as the donkey sanctuary weirdos. She scanned the marina and spotted an ice cream kiosk. "Bye then, I'm going there."

"Try Bobby's Dorset knob," said Judy. "Salty, but delicious." Kendal frowned. This was going too far.

Graham touched her shoulder. "Bobby's is the gourmet ice cream. Londoners love it."

"And Dorset knobs are a real thing," added Judy. "Mostly

people eat them dry. With cheese. But Bobby makes them wet."
She winked. It was getting worse.

"Mint Chop Chip for me," said Kendal. "I'm an old-fashioned
kind of girl."

Kendal ate a large, battered cod and returned to the library. No
sign of Clare, the librarian but, strangely, the homeless tattooed
man was slumped at the issue desk. Kendal moved straight to an
empty terminal and reluctantly opened her webmail account. The
bank was banging on again about the money she owed and the
interest she was accruing. She pressed Delete All and was starting
to Google maritime paintings like the ones in Clem's bedroom
when a new email arrived from Mad-Maxine, her flatmate-
landlord. Two red flags and URGENT in the subject line

> K – where are you? I've signed for a package for you from THRUm.
> It's an Exit document and a load of stuff about places to help the
> jobless. Have you been sacked? Cos, I hate to be a bitch, but you
> can't disappear. You owe me almost £2000. Let me know what's
> going on, pretty please. Or I'll come to Dorset and find you."

7

Gary left Jurassic Court early on Thursday wearing beige cargo pants with too many pockets. Despite the unappealing packaging, he still looked tempting striding across the lawn; healthily tanned, with no sign of grey in his thick hair; his strength and vigour accentuating the frailties of the old people who surrounded Kendal at breakfast.

The residents were excited at the imminent arrival of Hair By Barry. Philip was especially animated.

"Barry is a genius," he gushed through runny egg. "What he doesn't know about hair care and the human condition isn't worth knowing."

"Cheryl's coming today too. Those two can't keep apart lately," said Audrey.

"What are you implying?" asked Philip.

"Well either Barry's had a change of heart or she's a fag-bag," said Audrey adding jam to the marmalade on her toast.

"Hag, not bag," said Brian. "And I am not sure you can say fag-hag anymore."

"When you get to my age you can say what you like."

"Everyone's more gender liquid nowadays," said Brian.

Kendal giggled. It would be entertaining to meet the famous Barry, but she couldn't risk being recognised by Cheryl and having her grey hair revealed as out-of-a-bottle. Time to get into the countryside and combine nature research with a healthy workout; be match-fit and well-informed when Gary invited her on another trek. Perhaps to Dartmoor. Where she could watch him unwind.

Kendal left Jurassic Court at nine. She had no idea where she was heading, a familiar sensation after a drunken night out but strange on a Thursday morning whilst sober. She decided to find her way back to the bluebell wood and take it from there; she had water, sunscreen, crisps, and biscuits. She had all the time in the world. Sod THRUm, bugger off bank, get off my case Maxine.

The air was fresh, and the sea sparkled: dog walkers waved poo bags and electric bikes wobbled past mobility buggies. The prom was almost as busy as Ealing Broadway except no one held a phone in their face and everyone looked happy. And old.

At the top of the cliff path, Kendal stopped to watch rabbits nibbling the grass. In the distance a paraglider floated along the cliff, catching thermals like the gulls. She wondered what it would be like to fly. The breeze caressed her face. She got out her water and applied sunscreen. It really was a beautiful day and lovely to have no deadlines and no fear of an angry phone call.

She reached an empty bench and opened the crisps. Immediately a pair of seagulls landed beside her. Up close gulls were surprisingly big and ugly, with dangerous-looking beaks and powerful wings. One bird jumped on the back of the other, flapping its wings and squawking as it tried to keep balance. The bottom seagull lifted its beak towards the other and emitted an unpleasant crooning noise. This was useful material for Nature Notes, but was she witnessing mating or rape? Both gulls had the same markings and colour, so it could be homosexual seagull sex. No penises anywhere, not like when dogs or horses did it. She left them to it and turned inland.

The darkness of Almonds Wood was spooky without Gary and the cat pee bluebell scent overwhelming. Kendal skirted the edge, relieved to emerge into an open field with a wide easy track where she could walk at a pace, her eyes on the horizon. More rolling fields led into grassy pasture and soon Kendal was far from the coast with no humans in view except someone presumably driving a distant tractor in a brown field. The sky was cloudless; birdsong burst out of the hedges. She wished she could identify them; Gary probably could.

By midday, Kendal had drunk the water. She didn't care. The air, the emptiness, and the sheer greenness around was incredibly stimulating, like natural MDMA. Serotonin buzzed in her brain and her muscles tingled. She lay on a hillock and stared at the sky. It was crazy how her life had changed, and insane to be acting sixteen years older but in this moment, on this Thursday she was happy being a sixty-year-old heiress in a field somewhere in Dorset instead of a forty-four-year-old sales executive gazing bleakly at a screen in Islington.

"Are you OK?"

Kendal opened her eyes, but the sun was directly overhead.

"You're looking a bit pink," said a familiar voice. Posh West Country.

A slim woman in walking sandals stared down. Kendal's head and back ached and her mouth tasted metallic. "Fell asleep in the sun, I've walked a long way," she muttered. The woman handed her a water bottle. Kendal glugged.

"Do I know you?"

"I'm Clare. From the library. Have you walked from Bloscombe?"

Kendal stood unsteadily and groaned. Her back ached and she felt liquid rushing inside her baggy jeans.

"Shit! I've started my period. I forgot to bring anything."

Clare smiled sympathetically. "I'm well beyond periods but I've got a first aid kit." She opened her backpack and handed Kendal a large bandage and two sterile dressings. "This should stem it. I've paracetamol if you need it but I can only hand it over in a personal capacity. Not as a library service employee."

Kendal laughed. "Don't worry, I won't sue. I'm Kendal, by the way."

"I know," said Clare. "And you don't want any silver surfer training, I remember." Kendal, unsure if this was a joke or a jibe, said nothing. She stuffed the padding into her jeans, thankful they were charity shop ones, not her Levi high-rise skinnies.

"Even though you've a terrific silver bob." Clare smiled. "And it looks great."

Kendal smiled. It was a joke. This was how people made friends, wasn't it?

"It's quite a hike back to Bloscombe. I live in Plick which is ten minutes away," said Clare, pointing at the horizon. "Come and tidy up. I'm going into town later and can drive you back."

Clare's cottage had a thatched roof, and the garden was dotted with well-worn garden furniture. Despite feeling faint and slightly nauseous, Kendal had enough energy to smirk at the name on the door: Candida Cottage.

Two blue-grey cats sunbathed on the step. Kendal ignored them. She didn't do pets.

Clare led Kendal to a yellow and blue bathroom, drew a bath and laid out fresh jeans, a huge pack of sanitary towels, a mug of tea and a large slab of lemon drizzle cake. Kendal was used to showering in strangers' homes, but it was odd to be taking a bath in the afternoon in the house of someone she'd encountered via a public service. Whilst sober. She examined the shells, prints and bookshelves covering the walls. On the windowsill were candles, bath bombs and antique bottles. Books covered the armchair and a huge radio perched on the toilet cistern. She visualised other bathrooms she'd been in. None of them contained books.

When Kendal emerged, she found Clare in her shadowy sitting room, curled on a sofa reading, the cats purring by her knees. There were paintings, ornaments, and bookshelves everywhere. On the coffee table Clare had laid cheese, oat biscuits, olives and houmous. She handed Kendal a plastic bag for the stained trousers.

"Those stretch jeans look fab on you. They're Pamela's."

Kendal put her baggy, elasticated Cotton Traders in the carrier. Good to have her legs tightly covered again and feel tight-buns-best.

"How do I return them to Pamela?" asked Kendal. Too fashionable for the Pam at Jurassic Court.

Clare giggled. "They're mine, silly. Pamela is the brand. Pop them back to the library before you leave Bloscombe. You should get some, they're perfect for your slim legs." She handed Kendal a plate and a paper napkin. "Sorry about the lack of tampons. I've been keeping the STs for my granddaughter in case she starts when she's here."

Clare didn't look old enough to have a granddaughter, even one who'd not reached puberty but a forty-four-year-old could be a grandmother. She chewed the pitta bread slowly. If the baby she'd got rid of had lived and had a baby young, then real Kendal, as well as Fake-Kendal, could have grandchildren too.

"Quite a hike you did this morning," said Clare. "Especially in those gorgeous shoes. Are they Swedish?"

"They're orthopaedic. I got them in the Cancer Research shop." Kendal paused, her mind running through the crib list of boomer ailments she'd researched. "They're brilliant for plantar fasciitis." Clare nodded sympathetically and Kendal grinned. She'd remembered the foot ailment at the right moment with the correct pronunciation. "I need to buy some walking boots," she added. "Or maybe some walking sandals, like yours."

"These are marvellous," said Clare. "From Australia. Via John Lewis. Mind you, we can all get a bit obsessed with walking kit. Dorothy Wordsworth never bothered. She walked forty miles a day in huge skirts and leather shoes. It's what you see, and think, and feel on a walk which is important. Not clothes."

Kendal didn't know how to respond. Walking was what she did to get to the Tube. "Have you seen the bluebells at Almonds Wood?" she offered.

"Not yet, but they're always spectacular there. Stay clear of the stinkhorns though. Horrendous!"

Were stinkhorns animals or people? Kendal had seen a movie where cows trampled an adulterous husband, but stinkhorns might be travellers or, maybe, hippies. Librarians would hate alternative types, wouldn't they?

Kendal had never met anyone like Clare. Tricky to get a handle on her. She read a lot of books, and judging by the snacks, was probably a vegetarian. Or a vegan, like the drones at THRUm. There was something attractive about the librarian. Not in a sexy way. She seemed chilled but would probably be hopeless in London. Couldn't handle the top deck of the night bus like she could.

"Do you feel safe walking alone around here?" asked Kendal. Clare nodded.

"I've got my phone and I know my limits. Walking alone means I can stop and start when I like and let my mind, as well as my feet, wander. I like to imagine I'm Nan Shepherd climbing the Cairngorms or Virginia Woolf in Sussex. There are so many great walks around here. It's a shame you can't stay in Dorset longer." Kendal refilled her plate. She'd taken more painkillers and felt pleasantly relaxed.

"Actually, I am staying a while. I've handed in my notice. I'm living in my uncle's flat at Jurassic Court."

Clare frowned. "The retirement village? Don't you have to be a pensioner?"

Kendal tensed. She ran her fingers through her grey hair.

"You don't have to be a pensioner. Just sixty or older."

"Gosh, you don't look it. But then you've got that late menopause thing. Plenty of oestrogen to keep your skin and hair looking terrific. Been over ten years since the change for me. But I'm really glad I'm through it. All those up and down hormones. I get so much more done now and I haven't had a sick day for years. Best thing ever, the menopause! My husband didn't think so. But good riddance to him."

Kendal wished she'd included menopause analysis in her Ageing Insights research. She was out of her depth. She remembered something she'd learned at a Building Rapport workshop at THRUm. When out of your depth in a new conversation you need to ask a question.

"Do you like being at the library?" she tried.

"Love it, the books obviously, but also all the activities. Reading groups, poetry performances, you name it, we've got it. It's tiring sometimes and visitors can be a bit rude." Clare winked. Kendal frowned. Was the librarian hitting on her like Judy-the-gig-rower?

"Only teasing," said Clare. "Come on, eat up and then I'll drive you to Bloscombe. I've got my book group at five."

Kendal polished off the cheese and olives. She had no idea what Clare was talking about most of the time, but it didn't matter. Clare was smart, funny, and kind: they'd walked, done banter, drunk tea, ate cake. She'd discussed periods, divorce, art, and clothes (despite Dorothy Wordsworth's, whoever she was, dislike of shoe chat). And all this achieved whilst sober and at no expense.

Clare dropped Kendal at the Jurassic Court gates.

"I'll bring your jeans to the library, shall I?"

"Fine. And bring some ID so we can get you membership. A utility bill will do."

"I don't have any. Everything here was paid for by my uncle."

"A passport or driving licence then?".

"They're in London."

"A woman of mystery," laughed Clare. "Don't worry, we'll solve it."

8

A day on Dartmoor for Gary was like a week at a spa for Kendal; he returned with a deeper tan and even more positive, greeting every resident as if he'd been away for a month; praising new hairstyles and leaning precariously out of the window to hang extra fat balls on the bird feeders. His yellow T-shirt rode up his back and Kendal spread a thick layer of marmalade whilst feasting on the wide black waistband of his boxers. She dropped her eyes as Gary turned, dusting crumbs off his fingers.

"The birds don't need fat balls in spring but I don't like to waste them and they go off in the cupboard." Kendal wondered what was in a fat ball. Could she eat one if desperate?

"How was Dartmoor?" she asked. "Did you see the ponies?"

"Of course, and something even better." Gary paused. "Guess."

"An escaped prisoner?" said Audrey.

"Lost boy scouts?" sniggered Philip.

"The Ring of Bells Inn?" offered Brian. "Lovely spot, great beer."

Gary shook his head. "Incorrect. Kendal, what's your guess?"

Kendal looked up. The tan accentuated the whiteness of Gary's teeth. She paused and looked into his hazel eyes. He blinked. She visualised her Nature Notes pages.

"I'm guessing wildlife of some significance."

Gary clenched his fist. "Correct."

Kendal grinned. This was easy. "Was it, by any chance, the golden plover?"

"Indeed, it was. Amazing! A golden plover by the reservoir." He pronounced the bird's name differently: plover, to rhyme with lover, not clover.

"Gosh, how lucky are you," she enthused. "I am so jealous."

"Well, you must come with me next time," said Gary. Brian, Audrey, and Philip exchanged glances. Kendal smiled and reached for the last slice of toast.

After breakfast, Kendal searched Clem's Admin box-file. She'd remembered spotting a worn, leather wallet stuffed with membership cards. She smiled as she found a plastic library card, with peeling corners and a smudged barcode. She checked Clare's jeans for stains, folded them into a clean carrier, and wedged it between the empties in her trolley.

In the foyer, residents were mustering for another Well-being Walk. Brian, on the Rascal, had seized the front spot. Kendal gave him the logbook and a reminder to renew the insurance. Jennifer whistled through her teeth and drove quickly past.

Brian winked at Kendal. "Not joining us today? Don't let Jealous-Jennifer put you off." Kendal spotted Gary behind a clipboard and answered loudly.

"I'd love to Brian, but I am joining the library today. Keen to get some fresh naturalist publications."

Philip, who'd joined Brian by the door, lifted his stick and snorted. "Saucy mare! Hope you'll give me a peek. Even with this I can't get to the nudist beach."

Gary raised his eyebrows. "Behave, guys, ladies present." Audrey arrived, dressed in a towelling beach robe.

"Swimming season starting soon," she announced. "Hope you'll be joining the Bluetits, Kendal." Kendal scanned the men. No reaction. Was this banter?

"She means the ladies who swim in the sea," explained Gary. "Wild swimming. What we used to call swimming. Some of them do it all year round."

"I love swimming in the sea," said Kendal. "Bit too cold at the moment, isn't it?"

Audrey snorted. "Ridiculous, woman. A morning dip is a great start to the day. Keeps the immune system spick and span and the little grey cells alive and kicking." Audrey pinched the sleeve of Kendal's charity shop shirt. "Love your blouse. Wonderful Paisley design. Like giant sperms."

Bloscombe high street was the busiest Kendal had seen it. Shoppers queued outside the bakers like a scene from a second world war movie. It was the day after early closing. Maybe they hadn't heard of freezers? Kendal considered how much had happened since she'd arrived the week before. She'd lost her only relative and her job, found a love interest (currently off-limits), and been transformed into a home-owning heiress or an unemployed fraud, depending on perspective.

Carry On Camping was empty, and Kendal could try shoes on without annoying remarks from teenage staff like in London, or nosy volunteers as in the cancer research shop. Eventually she chose green leather sandals which the sales assistant assured her were ecofriendly and perfect for plantar fasciitis. Kendal wasn't bothered about the environmental footprint of shoes, but she thought Clare might be impressed.

As the sales assistant wrapped her sandals, Kendal examined the outdoor pursuit snacks. Behind vegan energy bars and gluten-free granola, she spotted a cardboard box of Romney's Kendal mint cake. Her stomach tightened recalling a school trip to the Isle of Wight when the class bully had brought a bar (despite the lack of mountains) and joked about eating Kendal, sucking Kendal, Tudge-the-pudge, fudgy Tudge. Kendal had grabbed the packet, eaten the whole bar, thrown up on the gangplank and had to watch vomit trickle through the slats into the sea. The horrible experience was made worse when the teacher told her parents. Kendal had screamed and shouted, demanding a name change; something pretty like Abigail or Kylie and a normal surname like Johnson or Clarke. Dad had spent a few days calling her Polo and Spearmint, but Mum had been kind and showed her a map of the Lake District explaining how Kendal was the town where her parents honeymooned. A magical place which had, and here Mum went a bit vague, conjured a wonderful baby which was why they had named her after it. Kendal, who knew exactly how babies were made, stomped out yelling they should have gone to Chelsea or Paris or at least used some contraception.

The sales assistant nodded. "Stuff yourself with Kendal and you'll be buzzing." Kendal sighed. It still hurt.

"I'll take two packets, please, and a walking map."

Next, Kendal visited the Co-op. She needed a stock of tampons and something to disguise her feet. Simple to age her face with powder, but harder to make her perfectly normal toenails turn old-person-yellow. She'd noticed Audrey's red painted toes peeking out of jelly shoes. If Audrey had painted toenails, then she would too. Wine-red.

She'd seen lot of feet at Jurassic Court. Resting unashamedly on footrests, with arthritic toes and bunions squeezed into sandals or pasty-shaped shoes. Everyone had small feet except fat-Albert whose blue, mottled limbs were encased in enormous tartan slippers held fast with dusty Velcro straps. Feet ailments were almost as popular a subject as the weather. Brian and Philip loved discussing corns and ingrowing toenails at breakfast. Their conversation made multigrain Cheerios difficult to swallow.

Kendal entered the library as Clare was changing the noticeboard. She smiled broadly. "I'll be with you in a tick. Too many ways to fill your days in this town."

Kendal strolled around the shelves looking for books on nature. Easier to study books than wait for the sticky computer terminal. She selected one about plants and another on birds then moved to the travel shelf and found a big volume about Dartmoor. Finally, she moved to the health shelves which had dozens of books about the menopause. She selected the only volume without a celebrity on the cover. Clare was helping a bent-backed, old lady use the self-service checkout. So much quicker if the old bat simply brought the books to the issue desk, but the stubborn crone was determined to master the machine, like the bottlenecking biddies at the Co-op's self-checkouts.

"So good to see you, Kendal. Are you feeling OK today? Not too burned or stiff. Quite a hike you did."

"I'm fine, thanks, Clare. It was kind of you to take me home." Kendal handed Clare the bag of jeans and a packet of mint cake. "A little thank-you present. To enjoy on your walks."

"Amazing. Haven't had some of this for years. I'll be a regular Nan Shepherd."

Clare hadn't joked about the Kendal name but was insulting the elderly ladies in the library. Kendal decided to go with the flow.

"You're so patient with the nanny shepherding, Clare. You deserve a treat." Clare looked puzzled. Kendal pointed to the bent old lady shuffling through the automatic doors, her newly borrowed books peeking from a Poundland bag.

"Oh, I see! Very funny. That's Lady Almonds. Bless her. Insists on using the automated checkout. I always have to help her, poor soul. Her son wants to close the libraries, but she won't let him."

"Can he do that? How?"

"As leader of the council he does what he bloody well likes. Privileged twat!"

"No one will let him close something so useful," said Kendal.

"You've got a lot to learn about rural communities."

Clare had a posh voice but appeared to be left-wing. It was confusing. Kendal wished she understood politics more.

Clare reached for Kendal's books. Kendal passed Clem's library card. The machine beeped angrily.

"Computer says no!" Clare examined the faded plastic card. "It's for Clement Tudge. You can't use this."

Kendal hugged the books.

"Tell us once," said Clare. "It's the best way."

Kendal's chest tightened. Was this how it was going to end? Exposed by a library card?

"It's a government service," said Clare in a kind voice. "Jurassic Court would have registered your uncle's death and then Tell Us Once notifies all official services, like hospitals, the pension people and libraries."

Kendal's chest relaxed. "I don't have any paperwork for the membership."

"No problem, Kendal. I know where you live and I'm in charge. At branch level, at least. I can make you a card now. New members help bump up the figures for Sir Anthony and his bean-counters."

"They're all nuts," said Kendal.

"Who?"

"The Almonds."

Clare burst into laughter. "You're hilarious." Kendal beamed. Nailing banter, at last. Clare touched Kendal's shoulder. "Hey, Kendal, why don't you come walking with me tomorrow? I'll show you my favourite place and we could eat your mint cake. See if our teeth fall out."

Gary wouldn't have another day off for at least a week and meanwhile, time spent with Clare gathering nature information would make her more attractive.

"As long as you're feeling OK and not still bleeding out," said Clare. "Bit worrying at your age."

"I'll be fine. I'd love to go walking with you and christen my new shoes."

"Shall I meet you at Jurassic Court around ten? Nice to see Gary if he's there."

"You know Gary?"

"Such a sweetheart. Went out with my daughter when they were teens. He should have stuck with her instead of the dreadful woman he got stuck with."

Kendal kept her face in neutral. Plenty of time tomorrow to glean Gary's history.

"Anyway, must get on. Got Books-On-Wheels to sort." Clare handed Kendal a new library card and glanced at the wall clock. "And my moment of bliss after work."

None of Clare's statements made sense but they were all intriguing. Kendal tilted her head into a questioning pose.

"Managed to bag an appointment at Bloho-Beauty. Lucky me." Clare waved her hands "Hallelujah, relief is on its way."

Kendal tried to imagine what might bring Clare relief. Over sixty, in work, well-fed? So not sex, money, or food.

Clare winked. "Goodbye winter feet. Hello summer. The minute the sun comes out everyone drags out their sandals. Then we're all gagging for a foot make-over."

A pedicure! "Ah yes, lucky you. Enjoy. See you tomorrow."

Wheeling the shopping trolley along the high street, Kendal monitored footwear. Clare was correct. Eight out of ten people had put on summer shoes: men wearing socks and sandals and women sporting slip-on sandals. No one had done their toenails properly. Yellow nails and crinkled corns adorned lard-white or raspberry-red feet.

Outside Peninsular-Pets, the pavement was blocked by a stunning pair of six-inch heels. Red stilettos. Higher than the chihuahua they stood next to. One person, in the whole of Bloscombe, with some shoe style. Kendal raised her eyes. A tall, gracious, elderly transvestite bowed. "Let the lady pass, Margot. Age before beauty."

"Thanks," said Kendal. "Love your shoes."

Chihuahua-owner winked. "Love your hair."

9

The ukulele club hand bell double booking was not the disaster Gary had predicted. The Coastal Campanologists rang the D and G bells to match the only chords the ukulele club had learned which meant a limited repertoire but a bearable sound. Kendal could endure *Drunken Sailor* on loop if it meant all residents were occupied and she could spend Friday afternoon alone.

After painting her toenails with the wine-red polish, leaving a few nails half-finished to emulate Audrey's messy toes, Kendal opened the library book to find out if she was perimenopausal. Two days since she started her period, but the flow was showing no sign of abating and she was sweating (though Jurassic Court was always overheated). There were horrible segments about facial hair, bladder infections, osteoporosis, and vaginal dryness but she learned that although rare to have periods at fifty-nine it wasn't impossible and Fake-Bleeding-Kendal could be a rarity, not seriously ill with polyps or uterine cancer.

Before meeting Clare, the only time she'd used the term perimenopausal was in relation to Dogbreath-Deirdre. Her self-righteous team-mates at THRUm were appalled at Kendal's use of the word as an adjective. They perceived Dogbreath-Deirdre's mood swings as constructive feedback. When Kendal moaned, they merely pointed at a giant mural above the desk: FEEDBACK – IT'S A GIFT!

Kendal turned to the Ageing Insights section of *The Tudge Transformation Toolkit* and started a new page:

Peri Pointers:
Heavy bleeding✓
Irregular periods? Can't remember
Memory loss? See above ✓
Weight gain? Difficult to tell with baggy clothes
Vaginal dryness —Too gross to think about

Kendal put on the new walking sandals and marched to the Co-op. She needed to self-sedate. In the corner of the store, on the dusty local produce shelf, she discovered a display of small bottles. Perry; old fashioned, and cheap. If she was perimenopausal, then Perry was the perfect, punning, accompaniment. She bought a six-pack. She wished she could share the joke about Perry. If her mother was alive, Kendal might have discussed the menopause with her and learned when and how it had happened. But her mum had died so young, she probably wouldn't have had it, and now she'd never know.

At supper, Brian, Audrey and Philip were discussing possible reasons why Albert had missed the music activity and hadn't appeared at the Well-being Walk.

"Maybe he's having a duvet day?" offered Kendal. "It's his choice."

Brian and Philip shrugged. Audrey whispered. "It's important to be seen." Audrey was a bit of a snob sometimes.

"Well, waste not, want not. I'll take his pudding," said Kendal. "Is there an activity tonight?" She was beginning to enjoy the free entertainment.

"Beetle drive," said Brian. "Stupid game, for stupid people."

"It's good for children," said Philip.

"My grandchildren can't do it," grumbled Brian. "They don't understand the dots on the dice. They're always on tablets."

Audrey slammed her fist. "It's the drug companies; they want them addicted. Kids should be taught yoga instead."

Jurassic Court's combination of biddies, bad hearing, and bonkers characters was entertaining but when you'd decided you might be perimenopausal it was exhausting. Kendal squeezed Audrey's shoulder and escaped to her room. She packed her backpack with snacks, water, sunscreen, tampons, and the new map for the next day's walk, opened another Perry and lay in the reclining chair studying the nature books. She was looking forward to the walk with Clare: a chance to find out about Gary, nail the late-onset menopause story, practise boomer banter, work off a bit of flab and practise her nature knowledge. With someone who was old, but not very old. Someone who might become a friend.

It was not the way Kendal normally spent Friday night, but with the sun streaming through the French windows, plenty of Perry, and Albert's bread and butter pudding in the mini-fridge, it was hugely pleasurable and, even if she was perimenopausal, she wasn't losing her memory because she'd remembered to put the vibrators on charge.

Kendal made sure to be in the foyer well before ten. Clare was still employed and not a pensioner, but she was a grandmother and technically old and, as Kendal was learning, old people were always early. Without a phone, Kendal stared at the garden while she waited. It was peaceful sitting on the sofa and counting the bluebells coming out in the garden. Even though they were incomers, not native. When she got a new phone, she must remember to adopt the oldie trait of looking at a screen only to make a call or take a photo. It wouldn't be difficult. She liked how not looking at phones made you see more. Obvious really, but something she never did in London.

A familiar figure hurried from the car park shouting into a phone. Nicola, the district nurse, looked even messier and more disorganised than at Clem's funeral; the red blotches on her face were merging and bandages were falling out of her open bag. She ran through the automatic doors and stopped in front of Kendal.

"Which room is he in?" she bellowed.

"Who?" said Kendal. The woman was trollied. Perhaps she'd taken opioids?

"The one with the blocked cock. I mean, faulty catheter?"

Kendal shook her head. "I don't know. What's his name?"

"You tell me. You're the manager."

Kendal stood, remembering to emit a tiny grunt. Her disguise must be effective if the nurse couldn't recognise her. The office door opened. Gary stepped out in Saturday shorts. Faded denim. Button fly.

"Morning ladies. Nicola, would you like to come into the office, and I'll update you on Albert?"

Nicola pointed at Kendal. "Who's she then?"

Gary took the nurse's arm. "This is Kendal, our newest resident."

Nicola scoffed. "And I'm the Queen of Sheba. No way is she a resident."

Kendal's heart lurched. The nurse stomped to Kendal and peered at her face. She was like the noisy, homeless guy Kendal used to avoid outside Ealing Broadway tube. "I'll give my pension to the marines if this woman is sixty. You've been hoodwinked mate. Once again."

Kendal smelled Nicola's coffee breath and heard the crackle of her tunic. Gary was shrinking into the carpet, clasping his hands and chewing his lips. Awkwardness made him even more alluring.

The automatic doors opened, and neat, clean, lovely Clare entered bringing fresh air and birdsong.

"Morning, wonderful day." She hugged Gary and stepped between the district nurse and Kendal. "Good to see you, Nicola."

Gary steered the nurse into his office and Kendal breathed. Clare lifted Kendal's backpack and held it for Kendal to slip her arms through.

"Ready for our Saturday jolly?"

Kendal nodded. Her heart was still racing.

"Right, let's get moving before Nicola gets out of Gary's office. Poor thing, she's got early-onset. I'm not sure if Gary's twigged it yet."

"Early-onset what?" asked Kendal.

"Dementia, of course, so sad. She's losing it. Not senior moments, like we all have. The full-on illness. She'll be incapacitated soon. Become a liability."

Kendal suppressed a smile. Such a relief. She remembered an

article she browsed in the library. "Makes people say outrageous stuff, doesn't it?"

"Indeed," nodded Clare. "No filters. You have to humour them."

Kendal pressed the switch for the automatic door and smiled. Early-onset dementia was rough for the district nurse but lucky for her.

The two women marched briskly along the prom until they reached the estuary and turned inland to follow the river. The route was busy with bird and wildlife spotters; some knew Clare and stopped for a chat, whilst others simply strode past nodding and making the oinking noise. They stopped in a small shed by the water and stared at the river. Clare was excited by some broken twigs on the opposite side, which she claimed was proof of beaver action. Kendal avoided inappropriate giggling by examining her new map (though contour lines, paths and rivers were difficult to tell apart). Weird how boomers preferred paper maps. Google was a thousand times better. Perhaps it made them think of the war. Their finest hour, blah blah.

After a mile, Clare turned off the track onto a wide path through farmland. Now Kendal could walk beside instead of behind Clare and steer the conversation. She remembered the Building Rapport course and began asking lots of questions: favourite books (Elena Ferrante), number of children (three), crops in the fields (peas, potatoes, maize). Clare asked lots of questions in return and Kendal was able to instantly retrieve convincing answers from *The Tudge Transformation Toolkit* back story. Building Rapport was easy if you prepared. Dogbreath-Deirdre had a point.

The walk finished at what Clare called the famous Seven Witches but was merely a heap of rocks. Kendal didn't care. She was glad to sit. Clare might be much older than Kendal but she was far fitter. They leaned against a rock witch and opened their backpacks.

"These ladies are not as old as they claim," said Clare, slapping the rock behind her. "They're masquerading as prehistoric, but are probably Victorian, dumped here by a misogynist farmer to make his land more valuable." She opened the mint cake and offered Kendal a mug of coffee from a pink flask. "I hate inauthenticity, don't you? So much of it around, unfortunately."

Kendal's hand shook and coffee spilt on her wrist. She winced and shook her head at the mint cake. It could still make her gag. "Watching my weight, Clare. What with my condition."

"Oh, I forgot. Are you still bleeding? Maybe you need to go to the doctor and get HRT or something?"

It was the perfect moment to build rapport, utilise the previous day's research, and cement her late-onset menopause alibi.

"I'm with Germaine Greer on this one. Us ladies of a certain age shouldn't have to take drugs and risk cancer to satisfy society's idea of how we should be. I'm acting my age, and proud of it."

Clare handed Kendal a nectarine. "Well, I'm not sure it's quite what Germaine Greer was saying, and she's always changing her mind, but I'm glad you're going the natural route. Swimming, walking, and gardening are better therapies than synthetic hormones. And free."

Kendal bit into the fruit and juice trickled onto her chin. "Yeah, Audrey at Jurassic Court is keen on getting me into the sea. She's an inspiration. Does yoga, understands *Pointless*, and I don't think she's lost her libido. Always hopping into Brian's flat."

Clare laughed and poured more coffee. "Jurassic Court has quite a reputation for romance. I've been to a couple of weddings there and, of course, Gary gets a lot of hearts fluttering."

Boom! Kendal had turned the conversation in the right direction again. The Building Rapport course never helped Kendal's telephone sales techniques at THRUm, but it certainly worked with Clare. Kendal gazed at the clouds, taking her time and mentally mining what she'd researched the day before. Two birds circled high above.

"Are those peregrines?"

Clare looked into the sky. "No, they're Common Buzzards. Interesting creatures. They mate for life. There are peregrines on this coast though. Further east, near Portland. I could take you one day if you like birds."

Kendal grinned. Rapport building was child's play. She'd like to share her childhood camping experience at Portland. It would be good to talk about her parents. They came into her mind a lot since she'd left London. But it was important to focus and accomplish the task she'd set out to achieve. She offered Clare a bag of popcorn.

"Can't do popcorn now. My teeth are dodgy. The last mouthful cost me six hundred pounds."

Kendal hadn't visited a dentist since her parents died but Mad-Maxine was always under the drill and it didn't cost anything half as much.

"Do you go to a private dentist, then?"

"There's no choice in Bloscombe. This government is desecrating the health service."

Clare was off on politics again and Kendal was not only out of her depth but getting further away from the topic she really wanted to discuss.

"So, what's Gary's story, then? You mentioned he went out with your daughter?"

"When they were teenagers. Used to write thank-you cards after Sunday lunch. Seemed like he came from another era and now he's with old people all the time. It's like he's found his niche."

"Why did they stop dating?"

"She went to university, and he went to the tech, and then his new girlfriend got pregnant. He married her, even though everyone knew the baby wasn't his. They moved to Plymouth and he got an engineering job. She went off with a marine. Took the child. We felt so sorry for him; he was unhappy, often drunk. He hated the secrecy at the MOD, he said it was full of liars. So, he went travelling and became an aid worker, building bridges, helping floods. Came back at the millennium and joined the

Quakers. He channelled his anger into surfing, got sober but he couldn't get an engineering job as technology had moved on. The only work was cleaning at Jurassic Court and now he's the manager, the best they've had."

Kendal was enthralled. Gary had been around the block. Lost a lot, like her, but remodelled himself. They had so much in common, except she still drank, and didn't hate lies.

"Did he meet another woman?"

"He's always working. Never going to find romance at Jurassic Court."

Kendal threw the popcorn packet into her bag and took out her lipstick. Clare trained her binoculars on the buzzards. Kendal thought about Gary amongst the rubble in an earthquake-hit hellhole. What a hero! A breeze blew across the hummocky landscape and the sun warmed the Seven Witches. The day was going brilliantly.

They returned to the estuary path and stopped in front of a notice pinned to the wildlife info-board:

Beaver Evidence Plan now published
Name your beaver for £50

"I'm tempted," said Clare. "But what to choose?"

"Diva Beaver?" said Kendal. "Or maybe Eager Beaver?"

Clare chortled. "It's been so long. Mine would have to be Leaver Beaver."

Kendal wondered if Clare knew about the two-for-one offer at Ann Summers. Not appropriate to mention yet, but maybe, at some point, they would be close enough to talk about stuff in a no-holds-barred kind of way. Laugh at the Perry drink and be real friends. Like she'd never had before.

"Thanks for introducing me to the Seven Witches," said Kendal as they entered Jurassic Court's gates. "A spellbinding day!"

Clare laughed and bent forward to hug goodbye. "It's been lovely. You're a fab walking buddy." Kendal tensed. So long since she'd been hugged when she was sober, or sex wasn't on the cards. She waved as Clare drove her perky Mini Clubman away.

Gary emerged from his office as Kendal walked through the automatic doors. It was almost as though he was waiting for her.

"Had a good time with Clare?"

"A lovely day, thanks, Gary. We went to the Seven Witches."

"Sorry about Nicola this morning. She's under a lot of strain."

"I understand. Clare told me."

"Yes, I should have known Clare would explain." Gary looked at his feet. "Did she tell you anything else?"

Kendal nodded. "Loads, she's a font of knowledge." Gary tapped his toe at a leaf which had blown in. Kendal waited. It was fun teasing. "I learned so much. For example, Dorothy Wordsworth was one of the first people to record a climb of Scafell Pike in the Lake District, Nan Shepherd is not a verb, she was a writer who climbed mountains in Scotland, and Stinkhorns are best eaten in an omelette."

Gary nodded and smiled. She wished she could hug him; not a Clare-friendly-goodbye-squeeze but a red-blooded clinch.

"Movie Night later. Philip's chosen *Some Like It Hot*."

Kendal opened the French windows and the last bottle of Perry. She dragged *The Tudge Transformation Toolkit* from under the bed and started a new page:

Bloscombe Business
Gig club (nothing to do with music)
U3A (a fancy acronym for oldies organising yet more clubs)
Books-On-Wheels (books for bedridden biddies who can't get to the library)
Dorset Knobs (triple baked lumps of dough made of flour, sugar, and water)

It was tempting to start a Gary Gossip page but more important to record insights which could be recycled – like nature facts or successful banter and by the time she'd added peregrines, beavers and the superbly named shags to Nature Notes, the dinner gong was doing its thing. Gary's story was to be kept, for the moment, under wraps. Besides, she wouldn't forget it. Perimenopausal or whatever.

Walking with Clare was excellent exercise and hugely educational. Clare knew about books, nature, and history, and quite a lot about Gary (though Kendal forced herself not to ask any additional questions in case it looked obsessive). Clare was over sixty and yet her clothes; hair, and skin looked normal. Yes, she had a few lines on her forehead and age spots on her hands, and allegedly dodgy teeth, but her blonde bob, well-defined eyebrows and cute daisy earrings placed her undoubtedly in MILF territory. Clare didn't have wobbly bits and made no sound when she got out of a chair or climbed over a style. When they climbed a hill it was Kendal who was puffing and when they descended it was Clare who kept her eyes on the horizon whilst Kendal peered at the ground to avoid rabbit holes and slippery stones.

Clare was young-old and Audrey, Prue and Jennifer, were old-old. When the money from the auction came through Kendal would amend her costume. Make it more appropriate for a sixty-year-old. Buy tighter trousers or some quirky earrings? Have a professional pedicure?

The best thing about Clare was how chilled she was. Clare didn't have a sarcastic word in her vocabulary; no moans about her ex-husband, no criticism of her children or grandchildren and nothing nasty about the people at work or the many clubs and societies which filled her life. Clare's pleasantness was authentic, not affected (like THRUm's goody-goody drones), and balanced with a dose of healthy nosiness and a sense of fun. Clare appeared to find Kendal genuinely funny; she too loved a pun and appreciated innuendo. Walking with Clare made Kendal believe she really was an intelligent, amusing, functioning pensioner who'd had a successful career and a well-balanced social life.

10

Philip had gone for a Miami nightclub vibe with paper umbrellas, cans of pineapple chunks, three bottles of Baileys and a rusty cocktail shaker.

"I'm your master misogynist!" he announced as the residents shuffled to their seats.

"You've never said you dislike women," said Audrey.

"He means mixo…," said Brian. "God, what is the word? Not the dead bunnies. It's a jumped-up bartender. You're getting mixed up, Philip."

"Yes, I'm mixing it. Like Tom Hanks."

"Cruise," corrected Kendal.

"Hate them," snapped Audrey. "Full of estate agents and second wives, and they make you seasick."

Gary arrived with the film projector. He'd put on a dinner jacket and bow tie and slicked his hair. Not as good as shorts but better than the cargo pants. Kendal accepted a sticky glass from Philip and sat next to a swarthy man in a velvet jacket.

"Good evening, I'm Sam," he said. "We haven't met, I've been on holiday."

Kendal nodded. "Flat 10, isn't it?" She gulped. Too relaxed.

"Indeed, how do you know?"

"Oh, Gary showed me round when I moved in. I'm Clem's niece."

"I know, everyone's thrilled you've moved in. Young blood is so welcome."

Kendal was about to explain that she wasn't young but Gary clinked his glass.

"Good evening, everyone. Welcome to the Bloscombe speakeasy. Before we start tonight's movie, I want to update you on Albert. He's been moved to the cottage hospital where he can receive appropriate care and be in a bariatric bed."

Everyone groaned. Audrey swore. Gary clinked his glass again. "Now over to our resident mixologist Philip who requested this film classic." Gary sat on Kendal's other side. She could smell his hair gel. Citrus and vanilla.

Philip, tumbler in one hand, ukulele in the other, marched to the front. "This film is a milestone in cinema. It's a funny film, one of the funniest. It's a movie about people faking it and…"

Philip turned towards Gary and Kendal. The pineapple chunk in Kendal's mouth felt gigantic. Was she going to choke?

"And nobody's perfect, especially Albert." Gary stiffened. Kendal relaxed; she was not the target. Sam poked her with his stick.

"Talk about people in glass houses," he whispered hoarsely. "He's been faking it all his life."

"What do you mean, Sam?"

"Philip, the silly bugger. Queer as a nine-bob note. Either he isn't aware or doesn't want us to know it. Either way, he's batting for the other side and always will be."

Kendal stared as Philip warbled through *Sweet Georgia Brown*. Off-key, but word perfect. Hard to imagine someone in their seventies could have desires, let alone suppress them.

Neat Baileys with pineapple was delicious, and the scent of Gary's hair gel intoxicating. Tony Curtis and Jack Lemmon were genuinely funny pretending to be women to hide from gangsters. Extremely weird to be spending Saturday night watching a film about two people faking identities, selected by a seventy-one-year-old who, allegedly, spent a lifetime masking his, whilst simultaneously faking her own.

Sunday brought blue sky and sunshine. Kendal skipped breakfast and donned white shorts she'd brought from London. Bit of a risk with the endless bleeding period but it felt good to have bare legs and a tightly covered bum. She dialled down the ensemble with the charity shop pearl earrings and padded gilet to create a wholesome, outdoorsy, possibly sporty image. Something to attract the attention of a nature-loving, athletic, spiritual, single, straight bloke.

Sunday was when the Quakers met at Jurassic Court. A week before this meant nothing to Kendal but Clare's revelation about Gary's involvement made the Quakers suddenly interesting. Who were these porridge people who'd saved the warden from a life of debauchery? Did they still wear funny hats? Only one way to find out.

The Quakers met in the Ammonite room at the western end of the complex where old DVDs, jigsaw puzzles and toys were stored. It was furnished with mismatched chairs, mug-marked coffee tables and a dusty cheese plant. The windows overlooked the car park and the bins whilst the interior windows onto the corridor had Venetian blinds which were easy to spy through. Replica ammonites hung on the walls, alongside three large words of wooden letters: PEACE   LOVE   JO

Kendal expected hymns; old-fashioned ones full of odd words like redeemer and feedeth. Yet, as she walked along the corridor, she couldn't hear any singing. There was no sound at all; perhaps she'd got the time wrong?

She crept to the window and peered through the slats of the blind. Audrey, Prue, Jacob, Jim and Jennifer sat on one side and five non-residents on the other. Gary was perched on a wooden chair with his back to the interior window. There were long hairs on his neck below the hairline which he probably couldn't reach when shaving. He needed someone to do it for him. In a shower.

Kendal watched for ten minutes but no one spoke, and nothing happened. Her legs cramped and she shifted against the window. Gary turned. He opened the door. "Good to see you. Come in."

"Just passing," mumbled Kendal.

"The corridor ends here."

"Yep, keeping up my step count."

"Well, this is the Quaker meeting, we're very friendly. We've got some Quakers from town who come too. There's no meeting house in Bloscombe so they join us here."

"I'm not good at meetings."

"You don't have to do anything. Sit with us."

Kendal entered the room. No one said anything, not even Audrey. The only sound a quiet fart. Kendal pushed herself into the chair and pressed her hands on the armrests. Her legs looked good in the shorts. She hoped she wouldn't suddenly shout something. At the corner of the window a cobweb had trapped two dead flies; in the car park, she could hear Carla and Emma laughing and then the growl of Carla's moped. She watched the spider slowly consume a fly. Doing nothing in a room full of other people was weirdly relaxing. Like a chill-out lounge but without the come-down.

Sometime later Kendal became aware people were leaving; a few hugged in the corridor but still no one spoke. Then Gary was standing above her.

"Thanks for coming, Kendal. I'm so glad to see you here."

Kendal wondered if she'd been asleep with her mouth open. She should probably speak. She nodded at the large wooden letters on the wall. "Who's Jo?"

Gary followed her gaze. "It's Joy, but the Y has fallen off. I'd stopped noticing it, to be honest."

Was a Quaker service an appropriate moment for banter? Perhaps with a spiritual slant? "We're all looking for the why in life, aren't we?" she ventured. Gary laughed. Nailed banter with a pious pun!

Kendal pulled herself out of chair, remembering to grunt. "Great movie last night. I enjoyed it."

"Good. I thought you were asleep. Your eyes were closed."

"Best way to appreciate the songs," lied Kendal. "Marilyn Monroe was superb."

"Philip made a good choice. Maybe you might like to select a film for Movie Night one week? Now you're a resident."

There was nothing alcoholic in her flat except the disgusting Noilly Prat so Kendal decided to see if she could get through the rest of Sunday without drinking. She made a cup of herbal tea, finished the first book in Uncle Clem's collection about a sailor called Hornblower and watched *Antiques Roadshow*. With her antiques waiting to be auctioned, and more hanging on her walls, it was suddenly must-see. A fireman from Swansea tried not to look too delighted as his grandmother's Gucci engagement ring was valued at five thousand pounds.

Sunday was a good day for him, as well as Kendal. She'd experienced joy (with a Y on the end), enjoyed boomer television, got into reading again and given Gary a good look at her shapely legs. Been entertained and admired. All without drink or drugs, and all for free.

Breakfast in London was something you grabbed on the way to work but at Jurassic Court it was an event as though the residents were delighted to have survived another night. Kendal had found their animated conversation a bit much first thing in the morning but when Albert disappeared, and the chatter fell away, she missed it, not simply because silence drew attention to the gummy chewing.

She escaped to her flat, opened the French windows and surveyed the dusty patio. It needed attention. New plants, or perhaps a sun lounger? But not yet. So many other priorities. She needed to focus.

It was good to have a clear head on a Monday morning instead of being hungover on the tube, knowing Dogbreath-Deirdre would be on her case the minute she arrived at THRUm. Kendal turned the deckchair towards the sun and started a list:

Kendal's Key Tasks
Get laptop
End flat share with Maxine
Pay debts — get money

Short, but daunting. Couldn't get one task done without the other, and none were fun. She needed to go to the library to access her email. It would be nice to see Clare too.

A discordant jangling erupted on the lawn. Eight chubby middle-aged men in straw hats, waistcoats, floppy shirts, and white trousers were skipping across the grass; seven had beards, one an accordion, and one, on closer inspection, was a woman. They carried thick wooden sticks, wore bells around their knees and were covered in red, yellow, and green ribbons.

Gary, in a blue linen shirt and dark jeans, appeared to appreciate the weirdos tramping over his lawn, shaking their hands, and slapping their backs.

"That's Gary's uncle, he's the boss of Tea Wrecks." Audrey had slipped in. Kendal had forgotten to lock her door. "I love these chaps. So much va va voom. They keep going for hours."

None of the group looked remotely like Marc Bolan or anyone in T Rex. Kendal closed her notebook and opened a deck chair for Audrey. The accordion player began to play, and the dancers jumped into action, frenetically skipping and beating sticks. For such old and large guys, they did have a lot of energy, and, even with beer bellies, were nimble and precise; no one missed a beat, and the sticks smashed each other, not faces.

Gary waved. "Happy May Day. Workers of the world unite!"

Kendal was confused. Was Gary a communist as well as a Quaker? She hoped he wasn't one of the weird dancers. Although, as Audrey pointed out, they had staying power which was a good trait in a hot bloke.

"The Morris dancers visit all the old people's homes on May Day, then every pub," said Audrey. "It would be fun to follow them, don't you think? We could be Tea Wrecks gropies!"

"Groupies," laughed Kendal. "What would Brian think?"

"None of his business," snapped Audrey. "I'm a free agent." She frowned, "But the pubs can get jammed on a bank holiday. I'm staying here."

"It's a bank holiday?"

"Yes, then there's another at the end of the month. Or is it June? Every day's a holiday when you live here."

"So, the library will be closed?" asked Kendal.

"What a bookworm you are. Relax! Carla's organising sitting-down maypole dancing."

"It's the computers there I want, not books. I need to do some emails and banking and I've broken my phone."

The Morris men wiped their faces with huge handkerchiefs. Gary opened a freezer box and distributed beers. Kendal imagined lying on the lawn beside him and cracking a few cans. Bank holidays in London could be fun, hanging out in parks and hooking up with fellow slackers. One Bank Holiday Monday she'd met a pony-tailed drummer who claimed he was a millionaire. They'd shared a joint, then slunk off to his flat where his fridge was full of champagne, coffee beans and Spanish beer.

"There's a computer for us in Jurassic Court," said Audrey. "Nobody uses it. No one knows how. It's part of the amenities."

"I've not seen a computer anywhere," said Kendal.

"It's in the Ammonite room, behind the puppet theatre. Which no one uses either."

"I'm not surprised," said Kendal. "It's an odd amenity in a place with no children. Is it because we are by the seaside?"

"It's so we can express any difficulties," answered Audrey. "A wakey social worker who was concerned we might be bullied. She thought we could act out our problems with puppets."

"No one could bully you, Audrey. It's woke, by the way, not wakey."

"Whatever! Not bothered." Audrey shook her head.

"But I am bothered about Albert. Still no news. Gary has done the wrong thing. He's too wakey as well."

"I'll investigate the computer," said Kendal ushering Audrey to the door. Could be hours if the Albert problem was on the agenda. "See you at lunch."

The activities board in the foyer had been updated. Kendal grinned. How things had changed. Her diary was on a wall now, not online.

Monday (BANK HOLIDAY)– Tea Wrecks & seated maypole dancing
Tuesday – Audrey's flower arranging class
Wednesday (Gary's day off) – Comfitoes Chiropodist. Book early.
Thursday – (Gary's day off)– Farming Chatter with Emma
Friday – Well-being Walk
Saturday – Movie Night – Brian's choice

No amusing spelling and disappointing to see Gary was going to be away for two days. She would join Friday's walk. Hard to stick to the slow pace, but a good opportunity to fraternise with the warden. She'd prefer an active session on Dartmoor, or somewhere secluded like Almonds Wood but, with the ending of the heavy period, she was approaching the lusty mid-cycle moment. Best to be with other residents, keep it slow, bide her time and focus on Kendal's Key Tasks. She slipped into the kitchen, grabbed a pack of Kit Kats, and marched to the Ammonite room which was always empty except for on Sundays. If it worked then she could use the computer whenever she needed. A bit exposed with the interior windows so not good for porn, or face-timing hot strangers, though recently she'd not felt the need for these internet activities.

The computer under the puppet theatre was ancient, but its keyboard was clean. Taped to the side was the password. GaryVaughan15.

Kendal wondered what fifteen meant to Gary. Perhaps he was partial to composite numbers which would be another thing they had in common. Maybe it was when he lost his virginity, or his house number, or collar size?

Pleasant thoughts about Gary's neck disappeared the moment Kendal opened her webmail. A red-flagged email from the bank announcing her card had been suspended was followed by seven messages from colleagues at THRUm. Such goodie-goodies, always running marathons and picking at healthy packed-lunches. Skimming through, Kendal decided they were probably cut-and-paste jobs dictated by Dogbreath-Deirdre as each message had suspiciously similar phrases, correct spelling, and no emoticons.

> Sending virtual sympathy for the passing of your uncle. I am sorry to learn you are leaving THRUm and wish you the best of luck in your new adventure. It has been fascinating working alongside you. We will all miss you, especially at the Christmas party!

Kendal punched the desk, and the PEACE, LOVE and JO wall letters wobbled. The dust made her sneeze but the pain in her knuckles felt good. Getting the sack was not the issue; she'd experienced it many times. She was angry at the hypocrisy and double speak of her young teammates who, she knew, despised her.

Being fired normally set Kendal off on a revenge-activity or shoplifting-bender. In Bloscombe, she could do neither. Disappointing, as well, to be denied an exit interview. Dogbreath-Deirdre was a total bitch and now she had no opportunity to tell anyone. Yesterday she was as chilled as it was possible to be whilst living a lie. Today, she was furious.

Kendal opened the cardboard doors of the puppet theatre. A bunch of glove puppets lay in a scrum. She slipped her left hand into Goldilocks (Kendal, when she was blonde) and the right hand into a witch (excellent casting for Dogbreath-Deirdre). Her departure from THRUm needed rewriting:

Goldilocks: Take your jargon-ridden job, your claptrap-key-performance-indicators, your shit-sandwich-feedback and go spread-sheet yourself into oblivion.

Witch: Kendal, be aware of the effect your behaviour has on your team.

Goldilocks: I don't care. You're all tossers. If the people who fund raise for THRUm knew how you operate, you'd be jobless too.

Kendal grinned. She was ready for Mad-Maxine and able to complete the second task on Kendal's Key Tasks list.

> Dear Maxine, apologies for not replying sooner. Been on a digital detox. I've decided to stay by the coast to find a more authentic way of living. Please rent the room to someone else. If you could possibly store my belongings, I will collect them asap. I've resigned from THRUm so ignore any letters.
> Hope all is well with the boyf.
> Love K.

Kendal smiled; the social worker had a point. Puppets were perfect for acting out trauma. Cathartic. She ate a Kit Kat as a reward for the progress she made on the Kendal Key Tasks list: got access to a computer; ended the flat share and now she had to get the bank off her back.

Begrudgingly, she used her final salary to pay off some of her credit card debt. There was still a few thousand owed, but it was a start.

Kendal was about to close webmail and treat herself to some Dartmoor browsing when a ping announced the arrival of a new email. Maxine was spending Bank Holiday Monday online. What a saddo!

> OMG K! You're alive FFS! Josh and I were frantic.
> No problem about the room, Josh is moving in!!
> Do need your money tho, hun.
> It's a month and a half rent, plus a percentage of the bills. Total: £1985.
> We're coming down to see you, got exciting news. Booking Airbnb now. Can't wait to see the sea…and you, natch.

Kendal frowned. Good news her flatmate-landlord wasn't demanding the three months' rent she actually owed but terrible news that Mad-Maxine and her posh prat boyfriend were turning up, in their disgusting, entitled real-life flesh which would expose her lie and then she'd be homeless. Why couldn't they leave her alone? She was enjoying her new life. Making friends and trying to get her shit sorted.

It was tempting to stuff her hands up the prince and princess for some cathartic puppet therapy but a speedy response was more important:

> Whoa M, don't come yet. I've still got loads of stuff I have to do with my uncle's passing. Once it's sorted, I can pay you in full and would love to welcome you. The sea will be warmer by then.

Kendal opened another Kit Kat. A Quaker poster caught her eye: "The best language has always come out of silence."

Those porridge eaters were brilliant! Mad-Maxine constantly banged on about spiritual development. Kendal added more lines.

"Also, I've joined the Quakers, and on a silent retreat.

Sounds weird, but it's helping my grieving. I hope you understand and can respect my efforts to grow and develop. I'll get in touch when I re-emerge."

Kendal ate the second Kit Kat finger. The computer pinged.

> Dearest K.
> Good to hear you're on a journey. Me too! Josh has proposed! We're celebrating with a week on the Jurassic Coast. Josh loves fossils! Bringing his SUV, so plenty of room for your stuff. Don't worry about being available all the time. We'll pop in. Found the Christmas card from your uncle so we know where you are.

Kendal hurled the puppets into the bin.

11

The mood at breakfast was edgy. Audrey's turban had a yellow stain, and Philip's eyes were red-rimmed. Albert hadn't returned from hospital.

"He'll never come back," sighed Brian.

"Gary's got it in for him," moaned Audrey. She pushed her breakfast plate away. "What in heavens name is Carla doing mashing fish fingers with eggs? Should be salmon."

"Can I eat it, Audrey?" asked Kendal.

Audrey nodded. "I've no appetite, not with Albert in hospital."

Kendal had spent an hour in the Ammonite room browsing wildlife sites to distract her from the arrival at Jurassic Court of Mad-Maxine and Josh.

"Did you know salmon are anadromous? They have high levels of mortality in their early stages but, if they survive, they show phenoptosis at the end of their lives."

"You swallowed a dictionary?" growled Audrey.

"Phenoptosis means programmed death. When certain circumstances cause an organism to rapidly degenerate and die." Kendal was pleased with how much she could remember.

"As in circumstances dictated by the warden," said Audrey, folding her napkin into tiny squares.

"Well, not exactly," said Kendal, reaching for extra toast. "With salmon, it's after they've spawned." She smiled. "Has Albert been spawning?"

No one laughed. Banter failure. Kendal changed tack.

"I'm looking forward to your flower arranging session this morning, Audrey."

"I can't do it with Albert at stage three."

Kendal gasped. "Has Albert got cancer? I thought it was, er, waterworks."

"Stage three, his third visit," whispered Audrey, her thin fingers grabbing Kendal's wrist. "Three strikes and you're out."

"This is Bloscombe, Audrey. Not the Bronx."

"If you're not upright, you can't stay here. It's in the rules. Didn't you read them?"

"I read the bit about being sixty and over."

Brian leaned in. "Jurassic Court provides care, not nursing. If residents can't look after themselves, they must move to the next stage. The final one. Nursing home."

Tears slid down Audrey's cheeks, dragging powder and rouge. "With nurses and winches."

"And assisted bathing," groaned Philip.

"Outrageous," said Kendal. "We own the flats. It's up to us, isn't it?"

"Read the Ts and Cs in your folder," said Brian. "If your needs change, then you're out."

"And no one comes back," sniffed Audrey.

Philip stood and tapped Kendal's head. "When you leave here, it's like the word you said. Beginning with p?"

"Pheno, phenotosia…" Three minutes ago she'd pronounced it perfectly. Was her short-term memory shot already? Classic perimenopausal symptom.

"I want to learn about flower arranging, Audrey," lied Kendal. "Keep the little grey cells active and make the world a prettier place. Don't abandon the class." Audrey wiped her eyes and brown eyeliner joined the smudged powder. "I'll drive you to the hospital after your session and we could take some flowers to Albert."

Audrey smiled. "Thank you, Kendal, you're so kind."

Kendal removed the Jurassic Coast welcome folder from the box file and scanned the small print. She'd not read the rules about physical dependency, and she didn't know Albert well, but she understood what it was like to be thrown out of happy places (night clubs, house-shares, beds). At her last THRUm personal development assessment Dogbreath-Deirdre had accused Kendal of lacking empathy (which was rich coming from her!). Kendal had professed not to care (empathy was overrated, she argued) but she did care about saving Albert for Audrey, Brian and Philip. They were sort of her friends, and she could help them.

She started a fresh list:

Assignment Albert – possible approaches
Persuade Gary to change the rules
Get Albert fit
Lobby Gary's bosses
Bribe hospital
Abduct Albert

Everyone except Jennifer turned up for Audrey's flower arranging activity. The day room smelled like a greenhouse and the residents looked a lot more cheerful than they had at breakfast. Buckets of flowers and foliage were lined up on a trestle table alongside vases, miniature watering cans, clippers, and string. Gary ferried chairs from the dining room. The residents ignored him but Kendal managed a discreet glance (aquamarine shorts, navy polo shirt). Audrey had fixed her face and turban and donned a clean, pink tabard. She waited until every resident had chosen a vase and taken a seat.

"Are you sitting comfortably?" Everyone, except Kendal, laughed. "Then I'll begin." Banter made no sense but needed noting. Audrey beamed, pulled her shoulders back, and swivelled her gaze round the room. Kendal wondered if Audrey watched TED Talks.

"The most important rule of flower arranging is to use an odd number of blooms. Trios are better than pairs. Like Brian, Philip and me!"

Kendal guffawed, everyone else nodded, straight-faced. Boomer banter was impossible.

Audrey selected nine stems and grasses, swiftly twisted them together and held out the bouquet for Brian to tie. Kendal was impressed. Audrey would be perfect for TikTok. Philip placed the bunch into a vase and Brian added water.

"Your turn, everybody," shouted Audrey. "Remember the rule of three."

Arthritic hands and poor eyesight hampered progress, but after an hour the table was heaving under an impressive array of arrangements. Audrey prowled round the display, clipping a stray asparagus fern or pussy willow and appraising each effort. Kendal had twisted together giant cow parsley, Spanish bluebells and purple tulips. It looked like something in a magazine, a world away from the pathetic bunches she occasionally took to Sussex where her parents were buried.

Audrey clinked a glass vase, and when everyone was watching, she opened her handbag and plucked out a red rosette.

Best In Show.

Kendal was forced to fake applause when Jacob won with a wobbly display of daisy, pansy, and catkin.

"I like to dedicate this rosette to my dear departed wife who did the flowers at St Bride's for thirty-three years," he said. "And loved pansies."

Brian and Philip sniggered. Kendal glared. She would not be recycling this homophobic joke.

The day room windowsills were filled with painted eggs from Easter and there was no room for the flower displays. The residents tottered to their flats clutching the vases like primary school children at the end of a school day.

"Would you mind carrying mine to my flat, Kendal?" asked Pam. "I can't risk falling and have the warden send me to hospital as well as Albert."

"Of course, Pam. Which number is yours?" replied Kendal. Best not to reveal she'd already visited.

It was hard to find a space for Pam's vase in Flat 17; the

surfaces were filled with bleached-out photographs and brown house plants, dirty mugs cluttered the coffee table, and pill packets spilled on the draining board. Kendal spotted an unused table, socketed below a larger one. She bent to pull it out.

Something glinted where the dusty carpet joined the skirting board. Kendal stretched her fingers and pulled the piece of gold free. It was an antique ring with a large blue stone and tiny diamonds. Diligent cleaners would have, should have, found it. They were taking advantage of Pam's glaucoma. Gary should have a word. The gold band was thick, but the hallmark was worn and hard to read; she needed a magnifying glass. Kendal slipped it into her pocket and returned to the day room.

"Kendal, you're so kind," said Gary, handing her a plate of cherry cake. "I've saved you a slice." Kendal scanned the room; the residents were still shunning Gary.

"It was interesting to see another flat," she said taking the plate but turning towards Pam and Prue who were bent over the jigsaw table.

Gary tapped her shoulder. "Did you discover anything?"

Kendal jumped. "Like what?"

"Residents organise their flats differently. Did you get any ideas for yours?"

"I went straight in and out. Don't want to be a nosy parker. But I noticed several flats are empty. I thought there was a waiting list."

"There is. A couple are owned by residents who come for respite care and the others are for overnight staff. Like me, sometimes."

"Also, I see there's no number thirteen. Bit superstitious?"

"I didn't design Jurassic Court," answered Gary. He surveyed the room; the residents still had their backs turned against him. He sighed. "And I don't make the rules."

Kendal licked her sticky fingers. She'd love to find out which room Gary used, how often he slept over, what he wore in bed, but Audrey was glaring. Not an appropriate moment to fraternize with Gary.

Kendal moved to the jigsaw table. The puzzle was a Victorian Christmas scene with big-skirted children sitting under a tree, surrounded by presents.

"We need the fairy," said Prue.

"Can you see it, dear?" asked Pam.

Kendal looked at the floor and spotted two pieces of jigsaw. Aware of Gary, she grunted as she bent. "Here you are ladies, your fairy was hiding."

Pam and Prue squealed as they completed the puzzle. Prue attempted a hi-five, but Pam couldn't see Prue's hand and left her hanging.

"I always feel sad when the puzzle's finished," said Pam. Kendal pushed her hand into her pocket and fingered the ring. Her heart was racing. She knew what she ought to do but the dizzying rush she used to get from three lines of coke, or a secret snog, was electrifying and made her feel intensely alive and not a perimenopausal faker with a massive overdraft.

"Would you like me to fetch you another puzzle. Keep the momentum going?" Prue and Pam squealed again.

"But no lakes, deserts or mountains," said Pam. "Too difficult."

Kendal closed the blinds in the Ammonite room and lay on the floor. What the hell had happened? Fake-Kendal had found an obviously valuable ring, probably belonging to a partially sighted old lady, and pocketed it which was wrong, wrong, wrong. But Fake-Kendal was not real. Real-Kendal had nowhere to live, no job, no pension, or money. Just debts, big ones.

From the floor she could see the large stack of jigsaw puzzle boxes and had a sudden memory of a map-of-the-world puzzle she'd had as a child which featured too many countries and complicated flags. Frustrated at not completing it she'd borrowed her mum's sewing scissors and cut the edges to make the pieces fit. Her parents had been cross and she'd never touched a puzzle since.

Kendal switched on the computer. More infuriating emails with red flags:

A link from Mad-Maxine to the Airbnb she'd booked; a list of equipment the THRUm operations manager said she must return; and a reminder from that the credit card company that despite the recent payment she still owed £5,459.

The final email was more welcome: a link to the catalogue for the auction. Kendal scanned it keenly; if every piece of her Royal Doulton met its estimate, she could count on £3,500. But the auction wasn't for six weeks, the credit company were screaming and Mad-Maxine required £1,985 immediately. Six weeks wasn't going to work. Kendal required £3,500 now.

Kendal took Pam's ring out of her pocket and Googled antique gold rings with sapphire and diamonds. Nothing was priced under one thousand and plenty were over six. If only she could use the ring to borrow money but this was Dorset and she didn't know anyone who lent money, even if she gave them the ring as collateral.

Kendal erased her browsing history, selected three boxes of puzzles, and hurried back to the day room. Pam and Prue were delighted.

"Thank you, Kendal," said Pam. "The forest scene is perfect. Contrasting colours and the sticker says all pieces are there. Isn't she kind, Prue?"

The third time in one day she'd been described as kind. Which was weird, since she was living a lie and had just pocketed an old lady's expensive ring.

"An absolute gem!" said Pam. "Do you want to join us?"

"Thanks, but no thanks," said Kendal. "I've got my own puzzles."

"Thousand-piece ones?" asked Prue.

"No, even trickier."

Kendal walked into lunch mentally listing her problems; how to pay the enormous debts, how to stop Maxine and Josh revealing her true age, and what to do with the antique ring inside her elasticated trouser pocket. Not forgetting, how to free Albert but at least that puzzle was shared with the other residents which made it bearable.

The Community Hospital was two miles from the centre of Bloscombe, at the top of a hill.

"Bloody stupid spot," grumbled Audrey. "The bus only comes twice a day and it's horrible. Full of old people."

"What, like you?" smiled Kendal. "And me?" she added.

"No, really old people," said Audrey. "Who smell."

They searched for a space in the car park. Kendal thought it best not to let Audrey witness her fraudulent use of Clem's disabled parking badge. At last, someone left and Kendal squeezed the Kangoo into a tight space, close to the hospital entrance.

The hand sanitiser pump was jammed. Kendal mimed rubbing her hands and steered Audrey to the League of Friends trolley. Audrey bought a box of liquorice and a Daily Mail.

"What's Albert's second name?" asked Kendal.

"Fry," said Audrey. "His favourite type of cooking, greedy bugger."

Kendal approached the reception desk. "Can you tell us which ward Albert Fry is in?" The receptionist scanned her screen and pointed at a sign for Almonds Ward.

"Thank goodness," said Audrey. "It's the best one for him."

"What do you mean?"

Audrey lowered her voice. "Only two wards in this tiny place. The other one means you're on your way to the big upstairs." She raised her eyes. One eyebrow was higher than the other. "Almonds is for the short stay patients. Mean's he'll be coming out."

Almonds Ward had six beds filled with crumpled, sleeping bundles. Silent, except for the bleeping from the medical apparatus, and the drone of a hedge cutter outside. No other visitors. Audrey scanned the room. "He's the huge one by the window."

Kendal reluctantly followed Audrey. Her mother had the bed by the window in the hospital before she was moved to a hospice. She couldn't remember where her father's bed had been. Things had got too messy by then.

A plump nurse arrived with a chair in each hand. "Here you go, ladies."

"You're fit," said Audrey.

"Dorset born, Dorset bred," answered the nurse. "Strong in the arm, thick in the head."

Her THRUm teammates would have been appalled but Kendal liked the pride behind the rhyme.

They examined the whiteboard above Albert's bed.

Patient's preferred name – "BERT"
Activity Goal – Walk to bathroom x 3
Next of Kin – Gary Vaughan

"It's not right," said Kendal, pointing at the board.

The nurse sighed. "I know. But we must have a goal. It's the system. Excellent care and all that."

"I mean, his name. Everyone calls him Albert."

The nurse handed Kendal a marker. "Be my guest."

Kendal added AL to BERT.

Audrey prodded the body but the only response was a snore.

"This place is like a morgue. Needs cheering up," said Audrey.

Kendal nodded. Hospitals were tricky. Kendal's mother seemed to be asleep all the time at her hospice and teenage Kendal had resorted to leaving notes on her bed full of lies about how well she was doing at school. After a while, Kendal stopped visiting and gave bundles of pre-written notes to her father to deliver. When he got ill the following year there had been little need for notes or visits; his decline had been swift. They'd both been out of it. But his drugs were legal.

"Come on Kendal, let's have a knees-up." Audrey cleared her throat and straightened her turban. "My old man said follow the van…"

Kendal tried. Anything to dispel unhappy memories. Audrey segued into a new song. "Show me the way to go home…"

Her screeching attempt at a Scottish accent woke Albert. He belched, coughed, and joined in.

"I'm tired and I want to go to bed…"

Albert and Audrey worked through a medley of golden oldies and one by one the other patients woke. Kendal marched up and down the ward, passing bed controllers, and pouring orange squash. She imagined how she would look in a nurse's uniform. A full-on Florence Nightingale type. Or maybe Mary Seacole? She wished she had a phone to Google cool nurse uniforms, but biddies didn't check stuff on their phones in hospitals. Or anywhere.

The patients were tiring of the singalong and started asking Kendal to switch on their screens or pass toffees. When a grinning Welshman requested a bedpan Kendal stopped being heroic and stomped back to Albert.

"It's knees, hips, blood pressure, the lot," he said. "They're not happy with me. The nurse is a tyrant. And the meal portions are minuscule." Tears trickled out of bloodshot eyes and gathered in between his chubby cheeks and nose. "I've had a good life, I'm ready to go." He pointed to the whiteboard. "They insist I walk to the bathroom, but I can't."

Kendal remembered the whiteboard at THRUm crammed with Dogbreath-Deirdre's stupid targets which Kendal always longed to erase. She patted Albert's puffy hand, dipped a tissue in orange squash, and rubbed out Albert's Activity Goal.

"Don't listen to the bossy boots nurse," she said. "Listen to your body. You're the man."

Albert squeezed her hand. Kendal squeezed the ring. She really needed a drink.

Audrey held it together until they returned to the Kangoo where tears and make-up flowed. Kendal remembered oldies didn't do make-up in public. She dropped the passenger sun visor and looked away as Audrey mopped her eyes with a lipstick-stained hanky. Kendal had a clean tissue, but it was in her pocket, wrapped around the sapphire ring.

"Are you ready to go back to Jurassic Court, Audrey?" Audrey needed a dose of *Pointless* and *Countdown* which anaesthetised her like a pint of wine sedated Kendal.

Audrey nodded. "Yes, dear. Let's go home."

Kendal switched on the ignition. The windscreen was misty. She wiped it hastily. Home was such an emotive word. Extraordinary! Audrey, Kendal, all of the residents had a home full of friends who cared, shared and loved a laugh. Kendal's eyes filled.

Driving through Bloscombe's rush hour (six minutes of gentle nudging in the high street) gave Kendal a chance to pump Audrey about the other residents and their histories. After describing Jennifer's role in the Inner Wheel Club, the newsagents Brian once ran, and the second-hand car dealership Jacob had managed, Audrey at last moved onto Pam.

"She's been around far longer than me. One of the oldies."

"Has she always lived in the same flat?" asked Kendal.

"I think so. Poor old thing, she never has any visitors. Why do you ask?"

"I, erm, think it has the best view," answered Kendal.

Audrey frowned. "It's the same as ours."

"How long have you been at Jurassic Court?" asked Kendal. Audrey gazed at the sea as they drove beside the prom. The gig club's wooden boat skimmed close to the shore and there was a queue of dog walkers outside Bobby's ice cream chalet.

"Four years, five months," said Audrey in a quiet voice. "Moved in after my Gerald died. The house was too empty. We had some marvellous times together. Won prizes".

"Ballroom dancing?"

"Waggiest Tail and Most Handsome Crossbreed."

"Gerald was your dog?"

"Of course! I've never been married. No man's going to put a ring on me."

It was good to see Audrey smile.

Back in the flat, Kendal peeled two Kit Kats, poured a large Noilly Prat (which was getting bearable) and started a fresh page in her notebook:

Sapphire Strategy
Sell in antique shop
Sell online
Take to auction house
Give it to Pam
Give it to Gary.

She attempted to calculate the benefits of selling in a shop versus an auction house (speed-plus-value versus probability-of-exposure) but all she could think about was Pam's cloudy eyes and her pathetic bouquet of flowers.

Why couldn't she decide? London-Kendal would have known exactly what to do. Sell the ring and pay off her debts. No one would know. Jurassic Court was weakening her. Perhaps it was the lack of food, alcohol, and sex. Whatever, Kendal Tudge needed to get tough or, like the dinosaurs, she'd be extinct.

12

The sun was high as Kendal hit the prom in sandals, striped Guernsey and Uncle Clem's floppy cricket hat. Five rugged swimmers, presumably Bluetits, poured flasks and admired each other's swimming robes. A hennaed hippy had opened a friendship bracelet stall, and there was a long queue at Bobby's ice cream.

With no family or close friends, Kendal had developed a world view where choices were easy; do whatever made Kendal Tudge feel better – and don't faff. Her current indecisiveness was uncomfortable but nine-thirty at Bloscombe was still nicer than battling crowds on the tube and panicking about the rent. Better to be indecisive by the seaside than in the city. Flotsam and jetsam at the water's edge, not litter on a chewing-gummed pavement.

Kendal bought a double-salted caramel ice cream and decided to explore Bloscombe properly to distract her from the Sapphire Strategy. She strolled the lanes and snickets criss-crossing pretty terraces of cottages and modern apartments. Behind the high street and sea front, there was another Bloscombe displaying signs of ordinary life: a primary school, medical centre, and a car showroom. It was reassuring to see people of all ages in Bloscombe. People doing jobs, running businesses, having families. It would be good to get a job and earn some money but jobs demand official stuff like P45 forms and filling in one of those would reveal her true age.

Kendal decided to miss lunch. Her stomach had been dodgy since she'd found the ring and the disgusting chiropodist was still in the foyer. Thirty-six feet at Jurassic Court: three hundred and sixty toes. Gross! She would visit the library, browse the cinema section for Movie Night and see her new old, but cool, friend.

Clare had shadows under her eyes, an upside-down badge, and was stamping books angrily. Clare was the most upbeat person Kendal knew. What was wrong?

"Hi Clare, all right?"

"Not really."

Kendal mentally listed Clare's possible concerns (library closure, redundancy, family?). Friends should offer upset friends lunch, coffee, or a drink, but these required money which she didn't have. What was that catch-phrase Dogbreath-Deirdre had for staff who were upset?

"What are the first steps you can take to address your problem, Clare?"

Clare threw the ink stamp into a bin. "Get rid of this before I break my wrist." Clare laughed.

Kendal smiled. Deirdre's coaching technique worked.

"Come with me to the office and I'll make us a coffee," said Clare. "Nothing's going on in here today."

Kendal scanned the library. Tattooed-homeless-man was asleep across two chairs, and three teenagers had colonised the computers. Clare nodded at the terminals. "They can watch as much porn as they can take. The filters never work."

Kendal really wanted to check out the teenagers but followed Clare through the Staff Only door into a room crammed with boxes, out-of-date magazines and a screen showing the library from different angles. The walls were covered in spreadsheets and notices about goals, objectives, issues, and income. Libraries clearly existed under the same tyranny of targets and evaluation as THRUm.

"How do you manage the library on your own?"

"I'm not on my own," said Clare, switching on a kettle. "We've lovely volunteers for books-on-wheels, empathy club, and silver surfers. And there's my library assistant, of course."

"I've never seen an assistant," said Kendal. "Where is he, or she? Or they?"

"Dear Dominic, he's not much use, to be honest," said Clare

pointing at the close-circuit screen. "There he is, bless him." The tattooed man was picking his nose. "But he understands the Dewey Decimal system, and it keeps him off the sauce." She offered Kendal a tin.

Kendal took two chocolate digestives. If it wasn't work upsetting Clare, perhaps it was something domestic? Kendal was determined to find out. It was what friends did for each other, right?

"Is something wrong with your family?"

"Sweet of you, Kendal. They're fine. It's Shelley and Keats. I don't know what to do with them."

She'd got this. The only Shelley she knew was a Zumba instructor, but Keats was a poet who banged on about bosoms and swelling gourds. "Put him in the poetry section, surely? Not sure about Shelley."

Clare smiled. "You crack me up, Kendal!" Kendal grinned. Not all her time at school was wasted then.

Clare began to gabble. "Cretaceous-Creatures is full; Paws-N-Claws have closed, and my friends won't help. They say the boys are too dangerous. Rebecca's relying on me, Oliver's on nights, and poor Collie's got SATS. I can't let them down."

Too many characters. Kendal had mined so much Gary-intel on their walk she'd forgotten to glean information on Clare. Rebecca was possibly the daughter (who'd gone out with Gary?) but who was Oliver and what did it mean if a dog got sats? Pause and Clause could be solicitors. Typical Bloscombe silly name. Important to get this right; an opportunity to usurp Clare's flakier friends and build solid rapport, even a proper friendship.

The chocolate kicked in. Kendal recalled the grey cats at Clare's cottage. Anthropomorphism was not only Audrey's silly game. Gerald for a dog, Shelley, and Keats for cats. Why didn't people in Dorset give their pets normal names, like Spot or Smudge?

"So, Shelley and Keats are the pussies?"

"Mad, bad, and dangerous to know," said Clare. "Like Byron".

Kendal had never wanted a pet. Pets take over people. Kendal returned to Dogbreath-Deirdre's solution-focused coaching. If she could help Clare sort this, there would be more biscuits, talk about Gary, and she wouldn't have to think about the Sapphire Strategy.

"What do you need to make this problem disappear? Who can you ask for help from?" Kendal had absorbed more THRUm twaddle than she'd realised.

"I need a cat sitter with balls!" said Clare.

"Tennis, wool, or fat?" said Kendal.

Clare's laugh was shrill, but she had, at last, begun to look normal. It was fun being a supportive friend; like being helpful in the hospital, but without the bedpans. Kendal took another biscuit.

"The boys didn't attack you last week," said Clare. "Wonder why."

"They recognised an Alpha pussy!" Kendal mimed a karate chop. "What do they usually do to your friends?"

"They're not too bad if I'm there but when I'm away they create havoc. Scratch, bite, steal. Donate fleas by the dozen. Once I went to Greece and a book group friend was feeding them. They disappeared for the whole two weeks. She was frantic. I've taken them to a cat psychologist, but it made no difference. No one will cat sit for me anymore. It's why I take the naughty boys to the kennels. But now I can't because Cretaceous-Creatures is full and Paws-N-Claws have closed."

"How long are you away?" asked Kendal.

"A week, from Saturday."

Kendal imagined the comfortable bath at Candida Cottage. The shower was super-efficient at Jurassic Court, but it would be nice to have an uninterrupted soak. Good to use her washing machine too. "I'd love to help you, Clare. Give something back."

Clare chewed her thumb again. "Oh no, I couldn't ask you to drive over there seven times."

"Why not? I've plenty of time. I could explore the village, find some new walks. The pub looks fun as well." Clare hesitated.

Kendal felt her face redden. It wasn't hot in the office. She hadn't blushed for years. She wanted to win this but didn't know why.

"I could water your plants too."

"Oh, Kendal! How wonderful. Are you sure?"

"No problem. I'll show those bad boys who's boss."

"Gosh, thanks. Shall I collect you from Jurassic Court after work tomorrow?"

"Don't bother. Quite fancy a drive in the countryside."

On the screen Kendal observed the library assistant at the issue desk surrounded by teenagers. Hoods up, shoulders hunched, Dominic was issuing stuff, but it wasn't books. No point telling Clare her assistant was dealing. It would derail the day. Leave him to it and let the teenagers get off their tits. Not much else for them in Bloscombe.

"I'll draw you a map of how to find me," said Clare.

"OK, but maybe you should get back to relieve your assistant. He looks stretched."

Kendal browsed the audio-visual section: five shelves for DVDs and four for CDs. Did people still access music and films this way? Must be the rubbish broadband. It would be good to choose a DVD for Movie Night and watch it first so she knew what to say when she introduced it to the residents. The ancient computer in the Ammonite room probably still had a slot for discs.

Kendal needed to choose a film which Fake-Kendal would have enjoyed in her youth. Something released in the nineteen eighties, then, with an upbeat tone like Philip had chosen. She spotted an empty computer terminal, ran a wet wipe over the keyboard, and Googled best comedies of the 1980s.

The only film available not featuring drugs, orgasms, or people pretending to be someone else was called *Trading Places*. She took the box to the issue desk. Clare had finished drawing the map and Dealing-Dom was asleep again.

"Ah this was terrific, wasn't it? Most of the actors are dead now though. My favourite was Bo Diddly."

"I don't remember, Clare. Senior moment."

Clare giggled. Boomer banter was lame, but good to hear Clare laugh.

"People only remember Eddie Murphy, but Bo Diddly was terrific in that movie with a cameo role as a pawnbroker. Good pub quiz fact."

Kendal felt a rush of excitement. Pawnbroker! Of course! A guilt-free way to get money. Not stealing. Borrowing. If she pawned Pam's ring instead of selling it, she could pay off Mad-Maxine and then buy the ring back from the pawnbroker when the auction funds came through. But were pawnbrokers merely a fictional device in 1980s' comedy films or did they exist in sleepy Dorset?

"Gotta go, Clare. Thanks for the DVD."

"Enjoy, and see you tomorrow, after five. Shelley and Keats will be waiting."

The Comfitoes van was still at Jurassic Court. Carla and Emma from the kitchen had laid on a special buffet for residents to enjoy between appointments. Kendal stacked two plates with quiche, dips and finger rolls, sneaked to the Ammonite room and Googled "Pawnbrokers near me".

Like milk in glass bottles, early closing, and apples sold by the pound, pawnbrokers still existed in Dorset and there was one in Bournemouth only forty miles away. Boom! It would be closed by the time she got there so Kendal agreed to join Audrey for a dose of her favourite detective show and a sherry.

Audrey, like all the residents, adored slow-paced detective series, especially if the actors were British. When new characters appeared, she ignored the plot to discuss which other programmes they'd been in and whether they were still alive. In this episode of *Morse* the murderer pretended to live in a college in order to attend a reunion his rival was attending. Another light bulb moment! Kendal could pull off a similar stunt (without the murder) and pretend to live in Clare's cottage when Mad-Maxine and PoshJosh came and then they wouldn't see her at Jurassic Court and ruin her disguise. She'd meet them at Clare's, wearing her London-Kendal clothes, pay the debt and return the funeral outfit. Her hair was grey, but this shouldn't matter since it was fashionable and Maxine, though mad, would know that.

"To absent friends!" toasted Audrey in the ad break. "To Gerald, the most loyal hound in the world, and Albert, the largest man in Almonds Ward."

"Absent friends means dead people," said Kendal. "Albert's not gone; he'll be back."

Audrey opened her *Countdown Dictionary* and read the definition.

"Absent; not present in a place, at an occasion, or as part of something. Similar adjectives: distracted, vague, absorbed, abstracted."

She downed her glass and giggled. "Could be any one of us at Jurassic Court."

Kendal would have liked to discuss the whereabouts of not-present Gary but Audrey was a canny old bird and she needed to be careful. She raised her glass.

"To Uncle Clem, our absent friend."

Audrey beamed. "To Clem, a wonderful neighbour."

The news began and Audrey switched off the television, wobbling as she stood. Kendal leapt to steady her.

"You're nimble tonight," said Audrey. "You really must join me in the downward dog on the lawn tomorrow."

"I'm not sure if I'm up to yoga."

"Then you'll have to go to Farming Chatter with Emma, and you'll never look at a sausage again after that."

Audrey was the master of persuasion. Surely Building Rapport courses didn't exist when she was young?

"You win, I'll come."

Audrey hugged Kendal. Her arms were bony but strong. Must be the yoga.

"It's good to have you as a neighbour after darling Clem. It's a Tudge dynasty," said Audrey. "Funny name, isn't?"

Kendal tried to smile. It still hurt, even if the perpetrator was twice her age and, it seemed, a friend.

In bed, Kendal opened *The Tudge Transformation Toolkit* at the Ageing Insights page and wrote:

How to talk about animals as though they are people
How to lose the plot in television detectives

She was learning so much about old people. She'd hardly spoken to one before, let alone have old-people-friends. If her parents had lived it would have been nice to watch detective series with them.

Kendal didn't want to think about her parents and the chaotic life she lived when they were ill, and then dead but visiting Albert in hospital had revived uncomfortable memories. What the THRUm snowflakes would call triggering. Despite the freedom, the car, and the empty house she could see now what a tough time teenage-Kendal had gone through. A trauma in THRUm-speak. At the time, she'd rebuffed the neighbours and volunteers at the hospice, calling them interfering old fusspots but now she could see they were only trying to help. Like she'd helped Albert.

All this introspection was exhausting. What was done, was done. She needed to distract herself or she'd never get to sleep with no drink, drugs or other body around. She began her favourite fantasy about the warden. Gary in Dartmoor: yomping through mud; climbing granite bosses, with lots of zips and ropes requiring tightening by a helpful female companion. It was hopeless. The hospital visit had crushed her libido as well.

But she'd nailed the Sapphire Strategy, and shown she could focus, empathise and finish tasks. Suck on that, Dogbreath-Deirdre!

13

Audrey's outdoor yoga session was nothing like the frenzied workouts Kendal endured in London where twenty- and thirty-somethings pushed limbs into painful shapes and filled clammy gyms with over-dramatic exhalations. Audrey's session had comfortable poses and the only sound was birdsong and delicate farts. Her moves were easy, but Kendal uttered an occasional groan to stay in role. Afterwards, Kendal felt ready to run to the river. Instead, she pretended to be worn out.

"You keep going with this and you'll live another twenty years," said Audrey as they rolled the mats. "Us pensioners need to use it or lose it. Minds as well as bodies. I wish other residents were as eager to learn as you, Kendal. Even Albert would be fitter if he moved more."

"Have you tried getting Brian or some of the others to join your sessions?" asked Kendal.

"Constantly," said Audrey. "But he's a lazy old dog and most of the others think yoga is painful or too hippy-dippy. They love Tavvy-Tina's seated sessions with pompoms and wooden spoons. But she costs money and Jurassic Court's budget doesn't stretch for her to come weekly. Mind you, the silly cow would probably give it away if Gary joined in with his shorts and muscles. She's mad about him."

Kendal didn't like the sound of Tavvy-Tina. "You're an excellent yoga teacher, Audrey. So fit and mobile. An inspiration," said Kendal, realising her compliment was sincere. No need for Building Rapport techniques with Audrey. It was built. It was a relationship.

Audrey and Kendal walked past the day room. Emma-from-the-kitchen was focussing her laser pointer on a slide of a cow giving birth. Jennifer and Jacob watched eagerly; the others examined coffee cups. Wendy and Shirley were asleep.

"Fancy a cuppa in my flat?" asked Audrey. "Ginger tea with ground pepper. The best cure for flatulence or morning sickness."

"I'll give it a go, Audrey, though I have neither." Audrey made the tea and Kendal watched the laundry service van drive through the front gate, an irritating strapline across its side: COASTAL CLEANING: WHERE WATER BREATHES LIFE!

Kendal snorted. Classic THRUm marketing twaddle!

The tea was delicious. Almost as stimulating as a flat white. Audrey handed Kendal a bowl of cottage cheese and honey. "A small reward for your efforts this morning," she said. "You're the first resident I've persuaded to join me for downward dogging. Most of the others think yoga makes you a terrorist or something."

The driver was opening the van's doors. Kendal winced at the messy message across the tailgate: COASTAL CLEANING (PREVIOUSLY KNOWN AS ABC WASHING).

At THRUm, the ponytailed-prat from marketing was always banging on about re-branding the charity, repeatedly sending emails with infuriating subject headings. If you can't change the customer, change the brand.

"Maybe you need a rebrand for your exercise class, Audrey?"

Audrey frowned. "Certainly not! Emma showed photos of branding at her last Farming Chat. It's disgusting and cruel."

Kendal was confused. Was this another case of talking about animals as though they are people? Audrey's cup wobbled.

"It's probably no more painful than tattoos. But I wouldn't want one of those either. Repulsive and degrading."

Kendal, grateful the charity shop trousers were too high to reveal her tramp-stamp, tried again. "Branding, as in giving your exercise session a different name or image. Something appealing to the residents." Kendal recalled some 1980s facts she'd researched. "Like when British Nuclear Fuels rebranded Windscale as Sellafield. Remember?"

Audrey dropped her spoon. "I do. To foil the echo worriers. They made it a visitor attraction, like the National Trust."

"Right, the power of a re-brand. A new name brings new attention." Ponytail guy would be proud. "They're ecowarriors, not echo, by the way."

"But yoga has been around for thousands of years. I shouldn't mess with it."

"Adapt and survive, Audrey. Or we'll go the way of the dinosaurs."

Audrey had gone glassy-eyed. Thinking of extinct dinosaurs or having a diabetic episode like the ones Kendal had read about in her Ageing Insights research?

"Are you OK, Audrey?"

Audrey blinked. "I'm fine. It's a good idea and I will brainsquall it after lunch. Carla's doing faggots. I have my best ideas after offal. Let's go."

Kendal had to get to the pawnbrokers and find a mobile phone shop. Faggots, bound to provoke homophobic remarks from Brian, were not going to hold her back.

"I'm going to the library," she lied. "See you at supper."

Google said the Derbyfield pawnbrokers was an hour's drive. Google can't have been to Dorset on the first sunny week of May, when every pensioner with a car decides to drive to Bournemouth. Kendal gave up trying to overtake and submitted to the views and the radio, which she still hadn't re-tuned.

Thursday afternoon was opera on Radio 3, and a woman was singing the part of a boy who was disguised as a girl. A barmy story, even stupider when you couldn't see the outfits. But classical music connected Kendal to Uncle Clem, so she allowed the radio to warble on. When green fields morphed into industrial estates and endless roundabouts, she spotted a retail park. At last she could buy a phone. She peeled off some notes from the Rascal sale and bought the cheapest in stock. Expensive phones, like hoop earrings and heels, were no longer part of Tudge world.

As she drove through the suburbs of Bournemouth, Kendal constructed a story about how she'd inherited the ring in case the pawnbroker asked awkward questions. It would be passed on from her great-grandmother to her grandmother, her mother and now, her. A simple plot. Unlike the opera.

Kendal had imagined something seedy: a three-golden-balls sign next to a bookmakers or brothel, but the Derbyfield pawnbrokers was a neat bungalow in a residential street with a modest brass plate on the gate. It looked like the dentist she visited as a child where the surgery was in the front room. Kendal polished the ring with her scarf; the blue stone glowed, and the diamonds glinted. She checked her reflection and opened the door.

Pawning a valuable piece of jewellery was simpler than it probably ought to be. Mr Field, the pawnbroker, wore a navy-blue apron and spoke in a kindly, respectful way. He didn't interrogate Kendal, or demand proof of ownership. He explained how the money he would give her in exchange for the ring must be returned in twenty-eight days and if she didn't then it would become the pawnbrokers to sell or keep as he wished. Kendal simply had to show her driving licence, sign a short form, and give him the ring. Like a childhood dental check-up, the visit was over in minutes but, instead of a sticker, she got two hundred twenty-pound notes. In cash! More than she earned at THRUm in two months.

It was tempting to explore Bournemouth. All Kendal had seen so far (roundabouts, tan shops, car dealerships) suggested Swindon-by-the-sea, but she had read that the town had rebranded itself as Bo-Ho. No longer simply a place for pensioners, Bournemouth boasted many digital start-ups staffed by rich, cool entrepreneurs who might be gagging to meet a silver-haired cougar and Thursday was the new Friday, wasn't it? Sadly, she was dressed in the charity shop clothes, needed the wedge of cash to pay Mad-Maxine's £1,985, and had a date with Shelley and Keats, the mad, bad pussies. Kendal turned the Kangoo westwards.

Clare sat outside her cottage holding a large glass. Driving to Bournemouth and back had taken four hours and the grunt Kendal made getting out of the car was genuine. A grim reminder to keep doing the yoga, re-branded or not.

"Wonderful to see you!" called Clare. "Fancy a G and T?"

"A small one," answered Kendal. "I'm driving."

No sign of the cats. Perhaps they were preparing an attack. Essential to show those bullies who was the boss. This was the moment to employ the dumping technique she perfected when women one-night stands got needy. The Tudge Trudge; look straight ahead, move heavily, avoid eye contact, and intimidate the victim with contained fury.

"This is so sweet of you," said Clare, returning with her drink. "Rebecca and Oliver are so grateful. Collie is thrilled."

Kendal wondered how a dog knew when a guest was expected. Maybe Rebecca went into a cleaning frenzy because her mother was due.

They sipped in the evening sun. Clare pointed out flowers and shrubs in her garden. Kendal nodded and tried to eke out the drink. Still no grey tail or ominous purr.

"You only need to come once a day. Feed, check their water and maybe hose the garden if it looks dead. The boys have a cat flap; they do their business outside so no stinking litter tray to change. Sometimes they leave dead birds or slow-worms on the floor. I'll leave a trowel and you can throw them in the compost. Best to lock the cat flap when you do because they can become possessive of their trophies."

A pair of white butterflies landed on Kendal's empty glass. "Cabbage whites," said Clare. "Symbols of change. Let's go inside and I'll show you the cat stuff."

The dry cat food was stored in a high cupboard in the kitchen. The sound of Clare lifting the packet shattered the peace. Slamming cat flap, crashing chairs, howling banshees. The cats head-butted Clare's legs, their yellow eyes glaring.

"Patience, puss cats. Remember your manners and say hello to Auntie Kendal. She's going to be looking after you while mummy is away."

The cats ignored Kendal; their gaze fixed on the bowls.

"Shall I feed them, Clare? To get them used to me?"

"Good idea. Keep them on side from the start."

Kendal stamped across the room and slammed the bowls on the floor. She clamped her hands over the food and looked at the ceiling. The animals stood quietly waiting until Kendal removed her hands. Calmly they ate and strolled away. Kendal ignored them, her legs firmly planted, her lips tightly shut.

"You're a cat whisperer!' said Clare. "Where did you learn that?"

Best not to tell Clare about the dominatrix she'd met in Berlin who had impressive rules about power dynamics.

"We had lots of pets when I was a kid," she lied. "My mum grew up on a farm."

Keats and Shelley jumped onto the sofa. Time to nail the alpha cat role. Kendal sat heavily beside them and the cats ignored her. Result!

"Good boys," chirruped Clare. "You like Auntie Kendal, don't you?" One cat (Keats?) yawned, revealing sharp, yellow teeth. The other (Shelley?) clawed a cushion.

"Do you have a vet in case something goes wrong?"

"I've put all the details in a file by the television including numbers for Rebecca and Oliver. Landlines and mobiles. Collie doesn't have a phone yet. She's only ten."

Clare was taking the anthropomorphic banter a bit far. Best to humour her. "Can't order a bone then!"

Clare frowned. "I'm not following you, Kendal."

"The collie, without a phone."

Clare squealed. "Collie is my granddaughter. Short for Colette, Rebecca's favourite writer."

Clare showed Kendal the fuse box, hoover, hot water tank, and outdoor tap. At last, she handed over the key. "I'll feed the boys before I go tomorrow and then you could come on Saturday. Whatever works for you. I'll be back the following Friday and I'll take you out on Saturday night as thanks."

It felt good driving in the evening sun with Clare's keys nestling by a bulging wallet and no antique ring scorching her pocket. Kendal stopped at the Co-op for fresh supplies of Prosecco, crisps, and coffee. At the fish and chip shop she slapped a twenty-pound note on the counter. The chippie recognised her and slipped in a free pickled egg. The day wouldn't stop giving.

In the flat, Kendal rolled a hundred twenty-pound notes into a toilet roll tube and hid it in the box file. The chippie had given her a huge portion. She ought to do some exercise, work off the calories. But it had been a long day with the yoga, driving, and the pretence of being a sixty-year-old as well as a dominatrix. Plus, her stomach was bloating. Better be the fish batter, not perimenopausal indicators. Kendal lay on her bed and messaged Maxine:

> I've left the Retreat and back in my lovely cottage in a village called Plick, seven miles north of Bloscombe. Not big enough to offer you a room but can manage tea.
> Got your money.

14

Albert had been discharged from hospital and was breakfasting with Audrey and Pam.

"Here's my Nightingale," he called, waving Kendal to the empty seat.

Kendal bent to hug Albert, careful to avoid the egg on his chin.

"Wonderful to have you back," she said opening a new box of deluxe muesli ignored by other residents (too many nuts for delicate teeth).

"I'm getting a new hip and they might do my knees for Christmas. Got new tablets too. I feel so much better. All due to you lovely ladies." Albert blew toast crumb kisses across the table. Kendal concentrated on the cafetière plunger. Hospital had not improved Albert's table manners.

"Good morning, ladies. I hope you are feeling proud of yourselves. Albert's been singing your praises ever since I collected him."

The plunger gushed at the sound of Gary's voice and coffee trickled over Kendal's hand. The warden had returned from Dartmoor, looking delicious in a pink polo shirt and pleated shorts combo.

"Let me do it for you," said Gary, wiping the pot.

"Did you enjoy your break?" asked Audrey, and Kendal was relieved to sense Gary's gaze move. It was disconcerting how her body was behaving. Her stomach had deflated overnight, but now she had sweaty palms, a rush of moisture and a creeping blush. Manifestations of the perimenopause or unmet lust? Probably mid-cycle hormones making her body misbehave. London-Kendal would have dealt with this level of lust at a singles bar or club. It was Friday, the perfect day for a pick-up. But intense desire could not be resolved at Jurassic Court. Maybe she should connect with the gig rowers? They were clearly up for it. But Bloscombe was a small town, and an anonymous encounter would be tricky.

Kendal patted Albert's arm and hurried to her flat. She locked the door and ran into the bathroom with both vibrators. The non-slip shower cubicle substituted for a racy wetroom the swinging rowers could have dragged her into, and with Audrey still at breakfast, Kendal could give full rein to the fantasy. The grab bars proved helpful.

Afterwards, Kendal recovered on the reclining chair and gazed at the view. She felt relaxed and pleased with the session. She'd not taken any risks or blown her cover and now she was extremely clean. Her new phone pinged:

Hi K. Plick sounds awesome.
See you Saturday afternoon.
Bringing all your stuff, including laptop.
Don't forget my black clothes you took.
Hugs
Maxine and Josh.

Kendal grinned. Good to get her laptop back. Cybersex with strangers might even be possible soon if the signal improved.

The phone pinged again. The creepy pawnbroker.

Official reminder – transaction Tudge-Derbyfield.
You have 27 days to return your loan."

Although she was only borrowing the sapphire ring her stomach lurched. The nausea was not from fear of being discovered. It was guilt!

The hardier residents had mustered in the foyer for Jurassic Court's afternoon Well-being Walk. Kendal wasn't keen to endure another slow procession around the park, but she needed to do something to stop feeling guilty. She could chat nicely to the residents and be helpful. She was ready to walk, talk, and be-well.

Or well-be. Whatever, she'd got this.

Walking in the afternoon, after fish pie and sweet potato mash, was a step too far for most residents. The buggy brigade had turned up (any chance to race their mobility scooters) but Audrey and Prue were the only walkers waiting. Kendal hadn't talked much to Prue. This was a chance to get to know more about Flat 6's ancient hippy who always dressed in yellow. Kendal lowered herself between the two old ladies. The sofa smelled of fish. Kendal hoped it was left-over lunch and not Prue.

"Do you think Gary plans to push us further?" asked Kendal. A lovely phrase, something to think about later.

"I hope he does," said Prue. "I'm sick of the park. We need to expand our horizons."

"We can't look further," said Audrey. "Nothing but the sea on Bloscombe's horizon." Prue pulled a phone from the pocket of her pinafore and waved the screen at Kendal.

"There's been another cliff fall at Almonds Chine," she said. "I'm desperate to go but scared on my own."

"Gary wouldn't take us anywhere risky," said Kendal. Prue pulled a hammer out of her backpack and Kendal tensed.

"There will be fresh specimens to find," whispered Prue. "Unless the Lyme Regis rockhound is there already."

"Fossil nerds, not bow-wows," explained Audrey, helpfully.

Gary bounded into the foyer. "Hi everyone, thanks for coming." He scanned the group. "The magnificent seven! Good to see you, Kendal. I thought our Well-being Walks were too tame for you."

Kendal rose out of the sofa remembering the quiet groan. "I want to join in with all the activities. I love JC so much." They were standing close. Sandalwood with top notes of spearmint. Better than fish.

Gary stepped back. "I'm glad the Quaker meeting appealed but, you know, mostly we don't believe in Jesus Christ. We merely follow his lifestyle."

"Why are we talking about Jesus?"

"JC, you said."

Kendal grinned. "As in Jurassic Court."

"Right," said Gary. "Top banter."

Audrey and Prue stood either side of Kendal and linked arms. Kendal tensed. They were simply being friendly. She must relax.

"Ta-da! We're the JCs," giggled Audrey. "The Jurassic Cautions."

"Going on a fossil hunt," chanted Prue.

Gary laughed. "Haven't you got enough, Prue?"

"Nope, I'm insatiable."

Kendal nodded. The hammer was for rocks. To find fossils. She pressed the automatic door button.

"You girls, ready?" shouted Brian, revving the Rascal. "Let's go. Va Va Vooms!"

The entrance to Almonds Chine was behind a shower block on the prom which Kendal had previously avoided as it looked (and smelled) suspiciously damp. The residents, however, loved it.

"Great sloping paths here for buggy-speeding," shouted Brian.

"The Bluetits are changing inside," added Audrey.

"The rock-fall looks promising," grinned Prue. "Full of treasures, waiting for me."

Gary's gaze moved from the racing mobility buggies to the muddy chine – he was unable to assess which resident presented the greatest risk.

"Do you promise not to climb anything, Prue?" he asked.

"I always follow the fossil collecting code of conduct," answered Prue, with a glint in her eye.

"I'll go with Prue," murmured Kendal. "Don't worry."

"Thanks Kendal, we're all grown-ups, obviously." He looked at Brian and Jacob reversing up the slope, buggy alarms bleeping in stereo. "Some more than others." He looked directly at Kendal. "And you are one of the most adult."

Kendal's blush appeared out of nowhere. "You saying I'm mature? Like cheese?"

It was Gary's turn to redden. "Um, not at all. I'm saying how considerate and empathetic you are with the residents. Carla told me how you managed the awkward situation with Sheila from the donkey sanctuary."

"Yeah" said Kendal. "I know a fake when I see one. Even her handbag was dodgy. There's two Rs in Mulberry."

"I should keep a stricter eye on what visitors are offering. Not enough hours in the day. I'm glad you're getting so involved. Maybe you could consider joining the Residents' Association? We could do with some fresh ideas."

Kendal didn't do groups. Meetings, agendas, and minutes were dull and complicated. But she'd do anything Gary suggested. "Sure, if you think I'd be useful. How does it operate?"

Before Gary could answer Prue screamed. Gary turned on his heels and sprinted towards her. Kendal followed, remembering to look at the ground as she negotiated the pebbles.

Prue clasped a rock against her muddy pinafore. "My best find yet!" she cackled.

Kendal and Gary bent to look at the dirty stone. A small dark disc, with a dimple in the middle. Nothing like the photos in Kendal's fossil book. More like hard dog poo, or one of Carla's faggots. Kendal kept her head low, pretending to be fascinated; a legitimate way to be inches from Gary's mouth. She closed her eyes. She could smell Gary's peppermint breath and feel his body heat.

"It's really rare," said Prue. "A backbone piece from an Ichthyosaur. There may be other parts nearby." She placed the burnt-faggot-dog-poo in her backpack and handed Kendal the hammer. "Get moving and look casual. We don't want the greedy rock hound coming." Kendal turned. No one in sight except Audrey and her swimming pals. Was Prue paranoid, going the way of Nurse Nicola?

"I'm going to check in with Jacob and the others," said Gary.

"You stay with Prue and give her a hand. Maybe you'll get lucky too."

Prue handed Kendal a hammer.

Getting lucky normally implied something more thrilling than rummaging in dirt but being told to smash stuff was appealing. Kendal struck the nearest stone. Chips bounced against her chin and sand flew into her mouth.

"Silly woman!" shouted Prue. "Be careful. Be strategic." Kendal clamped her lips. Another controlling old bag like Dogbreath-Deirdre. Any moment now, Prue would issue key performance indicators for digging.

Prue pulled Kendal's arm. "This bone comes from a giant reptile. It's from a backbone so the other parts should be close. Probe the neighbouring ground, try to sense what's there. Only use the hammer when you are convinced there's something inside a stone. Watch me."

The old lady scanned the pebbles; her brown-spotted hands stretched open; her eyes closed in an orgasmic swoon. "Feel the energy emanating from millions of years. Let the stones speak."

Prue was more woo-woo than Audrey. Kendal opened her palms and swept them slowly from side to side remembering the dodgy physiotherapist in Fulham she'd visited with a hurt wrist. He'd insisted she strip to her knickers then waved his hands over her breasts. Ninety pounds when all she needed was a gel-filled mouse pad and fresh batteries for her vibrator.

It was tranquil beside Prue, focussed on a task (if a bonkers one). Better than Friday afternoons at THRUm when Kendal would invent excuses (migraines, period pains, dental appointments) to leave early. Dogbreath-Deirdre was always saying Kendal lacked concentration. Yet, here she was, eyes closed, concentrating hard to help Prue discover backbone. Kendal felt a sharp tingle in her left palm. She opened her eyes to see if she had been stung.

"Keep still and follow the heat," ordered Prue.

Kendal lowered her hand onto a rock the size of a grapefruit.

"This feels hot," said Kendal, which was weird as they were in shade.

"Tap gently. Like you're opening a walnut."

Kendal wedged the stone between her feet and tapped it with the hammer's pointed end. The rock split and crumbles of clay dropped onto her shoes. Inside, was a tiny ammonite, the size of the blue sapphire, with each ring of the spiral standing proud. She blew off the dirt and polished the fossil on her trousers. Two hundred million years and finally seeing the light of day. She handed the treasure to Prue.

Prue shook her head. "It's yours. Finders, keepers."

"But you're team leader, Prue. You should take the credit."

Prue shrugged. "It's small and I've got loads. You keep it."

Kendal stroked the perfectly formed fossil. "Is it worth anything?"

"Not in money terms. But it's worth a lot to you."

"Why?"

"It's your first one." Prue grinned. "Everyone remembers their first time, don't they?"

Kendal didn't. It was long ago and she'd been far too drunk. She pocketed the ammonite, and stood, forgetting to groan or stretch.

"You're very flexible," observed Prue. "Like Audrey. Are you a yogi too?"

Kendal laughed. "No, but I might become one. Audrey's pretty persistent. I'm sorry I couldn't find you any more backbone bits, but I must make a move. I'm going to check how Audrey's doing."

"You are such a kind person, Kendal. God bless."

Audrey and her Bluetit friends were begging for buggy rides when Kendal returned to the prom.

"Is Prue all right?" asked Gary.

"She's well stuck in," answered Kendal.

"Oh Christ! It's terrible stuff this Blue Lias mud," said Gary, preparing to run.

"I meant she is concentrating on finding more backbone bits."

Gary sighed.

Kendal longed to help him relax. "Look what she helped me find."

Gary stroked the spiral rings of her fossil. "What a perfect specimen."

Kendal chewed her lip. Gary's mouth was so close. The atmosphere was charged and Kendal didn't hear Audrey arrive alongside, tugging at her elbow.

"You're breathing too fast, Kendal. Need more yoga."

"You've convinced me, Audrey. I'll be there tomorrow. I think I may have roped in Prue too."

"Good, now come and have a paddle with me. I've brainstormed with the Bluetits. The girls have a suggestion for the Brand New."

"You mean, the rebrand," said Kendal. "Go on then, tell me."

"Only when you've had a paddle." Audrey bent to remove her shoes and socks.

Kendal groaned. Audrey was holding out like the tedious big reveals put on by THRUm's design department when they tweaked the charity's brand. Always an anti-climax. Some minuscule change like THRUM to THRUm! Waste of time, money and trees.

They stepped into the water. Kendal's feet were agonisingly tender. The pebbles dug in and seaweed floated around her calves. The pain dispelled all fantasies about romping in Blue Lias mud with Gary.

"I've told the girls you're joining us for Bluetits bathing soon," said Audrey. "You'll feel so alive."

"I'll have a heart attack."

"Don't be ridiculous, you're far too young."

"I'm sixty, Audrey."

"And the average woman has her first heart problem at seventy," retorted Audrey. "Start now and your immune system will be unbeatable."

At last, Audrey allowed her to return to the shore. Kendal rubbed her feet. "So, how you are going to rebrand your exercise sessions then?"

Audrey winked. "You know what young people do on Dartmoor in the middle of the night. With drugs and disc jockeys? Raves, they're called." Kendal nodded. She'd been totally across the rave scene. Endlessly racing round motorways searching fields for secret gigs. A fantastic time she wished she could recall more accurately.

"I think I've seen them on the news," she said. "Dreadful."

"They leave a mess; the ponies get in a tizz, and farmers complain. But the more fuss the telly makes, the more the youngster wants to go. Controversy, you see. It attracts people."

Kendal had no idea where Audrey was going but pleased to learn Dartmoor had raves. Perhaps Gary attended?

Audrey bobbed with excitement. "What's the biggest controversy in residential homes?"

"The-three-strikes-and-you're-out rule? Exploitative donkeys?"

Audrey shook her head violently.

"Is it to do with food or activities? The annual charges?"

Audrey tutted.

"I give up."

Audrey raised her eyebrows which, today, were symmetrical. "End of life, of course? Going upstairs, kicking the bucket, passing over. Whatever stupid eupho-whats-it you choose. Everyone's scared of dying. Except Prue, of course, who looks forward to it. She belongs to Bloscombe Death Café."

Raves on Dartmoor, numb toes, death restaurants? For a moment Kendal missed the predictability of a THRUm meeting.

"We're terrified of drawing attention to it," said Audrey. "Look how upset all the residents got about Albert going to the hospital. It wasn't only concern for him; they were scared for themselves."

Kendal pulled her shoes on. "So, how does this connect with your classes?"

Audrey prodded Kendal's chest. "What is the point of exercise?"

"Get fit, have fun, make friends?" suggested Kendal (Ealing Leisure Centre gym was a great place for hook-ups).

"To stop us dying!" shouted Audrey. "Only we don't say it. We pussyfoot around." Kendal nodded.

"Exercise keeps us out of the grave. We need to stop fudging the issue. Get fit or die!" Audrey was on a roll.

"Right," said Kendal. "And the rebrand?"

Audrey opened her arms and shouted across the beach. "Audrey's Anti-Grave Rave! AAR, for short." She smirked. "Like a pirate."

Audrey, Prue, and Kendal walked slowly back to Jurassic Court. Kendal's feet felt like she'd had a pedicure but without the cost or awkward small talk with a teenage beautician.

"The Well-being Walks are so much better now you're here," said Prue.

"I think Gary thinks so too," said Audrey.

In Flat 4, Kendal washed her fossil and balanced it on a cork on her dining table. The ammonite reflected the shine of the polished wood; a perfect creature brought to the surface after millions of years buried in clay. It was ancient and mysterious (despite Prue calling it common). Cost nothing, and no one could be missing it.

15

Shelley and Keats emerged at the sound of Kendal's Kangoo and waited politely as she picked up Clare's post. One even purred as she filled the food bowls. The Tudge Trudge worked.

Kendal unpacked her London clothes and make-up and replaced Clare's family photo on the mantelpiece with Clem's photo of her parents. In flares and cheesecloth, her mum and dad looked very much at home beside Clare's candles and cacti. She placed two of Clem's Hornblower books on a coffee table. It was unlikely that Mad-Maxine and her dim boyfriend would make conversation about books, but, if they did, she was ready.

Clare had twelve packets of herbal teas in her larder. Kendal selected a hawthorn and eucalyptus mix for boosting digestion (Carla's porridge had been particularly solid). Clem's reclining chair was comfortable, but she'd missed the feeling of absolute abandonment you got from sofa-lying and Clare's was super-comfortable. A cat (Shelley was the bigger one, wasn't it?) threatened to jump. Kendal emitted a low growl and it slunk away.

The herbal tea was effective and Kendal was hungry again. In the fridge, she found creamy Devon goat's cheese which paired excellently with the crisps she'd brought. She switched on the CD player and Ella Fitzgerald sang 'Summertime'. Only May, but it felt appropriate. She felt her phone vibrate.

"Hi K. We've had a full English and ready to meet.

Lunchtime good for you? We could take you out.

Cheers, M and J."

Kendal grabbed an envelope and copied Clare's address into a text. Then she hid the post in the laundry cupboard, climbed the narrow stairs to Clare's bedroom and opened the wardrobe.

The Pamela jeans were still in the carrier bag. Kendal removed her charity shop clothes and lay flat to pull them on. Next came the crop top and shoes she'd worn when she first arrived, hoop earrings, eyeliner, thick foundation, and scarlet lip. So familiar; she could have dressed in the dark (and often had).

"Hello babe," she said to her reflection. "Good to see you again."

This statement wasn't true. It was good to see her tits, and legs always looked better in heels. But her belly was alarming, and the ivory foundation looked like slap Suspicious-Sheila of the donkey sanctuary might wear. There was something wrong about the black-ringed eyes too. Perhaps it was the lack of light? Clare's windows were small, and the thatched eaves blocked the sun. Kendal took the mirror to the window.

A black SUV was crawling along the lane, the driver peering at the names of the cottages. PoshJosh! Here already.

One of the cats sprawled on the landing as Kendal stumbled to the stairs. Kendal heard the clunk of the SUV's enormous doors. She must get in role. Be the forty-four-year-old party girl.

"Christ, this is narrow," whined Mad-Maxine outside. "Hun, park on the pavement or a bloody straw-chewer will key the motor." More grinding of gears.

Kendal hobbled to the larder and rattled the cat food packet. Shelley and Keats came running as she scattered pellets across the floor. As the cats started eating, she stepped swiftly out and slammed the door tight. Her heart was beating way too fast. Kendal channelled Audrey and lifted her arms to salute the sun in calm-inducing circles, mouthing:

I'm young, young, young.

"Hellooooo?" Mad-Maxine was opening the door. "Anyone at home?"

"Maxine, hiya hun!" squealed Kendal.

"Special K!" shrieked her ex-flatmate. "At last!"

PoshJosh, in tweed jacket and pink cords, burst through the

door. "How you doing, old girl?" Had he always called her old girl, or was it the grey hair?

Maxine thrust her ring finger under Kendal's nose. Three diamonds twinkled despite the darkness of the cottage. Kendal gushed appropriately.

"Nice manor, Kendal," said Josh. "How much this set you back?"

"I'm er, renting. Probate takes forever."

Maxine stared at Kendal's hair, her mouth opening and closing. "Cup of herbal? Hobnob?"

Maxine prodded Kendal's stomach. "It's gone midday on a Saturday. Why aren't you drinking?"

"Turmeric and ginger, do you?"

Maxine sniggered. "Are you really Kendal, or have you dumped her in a ditch?"

"I've changed. Like I said in the email."

"You look different too," said Maxine. "Doesn't she, Josh?"

Josh was scanning the bookshelves. "These all yours?"

"Not much to do in the countryside," answered Kendal. "I've had a lot of time to fill. The Hornblower series is classic. Have you read any, Josh?"

Josh frowned. "Books? Me? Same old Kendal! Banter central."

"Your hair is… different," said Maxine. Kendal put a hand to her head.

"Take us to the local, old girl," said Josh. "What's the beer like?"

A relief to be able to tell the truth. "I've never been," said Kendal.

The Londoners gasped in unison. "Now, I know you're not Kendal," hooted Maxine. "Come on! We're celebrating."

Kendal could hear the cats scratching from inside the larder. "Wait in the garden." She hurried upstairs, pocketed the cash-stuffed toilet roll, grabbed the bag of Maxine's black clothes she'd used for the funeral and checked her reflection. Bare shoulders and cleavage were too trashy for Plick, and the heels were lethal. She grabbed Clare's Seasalt cardigan, rubbed off the lipstick and slipped into trainers.

Maxine and Josh were in a clinch by the vegetable beds.

"You guys," said Kendal. "I'm so happy for you." She handed the wad of notes and the carrier to Maxine. "And I'm sorry it has taken me so long to pay."

Maxine unravelled herself. "I forgive you, Special K. I do."

There were four customers in the pub: two bumpkin types and a pair of hikers, all clutching glasses filled with cloudy beer. The Lazy Seagull didn't serve champagne, Prosecco, or even Cava so Josh ordered two pints of your finest ale and made a face when Kendal asked for a lime and soda. No ice, but paper straws decorated with ammonites. Prue would love them.

Maxine ordered a second round (not up the duff, then) which meant the next round had to be on Kendal, but her bank card was frozen and she'd given all her cash to Maxine. Maybe she could offer to cook something instead? Shelley and Keats couldn't have reached the bags of pasta in the larder, surely?

"Hun, we can't go to your place. We've ordered a hamper to be delivered to the Airbnb," drawled Mad-Maxine. "Curated by Hugh Fearnley-doodah. Come to us and I'll put it together."

Kendal considered the offer. She'd managed to convince them Candida Cottage was her home but, if she had more drinks, she could get confused about whether she was forty-four or sixty, or, worse, they might bump into someone from Jurassic Court. Also, PoshJosh and Mad-Maxine were even duller than she'd remembered; banging on about people she didn't know, places she hadn't visited and socials she'd never scrolled. She genuinely would prefer to spend the rest of Saturday at Jurassic Court enjoying Audrey's Anti-Grave Rave or Brian's choice for Movie Night. Good to get out of the tight jeans too.

Maxine patted Kendal's thigh. "Bloscombe's a sweet little place. But you must be bored?"

"I'm not," said Kendal. It was true. "How long are you staying?"

"Till Tuesday, and then we're back to town," said Josh. "I'm taking clients to Chelsea." Did he mean the football club or the flower show? Kendal couldn't remember Josh's job. He probably hadn't told her. Prats like Josh assumed everyone knew.

"Maybe we catch up tomorrow, you could show us around?" said Maxine. "Met anyone special yet?" She nodded at the other customers. "Or are they too old? Looks like the dinosaurs never went away."

The Londoners were unbearable. Patronising, metropolitan, entitled, unreal. Kendal had endured them for three hours. She must say something to make them go away. A Tudge Budge.

"Actually, they were never here. It's all lies. Like the moon landings," she announced.

Josh tittered. Maxine frowned.

Kendal crushed the ammonite straw. "There were no dinosaurs. The tourism people go along with it to attract people like you."

"Very funny, K," said Maxine.

Kendal was getting into her role. This was fun. "I've never been more serious. God created the earth, and He didn't include dinosaurs. I told you I went on a retreat. Been quite a journey, but now I know where I want to be. In God's garden, here in Dorset."

Josh groaned. Maxine shook her head.

Kendal pressed her palms together. "I wish you a wonderful life. Enjoy your meal and the rest of your stay. I won't see you tomorrow. It is the holy day."

Maxine gasped. "What about Monday?"

Kendal visualised the library notice board. "Poetry Appreciation in the morning. We're doing Shelley and Keats. Then Boarding School survivor group after lunch."

"Is that a thing?" asked Josh. "Why? I loved school."

So gullible. Almost too easy.

They walked to the SUV. Kendal asked polite questions about wedding plans and Maxine explained it would be quick since her fertility app was predicting dire percentages if they didn't get a move on with baby-making. Josh smirked and unloaded five bags of Kendal's London possessions.

"Your computer's there, with all the leads and plugs," said Maxine.

"I won't be using it," said Kendal. "The internet is toxic." She grabbed two bags and walked towards the front door.

"Sure," said Josh, following with the other bags. "But you'll miss the funny cat videos, right?" Kendal unlocked the door. Two grey missiles clamped claws into Josh's bare legs.

"Don't need the internet, Josh. Got real-life drama with these two."

Kendal grabbed the cat's collars and herded them into the house.

When the SUV was out of sight Kendal returned to the cottage. She put the charity shop disguise back on, replaced Clare's possessions and stacked the post neatly. Shelley and Keats wove around her legs. Kendal re-filled their food bowls.

"Good work, boys," she said. "Fill yer boots!"

The Quaker Meeting the next morning was comforting. It had been a full-on week; paying off a dangerous debt, successfully passing as both young and old, helping Audrey and Albert, arranging flowers, fossil hunting, masturbating in the shower and keeping it together with Gary. Kendal had a lot to be grateful for and this was the place to do it.

It felt good to feel chilled. Yesterday had been challenging; quite a performance acting her real age and pretending Candida Cottage was her home. The god squad bit was genius. Came out of nowhere. Or perhaps it didn't? Maybe she'd been visited by some kind of spirit? Uncle Clem, her parents or the million-year-old ammonite? She would have scoffed in the past at such woo-woo nonsense but now, well, everything was changing.

Gary sat opposite Kendal in a translucent linen shirt She could see his nipples and happy trail. Her body processed this information in a neutral kind of way, with a regular pulse, no blushing, or embarrassing moisture. Perhaps this was mindfulness, the much sought-after state everyone in London banged on about? Well, not everyone. Not people with genuine issues like poverty or cancer but THRUm tossers or pre-menstrual Mad-Maxine.

Kendal looked at the clock. Forty minutes already. No one had spoken. Sam, Albert, Pam and Shirley had their eyes closed. Prue and Jim were staring at dust mites. Wendy, a resident rarely seen outside of the dining room, slowly stood upright. She wore a fleece decorated with a picture of a howling wolf and white tufts of hair peeked out from under a black, lopsided wig.

"Friends, I offer my gift to bring joy to us all."

Everyone except Kendal stared at Wendy. Thirty years of late-night tubes had taught Kendal not to look directly at crazies.

"We have so much to be thankful for: the ocean, the beach, fishes, companionship. As Brian demonstrated with his cinema choice the world is full of mysterious and marvellous examples of God's grace."

Brian's choice for Movie Night had been *Titanic* and Kendal had watched it until the iceberg arrived. She'd been keen to unpack the clothes bags and computer and, besides, she knew how the film ended. Maybe she'd missed something, or perhaps Wendy was simply a massive Leo fan?

Wendy raised her arms. "I have created something to help us communicate joy. I hope you will join in."

Kendal hoped it didn't involve hand-holding as Gary was opposite, not beside, and she didn't want to touch anyone else. Wendy opened a Tesco bag-for-life and extracted a large two-pronged fork made of lipstick-stained, pink drinking straws.

"God has provided us with the why," she cried, and handed the plastic contraption to the warden. "Can you hang this, please?"

Gary held it warily. Kendal wondered if he found second-hand things gross too although Kendal's germ phobia had lessened at Jurassic Court. Germs hardly festered on the coast or in the countryside and Carla and Emma were intense about food hygiene. A dodgy prawn could annihilate Jurassic Court.

"Happy to help, Wendy," said Gary. "Where would you like it?" He scanned the room. His glance landed on Kendal and a rush of heat spread across her knees. His eyes darted from the sculpture to her. Not mocking Wendy but sharing the oddness. A special connection.

Wendy pointed at the damaged word on the wall. "It's to replace the letter Y that's missing on JOY. I couldn't get the same style, so I've made one from last night's cocktails. Picked them out of the kitchen bin."

Gary gently hung the pink Y next to the wooden J and O. Wendy beamed.

Kendal stayed to help Gary tidy the Ammonite room. "I've never heard Wendy speak before," she said. "She's quite a character."

Gary pushed the jigsaws straight. "Yes, she's been a campaigner for years and years. Lived at Greenham Common for a while. Done all kinds of protests. Young people think they've invented eco-concerns and blame the older generations for the state of the world. They forget about people like Wendy and Prue."

"Those straws are a bit nasty, though," said Kendal. "Could we have paper ones, perhaps?"

"The residents always vote against paper straws. They think they go soggy, like the ones they had as kids." Kendal nodded. Paper straws could be rubbish, especially when you snorted too hard.

"They have cool ones at the Lazy Seagull in Plick," she said. "With ammonites on."

"Do they?" said Gary. "Haven't been there since I was a teenager. Always turned a blind eye to under-age drinking. Must have gone a bit up-market."

"Well, they don't serve Prosecco. But I was there yesterday, and the straws are definitely paper."

"You could suggest it at the Residents' meeting next week. It won't be a walkover, though. There are plenty of climate change deniers here as well as ecowarriors."

"Does it need to be discussed? Why don't you just tell Carla and Emma to order paper straws?"

Gary had noticed the puppets in the bin. "Haven't seen these for ages." He put his hand inside Goldilocks, shook the white-blonde acrylic hair, and mimicked Trump.

"We live in a democracy. If the people want plastic, I can't force it."

Gary was a great performer. Witty and pretty. Kendal wished she could be funny in response but all she could think about was Gary's hand inside Goldilocks's skirt.

Gary returned Goldilocks to the box. The moment had passed. "You could put a suggestion on the agenda. Maybe bring some straw samples so residents could assess the sogginess."

Kendal nodded. Sogginess was a disgusting concept. Not like moistness which she was all too familiar with around Gary. "I'm feeding Clare's cats. The Lazy Seagull is close to her cottage. I'll ask them for a few straws. They won't have got rid of them. They're not busy."

"How do you know?" asked Gary.

Kendal adopted her best south London voice. "Seagull is lazy, innit?"

Gary threw his head back and laughed. A proper guffaw.

Boom! Warden-banter nailed!

Kendal felt her phone vibrate. The infuriating pawnbroker.

Official reminder – transaction Tudge-Derbyfield.
You have 25 days to return your loan.

Never a lull in the endless hassling. It wasn't fair. She simply wanted to be chilled with the kind, hot, honest warden.

16

The five bin bags delivered by Mad-Maxine and PoshJosh contained everything Kendal had owned before her uncle died. A pathetic haul. It was good to have the laptop (though technically it belonged to THRUm) and great to have the Kindle charger, but the rest was disappointing. The clothes were too trampy for a sixty-year-old in Bloscombe. They looked grubby and smelled of kebabs. There was a laundry service that visited Jurassic Court, but since the cost wasn't included in Clem's pre-paid lease, Kendal had not used it. No problem, she'd take her washing to Candida Cottage.

Shelley and Keats greeted Kendal meekly. Kendal refused to stroke them. Treat 'em mean, keep 'em keen. Good for cats as well as clingy lesbians.

Clare's washing machine was ancient but at least it used powder, not the stupid laundry eggs so adored by Mad-Maxine. She filled the tub with bed linen and underwear. This was going to be a double launderette session, like Sundays in bedsit land, but without a hangover. The cycle took fifty minutes. Perfect for visiting the Lazy Seagull to score paper straws which would be an easy win with Gary, and a tiny step forward for the globe.

The rustics were in the pub again, joined by four cyclists and a noisy family. Kendal had to wait to be served. The barman smelled of pork scratchings.

"Lost your mates?"

"They were visitors. I'm a resident." Kendal smiled. "I intend to be a regular."

"Good. Got to keep the Seagull going. We've been here for three centuries. Happy to serve all. Providing they're English."

Kendal clenched her teeth. Saving the planet was hard if your allies were racists. She ordered a lime and soda. "I'll do my best, but I'm not a great drinker. I do love these straws though. Where did you buy them?"

The barman examined the straw jar. "Brewery gives us them."

"Can I take a few extra?" asked Kendal. "For my friends? We're in a fossil club."

The barman bent under the counter and passed a large cardboard box. "Take these. Their straws are better than their pissy beer."

The washing machine was climaxing as Kendal returned but its position (under the eaves) meant no space for Kendal to hop on. She took the box of straws to the Kangoo, bundled the damp washing into the tumble dryer, and stuffed a second load into the washing machine. Fifty more minutes to kill.

Kendal tried practising yoga in the living room, but the ceiling was too low for tree pose and the cats dug sharp nails into her downward dog. She checked if the garden needed watering, but nothing looked dead and the cat shit smell was disgusting. She climbed the narrow stairs for a poop and snoop.

In the bathroom, Clare's scales accused Kendal of putting on six pounds since London. She stepped off quickly and opened the cabinet above the sink. Nothing desirable (like Valium, Adderall, or CBD oil) but Clare's bedside cupboard revealed a dusty wood hash pipe and a Rabbit vibrator (purple, waterproof silicone, well-charged). Go Clare!

Kendal opened the wardrobe. Clare's clothes were clean, smartly pressed and colour coordinated with easy-to-access shelves for underwear, trousers, bags, and shoes. She fingered the rolled socks and admired the neatly paired footwear. Librarianship was good for Clare. She had order and systems in her DNA. More surprising was Clare's choice of clothing brands; obvious oldie favourites like M&S, Regatta and Seasalt, alongside a spattering of younger labels from Urban Outfitter, Primark, and Nasty Gal.

Kendal began trying Clare's clothes. Some were too tight and others insipidly minimal (single colour, no pattern), but Clare was short which meant knee-length outfits became perfect minis on Kendal's cellulite-free legs. Kendal looked hot. Shame she'd deleted her profiles on dating apps: there would have been a right-swipe tsunami in these outfits, even without contoured cheekbones, red lip, or favourite hoops.

The charity shop trousers itched. Uncomfortable, unflattering, cheap, and full of static. Clare would never possess such horrible gear. Kendal sighed. She'd misjudged the disguise. She was pretending to be sixty, not over eighty. Old people should not be tied together in one elasticated lump. There was so much difference between Clare and Wendy, or even Philip and Brian now she'd got to know them.

Clare was a boomer, but she didn't seem to mind being old. Clare had a career, a family, a cottage, and probably a massive pension and her clothes were straight, but cool. Kendal should be a tad cooler, modify her sixty-year-old disguise and look more attractive? Gary, who'd been sending flirty vibes at the wake, had stopped flirting since she'd announced she was staying at Jurassic Court. She'd hoped it was the change of status from guest to resident, not the change in age. Clare was cool and over sixty. Surely, Kendal could find a way to have her cake, and eat it? Or have it eaten!

Kendal replaced Clare's possessions neatly (she could be tidy when she had to). She emptied the second laundry load, gave it a burst in the tumble dryer, fed the cats, and packed the Kangoo. She was looking forward to the fresh bedsheets. There'd been far too much sweating recently and single person sweat was not a good scent.

The hedges in the lanes were displaying white flowers. Something to research for Nature Notes. It was beguiling how Bloscombe was changing. She'd never noticed signs of spring in London. At a crossroads, Kendal was forced to wait while a gang of cows ambled past, the farmer prodding their bottoms and shouting unintelligible instructions. One dumped right in front of the car. A reminder that nature could be gross and she shouldn't get too bowled over by it.

At the Bloscombe roundabout, Kendal ignored the town centre and beach exits and turned into a retail park. It had normal shops: Pets-R-Us, Discount Furniture Warehouse, Lidl and Tool Station. Here, too, were ordinary people with kids and vape pens. Bloscombe was not only old people. It was more complex than people like Mad-Maxine and PoshJosh assumed.

She took a random turn and found herself in a large housing estate with small, modern homes. It was impressively neat and tidy. No dumped mattresses or abandoned shopping trolleys. Children played on scooters and teenagers kicked a ball around a basketball hoop. A pleasant Sunday afternoon with normal people. This must be what politicians meant by community. Kendal wondered if one of the boxy houses in the estate belonged to Gary. He might be hoovering his living room, changing a light bulb, or lifting weights and executing squats.

Gary was, in fact, still at Jurassic Court updating the activities board. Kendal blushed. The fantasy about Gary working out was fresh. She gave the board extra attention.

Monday Audreys Anti-Grave Rave launch AM
Tuesday "Ear Today" with EarWax-John AM
Knit and Natter with Philip PM
Wednesday Gardening Club AM with Gary
Thursday Fidget-blanket making AM
Residents' meeting PM
Friday Wendy's 91st Birthday Party AM
Well-being walk PM
Saturday Movie Night – Jennifer's choice.

"Another busy week for us, Gary," said Kendal.

"People who keep active live the longest," smiled Gary.

"You'll live a long time then, Gary. You're always on the go." Gary's turn to redden. So cute. Kendal wanted to prolong the moment. "Wendy will be ninety-one this week? Amazing! She seems so youthful."

"She's not the eldest. Shirley is. No one knows how old but she's got cards from the Palace, so definitely more than a hundred."

"I can't imagine being so old," said Kendal. "Hard to believe I'm sixty. Feel like I'm still in my twenties most of the time."

Gary replaced the marker pen lid and examined the board. "I can't believe you're sixty either."

Kendal froze. How dumb to draw attention to her fake age. She needed a diversionary tactic. "You've left off an apostrophe. On Monday's listing. It's Audrey-apostrophe-s."

She fled along the corridor, remembering to shuffle at the last moment.

Audrey and Brian went large on the Anti-Grave Rave launch event. Audrey bought glow sticks and borrowed a bubble machine and glitter ball, while Brian put Tom and Jerry cartoons on the Movie Night projector. Audrey wore silver leggings, a hi-vis vest, and a headset mic and stood on the wheelchair ramp to direct the residents. DJ Brian donned huge headphones over a back-to-front Bloscombe Rotary club baseball cap. He'd set his hi-fi and laptop on the jigsaw puzzle table and streamed music off YouTube.

The residents were totally up for it too: some on their feet; others with walking frames; only Albert, Pam and Shirley had to stay on the sofa but still managed some impressive hand-jiving. Mid-morning on a Monday, and Kendal was totally sober, but the noise, lights, bubbles, and goodwill, were intoxicating. Most residents adjusted their hearing aids to make the volume acceptable. Kendal surrendered to the sound and let her limbs take charge. She was pumped. She didn't want to talk, especially to poor Pam who looked sadder and cloudier than normal. .

Only Gary wasn't enjoying the daytime rave and, after forty minutes, he pulled the plug on DJ Brian. Groans turned into grins as Carla-from-the-kitchen served Mini Magnums and

Emma brought in a tray of iced tea. Kendal fetched the box of straws and gently offered them to the residents. Everyone agreed they were far better than the paper straws of their youth. Prue pointed out the difference between ammonites and belemnites on the pattern. Only Audrey struggled; her lip gloss was too sticky.

The residents returned to their flats clutching glow sticks and Mini Magnums. Kendal helped Audrey and Gary push the furniture back.

"Did you enjoy the rave, Gary?" asked Kendal. "I didn't see you moving." Gary opened the blinds and stared at the lawn.

"Not really, I was too anxious. From a health and safety perspective. All those flashing lights and the heightened level of possible slips and trips." His eyes followed a squirrel in a tree. "We've never done anything so active. Imagine the headlines if someone got hurt." The squirrel reached the end of a thin branch. Its head swivelled looking for the next landing stage.

Kendal was relieved Gary's bad mood had nothing to do with their encounter at the activities board the evening before. She offered a Mini Magnum. He shook his head.

Audrey prodded Gary. "We've got to take risks. Or we'll fade, like Pam, or get fat, like Albert. Tavvy-Tina's pompom workouts don't cut the bacon and cost too much."

"I thought it was awesome," said Kendal. "You're a regular rave bunny, Audrey."

Audrey beamed. "I'm going to need a nap this afternoon though. Exhausting being a goddess!"

"We'll see what feedback we get on Thursday," said Gary. The squirrel jumped from the tree and landed on a birdbath. "Then I'll check the trustees are happy for you to carry on."

"What's happening Thursday?" asked Kendal. The trustees sounded annoying.

"The Residents' Association," said Gary. "Where big decisions get made." He pressed the overhead projector controller and closed the screen. "The cartoons were great, though. Nothing dangerous about those."

"Well, I'm looking forward to the next Anti-Grave Rave," said Kendal. She smiled at Gary. "And then we want to see you make some shapes too."

Gary shook his head. "I'm a rubbish dancer. Two left feet."

Audrey cackled. "How do you climb rocks then?"

Gary walked toward the door. "I only have myself to worry about on a climb."

Poor Gary. It was lonely for him always being the one in charge. Kendal wished she could put the music back on and get him to relax. She pointed at the box of straws. "Shall I put these in the kitchen then, or wait for the meeting?"

Gary shouted over his shoulder. "I've put it on the agenda."

"I'm having a comedown," announced Audrey. "Come to mine, Kendal, for a chill-up."

Kendal had planned to spend the hour before lunch amending Ageing Insights; her observations about older people, their clothes, leisure pursuits, and attitudes needed updating. She'd got so many things wrong. Like spelling, there were general rules about ageing, and then there were exceptions. Like Prue, Philip, Wendy, and Clare. And, of course, Audrey. But Audrey deserved a debrief.

They sat in the deckchairs on Audrey's patio. Audrey ran through which residents had attended. Only Sam and Jennifer were no-shows.

"Sam sent apologies," said Audrey. "Had a pace-maker check. Jennifer is jealous."

"It was a massive turnout," said Kendal. "You'll need bouncers next time."

"Good idea," said Audrey. "A mini trampoline would be helpful for Albert."

"I mean security guards. You know, like doormen," said Kendal. "A joke."

Audrey frowned. Banter was a work in progress.

Audrey handed Kendal a Biro and a notebook with a lifeboat picture on the cover. "Let's storm our brains some more. While we're high."

"I've got one of these notebooks," said Kendal. "It was Clem's."

Audrey sighed. "We've all got loads. Clem was supposed to sell them for the lifeboats, but he was too polite to be a salesman, so he bought the lot himself and then gave them away." She pointed at a shoebox under the television table. "There's loads in there, along with Prue's chapped lipsticks in aid of the bumble bees, Philip's key rings for the dog trust, and Jennifer's crocus bulbs for polio. We keep selling to each other. The worst are Wendy's postcards for tramps. Nobody wants those."

"Can I have a look, Audrey? I love stationery and I think you mean chap sticks."

Kendal opened the box and removed a bundle of postcards. Bad fonts, garish colours and the kind of drivel adored by the Innovation team at THRUm:

I will press on until I achieve my heart's desires
Rejection will not deter me
Keep it Up, girlfriend/boyfriend!

Audrey snorted. "Rubbish, aren't they?"

Kendal turned the card over to read the back.

"For every affirmation card you buy, we'll give another to a homeless person."

"They're affirmation cards, Audrey."

"Don't care what they are," cackled Audrey. "They're absurd." She grabbed the pen and scrawled a message on the blank side:

Audrey's Affirmation.
Congratulations on being
One step further from the grave!

Kendal grinned. Hanging out with Audrey was genuinely fun.

17

Earwax-John was even more popular than Comfitoes Chiropodist.

"He makes everything clearer," enthused Philip.

"You feel more alive afterwards," added Brian.

"So much wax," said Jennifer. "And only forty pounds."

Kendal had experienced hearing problems after eight-hour raves but at Jurassic Court she could hear perfectly. Too perfectly at meals.

After breakfast, she researched older people's hearing and discovered older ears can dry and shrink. Not as horrible as vaginal atrophy, but nasty.

At lunch, the residents compared notes about the volume, thickness, and quality of the wax removed from their ears. The saffron risotto and marmalade mousse was too close in colour and Kendal decided to escape to Plick where the WiFi was excellent and nobody discussed any kind of discharge.

Kendal had hated Excel at THRUm, where even hot drink preferences were logged into little boxes, but now they must become her friends. They were perfect for storing and accessing wide-ranging data (and keeping it private). She fed the cats, made a turmeric tea and booted her laptop.

AI: Ageing Intelligence, Kendal's well-researched, lived-experienced observations and data about older people with a page for each decade starting with the 60-69 generation (Clare the librarian) and ending at Over 100 (Sleepy Shirley). Time-consuming but satisfying to insert hyperlinks to relevant websites and colour code data about Bloscombe, Banter and Nature. Dogbreath-Deirdre would have wet herself.

Kendal returned to her flat to rationalise her wardrobe. The tops Mad-Maxine had delivered were too revealing or decorated with slogans which Clare would never wear, but the trousers, shoes, and underwear worked when twinned with Clem's plain linen shirts. Wearing her own jeans and trainers made Kendal feel fitter and more energised. Maybe she'd start swimming soon.

"Shame you missed Knit and Natter," commented Philip at supper. "Excellent session. We could hear each other, for once."

On Wednesday, Kendal made straight to the lawn where Gary was creating an outdoor classroom for Gardening Club. He'd covered his blue shorts with a green boiler suit and added a studded tool belt adorned with dangling gadgets. His strong arms lifted a laden wheelbarrow.

"Need any help?" she asked. "I'm no gardener, but happy to hump."

Gary wiped his glistening head with a red handkerchief but failed to laugh.

"I mean, carry stuff," said Kendal. Perhaps he was still in a bad mood.

"Yeh, I got that." Gary frowned.

Kendal gulped. The sun, and Gary's swinging tools, were sending her into girly giddiness. She needed to get a grip. It might be safe to wear her rock chick jeans and trainers and still pass as a sixty-year-old, but she shouldn't start flirting like a teenager.

"What are we going to be doing this morning, Gary? The gardens at Jurassic Court always look so nice."

"Gardening Club is for the residents, not the actual gardens. It helps us physically and mentally. Joe and Linda, our professional horticulturists, tend the grounds. I'll pass your feedback on."

Kendal remembered an Ageing Insights article she'd copied when she needed distracting from a disturbing story about blocked ears and dry vaginas. "There's been some amazing research about what handling soil does to our neural pathways."

Gary smiled. "Yes, it's fantastic how serotonin can be released by specific bacteria in the soil. It's a natural anti-depressant."

"So are we going to all get mindful in the mud you're transporting?"

"Peat-free compost, to be precise. Can you help me erect the trestle tables?"

Kendal reddened. How teenage! Blushing at a semi-rude word!

She followed Gary to the garage, took one end of a folding table and concentrated on staring at the ground, pretending to be concerned about tripping. She could not look him in the face and walk backwards. He was just too attractive.

Carla and Emma brought more trestles from the day room to form a U-shape which reminded Kendal of the training room at THRUm where she endured pointless courses and endless workshops. Thankfully, there was no need for an icebreaking exercise or evaluation forms at Jurassic Court. Everyone knew each other and feedback was something that came out of the radio.

The residents trooped along the path to the outdoor classroom and waited for Gary to set the pots and planters. Only Wendy (hair appointment for her wigs) and Albert (new catheter tube fitting) were absent.

"This is my favourite club," said Sam.

"Makes me feel so alive," said Prue. "Flowers keep growing, whatever happens in the world."

"So do weeds," snarled Jennifer.

"Weeds have many admirable features," said Prue. "Like people who aren't beautiful, Jennifer."

Gary lifted heavy sacks of compost onto the table. Brian and Jim watched enviously.

"Not as heavy as the newspaper bundles I lifted in my shop," said Brian.

"Or the pigs I carried on one shoulder," sighed Jim.

"Not only men who carry weights," said Jennifer. "My twins were eight pounds."

Gary took a small knife out of his tool belt and handed it to Jim. "Can you use your butchering skills on the compost bags?" Jim's shaking hand slit each sack, peeling the plastic to reveal black compost. Gary waited patiently; the lawn behind him and the sea in the distance. The tool belt rested on his hips. His hair glowed. PoshJosh and Mad-Maxine might be at the Chelsea Flower show quaffing Aperol spritz, but Gary was far more intoxicating.

"Ladies and Gents, let the potting party commence," called Gary. "Grit first, then compost. I'm off to the greenhouse to get the seedlings. Then we'll prick out."

Kendal gulped. Gardening Club was intense. She watched him stride across the lawn to a hidden corner belonging to the gardeners. It would be very warm in the greenhouse. He might have to remove his boiler suit…

"Stop daydreaming, madam," said Sam. "Put your grit in, then pass me the scoop."

Kendal concentrated on preparing the large pot. Grit was simple to spoon but the lumpy compost wouldn't crumble with the trowel.

"Use your hands, woman," said Prue.

Kendal was not keen to get her hands in the dirt. Even without gels her nails were looking good. Clean, healthy, far better than they'd ever been in London.

"Feel the soil, sense the life force," urged Prue pushing Kendal's hands into the soil. Kendal gasped. The moist earth felt warm and soft and smelled of grass. She filled her pot easily and moved on to help Shirley (arthritic hands couldn't hold the scoop), and Philip (anxious about mud on his bow tie). Pam was struggling to see the edge of her pot. There'd been no mention of a lost ring but Kendal didn't want to get close to Pam in case her guilt manifested itself and she blurted something out. Happily, Brian, who had strong hands and good eyesight, took over.

Gary returned with a wheelbarrow full of seedlings and small plants. The pots were ready and waiting. "Much quicker than last year," he observed. "What's going on?"

"It's Kendal,' said Audrey. "She's helping."

Gary smiled at Kendal. She felt the heat of another blush.

"Beginner's luck," she murmured, wiping her hands on her jeans.

"Well done, everyone," said Gary. "Now it's time to choose which plants to put into your pots."

The residents could turn the tamest subject into a big debate: Jennifer was concerned about the vulgarity of dahlias; Prue hated anything white; Jim and Brian refused to say pansy, and Audrey claimed geraniums poisoned animals. They all hated lilies (too connected to funerals).

Previously Kendal had only considered patio pots as a place to hide a key or pee if she couldn't open a front door in time. At Jurassic Court patio pots were a way to signal status and express individuality. Like phones for teenagers or handbags for influencers.

When all the pots were filled, and the unwanted lilies donated to Carla and Emma, Gary dragged a yellow hose to the tables. He turned it to the lowest pressure and dribbled into each pot, his muscles swelling in the mid-morning heat. Kendal didn't trust herself and scurried away pretending to take a call on her mobile. She watched the residents as she pretended to talk on the phone; Audrey and Sam were attempting to sweep away spilled compost whilst Philip and Jennifer tried to fold the plastic sacks. It was sad how physically weak the old people were. Simple jobs became giant projects, but they persevered. Sweet how Gary and his staff made it happen, however long it took. He was patient, kind and sensitive. And hot. So hot!

The daily text from the pawnbrokers cooled her down:

Official reminder – transaction Tudge-Derbyfield
You have 22 days to return your loan.

"You all right, love?" asked Brian, when Kendal returned.

No one at Jurassic Court would speak on the phone in public unless it was something important.

"Just a junk call," said Kendal.

"A long time for a junk call," said Audrey, canny as ever.

"Sometimes I string them along," said Kendal. "Pretend I really am interested in insulating my loft or whatever they want to sell me. I enjoy wasting their time and money."

"They could be siphoning your bank account if you talk for long," said Brian.

Kendal rolled her eyes. There was nothing in her bank account.

Philip, Audrey, Brian, and Jennifer walked back to the foyer bombarding Kendal with examples of scams and hoaxes they had heard about in the *Daily Mail*, or on local television. It was the first time Kendal had witnessed Audrey agree with Jennifer about anything and Brian and Philip sounded vulnerable and confused. They were all nervous.

At lunch, Kendal listened to more examples of the evils of technology. It was so different from THRUm where everyone believed everything only meant anything if it was in an app or tightly packed into a spreadsheet. This was living representation of the digital divide. The residents appeared terrified of the internet and the criminals they believed controlled it, and yet none of them had been alarmed by Suspicious-Sheila from the donkey sanctuary who was clearly a far greater threat. Kendal wished she could find a way to challenge their scamming fears. The residents needed to be savvy about spam and more confident about new technology. She could help them, surely?

Kendal drove to Candida Cottage aglow with a sense of purpose and a buzzing mind. Of course Gary would have to endorse whatever she suggested and they'd have to have intimate meetings, strategic summits, in-depth analysis. For the first time ever Kendal felt enthusiastic about the prospect of a meeting. Blah blah, delicious, blah.

Shelley and Keats purred almost fondly when she opened the door. Keats (or maybe Shelley) tried to jump on her lap as she sorted through Clare's large pile of post. Crazy how much junk mail Clare was receiving; letters from four charities, three wealth managers, two hearing ad companies and one from a natural burial ground. Shocking how businesses wanted to exploit the grey pound.

As each day passed without the auction house getting in touch to say they had sold her antiques, Kendal was having to work hard to believe she could return the money to the pawnbroker and return the ring to its rightful owner. "Finders, keepers" was an excellent expression in relation to cupcakes, ammonites or even computers, but it wasn't applicable at Jurassic Court where there were no locked doors and everyone was honest.

Kendal fed the cats and drove straight back to Jurassic Court. Baths or more wardrobe investigations could wait. She had to get back and do some good. Block out the bad she had done with the sapphire ring.

A large yellow poster had been slipped under the door of Flat 4.

Jurassic Court needs you!
Tomorrow 1.30pm. Day room.
Residents' Association meeting
Bring agenda items and your opinions.
Kind regards.
Gary, warden of Jurassic Court.

Gary needed her! Yes, she was ready! Kendal had transformed herself (apart from the hormonal flushes and annoying new blush), and now it was time to transform the biddies, make them confident about tech and resilient to scams.

Kendal Tudge had a mission!

18

Kendal was curious about Thursday's Fidget-Blanket workshop (do they vibrate, are they warm, did she need one?) but returned to her flat after breakfast instead. She must decide how to help the residents overcome their tech and scamming fears and draft a proposal for the Residents' Association. Something about scams and con artists might work but it could also draw attention to the biggest fraudster at Jurassic Court. Herself! After spending too much time deciding where to put the apostrophe in Residents she'd only written the heading when the lunch gong pealed.

Kendal joined a table with Jacob, Jennifer, and Jim. They'd attended the Fidget-Blanket workshop and were keen to share.

"It could take weeks to finish," said Jacob. "Quite a task."

"Makes an enormous difference to poor souls with dementia," said Jim.

"There's folk here who should have one," said Jennifer.

Discovering fidget blankets were for people with dementia, Kendal was keen to change the subject – dementia was a favourite topic at Jurassic Court; it was a total mood changer and, after the daily Derbyfield text (21 days to return) Kendal needed something distracting.

"Are we all excited about this afternoon?" she asked brightly, as Carla-from-the-kitchen served plates of salmon quiche and finger rolls. Blank faces.

"Any opinions or concerns?"

"About what?" said Jim.

"The meeting," answered Kendal.

"What meeting?" asked Jacob and Jennifer in unison.

"They've all forgotten, Kendal," laughed Carla. "Be needing fidget blankets soon." Carla reached into the pocket of her tabard and handed out sachets of mayonnaise. "Unfortunately, Kendal, these lovelies are never interested in the Residents' Association meeting." Carla pinched Jacob's shoulder and winked at Jim. "Are you?"

"Thursday's is Westerns on the vintage channel," said Jim.

"And opera on Radio 3," said Jennifer.

"And I've got five miles on my exercise bike to finish," said Jacob.

"I can't open these bloody sachets," growled Jennifer. "Why can't we have a jar of salad cream?"

"Un-hy-gien-ic," said Carla, drawing out the word with her West Country burr. "And dead common." She opened the sachet for Jennifer, grabbed a glass, and tapped a spoon to draw attention.

"Ladies and gentlemen, there is no dessert for lunch today." The residents groaned. "But if you go to the meeting, you'll get a special pudding."

The dining room made a collective "ooooh".

"Spotted dick?" shouted Sam.

"Crumble?" whispered Pam.

"Tiramisu?" barked Jennifer.

"Better than those," said Carla, leaving a dramatic pause. "Knickerbocker glories with Baileys, followed by cheese platter." Carla wagged her finger. "But only for those who attend the Residents' Association meeting."

When Kendal entered the day room, every resident was present except Albert (couldn't trust himself with so much sugar) and Prue (offended by the alcohol incentive). Gary, in the black suit he'd worn to Clem's funeral, sat at a trestle flanked by a bald man in a striped suit and a blonde woman in a navy shirt dress. All the chairs were taken. Philip offered Kendal his seat, but she found a footstool and remembered to grunt as she lowered herself.

Gary introduced the visitors (bald-man was a trustee, blonde-woman from the council), whilst Emma pushed the trolley around the room. Kendal was familiar with the creamy kick of Baileys, but she'd forgotten the jelly-custard-tinned-fruit-synthetic-cream of the knickerbocker glory. She pushed her spoon deep into the goblet remembering a childhood holiday in Wales. Endless rain had forced the family into a steamy Wimpy where she had chosen this delicious-sounding sundae. It was impossible to finish, and eight-year-old Kendal had cried, but her parents ordered extra spoons and they'd all finished the glass together. Extraordinary how Jurassic Court and Bloscombe excavated memories that never appeared in London.

Bald-man burbled in the background, using nonsensical nouns – governance; agency; accountability; utilitarianism.

Blonde-woman followed with confusing verbs – safeguarding; interpreting; enabling, navigating.

Several residents followed Shirley's example and fell asleep, clutching napkins in limp fingers and dribbling custard. Sun streamed through the windows and Kendal's eyelids started to droop. Blonde-woman needed to modify her monotone. And stop touching Gary's arm!

"Thank you, Annabelle. Very helpful," lied Gary when blonde-woman finally stopped. "Before I read the minutes of the last annual general meeting, I want to check if there are any agenda items to add. I haven't had any sent in, but you can still raise concerns or suggestions now."

No one spoke. Sam snored. Someone farted.

"Any questions?" shouted Gary. "Or observations? What are we doing well, what are we doing not so well?"

There was a general stirring.

"Knickerbocker glories are top-notch," said Brian.

"Muesli is too chewy," said Audrey.

"The nurse is offensive," said Jennifer. "She should be struck off."

Gary took a sip of water. "And remember comments must not be personal attacks. We are considerate and understanding at Jurassic Court."

"Didn't know muesli was so sensitive," murmured Audrey.

Gary looked uncomfortable reading the minutes, constricted by their jargon and his unflattering suit. The meeting was as tedious as a THRUm training day, Kendal sipped a second Baileys and unpeeled a Babybel. At last, Gary reached the end.

"Can all acknowledge this is a true representation of last year's annual general meeting of the Jurassic Court Residents' Association?" said Bald-man. "Raise your hand to signal yes."

No one moved. All eyes had closed. Kendal remained silent. She wasn't at Jurassic Court last year, so how could she comment? Carla, rescuing empty knickerbocker glory goblets from stiff fingers and sprawling stomachs, clanged the metal handle of her trolley.

"Wakey, wakey, campers," she shouted. "Stir your stumps and vote."

A sea of mottled hands waved weakly. Jennifer stood to leave.

"Not finished yet, love," called Carla. "Got the agenda, then elections and AOB." Jennifer groaned and returned to her seat. "Over to you, Gary. I'll get the coffees," said Carla.

Gary nodded. He looked so awkward. Kendal willed him to do something anarchic; crumple the yellow agendas, rip off his tie, jump on the trolley.

"Thank you, Carla." Gary scanned the room. "Any other issues? Anyone?"

Sam coughed, and cheese cracker sprang across the carpet.

"Do we accept the plastic straws should be replaced with the paper ones Kendal brought?" shouted Audrey.

Gary smiled gratefully. The residents waved. "Right, passed. Anyone got anything to bring up?"

"Besides cheese crackers," barked Jennifer.

Audrey raised her hand. "You said we needed to backfeed about my Anti-Grave Rave to pass on to what's-his-name." She pointed at the trustee.

"Well remembered," said Gary. "Any feedback, ladies and gents, on Audrey's day-time rave."

157

Bald-man and blonde-woman stared at Gary, wide-eyed.

"I loved it," said Kendal. Time to use the line the residents overused. "Made me feel so alive."

"Me too," shouted Jim and Philip.

"Very good value," said Brian. "Better than Tavvy-Tina."

Gary nodded. "Passed then. Audrey's Anti-Grave Raves will continue. Any more items for discussion, or feedback for the trustees?"

Audrey, beaming with pride at the endorsement, raised her hand "Prue asked me to do one for her."

"A resident has to be in the room, or submit an item in advance," said Bald-man.

Audrey glared. "Then it's my item, not hers. I assume you'll allow another from me?" Bald-man nodded. "I propose all plastics be banned in Jurassic Court. We've made a great start with the paper straws, thanks to Kendal's efforts. No more swimming in rubbish, for the sake of turtles, polar bears, and my Bluetits."

The room erupted with opinions about what was plastic, whether recycling was pointless, why turtles didn't live in the English Channel, and the possible problem with Audrey's breasts.

"Can we take a vote on Audrey's proposal to limit unrecyclable plastic and aim to keep the sea unpolluted," bellowed Gary.

Everyone nodded except Jennifer (because it was Audrey's idea) and Jim (who thought it was a vegan conspiracy).

"Any final questions?" said Bald-man. Kendal had plenty but knew she needed to keep a low profile. Not draw attention to herself. She made a mental list instead:

Why can't people under sixty live in Jurassic Court?
Ditto, if they are obese and can't stand?
Why aren't residents learning how to deal with junk calls?
Does Tavvy-Tina stand a chance of shagging Gary?

"If there are no more items, we'll move on to the elections," announced Gary. "Jacob, are you happy to remain as secretary?"

Jacob patted the small recording machine resting on the arm of his chair and nodded.

"Brian, are you able to continue as treasurer?" Brian pointed at a pocket calculator on the arm of his chair and bowed.

"So we need to find someone to replace Clem as the Chair of the Residents' Association. Any proposals?"

The residents scrutinised their coffee cups.

"It's not a difficult role. Simply representing the views of the residents and keeping tabs on me, of course," continued Gary. "Clem did a fantastic job, for many years but anyone here could do it too. You don't have to be Clem, be yourself."

"I propose Kendal," shouted Audrey. Kendal's cup slipped across her lap.

"I second the proposal," shouted Sam. Kendal steadied the saucer.

"And me," chorused Jim, Jacob, Philip, Brian and Pam. Shirley opened her eyes and gave a thumbs-up.

Kendal had never been nominated for anything (except Girl-most-likely-to-bail at Freshers' Week). "Thanks for the offer," she said. "But I've not even been here a month."

"Then you'll bring a new approach," said Gary. "Wendy and Jennifer, what are your thoughts?"

It took Wendy a few minutes to emerge from the pile of cushions she was propped against. "I'm too old to care about such matters." She pointed at Brian, Jim, Jacob, Audrey, and Pam. "It's these young ones who need to decide."

"Kendal may be younger, but she is not equipped for this role," said Jennifer.

Audrey bristled. "She's as bright as a button. And very bendy! What's your problem?"

"Only men are equipped for positions of high responsibility," said Jennifer. "And Kendal is obviously a woman, if not a lady."

Only the district nurse had been rude to Kendal in Bloscombe, but she had early-onset dementia. Jennifer had no excuse.

"What about Margaret Thatcher?" said Kendal. "Are you saying she wasn't equipped to run the country?" Eyes swivelled. A heated debate! Even Shirley was alert.

Jennifer pursed her lips. "I admit she did a marvellous job. But I didn't elect her. I voted for our M.P. and he did."

"I've never voted," whispered Pam. "I wouldn't know how."

"Nor me," said Shirley. "My husband wouldn't let me."

"No point anyway, it's always the same in Bloscombe," said Prue.

Blonde-woman tapped her watch. Gary stood. "If there are no other nominations, then Kendal is elected unopposed, by a majority vote. Congratulations, Kendal. You're carrying on the Tudge tradition at Jurassic Court."

Bald-man and blonde-woman shook Kendal's hand. Brian gave Kendal a bear hug and Philip warbled *For She's a Jolly Good Fellow*. Carla unscrewed another Baileys bottle.

Kendal returned to her flat and lay on the reclining chair. She'd mastered Excel spreadsheets and been elected Chair of the Residents' Association. She had something to offer. She was valued. People liked her!

Kendal imagined a future where she became embedded at Jurassic Court, helping the residents and improving their understanding of modern society. If she was essential then she could get rid of the sixty-plus rule and live legitimately in the flat by the sea, with no worries about surprise visits from Londoners or accusations from Nurse Nicola.

If she was able to be her true self, she'd be able to register for a real job. She could go back to blonde, wear T-shirts with saucy slogans, go raving with Clare, agree to a threesome with Judy and Graham from the rowing club, and admit she had periods (and was still a potential baby maker).

It started to rain. Kendal hoped the patio pots were safe. She'd have to ask Gary about optimum water levels for dahlias and pansies. A harmless, unprovocative conversation. He had looked so ill-at-ease in the meeting. As chair of the Residents' Association, she would need to support him. He'd said the role involved keeping tabs on him which had a saucy ring.

She booted her laptop and watched videos about Dartmoor, the mythical destination she'd yet to visit. She wished she could go there with Clare or Gary. As a normal forty-four-year-old, who hiked all day and danced all night.

She'd succeeded at being Fake-Kendal, but it was a massive pressure and there was no downtime. It was tiring to be constantly thinking before she spoke.

Always performing, never herself. Except in the shower when Audrey was out.

19

Wendy's party was booked for mid-morning, the only time Gary was sure she'd be awake. Audrey and Kendal were still mid pigeon pose as Wendy's family walked up the drive clutching bouquets and giant nine and one-shaped balloons.

The presence of children and teenagers at Jurassic Court was as energising as the Anti-Grave Rave. Residents grinned indulgently through their French windows as small boys and girls threw gravel into the fishpond and tried to crawl through croquet hoops.

At eleven, the gong sounded and the residents ambled to the day room to join Wendy's family. Wendy sat upright on a chair graciously accepting cards and kisses and punching balloons when they swayed too close to her birthday beehive wig. Emma served Prosecco (with paper straws), Carla wheeled in a cake stand piled with macaroons, scones, and pink wafers, and Brian streamed his DJ set.

After two glasses of Prosecco, Kendal surrendered to the school disco vibe and crouched between Jim and Prue for *Oops Upside Your Head*. She wondered where the warden was on such an important occasion. More enjoyable to have Gary between her thighs than Jim.

Kendal had never been to a party so early but she had to admit it was fun. Wendy's six-year-old great-grandchild Adele led a conga down the corridor and even Jennifer joined in with the *Birdie Song*.

Jennifer was the only resident who hadn't been totally welcoming. In the past, Kendal didn't care if people disliked her. She expected them not to and, generally, the feeling was mutual. But Jurassic Court was not THRUm, and she had started to care about the people she lived with, and, as Chair of the Residents' Association, she ought to get on with the whole community. She turned her mind back to the Building Rapport training. Guidance for developing relationships with particularly difficult people stated it was important to praise them about something specific.

"Great hip syncopation, Jennifer," she shouted.

"I was county champion for ballroom and Latin dance," beamed Jennifer. "My cha-cha was the talk of Torquay Rotary."

"I can understand why," said Kendal. "Perhaps you could teach me one day?"

Jennifer beamed. "I would love to, Madame Chair."

Boom. Rapport built with one swift compliment. Politics was easy.

The party segued into lunch (mini-quiche, mini-hot dogs, giant-meringues) Kendal had never seen so much food served in one sitting at Jurassic Court. She wouldn't need to steal from the kitchen or buy chips, for once. Albert and the children kept refilling their plates, but Wendy ate nothing. Perhaps when Kendal was ninety-one her appetite might disappear?

When Brian played the *Macarena* for the fourth time, Kendal had to go. She thanked Carla and Emma, and hugged Wendy.

Gary, dressed again in the unappealing suit, rushed along the corridor.

"Am I too late? Been in meetings. Is Wendy still celebrating?"

Kendal grinned. "No one will let her stop."

Gary pulled off his tie. "Phew, I was worried I'd miss it. Her family are so lovely."

"Yes, her daughters did a great version of *We Are Family*," said Kendal. "There's fifteen family members here and, apparently, forty-four more who couldn't come."

"Good. The day room's too small. Health and safety nightmare," said Gary. "Coming to the Well-being Walk this afternoon? I'm going to see if we can get as far as the estuary."

Kendal's jeans (her real ones, not the charity shop elasticated-waist ones) were dangerously tight and she'd eaten two giant meringues. She needed exercise.

"I'll be there. Two pm?"

"Great," said Gary. "Now I better close the party before Wendy crashes. Want her to live another ten years and get a telegram from the palace, don't we?"

Kendal returned to her flat calculating how Wendy's dynasty could grow in if she lived another decade. If the precocious Adele had a baby at sixteen, then Wendy could easily have a great-great-grandchild when she reached a hundred. Meanwhile, the Tudge family tree terminated with her. Forty-four-year-old, single Kendal. It wasn't right. Or fair.

Only Audrey, Jennifer and Jacob joined Kendal and Gary for the Well-being Walk. The rest of Jurassic Court were asleep. When the group reached the end of the prom Audrey peeled off to chat to a fellow Bluetit and Jennifer and Jacob said the estuary path was too bumpy for mobility scooters. Ever since she'd transformed into a resident, instead of a guest, Gary had avoided being alone with her. Kendal hoped it was a professional safeguarding thing, like the hot chemistry teacher at school who kept a lab assistant close. Better not be sexist ageism making him gag at the thought of fancying a boomer. She assumed he would turn around and follow the buggy brigade. Instead, he suggested they take the path upriver together.

"I've been along the estuary before," said Kendal. "With Clare. It's fab."

"You know about the beavers then?" asked Gary, with no hint of a smile.

"I certainly do," said Kendal. She scanned the river. "Wrong time of day to see them. But I will, eventually." She mimed air quotes. "Good things come to those who wait."

They walked in silence, matching pace. Swans and geese glided upstream, and the breeze made the bulrushes whisper and sway seductively. Dark red cows chewed grass in a field and swallows zigzagged overhead. When they reached the path she'd taken with Clare to the witchy rocks, Kendal expected Gary to turn back.

"Have you been to the Seven Witches, Gary?"

Gary fiddled with the flaps on his rucksack. "Not for a long time."

"It's a magical spot. With buzzards. Do you have time?"

Gary gulped from his water bottle. Drips ran over his chin. Kendal opened her bottle. Shots would be more fun, but cute to share fluids in any form.

"I've been working non-stop. I would love to see the old ladies again."

"Busman's holiday, eh Gary?" He laughed. It was good to see him relaxing.

They reached the Seven Witches and Kendal executed a perfect grunt as she sat. Gary trained his binoculars on the birds circling above their heads.

"They mate for life," he said.

"Lucky buzzards," said Kendal. "Wish I could. Had, I mean."

Gary offered Kendal half a satsuma. "So do I."

The juice exploded in Kendal's dry mouth. Her heart began to race. She hadn't made up a relationship history for Fake-Kendal in the *Tudge Transformation Toolkit*. She didn't have a script. She needed to take control. Turn it back on him.

"Not much success in affairs on the heart, then?"

Gary sighed. "Got well and truly broken years ago. And it's too late now. I'm out of practice and in the wrong job to meet people. Don't get me wrong, I love working at Jurassic Court but it's never going to be the place where I meet Ms Right."

Tavvy-Tina was clearly not a runner. Kendal was delighted.

"What about the internet? The young people I used to work with were always going on about swiping right and left."

Gary frowned. "I don't want to meet someone online. Judging them by what they look like. Or have someone judge me. I'm not on any of those apps."

Kendal knew this. She'd checked his profile in the church on the first day.

"Lots of people meet each other at work," she said. "But it's not going to happen for you unless she's a nurse, a charity fundraiser or someone from the council."

Gary rolled the satsuma skin into a tight ball. "Ah, glad you mentioned Sheila from the donkey sanctuary. I was going to wait until we could have a coffee in my office."

Kendal would prefer to continue discussing his dating drought but was content to talk about anything except Pam's ring (still no mention), Jurassic Court's terms and conditions (maddening), immigration policies or global warming (too complicated).

"I took on board your comments and have informed Sheila she can no longer visit Jurassic Court. With, or without, the donkey."

Kendal whistled. Gary didn't faff around.

"And I was wondering whether you think I should announce this at a meal, or inform residents individually, or write a formal explanation. I know some people will be upset. After the cold-shouldering I got about Albert I'm not sure how to handle it."

Kendal smiled. A classic scenario in Building Rapport training. She'd got this.

"It's best to approach each resident individually, stressing points important to them, and talking in language they understand. Philip, for example, will only care about the donkey, so we could find another animal to visit. One of those dogs which answer doors or sniff for illness."

"We?"

"Happy to help," said Kendal. "Now I'm Chair Lady."

They walked back to the river discussing a Stop-Sheila-Strategy. Kendal did not flirt or make jokes about beavers and no unwelcome blushes invaded her face. She actively listened, asked relevant questions, and offered useful advice. Dogbreath-Deirdre would be gobsmacked. It was interesting to solve a problem for no personal gain. Perhaps it was why the boomers loved crosswords and sudoku. It was also the first conversation Kendal had experienced with a hunky straight guy which wasn't a precursor to seduction. Stimulating, but not in a sexy way.

"You know so much about each resident," said Gary. "Yet you've only been here a month."

"They all seemed the same at first. All old. But doing activities together means I see them more as individuals. It sounds a bit corny."

Gary beamed. "I wish more people were like you, Kendal. Society would be so much better. Some of our residents are so lonely with no family or visitors."

"I've got no family. I'm making friends at Jurassic Court instead," said Kendal. "With some people, not all."

"Well, some residents are easier to like than others," said Gary. "But they've all got good points."

"Who are your favourites?"

"I couldn't possibly say, Madame Chair. But Clem was definitely one."

"I wish I'd got to know him better," said Kendal. "Living in his flat, reading his books, drinking his drinks is strange. I'm even wearing some of his clothes. But I…" She trailed off. They'd reached the wooden observation hut. Gary trained his binoculars on the water.

"A little egret," said Gary. "Do you want to have a look? Clem was keen on divers. Shags especially."

Kendal slumped on the hard bench. Funny bird names weren't making her laugh. The hut smelled disgustingly damp. What was wrong with her?

Gary turned away from the river. "You've got a lot in common with Clem. He would be proud of you, I'm sure."

Kendal stood. No pretend groan. She was genuinely tired. And hungry. Time to get back to Jurassic Court.

A café on the prom had lit an outdoor pizza oven. A waitress laid candles on brightly painted tables and a bearded surfer fiddled with DJ decks. Almost evening, the light on the beach was hazy and the smell of garlic bread enticing. Gary pointed at the chalkboard menu.

"Great! The Albatross has opened for the new season. The cocktails and pizzas are amazing. Low prices too at the start. More expensive once the tourists arrive. Their margarita is really good."

Kendal's stomach growled.

"It's been a great afternoon, Kendal. Thanks for reacquainting me with the Seven Witches. I'm sorry I couldn't deliver a beaver for you." Gary was being playful, wasn't he?

Friday evening, the start of the weekend. They should be ordering pizza and A Slow Comfortable Screw on the Beach. And then have one. Kendal watched two seagulls share a polystyrene box of chips. Red sauce spilled across the shingle.

"Gotta go, Gary. Must feed Clare's cats. She's back tomorrow."

"When's your birthday, Kendal?" asked Gary, as she took a seat by Albert at breakfast the next morning. Kendal tensed. Was this a test? The moment she was unmasked? Stay strong, she'd rehearsed this. It was all in the *Tudge Transformation Toolkit*.

"Sixth of December," she said. "Why?"

Gary pointed at Wendy's balloons, feebly swaying in the corridor. The nine and one had deflated and were floating upside down.

"If it was imminent, we could have used those again."

"Taking the recycling to heart, aren't you son?" said Albert.

Gary smiled. "They look like sixty-one. Kendal's next birthday."

"Gary, lad. Word of advice. Never reveal a lady's age. You'll get into trouble." Albert buttered a slice of toast. "Kendal, sweetheart. You don't look a day over twenty-one to me."

The warden picked his nails. Clean and white with perfect lunula shapes. Kendal tried to remember what the connection between finger size and penis was. Probably best not knowing.

"Thank you, Albert, and you don't look a day over forty."

"You should have seen me then. We'd have got on like a house on fire. I had thirty acres and me marrows came top every year. All the maids were after me."

Kendal ate three rounds of toast as Albert talked, his tales of downy mildew on cabbages and root rot in tomatoes a welcome relief to comments about her age. Gary moved to another table and Albert began describing the blisters on unattended broccoli. Out of the corner of her eye, Kendal spotted Gary untie the sad balloons and lead them away.

"Time for me to make a move, Albert," said Kendal. "Got to take my books back to the library. It's been lovely hearing about your market garden. Maybe you could give a talk to the residents one day? With pictures? Like Emma-from-the-kitchen does?"

"Not much I don't know about vegetables," said Albert. "Wish I'd learned a bit more about women though." He stared at puffy fingers clasping the jam spoon. "Might have found one to look after me."

Kendal hugged Albert. "We're all looking after you now. Hope you're doing the exercises like they told you at the hospital."

Albert smiled. There was jam on the zip of his cardigan. "It's horse shit."

Kendal frowned. "Your fitness programme? Maybe Audrey could devise an easier one."

"No, love. The secret of my success with vegetables. Manure. As much as you can get. By fair means or foul."

After yoga with Audrey, Kendal packed eight of Clem's boat books into her shopping trolley and trundled to the library. Dominic, in a grubby T-shirt and baseball cap, was slumped at the issue desk cutting large letters out of fluorescent cardboard.

"Is Clare in?" asked Kendal. The library assistant shuffled the letters into a nonsense word:

S-A-V-E A-R-E L-B-A-R-E-E

"She's busy. Been on holiday."

"I know. I've been cat-sitting for her," said Kendal.

Dominic looked up. "Where's the evidence then?"

"What kind of evidence?" asked Kendal.

"War-wounds. Those feline devils always leave a mark."

"Not on me. I showed them I'm boss."

Dominic nodded at the staff room. "She's out the back. Knock first."

Kendal walked to the swing doors and tapped gently.

"Kendal, how wonderful to see you. Come through. We'll have a coffee."

The office was crammed with bunting and placards. Clare was full of hugs and gratitude. The week at her daughter's had gone smoothly and the cats and the garden were thriving. No mention of washing machine use or re-arranged wardrobes.

"I'm so grateful," gushed Clare "Such a relief having you look after those naughty boys. I hope I'll be able to help you in some way in return."

Kendal opened the shopping trolley and removed two books. "You could help me with these. They belonged to Clem. I wondered if they might be valuable."

"Yes, Hornblower is always popular here. Top condition too."

Kendal imagined going to The Albatross and trying the cocktail list. She'd start with gin-based ones and move on to rum. "And do I need to go into Exeter or is there somewhere closer?" she asked.

Clare frowned. "Here is fine."

"I could get rid of them today then?" She could buy a pizza for lunch.

"Yes, of course. You will be our first donor. We'll get a photo for our socials. Hold the books and I'll get the sign". She turned a placard around:

BLOSCOMBE
NEEDS BOOKS
S.O.L.

Clare wanted Clem's hardbacks for the library. As a donation! When all she wanted was information about where to sell them. For money. For cocktails.

"I hate having my photo taken, Clare."

"We need all the publicity we can get, Kendal. Sir Anthony and his cronies are announcing budget cuts any moment."

Kendal pursed her lips.

"Is something wrong, Kendal?" asked Clare. She offered the biscuit tin. "A trouble shared is a trouble halved."

Kendal sat. A biscuit was nowhere near as good as a cocktail, but it was something. "What's S.O.L?" she asked. "I hate acronyms."

"Save Our Library," said Clare. "I know what you mean but we've got to be succinct. The volunteers can't carry large placards." She nodded at the close circuit television screen. The library assistant was asleep. "And Dominic can't spell library, bless him." She touched Kendal's arm. "What is it, love?"

Clare's empathy was spooky. Kendal tried to summon some Tudge Trudge power but when Clare put her arms around Kendal's shoulder, it was hopeless. Kendal sniffed. She hadn't cried in front of a woman since she forgot the dominatrix's safe word.

"Men, managers, or money?" asked Clare. "No suitable men in Bloscombe for women like us, and you don't work. So, is it money?"

Kendal wiped her nose. "You should be in the police, Clare. You'd make a great detective."

Clare smiled. "Do you want to talk about it?"

Kendal took a deep breath. "Yesterday I saw the pizza place on the beach, and I really fancied, um, a night off from the soft food at Jurassic Court. But, until the solicitors sort out probate and stuff, I don't have any money and I'm too young for a pension."

Clare clapped her hands. "Phew, not a health scare. I'm so glad." She handed Kendal another biscuit. "The Albatross certainly provokes an appetite. Especially when Billy Whizz, the

171

DJ is there. I was going to suggest going as a thank you trip. If you're free this evening I could book a taxi and we could try the cocktail menu."

Kendal lifted her head. She'd told the truth and the world hadn't collapsed.

"But I don't think it's the best solution," said Clare.

The pizza and cocktail vision disappeared again.

"Better I pay you the fee I would've paid the kennels. It's fifteen pounds a day so that's..." Clare looked for a calculator.

Kendal had done the maths. A lot of cocktails, wine, or pizzas. "Oh no, Clare. I couldn't possibly take your money."

"Nonsense! I want to pay you. The kennels wouldn't have watered the garden as well. Or moved the post to deter burglars. Cat sitting is a proper job. You could get loads of work if you want it."

"Don't I have to be registered, or insured, or something?"

"You haven't got used to small-town life," laughed Clare. "Business is done through word of mouth." Clare checked the screen. A bent-over lady was prodding Dominic. "Gawd, Lady Almonds is here. I've got to go, Kendal. If you're free tonight let's hit The Albatross. My treat."

20

Portland looked magical on the horizon and Kendal could smell the wood smoke of the pizza oven as she strolled to The Albatross. Bloscombe was stirring for the summer. There was an expectant, fresh paint feel.

Kendal's chair was hard. Four weeks since she'd sat on anything not soft or with wheels to help the sitter shuffle to the table. Clare handed her the menu and Kendal creased her eyes to read the ridiculously tiny font. "I'm having a traditional margarita, but you go for whatever you fancy."

Kendal wondered if she needed to visit an optician. It would be another expense, but she'd have the auction money soon. "A margarita would be delicious. Haven't had pizza since I moved from London."

"They take a while here. We can start with the cocktails. What's your poison?"

"Aw right, ladies?" A twenty-something waitress smirked beside them. Kendal had forgotten how irritating young people could be.

"Very well, thank you," said Kendal pointedly. "And how are you?" The waitress waited. "What gin-based cocktails have you got?" Easier to listen than squint.

"Classics, like negroni, gin sling and Tom Collins," intoned the waitress. She glanced at the Harris tweed cap perched on Kendal's silver hair. "Or the house special, Messy Bird. Gin with salted caramel, sage, and soda."

Clare clapped her hands. "Like Coleridge's albatross. Brilliant!"

"Nah, messy like the waves," said the waitress.

Kendal nodded. "What gin do you use?" She hated craft-gin

show-offs but she needed to remind the waitress who was paying her wages. Which, technically, was Clare.

"Dartmouth, Deckchair, Annings; the cheapest is Plymouth."

"Plymouth will do," said Kendal, relieved to recognise a brand. "It's stayed the course, got legs, and is unpretentious." The waitress turned on her heel and Kendal grinned at Clare. "Like us!"

They were on their third round of Messy Birds when the pizzas arrived which, as Clare had predicted, were delicious; covered in fresh basil, heavy duty garlic and oozing chilli oil. So different from the food at Jurassic Court.

"Excuse me, Clare," said Kendal. "I need the loo." The door to the toilet was hard to spot since every surface was made of driftwood. At last, she spotted a mermaid and stumbled into the ladies. Kendal Googled Albatross as she peed. Why did boomers describe problems as an albatross around their neck? She scrolled through *The Rime of the Ancient Mariner* and learned that fishermen believed albatrosses carried the souls of dead sailors. Weird name for a restaurant!

Kendal fixed her lips and picked her way back to the table. "Coleridge did the albatross a disservice, don't you think, Clare? A beautiful bird. Forever associated with a problem."

Clare beamed. "Wordsmiths are wonderful. Shakespeare, Dickens, Thomas Hardy, they've all shaped our language."

"Coffee?" interrupted the waitress, the rising inflection in her voice even more irritating after four (or was it five?) cocktails.

"Nope. Two more Messy Birds. For tidy, beautiful women." Clare winked at Kendal.

Was Clare getting Kendal drunk? Why, Clare was one of the straightest women Kendal knew. Maybe she'd heard about Pam's missing blue ring? Kendal hadn't smoked weed for months but alcohol could make you paranoid too.

Clare took Kendal's hand and slapped a bundle of twenties onto her palm. "You have been superb with the boys. I am so grateful. And I am going to pay you, now before I forget."

"Clare, you really shouldn't."

"I'm so glad we've become friends, Kendal. You're different. A breath of fresh air. And I love that you know about Coleridge. An important figure around here."

The cocktails arrived and Kendal attempted to concentrate. Turned out Coleridge had lived close to Bloscombe. He and his mate Wordsworth (brother of Dorothy who could walk so far in long skirts) took loads of drugs and enjoyed plenty of sex. Clare shared her knowledge wonderfully. Who knew poets were such blowhards? She should start a page in *The Tudge Transformation Toolkit* about books though no one at Jurassic Court had mentioned literature so it wasn't strictly necessary as part of her disguise. Perhaps she could learn about stuff for its own sake? Like proper students, not ones who got kicked out of college.

"I've got a brilliant idea!" said Clare. "Come and try my book group. They've all got pets and are on the lookout for sitters. If you meet them, they'll be falling over themselves to employ you. They neglect their animals almost as much as their children."

"I've never heard you criticise people before," said Kendal.

"I don't normally. It's the booze. You can't gossip in small towns. Well, you can, but you shouldn't. Secrets are impossible to keep. I see lots, but I stay circumspect." Clare put her finger to her lips. "You'd be amazed what people read round here. I had to order fourteen copies of that S and M bestseller. County office got very shirty." Clare moved her eyes around the café and back to Kendal. "It's fascinating what people leave inside books as well."

Kendal frowned. Had she left anything in the Hornblower books? Something incriminating like an empty contraceptive pill case or a list? She needed to relax. The Albatross was a cool place, she could hear the sea, some people were dancing, the cocktails kept appearing. She was having a good time. Like friends did. She had a friend!

"Hi Clare. Out on the razz?" Graham and Judy, arms entwined, leered down.

"With our favourite sweet treat," purred Judy. "Good to see you again, Kendal."

"We hoped you would come to the gig club taster," said Graham. "We found a spare wetsuit which would fit you perfectly, Miss Mintcake."

"Yeh, I sluiced it till it squeaked," laughed Judy. Kendal blushed. There was no way the gig swingers could know about Flat 4's shower, was there? She needed to treat the smug twosome to some Tudge Trudge vibe.

"I'm not into sailing," she said. "Too many superstitions."

Graham frowned. "Not sure I get you, Kendal."

Kendal visualised her phone research in the loo, two (or three?) cocktails earlier. "It's all about control," she spouted. "The sea is dangerous, so sailors have superstitions to help them feel in control." Impossible to pronounce albatross after so many Messy Birds. "Like seeing certain birds as lucky."

"Brilliant, Kendal!" shouted Clare. She stood, clutching the table. "Let's dance."

Kendal shook her head. "I've had a fantastic evening, Clare but it's time for bed. Shall I order you a taxi?" For the first time it was Kendal calling an end to hedonism.

Graham and Judy lived near Plick and offered to drive Clare home. There was a lot of hugging to be endured before Clare had said goodbye to other diners, found her handbag, and danced on the decking. At last, she was ready and accepted Graham's steadying arm. Kendal waved goodbye and turned towards the prom.

Hearing the sea and counting the stars was a hundred times better than the night bus home from Hackney. The whole day had been good; she'd cash in her purse, found a way to earn more, and been wined and dined by someone not expecting a shag in return. And now she could even remember the passcode for the gate even though she was pissed.

Kendal wobbled up the drive. She hoped all the residents

were sleeping peacefully in their comfortable rooms. It would be good to know if Gary had missed her at Movie Night. Kendal stopped at the Jurassic Court activities board and giggled. She was genuinely keen to know what next week might offer.

Monday – Audrey's Anti-Grave Rave
Tuesday – Farming Chatter with Emma AND Albert
Wednesday – Bedding Out at Gardening Club
Thursday – Gary's day off – Visit from Jurassic Puppets
Friday – Wellbeing Walk PM
Saturday – Movie Night – Kendal's choice

Kendal felt a rush of tenderness for Gary's large scrawl. She was pleased to see Albert had acted on her advice but daunted to discover the next Movie Night was hers. She opened the whiteboard marker, inhaling the familiar chemical aroma. She licked her finger, erased the last words on Wednesday's activity, and added two new ones.

Wednesday – Bedding Out with Gary!

Nothing like her normal Saturday night transgressions, but a delicious thought.

Something was hitting the French windows, and someone was hammering on the door to the corridor. A terrible noise and a beast of a Sunday hangover whose symptoms (sweating, thirst, vertigo, sensitivity to light) had been absent from Kendal's world since she'd arrived in Bloscombe. She dragged herself to the door. Brian was in the corridor on his mobility scooter.

"Thank God! We thought you were dead," he said and reversed away. Kendal stumbled to open the blinds. Audrey was on the lawn, hand high with another batch of pebbles to hurl. Brian raced across the lawn and hugged Audrey dramatically. "She's alive. Don't cry, Audrey."

Kendal slinked onto the patio. "I'm fine," she shouted.

"Having a lie-in after my night out."

"Too many sherbets, old girl?" said Brian. "Or a dicky curry?"

"Pizza, on the beach. With Clare from the library."

Audrey made a loud pfft noise. "You've got twenty minutes till Quaker meeting. Get your skates on."

Sitting in silence with eight geriatrics was not how Kendal normally dealt with a hangover. It was usually duvet, sweet tea, buttered toast, and Season Two of Friends. But nothing in Kendal's life was normal now.

Prue, in lemon dungarees, broke the silence with a bible reading. "If I am guilty – woe to me! Even I am innocent, I cannot lift my head, for I am full of shame and drowned in my affliction."

The words crawled into Kendal's head. Her stomach heaved. She wished she could leave but didn't want to draw attention to herself. Why couldn't Prue stay silent? Why did she bang on about guilt? Kendal scanned the room. Shirley and Wendy were asleep. Pam held a tissue to her face.

At THRUm when she'd had a hangover, Kendal kept alert in meetings by making mental lists: capital cities she'd visited; people she'd snogged, favourite pubs. Prue's reading triggered a list of guilty secrets.

> Tudge Wall of Shame:
> Altering Gary's white board
> Invading Clare's wardrobe
> Pretending to be disabled to get free parking
> Not visiting Clem enough
> Getting chucked out of college
> Not being with dad when he died
> Not being with mum when she died

A sob sprang from across the room. Pam was crying properly. Gary cradled her gently. The sob morphed into a wail.

"She's lost it," said Audrey in a stagey whisper.

Kendal froze. "Lost what?"

"Her mind," said Audrey. "I'll tell you later."

Kendal stayed rooted to her chair. Now she felt guilty about the Wall of Shame list. She'd forgotten to include pawning Pam's blue ring. But should it be included on the list? It was shameful, surely, if she kept or sold it which she wasn't doing. She'd return it the moment the auction house money came through so was she guilty? What was the wanky term Dogbreath-Deirdre used for problems where she was too pathetic to make a judgement? Nuanced.

Kendal needed to get some spine. Be the Tudge Judge. She also needed coffee, fried eggs, and a bacon sandwich. She tiptoed to the door. Audrey followed.

"There was a right hoo-ha at breakfast," whispered Audrey. "Come to my flat and I'll tell you all about it."

"I need to get something to eat," said Kendal.

"I've got salmon skin chips," said Audrey. "Marvellous for reducing blood pressure. You look a bit peaky."

Kendal tasted a tiny bit of sick. "Thanks, but no thanks. I'm going to get some fresh air. Sorry to have worried you earlier. Sounds like breakfast was dramatic enough."

Audrey held onto Kendal's sleeve. "It was dreadful. Pam attacked Carla. Said Carla was in cahoots with the cleaners and claimed they were stealing her jewellery. She wants Gary to get the police in."

It wasn't acid reflux. Kendal opened the door to her flat and ran to the bathroom. As she lifted the toilet seat her phone pinged. Another text from the pawnbrokers.

Your loan of £2,400 is due to be paid back in 19 days.

The only sure-fire hangover chuck cure was carbs and fresh air. Kendal escaped to the beach and downed a pint of tea and two bacon rolls from a kiosk. The seashore was becoming beach-ready; the deckchair rental office had opened; beach hut owners were cleaning floors and hanging curtains; dogs raced across the shingle, chasing balls. Kendal hummed an old favourite of her parents.

"Oh, I do like to be beside the seaside, I do like to stroll along the prom."

Kendal marched in time, dismantling the Tudge Wall of Shame with each lungful of sea air. No way could anyone know Kendal had borrowed Pam's ring and Carla-from-the-kitchen was more than capable of sorting out any claims about thieving cleaners. Important to remember alcohol was a depressant and could be the cause of the extreme fear-and-loathing she'd experienced.

"Coo-ee, Kendal. Over here!" The pervy-rowing-duo lay on a rug near the sea surrounded by straw bags and a picnic basket.

"Fancy a cuppa, Mintcake?" shouted Graham.

"We've got buns," added Judy.

Kendal did fancy more carbs, even if it she had to endure the offensive nickname to get them. The couple rolled to the edges of the blanket and she was forced to sit between them.

"Get home last night all right, then?" said Graham.

"You and Clare were really going for it," added Judy. She giggled. "Took us quite a while to get Clare to bed."

"It was good of you to give Clare a lift. We'd both got a bit…" Kendal racked her memory for the appropriate boomer word.

"Pissed?" said Graham.

"Hammered?" said Judy.

"Tipsy," said Kendal. "A tiny bit merry."

Graham and Judy laughed. Graham opened a vacuum flask and poured tea into a plastic mug. Judy unwrapped a foil parcel and offered it to Kendal.

"Lemon drizzle, very moist," she purred. Kendal took a slice.

"Summer begins today," announced Judy. "Though, officially it's not till the end of the month when the dogs are banned from the beach. But I like to break the rules." She squeezed Kendal's arm. "And I think you do too, Miss Tipsy-little-bit-merry."

Judy unpacked a large rubber bag. "Still too cold to swim without help. We've brought all the gear for the first dip of the year. Neoprene gloves, hats, goggles, wetsuits, hydro booties, swimming buoy."

Graham opened the other bag "Dryrobes, towels, a hip flask, hand-warmers. So we avoid afterdrop."

"What's afterdrop?" asked Kendal. It sounded druggy.

"When you get cold and can't get warm," said Graham. "We're checking our equipment today to make sure nothing has perished in the winter."

"And check what fits," added Judy. She grinned at Kendal. "So, you're in luck. I've got spare stuff with me. So, no excuses Miss Peppermint Cream."

Kendal looked at the sea. It was calm and clear. Two children in rolled-up joggers paddled and squealed. Audrey and her Bluetits had been in the sea for weeks, and swimming was nowhere as dangerous as previous stunts she'd pulled after Saturday night benders. Audrey would be so impressed if she swam though. Gary might be too. Immersion in the ocean would clear her head. Wash away her shame. Like extreme baptisms.

"OK, I'm up for it if you think your wetsuit will fit me," she said.

Judy clapped her hands and waved a tube of Vaseline at Kendal. "If there's any chafing, I'll be more than happy to rub this on."

Kendal frowned. Sipping tea on a tartan rug on Sunday on a Dorset beach was as straight as could be but this couple were definitely coming on. In full daylight, with kids paddling and dogs gambolling. Pervy and pushy.

Judy handed Kendal a wetsuit and a towelling robe. "Keep your underwear and T-shirt on underneath, and we'll lend you a dryrobe for afterwards. You can bring it back when you come to the gig club taster. Next one's Thursday."

The wetsuit fitted Kendal perfectly. The neoprene smell, like overheated condoms, was disagreeable, but the tightness felt good.

"You look fabulous," gushed Graham, handing Kendal rubber boots and gloves.

"A Bloscombe mermaid," added Judy.

Kendal finished her tea as Judy and Graham pulled on wetsuits. The sun was warm on her face, and she liked the way the boots cushioned the soles of her feet from the pebbles. The swimming gloves too were comfortable, making her hands feel almost webbed. She smiled. She hadn't swum for years. She couldn't afford a private pool in London and the public one at Ealing sports centre was unbearably noisy, with the constant fear of a floating plaster. Or worse.

Judy and Graham stood on either side of Kendal. Judy took her hand.

"I'm perfectly able to get in by myself," said Kendal.

"Sorry, Mintcake," said Judy. "I'm encouraging you. Getting in is always the hardest part."

Kendal had tried wetsuits in the past, water-skiing in Greece and windsurfing in Portugal, but this one was far more comfortable. It was flexible, like a second skin, and she knew the red neon stripes would be accentuating her waist. Kendal felt strong, sexy, and excited.

The water was outrageous. It cut through like a steel knife. Kendal screamed, Graham roared, and Judy jumped in tiny circles. The paddling children cheered.

"Keep moving, Kendal," shouted Judy. "You'll get used to it soon."

"Think of your immune system" added Graham. "It's getting a wake-up call."

Graham began a perfect front crawl. Judy bobbed on her back splashing her legs. Kendal clenched her teeth. The wetsuit gave her extra buoyancy. It was getting bearable. She could do this. She cupped the gloves around her mouth.

"I feel so alive!" she shouted and plunged under the surface.

"Yeeha," shrieked Judy. Graham swam swiftly between them. "Well done, mermaids! Now let's not overdo it."

Judy draped a heavy dryrobe around Kendal's shoulders

and Graham poured tea, laced with rum. They stood in a smug triangle with red faces and tingling skin. Kendal hi-fived the free hands. The rubber gloves made the slaps sticky.

"Thanks, guys. Amazing. I can't believe I did it."

"We knew you were a goer," said Judy.

Kendal laughed. "I'm going to go home for a hot shower. Do you need the robe back now?"

"Bring it all back on Thursday," said Judy. "You're obliged to give us a try now."

"It's a date."

The flexible wet suit was easy to walk in and Jurassic Court was close. Kendal swapped the rubber boots for trainers and marched over the shingle. Lovely to think she had at least four months of sea swimming ahead of her, maybe more. She could go in the mornings before breakfast. The sea was warmer at the end of the summer than at the beginning. She'd managed it in May, so October should be easy. Perhaps she could go all year? Try long-distance swimming? Gary would be so impressed. He'd be attracted to her in a wet suit with its fantastic figure-hugging feature. She walked up the drive hoping to see him, but only Linda the gardener was around.

"You make the gardens look wonderful," said Kendal as she passed Linda kneeling by a shrub. "Thank you for all the work you do." The gardener jumped.

"I'm Kendal, I'm a resident here," said Kendal.

Linda wiped her hands on the grass. "Right, thanks. Good to meet you."

Kendal beamed. "Mustn't stop, don't want to get cold. I've been in the sea."

"Rather you than me," said the gardener. "Too many creatures."

Kendal stood under the hot shower for a long time. One of the great features about Jurassic Court (as well as the sea, the gardens and the warden) was the hot water which never ran out (unlike showers in all the dingy bedsits or flats she'd lived in before). Kendal wrapped her dressing gown over her clothes, made a cup of tea and lay in the reclining chair enjoying the sea view and reflecting on how much she had to be grateful for.

The Tudge Transformation had worked! She was getting away with it. She could stay in this free and friendly paradise for as long she liked. Tomorrow she would ring the Auction House and demand the money for her antiques. She could pay off the creepy pawnbroker, return the ring, and life in Jurassic Court would return to normal. No calls for police, no tears in the Ammonite room. There would be plenty of happy, smiling faces and a warden working closely with his Madame Chair to improve the lives of those happy, smiling residents. Perfect!

21

Kendal woke in a hospital in a wheelchair, with a tube of yellow liquid in her arm, yet nothing hurt. She was wearing a T-shirt and an appalling pair of trousers with an elasticated waist. Blue curtains surrounded her and there was a sink and bin for company. The wall clock said half-past two. Day or night? A machine beeped somewhere.

Kendal knew hospitals; the miserable visits to her parents, the teenage-right-of-passage stomach pump, the unpleasant hour in an abortion clinic, and recently the trip to Bloscombe Community Hospital to rescue Albert, but she'd never been in a hospital overnight. The artificial light and random beeping sounds were eerie. She looked at the clock. Three already? Time was disappearing. This was scary.

"Um, hello. Anyone there?" she called. The blue curtain concertinaed open.

"Hello pet," said a bald male nurse in blue scrubs. "How are you feeling? Do you know where you are or why you are here?"

"Have I had an accident?" Her voice was weak. She coughed. "Is it night or day? Why am I wearing these trousers?"

The nurse took her hand. "I'm Richard, I'm on nights. You're in Bloscombe Community Hospital. You've had an episode, but you're safe and sound. Tea?"

The mention of tea was comforting. They wouldn't be messing around with warm drinks if something serious had happened.

"I would love tea. And water, lots of it. Richard, right? You're Richard?" If she could remember his name, then she hadn't had a stroke. Strokes were for old people, weren't they?

"I'm Richard, yes and you're in A&E. We're waiting for your results. I'll get you your drinks. Don't move, love."

Kendal didn't know if she could move. Why on earth was she in the A&E ward wearing hideous baggy, violet-coloured trousers? She hated purple. Kendal closed her eyes and nodded.

Of course, the hideous clothes were a disguise! She, Kendal Tudge, was wearing charity shop clothes because she was pretending to be sixteen years older than her true age to live in the retirement apartment she had inherited at Jurassic Court, Bloscombe, in Dorset. Where she now lived, with Audrey, Brian, Jim, Jacob, Philip, Pam, Prue, Shirley, Jennifer, Wendy, Sam and Albert. Couldn't be too bad if she could remember all those names.

Richard returned with a jug, a cup, five packets of sugar and three wooden stirring sticks. "Anything to eat?"

Kendal felt sick at the thought of food. Of course! She'd been on a girls' night out with Clare the librarian. Her new friend. They'd got drunk. Had she blacked out or taken some dodgy pills? Clare was fun, but not a pill-popper.

"No thanks, Richard. Is it Sunday?"

"Early Monday morning, sweetheart. The doctor's coming soon."

The doctor's white coat was two sizes too big. She tapped the IV tube.

"Hello Ms Tudge, how are you feeling? I'm Dr Shobana."

"Are you a student?" said Kendal.

"No, I'm a qualified junior doctor and I'm older than I look," said the doctor. "Do you know how old you are, Ms Tudge?" She looked at her clipboard. "And your date of birth and address?"

Kendal did know all these facts but had no idea which version of herself to present in hospital. "Can you call me Kendal? I don't like my surname."

The doctor removed a pen from her lab coat and wrote a note. "Kendal, do you know why you are here?"

Kendal felt tears drip on her cheek. "I don't. I went out on Saturday night to a café on the beach called The Albatross with my friend Clare. We had pizza and a few drinks."

"Do you know how much alcohol you consume normally?" asked the doctor.

"Ten units a week," lied Kendal. "Sometimes less."

The doctor consulted her clipboard. "You were brought in by Gary Vaughan, the manager at Jurassic Court residential home. Do you work there?"

Kendal tried to pour a drink. The jug had an ill-fitting plastic lid, and she spilt the water. "I live there, I'm a resident."

"Then we both don't look our age," smiled the doctor. "Can you remember anything about Sunday morning?"

Kendal sipped the water. The bleeping seemed louder. Or quicker.

"The Quakers meet at Jurassic Court. I went to the meeting. I'm not a Quaker, I'm not religious but you don't have to be. You don't have to stop alcohol, you know. You don't have to eat porridge. You don't have to…"

"I know what Quakers do, Kendal," said Dr Shobana, touching Kendal's forehead. "What did you do afterwards?"

Tears slid down Kendal's cheeks. She blinked. "I don't know."

The doctor picked up the jug and poured a glass for Kendal.

"OK, try not to worry. We're going to run some more tests. You're in the best place here."

Three hours passed swiftly. Richard took blood samples, someone put her in the MRI scanner, more tea arrived. Then Richard waved goodbye, and the daytime shift arrived. Two nurses chattered behind the curtain.

"How was your weekend?" said one.

"Another baby shower," said the other. "We all wrote messages on white baby-grows."

"Awesome," gushed the first voice.

Kendal tasted bile at the back of her mouth. She groaned. The blue curtain opened. A nurse passed a grey cardboard bowl.

At last, Dr Shobana returned. "Kendal, your MRI and blood tests have come back." Kendal squeezed the wheelchair arms. Was this going to be the moment her life changed? Was it all over? She'd never even been to a baby shower. She wished someone was with her to hear the news. The doctor smiled. "There is no evidence of any heart or brain problem. We tested for diabetes too. Everything looks fine."

"So why am I here? I can't remember how I got here."

"We're pretty sure you've experienced a TGA," said the doctor slowly. "A trans global amnesia episode."

"But I'm not transitioning. I've dyed my hair grey. It's fashionable."

The doctor laughed. "Trans, as in transient. Loss of memory which happens for a short period. There's no obvious reason. The attack usually lasts a few hours. Patients know who they are, but they lose all memory during the period. You may not ever remember what happened. It's unlikely to happen again. We're going to transfer you to the ward, and they'll keep an eye on you."

A nurse arrived, handed Kendal a fresh sick bowl, and tucked a sheet firmly around Kendal's legs. "Right, we're going to Almonds Ward. Hold on tight."

Kendal grinned. Almonds Ward meant she would be going home soon. Home was Jurassic Court. In lovely Bloscombe. With wonderful friends. And gorgeous Gary.

Trans global amnesia? A banging club night in Ibiza, surely?

Gary and Audrey sat in low plastic chairs watching Kendal snore. She opened her eyes and smiled.

"Hello, Mummy Bear. Hello, Daddy Bear," she mumbled.

Audrey grabbed Gary. "She's worse," she whispered.

"Shush, Audrey," said Gary. "Give her space." He ran his free hand through his hair. His earlobes looked plump. Kendal wanted to nibble them.

"I'm kidding," she said. "The nurse gave me porridge and this bed is so comfy. I'm like Goldilocks and the Three Bears. Except there's only two of you."

Gary smiled. He was wearing walking trousers with zips and a faded hoodie but he was still gorgeous. Audrey clasped Kendal's hand, bumping the cannula in her arm.

"How are you, my lovely? We were so worried."

Kendal tried to sit upright. The pillows slipped to the side. "I'm fine, thank you. A bit confused. Serious senior moment, I think."

"Do you want help, Kendal?" said Gary. Fun to have the warden plump pillows, but she smelled rank. Gary pressed the controller button to raise the bed. Now she could see a perfect pink cherry blossom tree outside.

"Do you know what happened?" said Audrey, in a wobbly voice.

"Something called transient global amnesia," said Kendal. "But I don't know how it happened. Or why."

Gary was scrolling. Kendal had not seen him use a phone before. He looked almost teenage.

"You didn't come to supper, so I went to your flat," said Audrey. "You kept making odd claims. I got Gary." Kendal had no memory of Audrey in her flat. Or Gary. Or anything after the Quaker meeting and the hangover chuck-up.

"We think you might have been in the sea, Kendal," said Gary. "There was a wetsuit and dryrobe in your shower."

"I don't have a wetsuit. Or a dryrobe."

Gary waved his phone. "Do you want to hear what the NHS website says?' Anything was preferable than Audrey elaborating about odd claims. Kendal nodded.

"Possible triggers for TGAs are vigorous exercise or sexual intercourse or immersion in cold water," read Gary. He looked at Kendal. "Sound familiar?"

Kendal blushed. "Did we have an Anti-Grave Rave, Audrey? That's vigorous."

"No, it was supposed to be today," said Audrey. "But I'm glad you're remembering our raves because yesterday you didn't even

189

know you were a resident at Jurassic Court. You thought you were visiting your uncle."

"How weird," said Kendal. Her mind raced. What else had TGA-Kendal claimed?

"It was really sad," said Gary. "Because every time we told you he'd died, you got distressed. You kept asking where Clem was again and again."

"And you refused to believe how old you are," said Audrey. "Insisted you were forty-four. You got quite aggressive."

Kendal turned to the window. TGA-Kendal was a liability. Pink petals fluttered in the breeze. Blossom never lasted long. Kendal forced a grin.

"So funny how us girls are obsessed with youth. Even in a meltdown we're still pretending to be young."

Audrey raised an eyebrow. Uneven again. Gary's phone beeped.

"Text from Linda, the gardener," he said. "She's heard about Kendal going to hospital, and thinks she knows what happened. Shall I call her?'

Audrey nodded enthusiastically. Kendal blinked. "I need to go to the loo," she said. "But go ahead. I want to know."

The doctor had said the episode wouldn't happen again, but Kendal couldn't risk passing out on a toilet floor. She left the door unlocked, closed the lid, and sat on the seat. She groped in her dressing gown pocket and found a sticky Biro and a paper napkin. This chaos was crying out for a list:

Loo Review
She'd acquired a wet suit and Dryrobe (even though she had no money)
She'd revealed her real age (Audrey didn't believe her)
She was hungry and could take a red wine or two (therefore normal)
Audrey was a trouper and a true mate (but not a fool)
Gary was still hot and cared about her.

Kendal sniffed her armpits. She rubbed hand gel onto her shirt and trousers and opened the door.

A different doctor stood by her bed; a stethoscope hung over his checked waistcoat.

"Ah here's the daredevil," he barked, and held out his hand. "Dr Drake, good to see you." The hand gel had left a dark stain on Kendal's trousers. She climbed into bed and pulled the sheet high. "Don't make yourself too comfortable. These chaps will be taking you home soon."

Kendal looked at Gary. He nodded. "Linda said she saw you in the afternoon. You'd been swimming in the sea."

"Classic TGA trigger," said the doctor. "Though you are a bit younger than most people who get them."

"I'm sixty," said Kendal, groaning. She was back in role.

The doctor slapped his thigh. "Looking marvellous. Not being sexist, or anything."

"What's made me forget everything? I can't remember being in the water, talking to Linda, or coming here."

The doctor spoke slowly. "Think of yourself as a computer. Your brain, your heart, your bloods are fine. The hard drive is working. But the cold-water immersion closed you down and now you're having a re-boot."

Kendal attempted to unpack the analogy. What sort of computer was she: a newish laptop like the one she'd stolen from work, a sticky model like those in the library, or a clunky ancient dinosaur like the one in the Ammonite room? She shook her head. The doctor was still talking.

"Miss Tudge, you've lost the recent documents you were using, and they're not in the hard drive. Gone forever. But everything you saved from before will be in your hard drive and you'll retrieve them."

"Will she be in the mist?" asked Audrey.

The doctor frowned.

"She means the cloud," said Gary. "Metaphor needs finessing."

The doctor smoothed his waistcoat. "Anyway, you're free to go, Miss Tudge. We'll send a discharge note to the GP practice in town and they will organise a check-up at the surgery."

Kendal nodded. This was not the time to draw attention to name preferences or mention she hadn't registered with the medical centre. In the greater scheme of life, an annoying surname was not a big issue. Hadn't harmed Dr Drake.

Gary and Audrey waited outside the ward while the nurse removed the cannula.

"Take care, sweetheart. Don't be rushing back."

Kendal nodded. "Sorry for wasting the lunch I ordered."

"Don't worry, someone will eat it. When summer starts, we get loads of boomers who've fallen off electric bikes." She dropped her voice. "We love it when your Gary Vaughan collects a patient. Handsome and kind. Better than the men round here."

It was nice how the nurse said "your Gary Vaughan".

22

Kendal sat in the front seat with a rug around her. It was comforting to be driven by Gary. She wished they were going further. To Dartmoor, or Cornwall. He held her arm as she got out of the car and stood close as they walked to her flat. Once inside, he opened her bathroom door and pointed to a wet suit and Dryrobe hanging from the shower.

"See, you've got the gear for wild swimming."

Kendal shook her head. "I have no idea how."

"It'll all come out in the wash," said Audrey. "Now lie on your chair and relax."

"I can't believe how tired and hungry I am," said Kendal.

"It's shock," said Gary. "I'll ask Emma to bring you some lunch."

Kendal was asleep when Emma-from-the-kitchen entered carrying a tray.

"Rest now, lovely," she whispered. "We've missed you."

The supper gong woke Kendal. She lifted the lunch plate's cover. Cold potato, watery houmous and lumpy beetroot. As rank as her hand-gel drenched clothes and fuzzy teeth. But she was starving.

"You awake, Kendal? Coming to supper?" said a voice at the door.

"I'm not presentable," said Kendal.

Emma-from-the-kitchen peeked into the bedroom. "Would you like a tray? Oh, you haven't had your lunch yet. Let me take him away."

Kendal grabbed the handles. "I want this. Can you bring me a supper tray as well?"

"Right on, my luvver," said Emma. "Any special requests?"

"Whatever you've got, please. Could eat a horse!"

Emma grinned. "Not on the menu, Kendal. But I'll do my best. Wait till the others have done and I'll bring you a big tray. See you dreckly."

Something incredibly weird had happened to Kendal. At least thirty minutes for Emma to serve all the residents. Kendal needed to sort herself out and tap into her secret power, her alpha pussy mode. She locked the door, fetched her vibrator and stepped into the shower. It was no good, normal service was not to be resumed despite fully charged batteries and the promise of more food. She had changed so much at Jurassic Court. A good shower session always used to hit the spot and get her up and running. Kendal rinsed her vibrator and packed it away. It had never let her down before. She dressed in clean joggers and a T-shirt and opened her laptop.

There was not much information online about transient global amnesia. Far less than plantar fasciitis and yet both afflictions were experienced by older people, particularly women. Kendal suspected it was because there were no products to market (like orthopaedic shoes or Nordic walking poles). There didn't even seem to be a support group which was unusual since every other condition appeared to have one. Anxiety was reported as a possible cause. She must be more anxious than she realised.

Kendal started a new page in *The Tudge Transformation Toolkit*:

Tudge Terrors:
Fake-Kendal will be exposed and thrown out of Jurassic Court
Pawn-user Kendal will be arrested as a thief
Kendal will never have another orgasm
No sex likely with a person, especially Gary
No baby therefore
Forced to become a nanny for Mad-Maxine and Josh.
Be broke, alone, unemployed, homeless. Again.

She'd sneered at Mad-Maxine and the THRUm teammates when they banged on about anxiety and their mental health. But here she was doing the same bloody thing. She'd a lot of shit on her plate when what she needed was food.

At last, Emma arrived. "Three servings for you, love." She set the tray and turned to the door. "Carla. Bring in the contraband."

Carla-from-the-kitchen entered with a wine bottle in an ice bucket and three glasses. "Special delivery! Don't tell Gary." Kendal clapped.

"Doctor didn't say you couldn't drink, did he?" asked Carla. "Or she?"

Kendal shook her head and lifted a glass. Carla opened the French windows, pulling a packet of cigarettes out of her tabard pocket. "Do you mind if we have a quick one?"

"Go ahead. I'll enjoy the scent, for old times." Kendal finished two plates while Emma and Carla smoked.

"Nothing wrong with your appetite then?" said Carla. "Gary told us what happened. Must have been a terrible shock."

Kendal nodded. "We all have senior moments, but this was completely different. The doctor said I'll never remember what happened."

Emma re-filled the glasses. "Our greatest fear."

"What?" said Kendal.

"Running out of wine," giggled Carla.

"No, losing our memory," said Emma. "People are more scared of dementia and Alzheimer's than cancer."

Carla drained her glass. "Yeh, it's sad about the district nurse. She's really got it."

Kendal finished the second plate. "You've cheered me up."

"It's been a tough couple of days for all of us," said Carla. "You missed a right hoo-ha. Pam took a turn as well as you. It's horrible watching old souls decline."

"Which is why we're glad you moved in," said Emma. She loaded the tray. "Albert's been pestering me all week about our talk tomorrow and you're the one to blame. Livening up the place. Proper job!"

"Right, we're going on," said Carla. "Got the laying out for tomorrow to do. Take it easy, Kendal. No more swimming in cold water."

Kendal smiled at their cigarette butts in a flowerpot. Since moving to Bloscombe, she'd not had any kind of drug except alcohol. The Tudge Terror long list didn't make her want a cigarette but if Carla or Emma had offered her something stronger to smoke, she would have slipped, for sure. Kendal buried the butts in soil and sat on a deckchair. The sun was low, but still warm. It was pleasant to watch the sunset and feel slightly pissed. She remembered she was supposed to be choosing the film for Movie Night on Saturday. She moved inside, opened her laptop and began to scroll. Film selection could stop her thinking about the daily texts from the pawnbroker.

There was a soft knocking at the door. Nearly nine o'clock? Late for residents to visit. Only Audrey paid social calls and she never knocked quietly. Perhaps it was Gary, checking to see how she was, or driven crazy with unfulfilled desire, desperate to….

"Hello, dearie. I wanted to check in with you. Heard you had a nasty episode?" Prue, in a yellow kaftan with a golden headwrap, stepped into Kendal's flat.

"Oh, hello Prue, I'm fine now." Prue scanned the living room. She peered at the photograph of Kendal's parents.

"They look like good souls. Shame they passed so early." Kendal hoped Prue had heard this from Clem. Spooky otherwise.

"I miss them more here in Dorset than I did in London," said Kendal.

"I know, dear," said Prue. "But, like my Rumi says, anything you lose comes round in another form."

"I didn't know you shared your flat, Prue," said Kendal.

Prue looked puzzled. "I don't have anyone there, only spirits sometimes."

Who was telling Prue about lost things? Was it Pam? Kendal's heart began to race.

"Who's your roomie then?"

"Rumi is a thirteenth century poet and scholar." Prue grabbed Kendal's wrists and peered into her face. Her breath had a fishy tang. "He tells us to be true to yourself and be open to the truth."

Kendal stepped backwards. Prue was a bit of a witch.

"Thanks, Prue. I must go to sleep now. Don't want to miss Emma and Albert's double act tomorrow."

Prue pressed her hands together and bowed. "Namaste. Rest in peace."

A round of applause greeted Kendal at breakfast. Albert waved a sausage and Wendy fluttered her napkin.

"Welcome home, my dear," said Philip. "So sorry about your episode."

"Thanks, Philip. I feel fine. Incredibly hungry, though."

Philip passed the toast rack. His thin wrist shook. "Go for your life, Kendal. Emma's new marmalade is superb." He cleared his throat. "Had a few queer turns myself over the years." They were alone at the table. Was Philip about to out himself? A dinner plate of bacon, eggs, tomatoes, and beans appeared from above.

"This will do you the world of good," said Emma.

Kendal ate while Philip reported on the croquet game he'd played when the Anti-Grave Rave was cancelled. "I didn't do very well, my dear. Worried about our Madam Chair."

"There's spare commodes in the garage," said Kendal.

Philip frowned. "Not sure I understand, my dear. Are you having another turn?"

"Madam Chair, commodes. A joke?" said Kendal. Clearly too soon for boomer banter.

"And how is our Madam Chair?" said a voice from above.

"Ah, Gary, do take my place," said Philip. "I've had sufficient, and this lady needs looking after."

"I'm sure the warden has lots to do," mumbled Kendal. So cute how Gary's eyes crinkled and sparkled simultaneously.

"Actually, I don't," said Gary, wiping marmalade off Philip's chair. The table wobbled as he squeezed his legs in. Kendal tucked her feet away. Her buttocks gripped the seat.

Emma brought a fresh coffee pot and a clean mug for Gary. "There you go. What a lovely sight! The warden and the Madam Chair putting the world to rights together."

Kendal wiped her lips, folded the linen napkin, and attempted to push it through the serviette ring.

"Give it to me," said the warden. His hand encased hers. Dry, warm, firm. Kendal handed him the serviette. Gary rolled it into a tight sausage and squeezed it into the space. She crossed her legs.

"How are you feeling, Kendal?" said Gary, in a quiet voice.

"Much better, Gary. A bit embarrassed." She wished she could tell him how she really felt. Consumed by an adult crush, obsessed, off her head? Whatever, however, whenever….it was all pretty intense. Demanding huge levels of self-control. What if she didn't have any left?

"Kendal? What do you think?" Gary's eyebrows were raised.

"Sorry, I was miles away. What was the question?"

"What's your choice for Movie Night on Saturday?"

She was safe now, she'd got this.

"*The Graduate*," said Kendal. I watched some clips last night and it's still a great movie."

"Ah, yes," said Gary. "An older woman having a passionate affair with a younger man. Interesting choice, I'll see if I can download it. Will you be all right to say a few words about why you like it?"

Kendal nodded. Important to frame her talk along the lines of it being a nineteen sixties landmark rather than stressing the younger man with an older woman plot. Audrey and Philip were too sharp. She needed to change the subject with the warden too. Get herself under control.

"I was thinking about starting some technology drop-in sessions. To help residents feel confident to contact their relatives or long-lost friends, or research movies, poems or whatever they're interested in. And not be so scared about scams."

"Fantastic! I feel so guilty when they ask me to send emails or research something online because I never have enough time."

"Could we get boosters as well to improve the Wi-Fi?"

"Yes, we have budget for capital expenditure. Could buy some tablets too. I'll run it past the committee, to adhere to safeguarding protocols. Bound to be affirmative since improving digital access is one of our objectives this financial year."

Gary was talking like Dogbreath-Deirdre from THRUm but still looked hot. He put his hand on her arm again. "I'm glad you are back to normal. It was horrible to see you so distressed."

"Worse for you, than me since I can't remember it."

Gary stared into his cup. "You got so angry when we said you're sixty. Insisted you were forty-four. I let it go. But Audrey didn't. There was almost a fight."

Kendal swallowed. She should provide an explanation. "Maybe, it's because of the pass code on the gate. You know, 1-9-4-4? Forty-four, the special number for residents."

"You're special, Madam Chair," smiled Gary. "And Jurassic Court is grateful to have you here, whatever your age."

The dining room chatter faded, and outside, the ice cream van blared a new tune which Kendal couldn't place. Was this what Dogbreath-Deirdre called a leverage moment in the Building Rapport masterclass? The perfect moment to make the ask? Kendal took a deep breath.

"It's not true though, is it? I wouldn't be here if I was forty-four. The only people under sixty are you, Carla and Emma, the gardeners, and the cleaners."

Gary chewed his lip. "But we're the workers, here to support the elderly."

"Indeed. But it would be nice to have younger residents too. Make Jurassic Court a mixed community. So many benefits to being multi-generational."

Gary sighed. "We're an elderly community though."

He wasn't going to concede. Not yet.

Raucous laughter announced Emma and Albert's Farming Chat session had started in the day room.

Kendal stood, pretending to steady herself. Gary rose and opened his arms. Kendal flinched. He was going for an aunty hug when what she needed was a full-fat embrace, followed by full-on, full-frontal, full-works. Simple to demonstrate the benefits of a mixed community by shagging him senseless.

Senseless, however, was what she'd been during the trans global amnesia episode and she wasn't risking another by having vigorous sex with the hottest man in Dorset. Not yet.

23

The arrival of Wi-Fi boosters and tablets generated huge excitement at Jurassic Court with all the residents keen to participate in Kendal's Digital Drop-ins. Everyone was interested in the opportunities offered by the new, free facility. Some were thrilled to talk directly to their family members whilst others were fascinated exploring Wikipedia and Google Earth. Everyone watched cat videos.

At first, Kendal was concerned about digital safeguarding, but once she realised no one cleared their browsing history, she could monitor their searches every time they asked her to fix the machines. Which was often (and mostly only involved the Restart button).

Gary added an extra column to the whiteboard in the foyer for residents to book tablet time but insisted no one used them during collective activities such as Gardening Club, Farming Chatter, Anti-Grave Rave, and the Well-being Walks. This rule infuriated Jennifer who used her first session to order a pink laptop for herself not realising it was for children. It arrived the next day but she couldn't disable the parental control function and Kendal pretended not to know how.

It was fulfilling to be appreciated and give pleasure so easily. At THRUm the millennials had sneered at her slowness with technology but, at Jurassic Court, she was hailed as a digital guru with residents dropping in to Flat 4 so often she had to hang a sign on the door with Available on one side and Unavailable on the other.

Life would be almost perfect if not for the daily texts from the pawnbrokers counting down the day until she could no longer get the ring back. Fourteen, ten, eight... At last, the auctioneers put

Kendal's antiques on sale. The auction would be one day before the ring would legally belong to the pawnbroker. As long as they sold, she would be able to take the money and drive straight to Bournemouth and pay him off. It would be such a relief to get the ring back.

Fortunately Clare was correct about the high demand for pet sitters. Her phone pinged regularly with requests for cat care, dog walking, or tortoise tracking. The jobs were easy (apart from poo-picking), varied (interesting houses to nose around) and well-paid (cash in hand plus plenty of food and wine).

The shock of the trans global amnesia episode soon faded and the mystery of the wet suit in her wardrobe was resolved after Clare met Judy and Graham at Plick village's pot luck supper.

"They were virtually hyperventilating," she reported when Kendal popped into the library with Kendal's Pet Care cards. "Kept enthusing about your sea swim and banging on about how great you looked in Judy's wetsuit." Kendal couldn't remember wearing the wetsuit but was glad to know where it had come from. "But they're disappointed you haven't attended the gig club tasters. Are you avoiding them? I can't say I blame you. There's something a little off colour about those two."

Kendal packed the wet suit and dryrobe into her trolley, with a box of Maltesers from a grateful budgie owner and walked to the marina. The gig club boathouse was swarming with bearded men sanding, rubbing down, and doing boat-fixing things to two long wooden boats. Kendal was relieved to see no sign of Judy and Graham. She handed the wet suit, dryrobe and chocolates to the man with the longest beard.

"Could you get this back to Judy, please and apologise I've had it so long?"

"Right," said the man. "And you are?"

"A friend," said Kendal. "They wanted me to try gig rowing, but I've been ill."

"I need a name, love. Those two are always lending gear out."

"It's Kendal."

The man scratched his chin. "Like the mint cake. I'll remember."

Kendal smiled. She wasn't bothered any more. Not about her name, being sacked from THRUm, or even the onset of bloating and a hairy chin. Money was what bothered her. Selling books and pet sitting provided cash for sneaky fish and chip suppers, cocktails with Clare, or fresh roots at Hair By Barry but it hardly touched the big debts; a credit card bill edging towards six thousand pounds and the £2,400 loan from the pawnbroker. Kendal's Pet Care would need to deliver five hundred and twenty dog walks, four hundred cat sittings and three hundred tortoise check-ups to get anywhere close.

Kendal didn't care about the credit card bill. It was bearable, like hay-fever or herpes. The pawnbroker debt, however, was agonising. Pam had retreated to her room and was refusing to attend any activities. It was worse than the guilt Kendal felt about Clem dying which wasn't even her fault. She was totally to blame and she needed to fix it.

Four days away from the pawnbrokers deadline, the knock on the door Kendal had been dreading, arrived.

"Kendal, I'm praying you can help." Pam, in her dressing gown at three in the afternoon, wobbled on two sticks in the corridor, clutching one of the Jurassic Court tablets.

Kendal cursed herself for not turning the sign to Unavailable.

"Can you show me how to search the intercloud for my ring? I want to find out if it has been put up for sale by Carla or one of her cronies."

Kendal showed Pam to the table and switched on the tablet with a shaking hand. Her mouth was dry. "We need some words to enter first, then Google gives us possible answers. Pam, speak to Siri and ask a question?"

Pam frowned. "Siri, find my special ring piece."

Possibly the only advantage to Pam's extreme glaucoma was she couldn't see the inappropriate sites this request yielded.

Kendal closed them all and pretended to keep searching. After twenty minutes Pam was exhausted.

"My great-grandson Arlo said people find things in the cloud. I'm sorry to have wasted your time, dear Kendal."

Kendal blushed and gently led the old lady to her door.

The day before the auction Kendal rang the pawnbroker. "I'm getting the money tomorrow. A big windfall from an auction. If you go online and look at the Royal Doulton you'll see the pieces I'm selling."

Mr Field, the pawnbroker, sighed. Kendal could hear the faint tapping of a keyboard. "Have you dealt with the auction house before Ms Tudge?" he asked. Was it more advantageous to appear expert or novice? She remembered a rhyme from childhood:

"Oh, what a tangled web we weave

When first we practise to deceive."

The lines had always sounded lame but continually telling lies was exhausting.

"This is my first time."

"I thought so," grunted the pawnbroker. "Ms Tudge, I'm sorry to inform you but sellers don't receive the money immediately. It's not like the movies. You need to read the small print."

Kendal felt sweat dribbling down her cleavage. The perimenopausal symptoms were getting worse.

"My problem is the ring belongs to a very old person who desperately needs it. I promise to pay extra when my money comes through. As much as you like."

The pawnbroker sighed again. "You've no idea how many times I have had this kind of conversation. Rings needed for weddings, engagements, christenings, funerals even. I'm sorry but I can't make an exception. You're missing the deadline so I will be selling tomorrow. It will go fast. A beautiful piece."

Someone was knocking on Kendal's door. She'd forgotten to turn the sign again. She tip-toed into the bedroom and closed the door behind her. Clem's boat paintings hung in a neat formation on the wall of the bedroom. They must be worth something.

"What if I gave you something else as payment?" she whispered.

"No thank you. My wife wouldn't be happy."

The guy was such a creep. "I meant an object. Valuables. I've got eight maritime paintings and a collection of medals. I was planning to sell them later, but I could pawn them with you instead. For the return of the ring."

"An interesting proposal, Ms Tudge, but I need to see what you've got first. Get here before the end of tomorrow and I'll decide."

Kendal fist pumped the air "OMW, Mr Field. OMW!"

"What?"

"On my way."

She used an acronym. She hated acronyms but Kendal wasn't bothered. TBH.

Kendal ignored speed cameras, overtook tractors, roared across roundabouts and reached Bournemouth in a record forty-five minutes. She grabbed the maritime paintings and medals from the back seat and ran to the pawnbroker's door.

"You were quick," said Mr Field.

"Didn't want to keep you waiting," replied Kendal. "Keen to do the business."

Mr Field stroked the medals and ran his eyes over the paintings.

"Not as liquid as jewellery. Too niche. As collateral on your previous pledge, they're adrift."

Kendal watched him run a grubby finger along the frame of her favourite painting. He wiped the dust on a spotted handkerchief. She shivered.

"My uncle was a very experienced collector," she said. "He was a naval officer."

"I'm running a business here, Ms Tudge. Not a social service and I'm not confident these would equal the amount you owe."

Kendal smiled, remembering her favourite training day mantras at THRUm. She'd never used them at work, but they had proved useful on dates:

The four stages of negotiation:
* Information Exchange
* Bargain
* Conclude
* Execute

She and the pawnbroker had exchanged information. Now she needed to bargain. Kendal pulled her chair close to the pawnbroker's desk.

"What will it take to anchor the, er, collateral?"

Mr Field put down his magnifying glass and blinked at Kendal.

"Well, there is something I need," said the pawnbroker. "How fit are you?"

"Fit enough."

"I need a girl to do some work."

"I have a small personal business already."

"Delighted to hear it, Ms Tudge. Do you have spare capacity?"

"Possibly."

The pawnbroker moved around the desk to stand next to Kendal. All she could think about was Pam crying. She closed her eyes. She could smell the leather of his trouser belt.

"I'll give you a month's leeway if you sort this out for me."

This was her punishment. She was going to have to make the ultimate sacrifice. Her heart was racing from the dangerous driving. She wished she had a drink. Ten drinks. How long would it take for the horrible old creep to, er, conclude? Slowly, she nodded.

Something heavy slapped onto her lap. Kendal winced and looked down. A box of advertising flyers. Bad font, clashing colours.

Struggling to make ends meet?
Derbyfield's Pawnbrokers can help.
Favourable terms, fair prices.

"I'm not a graphic designer, Mr Field."

"Don't need design. It's a distributor I need." He handed Kendal a map, a list of Bournemouth venues and bars, and a jar of drawing pins and grubby Blu-tack. "Send me photos of my leaflets in situ and I'll hold off selling the ring. I'll keep the paintings and the medals as further collateral."

Kendal hugged the box of leaflets. "Deal." They'd concluded, and she'd survived.

Back in the car Kendal entered the postcodes on the pawnbroker's list into her phone to establish the best route to visit all the venues. She must execute her side of the bargain and the sooner the job was done, the quicker she could rescue the ring to stop poor Pam's misery. Life would be so much better without the guilt she felt. Almost perfect. First, she needed to cancel that afternoon's Digital Drop-in.

"Jurassic Court, Gary Vaughan speaking." Kendal pictured the warden at his too-small desk, his long fingers stroking the keyboard. Lovely to hear his phone voice again. She swivelled the rear-view mirror to check her appearance.

"Gary, it's Kendal."

"Hello, Kendal. All right?" The warden's voice was odd. Flat. Perhaps he was missing her. Kendal opened her make-up bag

"I'm delayed in Bournemouth and I'm booked to do a session with Philip this afternoon. Can you let him know?"

"I'll try. But I can't promise."

"He's been excited about this session for ages. I don't want him to lose motivation,"

"Yeh, I understand. Sorry Kendal, there's a lot going on here."

"What's going on?" said Kendal, refreshing her lipstick.

"I'm not sure I can say."

"But I'm the chair of the Residents' Association."

"There's been er, an incident."

Someone moved behind her reflection in the mirror. Two youths in hoodies swaggered up the pawnbroker's path.

"What kind of incident, Gary?"

Gary swallowed loudly. "It's something we have to expect here but still a shock when it does. I never get used to it."

The hoodie boys were hammering on the pawnbroker's door. They must be as desperate as she'd been a few minutes before. Well, they were too late if they hoped to pay the pawnbroker by working. She'd got the job, and she would deliver.

Mr. Field came to the door with a napkin hanging from his collar. He was chewing.

"A resident has, um, reached the end of their journey." Gary made a sound like a dog whimpering.

"What! Oh no," said Kendal. "Who?"

The tallest teenager pulled something shiny out of his pocket and lunged at the pawnbroker. The napkin fell.

"Oh my God! I've got to go."

The men pushed Mr. Field aside and stormed into the house. Kendal jabbed at her phone and dialled 999.

"Emergency, which service?"

"Police!" shouted Kendal.

Kendal gabbled the address down the phone, jammed the key into the car and roared away from the quiet road. She'd do the leaflet distribution tomorrow. Something terrible had happened to someone at Jurassic Court. She must get there.

Kendal hoped the police could get to Mr. Field in time. The guy was cheesy, but he didn't deserve to be robbed, or, even worse, stabbed. She'd never get the ring back if the low-life hoodie-boys stole it. What if her phone was traced because she was the only witness? She couldn't risk police arriving at Jurassic Court with questions about a burglary at a pawnbroker's. She couldn't go to court; she'd have to admit her true age. This was a total mess. Her heart was rushing in a horrible way and her head seemed to be floating over the high, green Dorset hills bordering the dual carriageway. Was she having a panic attack like the millennials at THRUm constantly claimed to experience?

Kendal veered into a layby, opened her phone, and snapped the sim card into two pieces. Impossible to track her now. At the end of the layby was a parked van and a beach umbrella. A swarthy man was selling strawberries. He leered at Kendal and pointed at the flimsy sign on the table: LOCAL STRAWBS PIKKED TODAY

She shook her head and closed her eyes. She had to calm down, get a grip.

Kendal breathed slowly and unpacked the terrible news from Jurassic Court. Gary had said a resident had reached the end of their journey. Jurassic Court code for die. The most likely candidate to drop dead was Albert, though he'd got healthier lately. Wendy or Shirley were the oldest residents, but optimists live longer than pessimists, and they were glass-half-full people. What if it was Philip and his last experience was her cancelling the Digital Drop-in? Or Brian? He could have had a crash on the mobility buggy she'd sold him. Audrey would be devastated; she adored Brian. What if it was Audrey? Too much yoga putting a strain on her heart. Kendal gazed at the view of Portland in the distance and remembered Audrey suggesting they went on a trip to see the lighthouse.

"There's a hundred and fifty-three steps," Audrey had said. "Keep practising yoga and you'll keep up." She'd bowed her head in prayer position and cackled. "Not like Brian."

Terrible not to see Audrey again. No more Anti-Grave Raves or *Midsomer Murder* marathons. Was there mist on the windscreen? She switched on the radio. The music was slow. In a minor key. It wasn't mist clouding her vision. She was crying, full on.

Everyone she loved died and every time it happened she wasn't there.

Jurassic Court was deserted. No one in the gardens, the foyer, or the day room. Even the kitchen was empty. Kendal stood outside the warden's office. What was her story? Could she have been to Bournemouth to visit a friend? What if Gary noticed the bare spaces on her bedroom wall where the paintings had hung? He'd never been in her bedroom and, if he did, Kendal hoped he wouldn't be looking at the walls, but best to be safe. She'd tell him she'd taken Clem's paintings to be valued at a specialist auction house in Bournemouth. Almost true.

Kendal opened the office door. A pale Gary jumped up, rushing towards her, then pulled back. "Thank goodness, you're here. I tried to call you, but your phone is dead."

"Classic boomer. Forgot to charge it last night." Kendal tried to remember what she had done with the sim card. Extreme anxiety was triggering genuine senior moments.

"Never mind, you're here now," said Gary. "Sit down. Do you need a drink or anything? Tea, coffee, something stronger?"

Kendal wished this exchange was taking place in a normal household. They could be flatmates, moaning about their jobs, or another housemate. Getting smashed then forgetting about it in the morning. Instead, she was living an old people's home, and he was about to tell her which of their roommates had died.

Everything seemed slower. Things were happening at two levels. She felt hyper aware of how she was interacting with the warden. She looked out of the window. Seagulls were fishing for goldfish in the pond. She had to be calm.

"Where are the residents?"

"Gone to their rooms. They're all in shock. It was so horrible, Kendal. It was as though..." Gary's voice faltered.

Kendal shivered. "Can I have a drink? For the shock."

Gary opened a deep drawer and brought out a bottle of Laphroaig and two glasses. "For medicinal purposes," he said. "A terrible day." His hand trembled as he poured.

Kendal couldn't wait. "Is it Audrey?" she shouted.

Gary shook his head and offered a glass. Kendal swallowed and felt the heat hit her throat. "Thank God," she said, sinking into the chair. "This is good stuff."

"Yes, Clem gave it to me for Christmas. I tried to stop him, but he insisted."

"To Uncle Clem, who brought me here," said Kendal. Her eyes were misting again. She turned to look at the warden. His cheeks were damp. Gary was crying.

"Oh my God, what's happened, Gary? Has there been an accident?"

Gary pushed his hands into his eyes and shook his head.

"A murder?" Unlikely, but there had been those bestsellers about murders in an old people's home.

"No, not that bad. But the coroner has been informed because she hadn't seen a doctor for months. It makes things even more upsetting. Especially for the family."

"She?" The whisky burned in Kendal's stomach. It wasn't Audrey. She stared at the warden. "Who has died, Gary? I need to know. I can help you."

Gary nodded. "It's poor Pam."

Kendal's stomach lurched. "What happened?" she whispered.

"Apparently, she went into the kitchen after breakfast and shouted at Carla again, then stormed off to her flat. When Emma checked in on her she was on the floor. Completely cold. Heart, probably."

Kendal stared at the floor. There were no rugs in Jurassic Court (too risky) but the carpets were thick and springy. She could curl under Gary's desk and go to sleep. It was clean under there. Not dirty like the dust corners in Pam's flat.

If only she had left the ring in its dusty corner. If only, if only…

"It started when you were in hospital. She was so upset about her lost ring. She wouldn't let it lie."

The waistband of Kendal's trousers felt painfully tight. And her bra. And her pants. This was bloating in a big way. A perimenopausal symptom or a response to her extreme guilt? Whatever, she needed to get to her bathroom. Fast.

24

It was just like Uncle Clem's funeral: same time, same place, same tiny congregation but now it was Pam's great-grandson who stood next to Gary. Arlo, in a shiny suit with a giant tie, looked shell-shocked as the parade of old people shuffled past.

Kendal remembered being in the same position, thinking these are the poor buggers your relative died alongside. He might be feeling he hadn't visited often enough like she had. He wouldn't be fantasising about the warden like her or, if he was, he would be far better dressed.

So much had changed for Kendal since Clem's funeral. These same old people had become individual characters, with histories, likes and dislikes. And now, in Arlo's eyes, she was one.

Arlo was a better relative than Kendal. He'd accompanied Gary to the crematorium, returning to Jurassic Court with an urn containing Pam's cremains which he held awkwardly. Gary gently placed it on the mantelpiece and handed Arlo a glass. Kendal stared at the urn and wondered what had happened to Clem's ashes. She'd never asked, he'd never said.

The wake was the first time the district nurse had been spotted since her outburst at Jurassic Court. Nicola's black coat was splattered with mud and her hair hung in greasy bunches.

"She needs a fidget blanket," whispered Audrey as they waited in the queue to pay their respects. Ahead of them Albert was taking a long time to tell Arlo how much he'd admired Pam.

"Your great-grandmother was a trouper. If she couldn't see something clearly, she would simply guess. The ideal person to ask if I looked like I'd lost any weight."

Arlo smiled and shook Albert's hand.

Kendal took a deep breath as she took Albert's place.

"Pam was very proud of you," she said. "She loved talking to you online."

Arlo grinned. "Ah, you're the digital guru. Thank you so much for what you did for her. I was always trying to get her to use new tech, but she refused to learn. You must be a great teacher."

"Are you, I mean, were you Pam's closest relative?"

"Yes, I am. My parents have passed, and my cousins live abroad."

Kendal nodded. So, Arlo would probably inherit Pam's estate. If she had any.

"Please accept my condolences during this difficult time," said Kendal. The words were formulaic, but she meant them.

Arlo bowed his head. "Thank you, I appreciate it."

Kendal blinked and walked to the drinks table. The wine was screw top, not the posh stuff with corks Clem had ordered. It didn't matter, it was alcohol and free. She grabbed two glasses.

"Woah, Kendal. Pace yerself, luvver," said Emma-from-the-kitchen. She nodded at the district nurse. "Or you'll be as confused as her." Nicola was licking the insides of vol-au-vents and placing them back on the table. "Poor soul, they've pensioned her off now."

Kendal felt wobbly and loose. Her legs, her tongue, her bowels.

"You look as white as a sheet," observed Emma. "Not going to have another funny turn?"

"I'm sad about Pam. I feel so guilty about her ring."

There, she'd said it out loud, and the world was still spinning. Emma stared hard. "Why?"

"Well she asked me to look online for it, but it was hopeless."

Emma put her arm around Kendal's shoulder. She smelled of sausage. "There probably wasn't any ring at all, love. She had gone gaga, to be honest. Look at the palaver about Carla and the cleaners being in cahoots. Now, lay off the wine, take these sausage rolls, and circulate. That poor lad Arlo needs carbs."

Kendal walked the sausage rolls around the room. Moving helped take her mind off Pam, the ring, and the pawnbroker. Arlo took three. Not his great-grandmother's ring, but good to give him something. Albert pocketed four. Bad for his health but not worth fighting about. Gary leaned against the wall holding an empty plate.

"Can I tempt you, Gary?"

"Always," said the warden. He swayed as he reached for a sausage roll. "Haven't seen you for ages."

Kendal sighed. "I've been watching a lot of television." This was kind of true. She'd been scanning online sites and watching the local news. The burglary had been reported but no details about what was stolen or descriptions of witnesses.

Gary downed his glass. "I hope you're not avoiding me."

"Of course not, Gary. You've been busy with the funeral, and I've been busy with the Digital Drop-ins and pet-sitting. I'm helping Clare at the library too. She's running a publicity campaign to stop the council's spending cuts."

Gary slumped into a sofa. "You missed Gardening Club. We analysed the seed in Linda's no-mow bush area."

Kendal smiled. Jurassic Court still provided comic moments, even in a funeral. "I went to the Auction House. I've sold Clem's Royal Doulton. You were right, they were valuable."

"And you haven't been on any Well-being Walks. I wanted to show you the Painted Ladies." Gary raised his glass. "To the beautiful migrants you missed."

Kendal slammed the plate of sausage rolls onto a coffee table and perched beside him. Even allowing for drink and grief, Gary had no right to be offensive.

"Best not to judge, Gary. It could be their economic situation forcing them."

"Judge what?"

"Ladies of the night, prostitutes. Migrants get all the rubbish jobs."

Gary closed his eyes.

Kendal experienced the two-level-functioning feeling again. She was performing whilst simultaneously observing herself from above. Was this her fourth or fifth glass? She stared at Gary's crinkled eyes, squinting at three wayward hairs escaping his eyebrow

"What are you doing, Kendal?" Gary had opened his eyes.

"Nothing. I thought you'd passed out."

"I was trying not to laugh. Inappropriate at a funeral." Gary swiped his phone and showed Kendal the screen. "Painted Ladies. A rare type of butterfly which visits Dorset. From overseas. Prue was in seventh heaven when we spotted them on the walk."

"Sorry, classic misunderstanding," said Kendal. She'd not done any Nature Notes for a while. Too busy searching for robbery news.

"I love your misunderstandings. I've missed them. It's been such a difficult time with Pam's passing. You'd think I would get used to it working here, but I don't."

Kendal patted his arm aunty-fashion.

"Gary, do you mind if I ask what you did with Clem?"

"With his cremains? I followed his wishes and left them to be distributed at the crematorium."

Cremains! What an awkward, blended word. Like tiny diamonds in Pam's ring, cremains stayed hard forever. Poor, poor Pam. Kendal had to change the subject, stay alert. Gary was falling apart, she mustn't.

"It was a good funeral, though. Like Clem's."

The warden lifted his head and sighed. "Two funerals per year is average. Better be no more, or the trustees get twitchy. Bad for business."

"But you can't control when residents, um, check out."

Gary closed his eyes again. "I know, but there are a whole host of key performance indicators for this place."

Kendal frowned. Targets for limiting deaths in a retirement home? Jurassic Court was worse than THRUm.

"Well, I won't be checking out. And no one could have predicted Pam's weak heart. You said she never went to the doctors, only the opticians."

"She was in great condition, except for the glaucoma. But it's only June and we've winter to get through." Gary scanned the room. All the residents were chewing and drinking, their plates piled with scones and cakes. "Bloody hope Albert isn't eating too much."

"Grown-ups make their own choices," said Kendal. "Albert will be fine."

"Thanks, Kendal. It's been good to share, Madame Chair."

Kendal wished she could unload in return. But the ring problem was impossible to share. She poured two more glasses. Drinking didn't solve her isolation, but it blurred the edges.

"Anyway, how did you get on at the auction?" asked Gary.

"Clem's pieces did really well. Much better than predicted."

"Great news," said Gary. "You can buy your own wet suit now."

"Very funny," said Kendal. "But it takes a while for the money to come through and I've got some big bills to pay."

"Well, nothing to pay here, remember? Not until January. So, you can plan ahead."

Kendal had never been much of a planner. Maybe she should start now, be more grown up? "How much are the costs after January, Gary?"

Gary narrowed his eyes. "Around eight thousand a year."

Kendal gasped. "Why? The flats are tiny, and nobody eats much, apart from me and Albert."

"There's electricity, heating, maintenance, gardens, activities and, of course, staff. We may have to raise fees with all the energy and food price rises. The minibus needs work too. We've spent a bit on all the tech, and we need to spend more because it's so popular and helping the residents. If the medical centre doesn't recruit some more nurses, we may have to start paying for agency visits and then…"

Gary's picked up his glass, shaking his head.

Kendal longed to distract him from budget worries. Her fingers itched to stroke his brow and then some other parts. But they were at a wake, in an old people's sheltered complex where she was a resident, with Audrey and Philip watching with their beady eyes. The weird disassociation feeling had returned, and high-above-Kendal was witnessing down-below-Kendal losing control.

"We'll get through this, Gary," she said. "I'm good at budgets." A lie but delivered with the best of intentions. "I need to go back to my flat before I make a fool of myself. The last thing Arlo needs is me crying at his great-gran's wake."

Gary tried to stand. "Thanks, Kendal. It's so easy to talk to you. Like when we walked to the Seven Witches. I have to remind myself sometimes you're a resident. You're so different from the others."

Kendal shook her head. "I'm not, Gary. It's simply because I stopped working very recently and am more familiar with work-place pressures. Most of the residents haven't been employed for decades. Key performance indicators hadn't been invented then."

"Yes, Kendal. You're not like the others because you understand about contemporary issues. Jurassic Court is lucky to have a younger resident. We need more residents like you. I need…"

Gary's eyes were closing.

Kendal had replaced her sim card and there'd been no word from Dorset police. She'd called and emailed the pawnbroker, but no one answered, and the emails bounced back. The Derbyfield flyers sat undelivered in the car. There was no point distributing them if the pawnbroker was out of action. The whole situation was horrible. All because of her lies. Lies caused chaos and were exhausting. She had to be more honest now. With the small lies, anyway. At least she could turn the lie about helping Clare into a truth. It would be pleasant to get out of Jurassic Court. She left for the library straight after breakfast.

"So good to see you," squealed Clare. "You've been so elusive since Pam passed."

"Yes, sorry. I've come to offer help with your campaign."

"Brill! Well, we've got nine hundred signatures including all the local councillors, plus hundreds of book donations, and Dominic is organizing some kind of flash mob with excluded teenagers. I'm waiting till budget day at the council when I can lobby the bastards." Clare squeezed Kendal's arm. "But I am really pleased to see you. Free tonight?"

"Possibly. Movie Night's been cancelled. Gary thought *Diamonds Are Forever* inappropriate after the wake."

Clare frowned. "James Bond's loss, but your lucky break. Our book group is meeting, and we need a new member."

Kendal groaned. "Not my thing, Clare."

"I promise you'll enjoy it. They're a lovely bunch of ladies. Not like the one I used to belong to. Wittering on about unreliable narrators and story arcs. This group is fun. The books play second fiddle to the eating and drinking. Especially the drinking."

"Are you saying I'm a bit thick? Or an alcoholic?"

Clare giggled. "Of course not. I thought you might like a change of scene, meet some new people."

"But I haven't read the book."

"Most of them won't have either. They Google it beforehand. It's *On Chesil Beach* by Ian McEwan. Set on the long bit which leads to Portland. Do you know it?"

"The book?"

"No, Chesil Beach."

"My parents took me there years ago. It's one of my best memories of them."

"Then you must read it."

"I couldn't read a book in an afternoon, Clare."

"You could read this one. It's short. More of a novella."

Kendal didn't know what a novella was (a book for females?) but Jurassic Court was a depressing place after the funeral. The residents were all wondering which of them might be next. A change of scene would be good.

"How old are the members?"

"Rosie and Erica are in their seventies, but Anna and Phyllida are about our age. The food will be delicious, and there's always loads."

Good to be away from Gary too. The Kendal-above-looking-at-Kendal-below feeling was exhausting. "All right," said Kendal. "Where is it?"

"At Phyllida's. Near the croquet club. Meet at Jurassic Court and I'll walk you there. Six-thirty good?"

"Let's meet at The Albatross and have a cocktail," said Kendal. "It's such a lovely day."

"Fine, but only one," said Clare. "I don't want to be taken home by Judy and Graham again." She pulled out a paperback. "Here you go. You'll get through it easily and, if you don't, read a review. Or watch the film."

Kendal power-walked to the bird hide on the estuary path. She opened the book and began to read, calmed by exercise and the rustling reeds. Twice, a bird watcher popped in, nodded hello, and slipped out.

A swan circled slowly, a baby bird nestled inside the wings, its dingy brown feathers fluffing as the mother moved. Reminding Kendal of a song her parents used to sing:

"You're not such an ugly duckling, with feathers all tattered and torn…"

Kendal stuck her head through the narrow window of the hide. The swan hissed.

"And the other birds, in so many words, said quack, quack, get out of town."

It was almost midsummer, the days were long, the river alive with birds, insects, fish, and all things natural and watery. She would make amends somehow. Do more Digital Drop-ins, participate in all the Well-being Walks, support Clare to show the value of libraries and never flirt with Gary again. She would try to act her age. Become a person who could identify every butterfly, willingly discuss feet, ears or the weather, and recognise when borrowing was stealing. Who couldn't be told get out of town. She would do her best to live well. For free.

A tiny splash interrupted the stream of penances and promises. Kendal froze. A brown creature, with a large head, long front teeth, and scaly tail. A beaver. At last! It bit through a low-hanging willow branch, pulled green leaves into the water and began to nibble.

25

Kendal was applying lipstick when someone hammered on the door. Kendal's hand jumped, leaving an old-person lipstick smudge.

"Caught you at last," said Audrey as Kendal opened the door. "Where are you off to, and where have you been?"

"And hello to you, too, Audrey. How are you?"

"Concerned about my errant neighbour, is how I am. I've hardly seen you since poor Pam went. You've not been at yoga, or any of the activities. Life goes on, you know. Pam wouldn't have wanted us to be miserable all the time."

"Sorry Audrey, my back's dodgy and I can't manage yoga at the moment." She hadn't totally nailed truth-telling.

"You look perfectly well to me, except your make-up." Audrey prodded Kendal. "Are you seeing someone, you wicked minx?"

"I am, actually."

Audrey's widened her eyes. "Ooooooh." The eyebrows were equal.

"I'm going to a book group. Friends of Clare, the librarian."

"Well, don't sign for too many. I've still got Tupperware from the seventies."

"A group where you read a book, Audrey. You don't buy them."

"Why read a book with strangers? You're odd, Kendal Pudge."

"Tudge, Audrey. It's Tudge."

Billy Whizz twiddled his knobs and Clare sipped something orange as Kendal arrived at The Albatross. The DJ winked, Clare hugged, and the teenage waitress smiled politely. Kendal ordered a gin Mint Julep.

"With Plymouth Gin?" asked the waitress. She'd remembered.

"I read the book this afternoon, Clare," said Kendal. "It was short, like you said. I loved the bit about …"

"Save it for later," interrupted Clare. "We haven't got long till we need to leave."

"I've had a lovely afternoon. Walked the estuary path and read the book by the river. Spotted a beaver at last."

"Impressive," said Clare. "Might be dolphins to spot this summer. One of the few good things about global warming."

"And one of the few animals who have sex for pleasure," said Kendal (some Nature Notes were easier to remember than others). "Their clitorises have lots of nerves, like humans."

"Oh Kendal, you are a one! I'd love to spend the whole evening drinking cocktails and discussing the sex lives of dolphins, but we better get moving."

Phyllida's front garden featured flowers in rowing boats and lobster pots around the front door. Clare and Kendal stood on the doorstep and listened to the laughter inside.

"The book's going down well," observed Kendal.

"The wine, more likely," said Clare. "You ready?"

"Should we have brought a bottle?"

"No, whoever hosts the evening provides refreshments."

"But I can't offer a meal. Carla and Emma wouldn't let me cook."

"You're looking for excuses," laughed Clare. "It won't be your turn for ages, and you can always do it at my place instead."

"Door's open," someone shouted.

Kendal followed Clare into a bright conservatory. Four smartly dressed women sat round a table piled with salads, dips and cold meats. In the back garden were more lobster pots and a fishpond with a model lighthouse.

"This is my new friend Kendal Tudge," said Clare. "She's recently moved to Jurassic Court and is going to give us a try out. So best behaviour, girls."

The women raised giant glasses full of Cava.

"My Dad spent his last years at Jurassic Court," said Phyllida. "He loved it. Independent, but surrounded by company when he wanted it."

"My cousin Joe gardens there," said Anna. "Says the manager never rips him off. Not like some of the other retirement homes."

"Yes, the manager is a sweetie," said Erica, winking as she poured more wine. "He went to school with my eldest. Developed muscles far earlier than Matt. Gorgeous."

The women groaned. "Erica, you're so inappropriate!" said Clare, with a giggle.

Rosie, the oldest member of the group, whispered into Kendal's ear. "I'm on the waiting list. For a rental, not a purchase. Maybe you could put a word in for me?"

Kendal nodded. "A resident has, um, vacated their room recently, but I don't know if it's for sale or rent." The women began discussing their children and pets. Like everyone Kendal was meeting in Dorset, it wasn't clear when they were talking about humans or animals. Phyllida switched on fairy lights in the conservatory roof. Kendal downed another giant glass and watched the model lighthouse which had begun to flash. She felt more relaxed out of Jurassic Court with its constant reminders of Pam and the lost (well, to be honest, the stolen) ring. Book group was easy, and no one thought it odd to live in a retirement complex. Best of all, no one had commented on her name.

"Perhaps we better discuss the book?" said Clare.

"Yes," shrieked Erica. "Before I lose the plot!"

Kendal straightened herself on the cane armchair. She wished she had her back to the garden. The flashing lighthouse was unsettling.

"Comfort break first," shouted Erica. "Two per loo."

Kendal grimaced.

"Nothing to worry about," whispered Clare. "We'll go to the top floor one."

Kendal gripped the banister. It was a struggle to stand straight.

"You, OK?" asked Clare emerging from the bathroom.

"I think so," answered Kendal. She sat on the toilet and focused on a dolphin-shaped electric toothbrush. Could be a vibrator. Nice to think women like Phyllida were still pleasuring themselves. Even better, that she kept it clean in the bathroom.

Returning to the conservatory, Kendal saw her glass had been re-filled. The women were brandishing their copies of the book.

"It's tragic," declared Phyllida. "Someone should have explained about sex before they got married."

"It's set in the sixties," said Anna. "So, you'd think they'd know. Hardly anyone is a virgin when they get married."

Rosie raised her hand. "I was," she said. "We didn't swing in Dorset then."

"The film's better," said Erica. "Explains why she's not into sex."

"Which is only hinted at in the book," said Clare.

"She's messed up because she's keeping a secret," said Anna. "And secrets always come out and cause trouble."

The lighthouse's flashes seemed to be getting faster.

"What's your take, Kendal?" asked Erica.

Kendal remembered her response at job interviews when she didn't know the answer.

"It's all about timing."

The conservatory erupted with a chorus of agreement. Boom!

Phyllida brought in a tray of desert bowls. Kendal decided she must be very drunk because her spoon couldn't hold the grapes. The cane chair wobbled. She seemed to be on the roof of the conservatory looking down at herself. Flying-Kendal was observing Fake-Kendal pretending to know about books as well as sixteen years older than she was. Fake, fraudulent, pissed.

"Apologies ladies, but I've got to go. The gates close soon at Jurassic Court, and I can't remember the code."

Kendal crossed the prom and collapsed on the shingle. A full moon shone over a calm sea. Easy to stride straight in and sink into the inky water.

"Wait for me." Clare was running towards Kendal. She grabbed Kendal's arm and guided her to a bench. "You were a great success tonight."

Kendal's head lolled. Her face ghostly. Clare tried again. "Did you enjoy the book group? Erica is such a hoot, isn't she?" Clare peered at Kendal. "Are you crying?"

"No. Tired." A loud sob escaped. A man walking a Dalmatian stopped.

"You OK, ladies?"

"We're fine, thank you," said Clare. "Women's problems." The dog walker tightened the lead and hurried off. Clare poked Kendal. "Mention periods and men run a mile."

"I'm due mine," mumbled Kendal. "It's making me crazy."

"Gosh, your perimenopause thing is dragging on," said Clare. "I'm so glad I got mine at fifty. Much easier I think."

Kendal wiped her face with her sleeve, stood unsteadily, and lurched towards the sea, collapsing by the water's edge. Stones crunched as Clare lay beside her. A satellite passed over their heads. Clare nudged Kendal's knee with her foot.

"Did you know Ian McEwan took some pebbles back from Dorset to London when he wrote the book we read. There was quite a hoo-hah, and the council made him return them."

"A PR stunt," growled Kendal. "They were always doing that kind of shit where I used to work. People are so gullible."

"What's going on, Kendal?" said Clare. Kendal stared at the moon. Clare waited. Kendal shifted on the cold stones.

"It's like what Anna said. I'm messed up because I'm hoarding a secret, and it is doing my head in. I always mess up but this time is the worst. I feel like walking into the sea again."

Clare took a packet of tissues from her bag. "Do you want to share it, Kendal? I promise not to judge. I'm unshockable."

A flock of seagulls skimmed the water, their white backs shining in the moonlight. Kendal blew her nose.

Clare waited.

"Are you falling asleep, Kendal?" she said. "Probably best not as it will get cold, and you won't feel yourself in the morning."

"I'm not myself," whispered Kendal. "I'm living a lie."

Along the beach a group of teenagers laughed and shrieked. Clare took Kendal's hand. Her palm was cold, her fingers short.

"No one needs to live a lie these days. Things have changed. Even in Dorset. You don't need to lie about who you are."

Kendal turned to face Clare. "I'm lying about my age."

"Is that all? I thought you meant a sexual secret. Like gay, bisexual, or the one beginning with Q." She squeezed Kendal's hand. "Loads of women drop years. It's our patriarchal society, as my Rebecca would say. Young women are more desirable."

"I'm not dropping years, I'm adding them. Pretending I'm your age when I'm really forty-four."

Clare's teeth gleamed in the moonlight. "What on earth for?"

"To stay at Jurassic Court. They don't let anyone under sixty live there, so I lied and added sixteen years to my age."

Clare clapped her hands. "Oh, my lord, this is priceless. You're a case, Kendal Tudge. I adore you whatever age you are."

The sweet scent of teenage dope drifted along the shore. The moon had moved further towards the horizon. The shingle was shifting into place around Kendal's thighs.

"I could sleep here," she said. "Like a fossil."

Clare stood and pulled Kendal's arms. "Let's get you home, old thing. I mean, young thing. No, middle-aged thing. That's what you are. Come on."

26

The silence at the Quaker Meeting was heavenly. Kendal felt almost relaxed. She'd no hangover (Prosecco was for lightweights) and no concerns about confessing her secret to Clare. She was lighter, relieved by Clare's response, hopeful that other people would feel the same. It would have been even better if she'd had the courage to tell Clare both her secrets, but Kendal was hoping she could still get the ring back and then she wouldn't need to. Someone as wholesome as Clare might not appreciate the nuances of borrowing and stealing.

It felt good to sit in the silent space, with people. Not alone but not having to talk either. Almost as peaceful as the wildlife spotting hide on the estuary. Kendal bathed in the stillness and imagined the beaver and swan swimming in the river. She wasn't separating from herself in that horrible way that had been happening recently. Her mind was clear and she understood the difference between finding and keeping. She, Kendal Tudge, had stolen the ring. It was a fact. She could still be run out of town.

Kendal tried to empty her mind, but Gary wore a blue linen suit she'd not seen before which fitted well and complemented his tan. Better than the black one he wore for funerals.

Prue grabbed her elbow as they left the Ammonite room.

"I'm going fossil hunting this afternoon. It's full moon day. Do come. There's so much energy coming off you. It could help me find a big belemnite."

"Sorry Prue, I've got a Digital Drop-in booked with Albert. He's starting a blog about dung."

Prue shook her head. "I disapprove of all these computers in Jurassic Court. We'll all get brain tumours." Kendal heard a laugh. Gary was following.

"I'm glad some of the residents are not wild about tech," he said. "Otherwise, we'd have to buy more equipment."

"Or clone Kendal," said Prue.

"There could never be another Kendal," said Gary. "She's unique."

Kendal studied the warden's face. He looked sincere, though it might just be the suit.

"Cheerio, you two," sang Prue "Enjoy God's special day."

Kendal felt vulnerable standing alone with the warden, as though the Quaker Meeting had somehow stripped away her all her defences.

"Off somewhere special?" she asked.

Gary reddened. "Kind of. Meeting someone for lunch."

Kendal felt a sudden pain in her stomach. She'd had an enormous breakfast, done twenty minutes yoga and stayed calm in the meeting. What was wrong with her? Was it guilt? No, it was not that. It was simply that Gary had confessed to dating and she, Kendal Tudge, creator of the Tudge Trudge, was literally gutted. She patted his arm. "You look great. She'll adore you."

"How did you know I'm on a date?"

"Been there, got the T-shirt."

"I'm finding it hard. Not the technology. The system," said Gary. "Perhaps I could learn from you?"

"It's been a while," lied Kendal. "I'm into animals and plants now, not people. Had a lovely walk at the estuary yesterday. I spotted the elusive beaver."

"Really? Lucky you, well done. I'm going to Dartmoor again on Tuesday. I promised you a trip. Have you been yet?"

Beaver-spot, a full confession to Clare which hadn't brought the world to its knees, and now a date on Dartmoor. If it wasn't for the nagging guilt about Pam, Kendal might be allowed to think the universe was on her side.

"Let me check my diary," said Kendal (no one looked at phone calendars at Jurassic Court). "I'll let you know."

"I'll be in the foyer," said Gary. "Writing up the activity board. Got so many clashes. Hope it's going to work."

Kendal smiled. "Jurassic Court's range of education, self-care, and entertainment activities work well, Gary. You're a terrific organiser."

The warden was chatting to Audrey at the white board when Kendal returned. She scanned the programme.

Monday AM – Audrey's Anti-Grave Rave + Farming Chat with Albert
Tuesday AM – Hair By Barry + Toes Are Us (Gary's day off)
Wednesday AM – Gardening Club + Fidget Blanket
Thursday AM – Patriotic Pompoms with Jennifer + Chat Rickshaw
Friday PM – Advanced Wellbeing Walk + Beginners Ukulele with Philip
Saturday PM – Movie Night: *Eat, Pray, Love* (Prue's choice)

"Who's Chat Rickshaw?" asked Audrey. "The dreadful piano player we had at New Year? Breath like a pig."

Gary shook his head. "Not a person, it's a thing. Well, not a thing, an initiative."

"Talk properly, man," shouted Audrey.

"It's a social transport vehicle which takes two people for a ride. The pilot sits behind and gets them talking as they look at the view. Good for residents who can't move far."

"Another of Kendal's ideas, I expect," said Audrey. "She's really livened up this place." Kendal smirked. Being praised in front of Gary was fun. She'd take it.

"Actually, it's from the medical centre. They're giving us a free trial. I'm going to be their test pilot."

Audrey frowned. "You hate flying, Gary Vaughan. I'm going to be busy on Thursday."

"You could make a pompom with Jennifer instead," said Gary.

"Definitely busy."

"Activities aren't compulsory, as you well know," said Gary.

Audrey cackled. "Yes, sir. Have a lovely lunch date. Don't do anything I wouldn't."

Kendal touched Gary's arm. "I would love to come to Dartmoor on Tuesday."

"Great. I can't promise beavers. But we'll see lots of other attractions."

A hot blush was threatening. Kendal was relieved to spot Carla-from-the-kitchen striding towards the gong.

"Better get a move on, Gary. Women hate waiting in pubs on their own. Your pub lunch won't be as good as ours. But at least you can eat later for a change."

"The residents choose to eat early, not me," smiled Gary.

"Yeh, well, when I've finished this afternoon I'm choosing to take up residence on my sofa, do end-to-end *Friends* and a gallon of Old Rosie," said Carla.

"Well, I hope you'll be bright-eyed and bushy-tailed on Monday," said Gary.

"Back at you, boss. Good luck with the date."

Gary sighed. "Impossible to keep secrets in Jurassic Court."

Kendal nodded in agreement. Though she knew it wasn't.

The new schedule was problematic. Albert wanted to show tractor slides during the Anti-Grave Rave, but Brian was taking all the power for disco lighting. Jacob had purchased a powerful battery for the Advanced Well-being Walk and new strings for his ukulele and was distraught at having to choose one activity over the other. Shirley said she didn't have enough energy for a perm and a pedicure on the same day and Prue worried fidget blankets would get muddy at Gardening Club

Everyone was confused about the Chat Rickshaw.

"Nasty, foreign vehicles! Should be banned from British roads," said Jennifer.

Kendal didn't care about the clashing activities but, as chair of the Residents' Association, she now had a responsibility to help spread harmony. Be solution-focused, as the drones at THRUm liked to say.

"Maybe we could locate one event in the day room and another in the Ammonite room?"

"Well said, Madame Chair," said Philip.

"She's waxing gibbously. Like a moon goddess," added Prue.

Kendal heaped Yorkshire puddings onto her plate, hoping Gary's date ate lots of carbs too. Jealousy was an ugly emotion, but she'd take it. Made a change from endless guilt.

Audrey and Albert were still squabbling about who should have the day room during their activity clash.

"We need more space than the Ammonite room can provide," argued Audrey.

"But I need the screen that's in the day room," complained Albert.

Kendal put down her fork. She must channel Dogbreath-Deirdre and be solution focused.

"Guys, here's a thought. Show the photos at the same time. You could choose some farming related music to accompany them. Let's watch a slide, then dance, then watch another slide, dance some more. Everyone will stay awake if they move between your stories."

It was satisfying solving problems. Kendal Tudge was living her best life. She nodded as Carla offered another tray of roasties.

The next morning Kendal opened her laptop to see the longed-for email from the auction house had arrived. They'd paid in the money from the sale of the ornaments. £4,880 for those simpering shepherdesses and ugly sailors. Amazing! Now she had money to pay the pawnbroker (if only he'd answer the phone), pay part of the credit card debt and have enough left over to pay Jurassic Court January fees when Clem's payments ran out.

It was tempting to rush to the beach and reward herself with every cocktail The Albatross could invent. Instead, Kendal forced herself through the daily Find-the-Ring scenario, trawling local news for clues to the whereabouts of the pawnbroker whilst simultaneously ringing his number on speed dial.

Kendal didn't know what she would do with the ring once she'd got it. She couldn't give it to poor dead Pam, and she wasn't certain that Arlo was inheriting Pam's estate, and, even if she did know, how would she get the ring back to him? What would be a feasible explanation for having it?

Kendal wished she had someone to share her problem with but anyone she talked to would be shocked to learn that Kendal was the kind of selfish person who had found jewellery in a partially sighted, vulnerable person's room and taken it to a pawnbroker. She had to admit she'd shocked herself. Yes, she was desperate to pay off Mad-Maxine and live for free in Jurassic Court, but it was still wrong. It was stealing, not borrowing, and it was wrong. Lying about her age was also wrong, but it wasn't hurting anyone.

Kendal touched the photo of her parents. They'd tried to raise her properly: camping holidays, knickerbocker glories, and jigsaws. It wasn't their fault they got cancer. They didn't even smoke! It wasn't the school or sixth form college's fault she didn't have any qualifications, and it wasn't anyone's fault she didn't have friends, or a career. Maxine wasn't even Mad, just organised and Deirdre was just a middle-aged woman trying to motivate an unreliable, resentful sales exec.

The sun streamed through the French windows. Kendal opened her mini fridge to find something to dull the pain. Nothing but half a Kit Kat. She had to get outside. The countryside was the best drug. It was free, close-by and didn't have calories.

27

Kendal spent Monday at Carry On Camping's end of season sale buying comfortable walking boots, a sensible waterproof, Thermos flask and a pair of figure-hugging three-quarter length walking trousers. With the paisley shirt over a tight tee she looked totally fit, but not slutty. She smiled at her reflection in the mirror. She looked capable, organised, decent. She still had enough cash and time to pop into the expensive clothes shop next door and buy two pairs of new knickers. Just in case.

Gary met Kendal the next morning in the car park wearing firm-fitting, black trekking trousers and a wide smile. He looked much cooler than when he went to Dartmoor alone and had worn the grungy cargo pants. Perhaps he was dressing as carefully for her as she was dressing carefully for him?

"Great boots, Kendal," he said, and opened the passenger door. "Perfect for Dartmoor." He worked his way through the gears, and she made sure to keep looking forwards, not at him. Her new underwear was stimulating, she needed to calm down. Only when he walked across a garage forecourt to pay for petrol did Kendal allow herself a peak. Yep, he was hot to trot. Lucky she'd packed both pairs.

"How did your date go on Sunday?" asked Kendal. Jealousy needed to be lanced as quickly as possible if she was to enjoy the day without an aching stomach.

"A disaster, to be honest," said Gary. "The moment I said I worked at Jurassic Court I was off her menu."

"She sounds shallow. Better off without her, for sure."

Easy to keep the conversation flowing. It helped they were sitting beside each other instead of opposite. Gary was keen to review Pam's funeral, and Kendal was prepped with details about

Dartmoor's geology, history, and wildlife. By the time the car bumped over the first cattle grid marking the start of the National Park, they'd established a comfortable relaxed atmosphere. Away from Jurassic Court, with its complicated warden-client vibe and the constant gaze of residents or staff, Gary and Kendal could be two friends, sharing an interest in nature and the great outdoors.

They drove higher and higher, stopping only for ponies and sheep that wandered casually over the road. At last, they reached the car park. Gary unwrapped a flask. Kendal pulled out hers.

"Snap!" she said. "Great minds think alike."

"I've brought my special roast. Tastier than Carla's coffee."

"Mine's hot chocolate. In case we get lost and need sustenance."

"Unlikely, I've been walking up here since I was eight. Did the Ten Tors when I was fifteen. You'll be safe with me." Gary pointed at his rucksack "Map, compass, tick-remover, hypothermia blanket, water, everything."

Gary's enthusiasm was adorable. Kendal focused on the view. Unmarked roads stretched across heathland towards the horizon. Sky and moor, stone walls and mini mountains. She pointed to the nearest.

"One of the famous granite tors of Dartmoor, I presume?"

"That's where we're going. Bowerman's Nose. Supposedly the inspiration for Sherlock Holmes's *Hound of the Baskervilles.*"

"Glad we're here in daylight then." Banter was so easy.

Gary locked the car. "Let's apply our detective skills to nature."

Kendal grinned. Walking on Dartmoor was going to be a Building Rapport masterclass.

The path was springy, and a light breeze kept them comfortable. Gary stopped frequently to point at tors, tracks and birds, and Kendal remembered the correct way to pronounce plover. They reached the base of Bowerman's Nose tor and Gary handed Kendal a retractable hiking pole.

"I don't need a stick, I'm not that old," said Kendal.

"It's to steady you. You don't want to turn an ankle or knee. I'm going to use one as well." Gary pulled out the pole's twin and extended it expertly.

"Funny to think the others are having a perm or getting a corn removed."

"I'd rather not. Come on, let's get to the top."

Gary thrust his pole into the ground and pushed forward. It was a short, but steep ascent. When they reached the top he cupped his hands.

"Hello world!" he shouted. "You're looking beautiful."

Kendal smiled. He was so playful away from work.

They relaxed against the smooth, warm rocks. Gary trained his binoculars on a speck of a distant bird.

"A skylark. Amazing how they rise."

Kendal visualized the bird spotting sites she'd Googled.

"Second most numerous breeding bird on Dartmoor, after the Meadow Pipit."

"Phenomenal, well done."

Kendal pretended to look modest. "And one of my favourite pieces of music."

"I know this one," said Gary. "My grandfather's favourite too. *Lark Ascending.*" He whistled the soaring melody of Vaughan William's symphony. Kendal closed her eyes enjoying the sun on her face and a pleasant ache in her thighs. "Grandad took me here when I was small. He said it was better than all the rest of the tors."

"All one hundred and sixty," said Kendal.

"You love your numbers," laughed Gary.

"Numbers never let you down," said Kendal. "Tell me about your grandfather."

They ate hard-boiled eggs and apples while Gary talked about his grandparents who'd run a post office in Plymouth and looked after him during holidays.

"They sound really lovely," said Kendal.

Gary nodded. "They were. I miss them." He started to cough. "Sorry, getting a bit emotional. I don't normally talk about myself. Let's get moving. I want to show you a leat. A fantastic bit of engineering. Have you got some sunscreen?"

Kendal passed her tube of Factor 50. He rubbed it onto his face and neck and turned to face her. "All gone?"

"A bit on your nose."

Gary bent towards her. The sunscreen smelled delicious. She pressed her finger onto his warm skin. She could feel him watching but kept her eyes on the cream.

"All done, you're safe."

They began the descent. The hiking poles were, indeed, useful as stones slipped away and bracken concealed the many rabbit burrows. When they reached the flat path, Gary consulted his map and began walking towards a pine wood. A pair of butterflies danced in front of them. Kendal didn't want to risk another plover-lover mispronunciation. She should have practised how to say Fritillary.

"Are those brown, marsh, or pearl-bordered?" she said.

"Top spotting, Kendal," said Gary. "I think they are Marsh Fritillaries."

Now she knew the pronunciation. Like distillery. Easy to remember.

"Are we going to the pub later?" she asked.

"We are going to the best pub ever," said Gary. "But first you have to see a leat." He pointed at narrow stream with man-made stone walls. The gradient was so slight it was almost impossible to decipher which way the water flowed. "They carry water all the way to Plymouth."

Kendal washed her hands in the freezing water and opened her water bottle.

"Don't," shouted Gary. "Could be a dead sheep upstream."

Kendal grimaced. "Better get to the pub then."

The pub looked bleak, the kind of place where locals stopped talking as you entered. Good to use the loo though. Her sexy pants were quite uncomfortable. She hurried across the car park.

Gary was sitting by an enormous fireplace when she came out, his head below a large sign in Gothic font.

Our fire has been burning since 1845.

The barman added a log to the embers.

"What can I get you, guys?"

Smoke spiralled as the embers greeted the dry log. Gary ordered two pints of Black Tor, and a pasty to share. Kendal ate eagerly.

"That was fantastic. Must be the exercise."

"Or you're a proper lush local! Fancy another, Kendal?"

Kendal nodded.

"Pasty or beer?"

"Both."

Gary returned with a beer and a pint of orange juice. "Can't risk being over the limit. I did when I was younger, though. With mates from school. We'd drink all night, then drive home drunk. Hit a sheep once."

Kendal stared at the fire. The single log smouldered gently. It was cosy, even in the middle of June.

"Bit of a hell-raiser when you were young, then, Gary?"

"Worse in my twenties. The teenage stuff was pretty average."

Kendal knew Gary's messy past from Clare but was happy to hear it from the horse's mouth.

"I was hurting, Kendal. Dysfunctional family and all that. Didn't get inspired at school, hated Bloscombe. I should have gone away, but it was difficult. Plymouth was about as exciting as it got."

Kendal nodded gently as Gary's described his drunken rampages in dockyard pubs. Far tamer than Kendal's forty-eight-hour raves or regular coked-up nights in London. Best not to say that, she knew.

A cycling group clumped towards the door in weird shoes. Kendal sipped another beer. Gary had opened up. They'd built rapport, the day out was going wonderfully.

"It got worse though," said Gary. "I tried to create my own functioning family. Got married, had a baby, got a proper job. We got a mortgage. I thought I was grown-up."

"What happened?" asked Kendal, although she already knew.

"We split. She took the baby, and I went properly bonkers. Took the drinking to another level, smoked too much weed, lost my job, the house, and had a total meltdown." He placed a fresh log onto the fire and smiled at Kendal. "I'm bringing the day down. Sorry. You're so easy to talk to."

Kendal put her hands under her thighs, determined not to interrupt. The fire crackled as the new log caught. The cyclists looked at their phones, mounted the machines, and disappeared.

"There is a happy ending," said Gary "The boss who fired me kept in touch. He got a job in Singapore and kept sending photos. Banging on about islands and beaches and amazing food. Said he had plenty of space in his flat and I should come and visit. My ex wouldn't let me see the baby and I didn't have any rights because it turned out he wasn't mine so there was nothing for me in Devon. I'd never been further than the Isle of Wight. I hate flying and ferries, but I forced myself to get on a plane. That trip changed my life."

Kendal nodded. "Travel broadens the mind, doesn't it?" she said, trying to recall something transformative she'd done abroad other than drugs.

"Put my troubles in perspective, seeing how people live over there. My boss got me a job at a turtle sanctuary in Malaysia. A Muslim country – got me off the booze. Then I went to Sri Lanka and helped in an orphanage. Then to Sarajevo to help after the war. When I finally got back to the UK, Bloscombe was bliss: the dullness was suddenly very attractive."

Kendal tried to remember where Sarajevo was.

It was hard being an old person who never looked at their phone in public.

"Where do you go for a holiday now?" she asked, hoping it would be somewhere she knew. Mallorca, Ibiza or even London.

"I don't really do holidays. Hate flying and don't like being away from Jurassic Court for long." Gary pushed his lips tightly together. "So now, Madame Chair, you know the full dissolute history of your warden. Hope it wasn't shocking. Or boring?"

"Not at all, Gary. It goes a long way to explaining why you are such a caring, responsible, and energetic manager."

Gary looked at his watch. "If you don't mind missing supper I could drive us home the long way, so you get to see some other favourite spots."

"More moor! I'd love to!"

"And you can tell me your life story."

28

They drove across Dartmoor in the afternoon sun and Kendal delivered a sanitised account of the countries she'd travelled to, putting culture instead of hedonism at the centre of each story. Gary had to keep stopping and reversing to let camper vans squeeze past and didn't notice the pauses as Kendal struggled to remember the names of famous cathedrals or castles she might have visited.

They reached a car park by a fast-flowing river.

"Could you manage an ice cream, Kendal?" asked Gary.

Kendal nodded. It had been exhausting talking about her fake past. She deserved a treat.

Every seat in the café was taken by sweaty cyclists. Gary pointed to an empty bench on the other side of the river. "Let's go there. It's got a great view up the valley."

"Don't want to go in cold water again."

Gary's face crinkled with concern. "Of course, I'm so sorry. But don't worry, there's stepping-stones. Been there hundreds of years. Tourists used to dare each other to cross them. A Victorian version of bungee jumping or running with the bulls."

The riverbank was firm, the stones easy to step onto. They reached a large rock in the middle of the river. The water rushed, spritzing tiny waves and bubbles. Kendal swallowed the last mouthful of salted caramel and lay back on the warm rock.

"Kendal, sit up," whispered Gary. A streak of blue sped past. "Amazing, a kingfisher. With so many people around, you'd think he'd hide away. Keep still. He may come back."

Kendal shaded her eyes. "Perhaps we'll see an otter."

"Not on this river. It's too fast and public. If Prue was here, she would say the kingfisher is your spirit animal. Kingfishers are full of wanderlust. Like you! Kendal the kingfisher."

Kendal laughed. "I'm not fast enough to be a kingfisher."

"Kendal the kestrel then. But they can be terrifying."

Kendal was getting damp, and it wasn't just the river spray. She needed to get a grip. Dial it down, as the THRUm drones liked to say.

"What are your favourite birds, Gary?" Primary school level Rapport Building, but safe.

"Well, the Cornish chough is cool. The jenny wren is cute with her ability to make so much sound in relation to her size, and I love the sea parrot, the good old puffin."

"And which do you like the best?"

Kendal adopted the listening face she perfected at THRUm strategic review meetings while Gary delivered a comparative analysis of puffins, wrens and choughs. More interesting than football, cars or investment opportunities as delivered by the men in London bars but boring enough to calm her lust.

Just one more question and she'd be able to trust herself in the car again.

"Where's your favourite bird spotting place?'

"There're good places around the river Exe but if I was better on boats, I'd go to Gull Island. More than a hundred and thirty different species there. Sadly, I'm a terrible sailor so I don't go."

"Never heard of it," said Kendal. "Tell me."

By the time he'd detailed the wildlife and history of a tiny island off the coast of Wales, Kendal was back in a safe bubble of fresh air and platonic friendship.

"It's been great talking to you," she said. "You share your knowledge so generously."

"I do like a nerd fest," nodded Gary. "Not great for my personal life though."

They walked to the car and Kendal retrieved her Thermos flask. "Fancy a hot chocolate for the journey home?"

"Perfect," said Gary. "More sugar."

"How reckless we are," giggled Kendal.

They sat in the car, sipping side by side, looking at the view. The kind of thing her parents used to do. Innocent, but intimate.

A minivan entered the car park with a group of teenage boys who burst out of the doors followed by two anxious teachers. The youths charged to the river and began to leap across the stepping-stones.

"It'll end in tears," said Kendal.

"More stressful than a Well-being Walk," laughed Gary.

"I'd completely forgotten about the others. This is the longest I've been away from Jurassic Court since I arrived."

Gary wagged his finger. "Watch out, you don't want to become institutionalised."

Kendal frowned. "What do you mean?"

"No offence, Kendal. It can happen. Everything is laid on for residents at Jurassic Court and they can start to lose their ability to make decisions or express themselves as individuals. It helps to have other contacts or experiences outside of residential care."

A tall, ginger youth pushed a smaller, blonde boy into the river. One teacher shouted. The other removed his socks and shoes.

"I do have contacts outside of Jurassic Court," said Kendal. "There's Clare in the library and I've joined a book group. Aren't you being a tiny bit patronising, warden Gary?"

"Sorry. We've shared so much it feels I can say anything." He emptied the dregs of the hot chocolate. "To be honest, Kendal, a book group where one of the members wants to move into Jurassic Court is not exactly uncharted territory."

"How do you know who's in the book group? There are loads in Bloscombe. You can't know them all."

Gary sighed. "Sadly, I do. Bloscombe is a very close community; that's why I like to get out to Dartmoor or Cornwall. I could get institutionalised as well."

The teenagers jeered at their teachers. One pushed a bench over. Another kicked a litter bin. Gary gripped the steering wheel.

Kendal's head had begun to throb, and her stomach was cramping. She'd consumed too much sugar and carbs. "You don't know everything, Gary Vaughan." Her voice seemed to belong to someone else. The disassociation thing was starting again.

A teacher dragged the blonde boy out of the river while the other tried to right the bench. A seagull appeared out of nowhere to pick at the fallen rubbish. Gary clasped the door handle.

"Those lads are well out of order."

"Leave them, Gary. The teachers can handle it."

"It's not right." His lips were white.

Kendal grabbed his arm. "You can't control everyone, Gary."

"I don't." Gary rammed the key into the ignition and stamped on the accelerator. The car lurched forward.

"Steady, Gary!" she shouted. "You're a Quaker."

They drove across the moor without speaking. Kendal tried to count the sheep. The noisy bump of the cattle grid at the edge of the National Park shattered the silence.

"Sorry," they said in unison.

"I was being ridiculous," said Gary. "Vandalism does my head in."

"I was having a sugar rush," said Kendal.

The road wound through a thatched cottage village. The sun had dropped and was shining directly into the car. Kendal reached for the sun visor.

"Bit of a technique with that. It's broken," said Gary. He reached across and tugged at the shade. His arm was inches from her breast. She counted the hairs. A tractor pulled out in front of them and Gary slowed. The tractor was slower than Jennifer's mobility buggy.

"So, what should I be studying then?" asked Gary.

"What do you mean?" said Kendal.

"You said I didn't know everything. Be honest, Madame Chair. What should I know about?"

They chugged past the village green. An elderly couple threw bread at a duckpond, and the evening sun trickled over chimney pots. It was even prettier than Clare's village.

Clare was a cool person. Sixty, but chilled. Clare was kind, understanding, sweet. Clare had not freaked out when Fake-Kendal told the truth.

Kendal took a deep breath.

"It's not something you need to learn; it's something I must confess."

The tractor turned into a field. The driver waved.

"But I'm worried you might get angry again."

Gary waved back at the tractor driver. "Don't tell me you're a litter lout."

"Worse," whispered Kendal.

The road was empty. The hedges were higher than the car. Nothing to look at except the road. Gary opened the window.

"You think I'm too nerdy?"

"It's not about you, Gary," said Kendal. "It's me. I haven't told you the truth."

Gary rested his arm on the window. He waved at the hedgerow.

"The elderflower is fantastic."

Kendal sighed. She raised her voice. "I've lied to you. Please listen."

Gary slapped the side of the car. "You didn't visit all those countries? Made a good story though."

"No, I did visit them, but not as long ago as I said."

"It's easy to get dates mixed up. Especially as we get older."

Gary slowed the car as they approached a main road. This was it. They'd had a wonderful day; it was now or never. Kendal took a deep breath. "I'm not old."

"I'm often mixing up dates and I'm only forty-six."

The sound coming out of Kendal's mouth didn't sound like her. It was as though she was watching from above. Watching someone with a loud, ugly tone. "I'm younger than you! I'm forty-four."

"What?" The car stalled. Kendal lurched forward. The seat belt dug into her chest. Gary lowered his head, searching for the ignition. His hand shook on the gear stick.

"What? You mean you're not sixty?" Gary swore as the engine protested. "Are you saying you lied to me?"

Kendal longed to touch his hair, kiss the back of his neck, do anything but speak. Her eyes burned.

"Answer me!" shouted Gary.

Kendal crumpled. Now her voice was small. Childlike.

"I wanted to stay at Jurassic Court, and you said residents must be sixty-plus, so I added on extra years. Sixteen, to be precise. I'm forty-four."

"You lied. That's appalling. I don't... I'm not... oh my God!"

Gary pumped the accelerator and rushed onto the main road. A pantechnicon roared behind them. Kendal gripped the edge of her seat. She had to shout over the noise of the lorry.

"It's all so lovely at Jurassic Court. You run it so well, and I wanted to stay, and I didn't have anywhere else to live, and I've been wanting to tell you for ages, and we've had such a great day, and..."

Her words were obliterated by the overtaking lorry, its horn blaring and lights flashing. Gary began racing the enormous vehicle. His lips were white again. The car whined as he pushed it faster and faster. The lorry slipped behind.

"I'm so sorry, Gary. Please don't be angry."

The warden leered at the lorry in the rear-view mirror.

"Bloody moron. Eat dirt, mate."

They were nearly at Bloscombe. Gary had not spoken for forty minutes. Kendal trembled. This was horrible. Worse than the ring tragedy. She gritted her teeth.

"Are we OK? Gary?"

Gary gripped the steering wheel, staring straight ahead and saying nothing. They passed the business park and the tennis courts. Gary swerved into a lay-by and slammed on the breaks.

Dirty plastic bags spilled around a bottle bank. He snapped his seat belt and glared at the mess.

At last he spoke. "I hate lies, more than litter, Kendal," he announced in a quiet monotone. "You've lied to me, the other residents, all of us. Made a complete and utter fool of me. And you've committed fraud. I don't know what to say."

Kendal opened her mouth. Nothing came out. Angry people were the worst. They should be avoided. Given the finger. Walked away from. But she couldn't. She adored Gary. He was the kindest, most interesting, hottest, straight, single man she'd met. Ever.

But now he was standing in a pile of rubbish, picking up bottles and hurling them into the recycling skips. He was dangerous. Violent. And weird.

The warden efficiently separated green bottles from the white and brown. Furious, but still following the rules.

Hot tears ran down Kendal's cheeks. There was a stabbing pain in her stomach. She dug her nails into her arms and swore under her breath. Using the worst words she could think of and aiming them at herself.

Gary scrutinized a black bottle. No skips for black glass. He sneered at the bottle, hurled it into the green glass hole, wiped his hands on his trousers, and returned to his seat. The car shuddered.

"I will be informing the trustees about your deception immediately. It's up to them whether they take the issue to the police."

"The police? Don't be crazy, Gary. I'm not a criminal. Women lie about their age all the time. You're over-reacting."

"You have deliberately committed fraud, Kendal. Taking accommodation away from the people who need it. It's as bad as benefit fraud which people go to prison for. I'm sorry, but you will have to go."

"Look at me," shouted Kendal. "It's me. Your friend. The same person you were sharing pasties and jokes with. The person you told your life story to. For God's sake, Gary!"

Gary started the car and drove to Jurassic Court in silence. He pulled up outside the gates.

"I'm not coming in," he barked. "It's still my day off. Goodbye Kendal. Don't come to Gardening Club tomorrow."

"But Gary, can't we talk about this?"

The warden pushed across her and yanked open the passenger door. The hairs on his arm were threatening, not attractive. Kendal grabbed her bag and climbed out of the car as quickly as she could. No point moving slowly or grunting any more. Before she'd keyed in the pin code, he'd gone.

29

Kendal woke with period pains, hot flushes and a hangover. Her preference would be to spend the next day, week, month, or even decade day-drinking, but you couldn't clutch a glass of anything stronger than ginger cordial before twelve in Bloscombe without attracting tut-tut noises and stares.

Kendal trawled through the London clothes and selected a crop top, silver jeggings and strappy, gladiator sandals. She found her old make-up case and covered her pale face with deep tan foundation, thick eyeliner and scarlet lip.

The new reflection didn't look as good as she'd hoped, and the massive hoop earrings were agony. Kendal rubbed away a few layers of foundation and slapped Warm Nude on her lips to lessen the garish red. She still didn't look right. Perhaps it was the hair? She rummaged in the London bag and pulled out a floppy sun hat to cover the grey she'd spent so much time and money perfecting. Twisting in front of the mirror she peered at her bum in the tight jeggings. The crop top had revealed her black and white bird tattoo hidden for two months.

"Hello there, little swallow," she whispered. "You've had a good holiday in Bloscombe." She shook her hips, and the bird moved. "But you need to fly away now."

Outside, Kendal could hear Carla and Emma setting up the outdoor classroom for Gardening Club and the Fidget Blanket workshop. They were great women, friendly, fun, unjudgmental. Not like the alpha females at THRUm, always running marathons, detoxing and going on leadership courses. And now she had to leave them. All because of Gary.

Someone was knocking, despite the Unavailable sign. Kendal closed the blinds and tiptoed into the bathroom. She couldn't escape over the patio wall without bumping into Carla and Emma, and she didn't want to risk an encounter with the warden. It was probably Audrey, nagging her about missing yoga. She never gave up. Kendal stomped to the door.

Prue stood in the corridor, clutching a house plant. She thrust the pot at Kendal.

"A Boston fern."

"Very nice, Prue but I'm on my way out," said Kendal.

"You look exhausted, my dear," said Prue. "Let me feng shui this plant in your home. Won't take a moment." She side-stepped the clothes and placed the plant next to the ammonite on Kendal's table. "This beauty will help you sleep. Remove the toxins in the air." She scanned the room. "You need some living things to care for."

"Kind of you, Prue but I am late for an appointment at, um, the hairdressers."

Prue studied Kendal's face. "But Barry was here yesterday."

"I know," said Kendal. "But I was out. Went to Dartmoor."

Prue frowned. "With the warden?"

Kendal nodded.

"Did something happen? He had a terrible aura at breakfast too."

Kendal touched the fern. Its feathery leaves were soft and cool. Outside the residents were arriving for the activities.

"He doesn't like Carla's coffee," she attempted to joke.

Prue didn't laugh. "He's a very sensitive soul. I'm going to give him a Boston fern as well. They symbolise happiness. You two can have a competition. See whose fern grows the best. Keep it moist and feel contentment breathe into your space."

"Like that's going to happen," growled Kendal.

"What dear? Not sure I understand you," said Prue.

Kendal grabbed her backpack and rammed on sunglasses.

Wednesday was coach party day in Bloscombe, and the high street was rammed with slow-moving boomers gawping and taking up too much space on the pavements. Kendal stepped into the road. Better to be mowed by an electric bike than crushed by zombie pedestrians.

The library doors seemed even slower. Dominic, the library assistant, was tidying the noticeboard.

"Where's Clare?"

The library assistant dropped a tin of drawing pins. He slouched to the floor.

"Not in," he mumbled.

"So I bloody see," said Kendal, stamping her foot. She removed the sunglasses. A pin had stuck to the heel of her sandals. "Where is she then? It's urgent."

"At the council for an all-day meeting." Dominic crawled behind Kendal to reach a pin. "Can I help?"

"It's personal," said Kendal.

Dominic looked up. His pale face broke into a broad grin. "Love your tattoo. Like a swallow, do you?"

Kendal glowered. A gladiator sandal with drawing pin could do serious damage but Clare, her only friend, wouldn't want an injured assistant. She turned on her uncomfortable heel and limped to the prom.

The scratching pin put her teeth on edge. Still too early for a drink. She found an empty bench and texted Clare:

Hope you're nailing the council bastards.
I've told Gary about my true age. Massive mistake.
Desperate to talk asap.

The phone pinged. Not a reply. A reminder:

Walk Erica's dogs

Kendal pressed delete. Sod the stupid, pet-care business.

On the beach, a group of pensioners were erecting deckchairs and windbreaks whilst their small children unpacked buckets, spades and footballs. Boomer grandparents babysitting while their lucky children did proper jobs, earning normal salaries and living in houses they could afford. Safe, secure, and privileged.

She walked to her favourite bench. Almost eleven. At Jurassic Court the residents would be arranging flowers at Gardening Club, Audrey and Brian exchanging banter with Albert and Sam, or puzzling over the symbolism of dahlias with Prue. There would be one of Emma's special cakes and Kendal could have helped Wendy and Shirley whose fingers were not so nimble. Gardening Club was the perfect combination of learning and laughing. No PowerPoints, spreadsheets, or passive-aggressive feedback. Fingers in the mud and patience.

Just when she'd got into gardening, it was being taken away.

The bench wobbled. Someone had sat next to her.

"What's with the sad face, Mintcake?" Gig-club-Judy squeezed Kendal's arm. "Haven't seen you since our picnic dip. Hope you've recovered from your amnesia episode."

Kendal shifted along the bench. "I'm fine. But don't ask me to go rowing or anything."

"Anything in the sea, or anything physical?" said Judy, inching closer.

Kendal sighed. This woman never gave up. She was irritating, but at least she lived in the town, not Jurassic Court proving Kendal wasn't as institutionalised as pompous know-it-all Gary had claimed.

"How's Graham?" said Kendal.

"Busy, as ever. We've got the Gig Rowing Championships soon and he's instigated a tough regime. My muscles are getting tighter by the minute."

Judy held out her arm. "Feel my biceps." Kendal pinched her lightly. Judy squealed, and a passing deckchair attendance winked.

Judy pushed her thigh against Kendal's leg.

"Love your leggings. Wild for a Wednesday."

Kendal jumped away from her grasp.

"Ooh, and a sexy tramp stamp too. You're not a conventional Jurassic Court resident, are you Mintcake?"

Judy ran her finger over the wings of the bird tattoo and dipped down under Kendal's waistband. No one had touched that erogenous zone in two months. Kendal gauged her level of arousal. If day drinking wasn't feasible, maybe she could self-medicate with meaningless sex.

"You should get a kingfisher for your next tat," said Judy. She poked her finger in the groove between Kendal's buttocks."

Nothing! Her body was dead to the touch.

"Kingfisher blue is so vibrant. Like you. That'll cheer up the old biddies at Jurassic Court."

"I won't be there much longer. I've got to move."

"Worn Gary Vaughan out? Tragic."

"I've done nothing with Gary Vaughan," snapped Kendal.

"All right, keep your lovely hair on. Where you off to?"

"I don't know. I've got to find somewhere," mumbled Kendal.

Judy frowned. "It's the start of the season so all rentals will be booked by grockles. Mega expensive until September."

She thrust her arm through Kendal's. "Come on, let's walk. I'll get you a cornet."

Ice cream was as unappealing as sex with Judy. "I've got an appointment. At the hairdressers."

"Sad-face me," drawled Judy, pressing her forefingers into the sides of her mouth. "See you around, Mintcake."

Kendal's feet were starting to ache. The gladiator-sandal-drawing-pin combination was agonising. She missed her comfortable walking sandals and orthopaedic shoes. Hair By Barry was only five minutes away. She could see if they had a spare appointment. One less lie, and a chance to kill time until she could day-drink unjudged. It would be soothing to sit in the salon and let her feet recover.

Cheryl was vaping outside the salon. She nodded and held the door open. Kendal pulled off her sandal and examined her punctured foot.

"Vicious beasts," said Cheryl. "Fashion hurts, don't it love?"

Kendal pulled off her hat. The hoops jangled.

"Do you have space for me today?"

"Got a yummy mummy with twins at one, but nothing until then."

It was calming to sink into a chair and breathe the sweet chemical salon smells. Bloscombe and its boomers melted as Cheryl ran her fingers through Kendal's hair.

"Your roots are showing but the cut still works. You could have a full head or get away with a demi. If you're feeling flash, there's time for a balayage. I've plenty of slate, you could add a bit of steel. Your choice, love."

Kendal bit her lip. She wanted to be party-girl-Kendal again. A goddess who didn't give a damn about terms and conditions or tight-arsed blokes in one-horse towns.

"I'd like to go back to how I was before the, um, transition."

Cheryl grasped Kendal's ears. "The bleached blonde?" she gasped. "But it's so ageing. The silver is much better. Takes years off you."

Heat spread across Kendal's chest and sweat trickled between her breasts. The perimenopausal thing was infuriating.

"I want to be who I really am. Who I was."

"I can't stick the straggly hair back," said Cheryl. "But if you really want to be blonde again. I can change the colour."

Kendal stared at her reflection. Her face was scarlet. Would blonde go well with her perimenopausal complexion?

"Yes, please. Back to blonde."

"I'll get you a cuppa and mix the product. I'll switch on the fan too, love. Terrible thing the menopause, init?"

Kendal nodded. How did Cheryl know what was happening to Kendal when she didn't know herself? Yes, she had perimenopausal symptoms but she was only forty-four. Then again, she'd been young apparently to have the trans global amnesia episode. To find out if she was perimenopausal she would have to go the doctor probably. Horrible to think she would never get pregnant, not that she especially wanted to, but it was good to know she could. If Judy was right about the impossibility of finding somewhere to live in Bloscombe during summer, perhaps she should go back to Ealing for a while. At least she had a doctor there. She wouldn't have to lie anymore about her age.

Kendal got out her phone.

Hi M, hope you and Josh still loved up?
I'm moving out of Bloscombe. You were right about the dinosaurs.
I need to get back into reality. Can I have my room back, please?
Happy to pay a bit more if that suits?
K

Kendal sipped sweet tea and ate a plate of biscuits while Cheryl applied the bleach. She'd didn't like tea with sugar but in the old-fashioned hair salon, it tasted delicious. She closed her eyes and recalled the salon her mother went to when Kendal was very young. Probably pre-school. All the women were kind and friendly. They'd sit Kendal on a stool and feed her chocolates.

Her phone pinged. She'd forgotten how quickly millennials replied.

So Sorry K, no room at the inn here
Delighted to report I'm preggers already so we're moving out.
Josh's parents helping us buy a proper house. Yeh!
You should try it, hun.
M. xxx

Kendal swore and threw her phone into her bag.

"Bad news, love?" said Cheryl.

"Yeh, though probably good, to be honest," sighed Kendal. It would have been infuriating meeting Mad-Maxine and Posh-Josh again. Over-privileged, entitled twats.

"Just my bossy ex-landlord," said Kendal. "Always telling me what to do."

"There comes a time in life when you do what you want, not

what folk tells you," proclaimed Cheryl. "Like me, for instance. I'm done with perms. Don't want to do them, so dumped the stuff. No going back."

Cheryl would make a superb life coach. Or a masseur. Her fingers were incredible. More enjoyable being touched by Cheryl than swinger-Judy.

"If you're not doing perms won't you lose customers?"

"Get new ones, love. People like you who keep changing their look!"

There was an appealing warmth to Cheryl. Her jokes were easy to understand. Kendal smiled for the first time since exiting Gary's car.

Cheryl brought another cup of tea and a doughnut. "I'll give you a little trim, get the layers tidy, shall I?" Kendal nodded. Anything to stay in the chair and be cosseted. Soon she'd be back in the real world dealing with the consequences of her fraud. In two months, this sleepy Dorset town, with its strange shops and peculiar clubs and societies, had become more real than London. The beach, cliffs, and river so much more attractive than Ealing, or Islington, or any of the noisy, crowded places she'd lived in. The Albatross was more enjoyable and cheaper than any clubs in Hackney. Being by the sea transformed everything. And now she couldn't stay.

"Right, love. You're all done."

Kendal opened her eyes. A hairdresser was smiling over the shoulder of a trying-too-hard middle-aged woman with brassy yellow hair, cheap gold hoops, and a heavily made-up face. Mutton dressed as lamb. Kendal stuffed the doughnut in her mouth. She looked like trash so she might as well eat it too.

"Thanks, Cheryl, you're a star."

"If you say so, love. As long as you're satisfied."

Kendal squeezed her feet into the gladiator sandals. There was a swelling on her toe joint she'd not noticed before. Perhaps she was developing a bunion. Or arthritis. Delphine in the charity shop had been right. Orthopaedic shoes were far better.

"You can take a photo of my hair from the front this time if you like," said Kendal.

"Nah, you're alright," said Cheryl. She seized a broom. "Come back when you're in your next phase. Black, red, brown, whatever. Anything but green. Don't do green."

Kendal went to hug the hairdresser. Cheryl pushed the broom handle between them. "Cheers then," she said, and began to sweep.

Outside the salon, Kendal checked her phone. Nothing from Clare. Only an email from the council:

Dear Ms Tudge,
We have been informed by the warden of Jurassic Court that you do not meet the requirements for eligibility to reside in the retirement village.
With regret I must formally issue you with an eviction notice.
You must sell or sublet Flat 4 within one month or we will be forced to notify our legal partners.
On behalf of the management team and trustees of Jurassic Court, I would like to thank you for your efforts to improve the facilities and the support you have provided as Chair of the Residents' Association.
Yours sincerely,
Annabelle Mitchell
Senior Quality Assurance and Improvement Officer.

Gary hadn't wasted time; running to the blonde bitch at the Residents' Meeting with her grins and inappropriate hand touching and making her deliver his message. He was pathetic!

Doughnuts, sweet tea, and bitter fury did not mix. Kendal's stomach churned. She no longer craved day-drinking. She hurt all over; earlobes, toe joints, stomach, pride, heart but she simply wanted to remove the gladiator sandals, down some painkillers, and drink ginger tea.

Back at Flat 4 Kendal extracted her notebook from underneath the bed. A thin layer of dust lay on the cover. Kendal started a new page. Her final chapter at Jurassic Court:

Tudge Exit Strategy.
Find a job
Sell or rent Flat 4
Get the ring back
Punish Gary

Kendal didn't appear at Wednesday's supper or Thursday's breakfast so Audrey placed her yoga mat beside Kendal's patio. When her neighbour's clicking hips and dramatic exhalations became unbearable, Kendal pulled on leggings and slid open the French windows.

"Okay Audrey, I give in." Audrey feigned surprise and rose slowly. Her eyes focused on Kendal. For once, Audrey was speechless.

"Do you want a coffee?" said Kendal. "It's the good stuff?"

Audrey attempted to climb over the patio wall, but her exhausted hips would not allow it. She waved a finger in a hoop to mime she would walk the long way round. Plenty of time for Kendal to hide the empties and stuff the Tudge Exit Strategy into the box file.

"What in hell's name have you done to yourself?" said Audrey. She poked at a gold hoop.

Kendal grinned. "You don't approve of my new look then?"

"I certainly don't," said Audrey. "Who on earth did your hair?"

"Cheryl, at Hair By Barry," answered Kendal. "Sit down, I've got something to tell you. It's important."

"I knew something was up," said Audrey. "You wouldn't miss supper and breakfast otherwise." She reached for the mug with a shaky hand. Coffee spilled on the dining table. Audrey fumbled for a tissue and attempted to wipe the wood, her fingers wrinkled, the joints stiff and swollen.

"Don't bother," said Kendal. "This table will be going soon. And so will I."

Audrey gasped. Both eyebrows crazily high. "Are you ill? Have you had a relapse of your tranny global thing?"

"I'm fitter than I've ever been." Kendal touched Audrey's hand. "Your yoga and daytime raves keep me flexible but, I'm afraid, it's all got to stop. I'm leaving Jurassic Court."

Audrey's pale eyes filled. She pressed the coffee-stained tissue to her nose. "Why? I thought you liked it here. Is it Jennifer, has she upset you? I'm going to have a word with the old bat. More than a word, several words. And some will be rude ones."

Kendal shook her head. Audrey was not so canny. "It's not Jennifer. It's Gary. He's asked me to leave."

"What! Why would he throw you out? You're his favourite. He adores you."

Kendal reached across the table and patted Audrey's arm. She could feel the bony elbow. Not an inch of spare flesh. "Calm down, Audrey. It's all right. It's my fault, to be honest. Drink your coffee."

Outside, the ice cream van played the *Just One Cornetto* theme, which, thanks to all the music she'd listened to in the Kangoo, Kendal knew now was really called *O sole mio*. If only she was driving somewhere, listening to opera, and not having to talk to anyone.

Kendal took a deep breath, poured another coffee, and slowly explained why and how she had lied about her age. Audrey listened, eyes wide and lips trembling.

"I always thought there was something odd. You downward dog far too easily."

Kendal nodded "I'm truly sorry, Audrey. I wanted to stay here, and it seemed the only way to get round the rules."

A crunching sound was clashing with the ice cream van. Kendal gazed out of the French windows across the lawn. The warden was on the drive pedalling a rickshaw containing Brian and Philip waving like royals.

"Looks like the Chat Rickshaw is a success. Quite a queue. Jennifer's going to be cross if no one goes to Patriotic Pompoms," said Kendal. No comment from Audrey.

Kendal turned. Audrey was shaking with silent sobs, hands tight across her face, her breathing fast. Kendal froze. She wished Clare was with her, but the librarian hadn't been in touch since Saturday. Gary would know what to do but he was the last person she wanted in her flat.

She pushed the Boston fern towards Audrey. "Prue gave me this yesterday. It's for happiness. What do you think?"

The sobs had turned noisy. Deep and growling.

"Please stop, Audrey," pleaded Kendal. "It's horrible to see you so upset. Do you want me to get Brian?"

Tears streamed down Audrey's face, cutting a deep path through her face powder. She covered her eyes and whispered. "You're the same age as Brenda."

Kendal ran through a mental list of Audrey's favourite news and weather presenters. None of them were called Brenda. Could a dog live to forty-four? Perhaps it was a tortoise?

"Who is Brenda?" she asked. "I'm sorry, I've forgotten."

Audrey uncovered her eyes and stared at the floor. "My daughter."

Audrey had never mentioned children. No photos of girls in Flat 3. Audrey was well into her eighties. How could she have a forty-four-year-old daughter? Kendal was confused. She squeezed Audrey's shoulders and Audrey rested her head against Kendal's chest. Audrey's hair was soft with a sweet bubble-gum scent.

"I got pregnant at thirty-eight, which was ancient then. The father was married and wouldn't leave his wife. Same old story. I had to give her away. I didn't want to, but he made me. A beautiful little girl. Brown eyes and perfect fingers."

The ice cream van was out of hearing. No sound from the gravel drive. Everything was still. Kendal stared at her friend.

"I had three days with Brenda and then she was taken. They said the family was very nice. I think about her every day."

"Audrey, I'm so sorry."

Audrey wiped her eyes. "I thought we got on so well because you're Clem's kith and kin and he and I were such good friends. You don't have brown eyes, but, perhaps, you fill the space Brenda left. She would have been forty-four."

Jurassic Court had introduced Kendal to walking, classical music, Quakers, gardening, and the joys of wildlife spotting. It had also rooted out an empathy muscle which Dogbreath-Deirdre claimed was missing in Kendal. Audrey was sarcastic, bossy, and the way she mispronounced words was infuriating but, Kendal realised, she adored her.

"Perhaps I'm transmitting Brenda onto you?" said Audrey.

"You mean transferring."

Audrey frowned. "Transfers are like tattoos, aren't they? Except they wash off."

Kendal tugged the waistband of her jeans. "This one won't."

Audrey peered at the swallow on Kendal's lower back. She clapped her hands.

"Wonderful. My Brenda would have had one of those."

The two friends stood by the windows. It was Jim and Albert's turn in the Chat Rickshaw and Gary was struggling. Kendal tried to hide behind the blind.

"Don't be a sunflower," said Audrey. "Gary, and the stupid trustees, are ridiculous. You've nothing to be ashamed of." Kendal smiled. Gary did look a bit silly. He'd removed his shirt and was slumped on the saddle, semi-naked in a hi-vis vest and pink helmet.

"I think you mean wallflower, not sunflower," said Kendal. "But thank you."

"I don't care if you are forty-four, or ninety-four. I will always be your friend."

Kendal put her arm around Audrey's thin shoulder "You won't be around then."

"No, but I'll be keeping an eye on you," said Audrey. She wiped her nose on her sleeve and gazed at the cloudless sky. "From the great yoga mat up there."

30

Audrey spread news faster than any online platform. By the time the lunch gong rang every resident knew the warden had ordered Kendal to leave Jurassic Court. When Kendal entered the dining room all chatter stopped, reminding her of when her dad had died, and she'd entered the classroom officially an orphan and unofficially a tiny bit stoned.

Kendal sat at an empty table by the serving hatch with her back to the room. She could not face the people she'd fooled but she knew she had to eat. Later, she'd find a bar and drown her sorrows in private. Carla-from-the-kitchen placed a large plate of omelette and chips in front of her and whispered in her ear.

"Emma and me, we're gutted. It isn't fair and it isn't right." She pulled a mini bottle of Prosecco from the pouch in her tabard. "Knock this back, hun. We've got a secret stash for emergencies."

Kendal grinned and attempted to undo the screw cap.

"My dear, let me help." Philip was at her side.

"I'm better at bottles," roared a voice from behind. Brian had manoeuvred his walking frame past Philip. "Let me do it."

"Drinking, not opening them," boomed an even louder voice. Albert had joined the throng. "Give it to me."

Emma-from-the-kitchen thrust her face through the hatch. "Calm down, gents! Give the lady air."

Kendal twisted the cap herself and took a slug straight from the bottle. The bubbles hit the back of her mouth. Daytime-drinking. It had been a while.

"What's all the fuss, guys?" she giggled. "Too much Chat Rickshaw excitement?"

Philip gripped the salt and pepper pots. His knuckles were white, and his wrists flailed. Salt spilled across the tablecloth.

"Audrey's told us the dreadful news," he said. "And we're all very cross."

Kendal cut a corner off the enormous omelette. "Guys, I'm sorry. I didn't mean to deceive you."

Brian squeezed her shoulder. Albert patted her head.

"There, there, pet," said Albert. "We're not cross with you; we're cross with the warden. Gary's being ridiculous."

Brian shook his fist at his walking frame. "If I had more strength, I'd give him what's what."

"Me too," said Albert. "He's forgotten who pays his bloody wages."

Kendal forked a chip. "Are the others angry?"

Philip nodded. "Not with you, my dear. With Gary and his pen-pushers."

Kendal poured the mini-Prosecco into a water tumbler and swivelled to face the room. Everyone, even Jennifer, was grinning. Prue lifted her water tumbler in a toast.

"Here's to our marvellous Residents' Association Chair-Madam."

"Hear, hear," chorused the room.

Kendal tried to smile. She pushed the plate away, swallowed the last of the Prosecco and stood. She needed to breathe sea air and run properly. Get away from these kind, sweet, caring oldies.

Her phone vibrated. At last, a text from Clare.

A thousand apologies – it's been bonkers at work.
Will be out by three. Shall I meet you at The Albatross?
Hope you're OK. This will pass.
Big hugs.

Kendal worked steadily through The Albatross's Thirsty Thursday cocktail menu, only omitting number four since it was obvious Jurassic Cliff Collapse was merely a tarted-up Mudslide and she'd avoided creamy cocktails since a fridge in Magaluf cultivated bacteria even Spanish vodka couldn't kill. She'd reached number six when Clare arrived, red-faced and breathless.

"Fancy a Bloscombe Barney?" said Kendal as Clare collapsed into the seat. "On me."

Clare frowned. "I'm on your side, Kendal. Let's not argue."

Kendal waved the menu at Clare. "You numpty! It's a cocktail. With rum, coke, and Cointreau."

"Oh right, um, no thanks. Bit early for me. A cup of tea would be lovely." Clare waved at the waitress. "Tea for two, please." Kendal was swaying to the background jazz. "And something with carbs."

The waitress nodded sympathetically. "Freshly baked banana bread on the way."

"I'm so sorry this is happening, dear Kendal," said Clare. Kendal stared at the sea. Her hand reached across the table seeking the glass but finding a teacup.

"Where's my drink?"

Clare patted her hand "It's finished, love."

"So am I."

Clare pushed banana bread at Kendal. "There's no problem in the world can't be solved by a piece of cake."

Kendal shook her head. Bleached blonde hairs fell onto the plate.

"I hate banana bread! Hate my shitty hair. Most of all I hate…"

Clare took Kendal's hand. "Not me, I hope. I'm so sorry I couldn't get back to you."

"I hate Gary. What an arsehole!"

Clare gasped. "Gary Vaughan? What's he done? Oh my God, has he been, um, inappropriate?"

"He's thrown me out. Says I can't stay because I'm too young. Got the committee to cover him. He even threatened to bring in the police." Kendal waved her phone at Clare's face. "And Mad-Maxine, where I used to live, needs my old room because she's up the duff. I've got to find somewhere to go. And fast."

Clare moved her chair around the table and tried to hug Kendal. "You can stay at my place. Rebecca's down for half-term and leaving Colette with me, but I'm sure we could make room. I'm really surprised by Gary being so heavy. Not like him. To be honest I thought he had a bit of a crush on you."

"Only when he thought I was his age. Once I told him I was sixty he didn't give a toss." She tried to remember if Colette was dog, cat or child. "I've stopped doing the pet sitting. Can't be bothered."

"Explains the emojis Erica's been sending. You need to let your clients know your plans." Clare drained her cup. "Anyway, if Gary knows your real age won't that, um, rekindle his interest?"

"It has not. He is furious. He hates lies. It's all he sees. One big fat Tudge lie. Sorry, Clare but I can't stay in Plick. Or Boscombe. Or anywhere in Dorset. I can't be near Gary Vaughan. Pathetic, pompous, and scared of rules. Gutless. I've got to get away from him. Act fast."

Clare smiled. "Well, you're good at acting! You fooled all of us."

Kendal licked her finger at the crumbs. "Shouldn't have bothered. Got me in a right mess."

The waitress appeared. "Do we need more tea?"

Clare shook her head. "A Bloscombe Barney for my friend and a Messy Bird for me."

"And two more banana breads," cried Kendal. "Please."

Kendal scanned the beach. A jet ski buzzed along the shore and a red microlight whined over the cliffs. The sea was gloriously blue and calm. She sighed, grabbed her cocktail, and bit into the fresh cake.

"Anyway, Clare," she mumbled. "How's your campaign? Did you nail the bastards?"

"I think so. We had some powerful endorsements. Lady Almonds, the parent-toddler network and the Silver Surfers. I presented a convincing case, with spreadsheets and they liked the income we'd got from people like you donating good quality books. The best bit was when Dominic waltzed in and Super Glued himself to the ceremonial mace. That put the cat amongst the pigeons, I can tell you. They need it for the town criers' competition."

Hard to imagine the library assistant doing anything active.

"So will they close the library?"

Clare grinned. "They're going do another strategic review. Keep the pen-pushers busy till the next time the council needs to save money. Hopefully, I'll be sixty-seven then and get my pension."

Kendal attempted a hi-five. Failed. Didn't matter.

"You need a campaign too," said Clare. "To change the rules at Jurassic Court."

Kendal snorted. "No one's going to save me. I'm not something useful." She waved her hand in the air, but the waitress was looking at her phone. "Twenty-three years until I get a pension and they'll have raised the age again then, so probably loads more. Bloody Gary Vaughan. I hate him! Putting me out on the street because I lied about my age. Women lie about their age all the time. I just did it the other way round."

Clare stroked Kendal's shoulder. "Yes, Gary needs to get off his high horse."

"I've got to find a job and somewhere to stay pretty quick."

The sun was shining into Kendal's eyes. Kendal was sweating and her face was flushed. Alcohol and sun were perfect together in Spain in your thirties, but not in Dorset when you're probably perimenopausal.

Clare signalled for the bill. "Summer is the time to find employment that has accommodation provided. There's loads of tourist places looking for seasonal workers. You don't have to see it as a job, more like a working holiday."

Kendal rested her head on the table. "I don't have the energy for a working holiday, Clare. I'm too old."

Clare laughed. "Don't be ridiculous, you're in your prime."

Stumbling back to Jurassic Court, Kendal phoned the pawnbroker for the forty-fifth time. Still no answer. She collapsed into her bed and stared at the blank spaces on the wall where the maritime paintings had hung. She might never get them back either.

Sorry Pam, sorry Uncle Clem, sorry Audrey.

Sorry lovely residents and staff.

Not sorry, Gary.

The next morning Kendal woke with a mid-level hangover which Carla's special fried breakfast and a walk along the prom quickly sorted. She was tempted to throw Flat 4's key at Gary, drive to Exeter airport and buy a ticket to somewhere hot and happening. But alongside minor snags (overgrown beaver, no free parking at the airport, lack of intel about the happening places), were major problems making foreign escape tricky (credit card debt, out-of-date passport and the missing ring). Plus, Kendal realised she no longer wanted to be anywhere noisy, busy, or overpopulated. She preferred beaches, rivers, woods, and quiet little villages. It was genuinely fun to learn about fossils, beavers, and butterflies and she had to admit she didn't like getting wasted, feeling ashamed. She'd reconnected with childhood holidays and re-learned how much she loved being by the sea and breathing fresh air.

In the flat Kendal picked up the ammonite and held it tightly. The fossil had become a distraction tool, like a cigarette lighter, phone or vibrator. She made a large cafetière and started a fresh list in the *Tudge Exit Strategy:*

Live-in job preferences:
By the sea
No sharing rooms (or bathrooms if possible)
Not in Dorset or Devon (where might bump into Gary).
Remote (to deter Maxine and PoshJosh and their baby ever visiting)
Not involving solely old or young people. (A healthy mix where I can fit in).

The list was pleasing. Short, clear, and, hopefully, feasible. If only men were like lists (except the short bit).

Outside, residents gathered for the Friday Well-being Walk. Kendal peeked through the window. Prue, Audrey, Brian, Philip, Albert chatted and laughed. Kendal trickled water onto the Boston fern. Bit pointless really. Who cared if it died? Prue would, of course. But horrible Gary would probably gloat.

Kendal began researching jobs by the sea and discovered a bespoke site for southwest-based jobs called Wheresitto.com.

Clare was correct about the abundance of live-in jobs on offer. Some were dodgy (gentleman seeks flexible housekeeper) whilst others demanded skills even Kendal couldn't fabricate (expert orchid horticulturalist and cordon bleu chef). Most sounded like hard work in uncomfortable accommodation (fruit pickers, chambermaids, holiday park redcoats) which were fun for teenagers, but a nightmare for a middle-aged women craving her own bed, bathroom, and kettle.

Seconds later a headline caught her eye. Proper Job! As Carla and Emma would say.

Seasonal Staff roles at Gull Island
in The Mermaid Tavern and the island shop.
You may also be invited to join the auxiliary coastguard
or the island fire-fighting team
Ensuite bedroom accommodation, in stone-built cottages

Gull Island was the place Gary had raved about with loads of birds that he'd said he wouldn't visit it because he was a bad sailor. It was twenty miles off the coast of Cornwall and there were only two ways to get to there. By helicopter (Gary hated flying too) or by boat. Plenty of sea, lots of nature, a pub, a chance to meet firefighters but not Gary. She clicked the link for more information.

Yes, she was comfortable dealing with a wide range of people, she'd had a lot of fun with fire-fighters at a fireworks display in Clapham. No, she didn't have experience related to coastguards, but she'd used Clare's binoculars and looked at the coast. Big yes, she knew loads about pubs and working in teams.

Kendal downloaded the application form and texted Clare the link to the job.

You OK to be my referee?
I promise I won't let you down.
And let me know how much I owe you for yesterday"

Clare responded immediately. So it wasn't just millennials who did that.

> Of course. Great choice.
> Escape to an island. It's like Enid Blyton.
> I'll come and visit you there. Always wanted to go.
> PS The drinks were on me!!!"
> Followed by four gull emojis and three cocktail glasses.

The next Exit Strategy task was dealing with Flat 4. Kendal paced around the apartment imagining it through the eyes of a potential buyer or subletter. The furniture, books, and photographs were warm reminders of Uncle Clem to her, but a stranger might see mere clutter.

She packed the remaining hardbacks into the shopping trolley and filled her rucksack with Clem's knick-knacks. She wrapped the charity shop beads, brooch and pearl necklace in the floral scarf. She would keep the studs. They'd be good in an outdoorsy kind of environment like Gull Island. Plus, she had to admit, they were way more comfortable than hoops.

The residents were eating as Kendal pulled her trolley along the corridor. A couple of reedy voices called a greeting, but she'd spotted the warden's tight shorts leaning over Shirley to open a jar and she couldn't witness him being kind. She had to think only nasty things or she would dissolve. No more Gorgeous-Gary. He was Glowering-Gary, or maybe, Gutless-Gary? Psycho-Gary?

Passage to Pages, the second-hand book shop, was closed, and the library had a sign on the door, presumably written by dyslexic Dominic: NOMOOR HADBACKS THANKS ATM WEAVE RUN OUT OF SPACE.

The shopping trolley squeaked horribly. Kendal needed to dump the books.

Delphine, the volunteer sales assistant in the cancer research shop, greeted Kendal enthusiastically. "Hello again, lovely lady. Wonderful to see you."

Kendal pushed the trolley forward. "I've got books to donate."

Delphine frowned. "Big sellers?" She waved around the shop. "Don't have room if they're not."

Kendal nodded. "Er, yes. They're huge."

"Can you leave them in the sorting office at the back? Dolly-the-book-volly isn't in till Monday."

The back room was crammed with clothes rails, bin bags, and plastic crates of old toys. Dust motes spiralled from ill-fitting carpet squares. Two women in tabards cleaned trousers with a hissing steaming tool while an old man in a blazer and tie examined boxes of jigsaws. They all turned to look at Kendal.

"Better be good stuff," said a tabard woman.

"Not rags," added the other.

"And no missing pieces," barked the man.

"Books, in good condition," she said. "Bestsellers,' (true, half a century before). "I'll leave them here. You can have the trolley too."

The tabard ladies clapped. "Trolleys always sell."

Kendal handed the trolley to a tabard lady and emptied the knick-knack filled rucksack onto a shelf.

"Very generous," beamed blazer man. "Your donation will save lives."

"Right," said Kendal. "You can't keep my rucksack though." She grabbed the empty rucksack sending plastic horses and towelling teddy bears onto the carpet.

Kendal picked up a plastic horse and a vivid memory popped up of from childhood when she'd been desperate for a blue My Little Pony and sulked all Christmas Day when a pink one was unwrapped. It was one of the rare times she could remember her dad shouting. It was scary. Looking back, he'd been right to be angry. The tumour which would kill her mother was probably already pushing onto her brain. Gutless-Gary had no excuse to be so angry. His anger was disproportionate to her mistake. What was the insult people hurled at each other now? Oh yes. Gutless-Gary was a narcissistic knob!

At the fish and chop shop Kendal ordered cod, chips, and mushy peas, with two cans of orange. She packed the food into her rucksack and strode to her favourite bench. The batter was crispy and peppery, the fish moist and firm. The sea gulls kept their distance.

Kendal's phone buzzed. With greasy fingers she pressed accept.

"Ms Tudge?" Welsh accent. Not a junk call, then. They were never Welsh.

"Yeh," said Kendal, through a mouthful of chips.

"Cai Evans here. Gull Island Operations Manager. About your job application."

Kendal swallowed. "Hi, Cai," she said and giggled. The greeting sounded like a cocktail or a martial art. "I mean, hello, Mr Evans."

"We got your application. You're the right kind of person for us. And the right kind of age too, if you don't mind me saying."

There wasn't a question about age on the form. It was discriminatory, wasn't it?

Mr Evans continued. "Senior people get too tired, and young people, who might be fitter, can't handle the insular nature, if you get my drift. But it looks like you're in the middle, judging by your job experience. Am I right?"

Kendal zipped the rucksack to protect the fish and chips.

"Ms Tudge? Are you there?"

"Yes, sorry. Please call me Kendal. Yes, you're right. I'm forty-four. I am in the middle. I'm middle-aged. But very fit and I've been in living in – um – an insular community for three months."

"Thank you for being honest, Kendal. Lovely name, by the way."

"It's where my parents met. They loved the great outdoors and nature." She stared at the sea. The rowing gig was gliding westwards. "And so do I."

"You'll love it here then. We have plenty of weather." Mr Evans laughed. "One more very important question. And call me Cai."

Kendal pushed the phone close to her ear. She hoped it wouldn't involve sales targets, food hygiene legislation, or a request for a referee other than Clare.

"Yes, Cai. Go ahead. I'll answer as best as I can."

"When can you start?"

31

Kendal had rung the pawnbrokers ninety times. There'd been nothing more about the robbery on the news. The police wouldn't be watching the building. It was time to act. She'd got a job, cleared the flat, and now she must get the ring back.

Kendal pocketed the comforting ammonite and drove to Bournemouth as fast as she could. She was rushing, but took care to observe the speed limits, wary of adding motoring offences to the list of crimes Gary had accused her of.

The suburban street was empty, the pawnbroker's curtains tightly drawn. Kendal stood on the doorstep and rang the bell. Nothing. She knocked. Nothing. She peered through the letter box but a thick draft excluder blocked any view.

"Hallooo, anyone there?" she called. Nothing. She dialled the pawnbroker number and listened to its ring inside the house.

After twenty minutes Kendal returned to the Kangoo. In Audrey's police dramas the next scene generally involved police officers knocking at doors but this wasn't going to happen. She would have to solve this herself. She walked up the path of the next-door bungalow. What if someone there recognised her? She rang the neighbour's bell.

In the corner of her eye something moved. A curtain in the pawnbroker's!

Kendal stomped back to the pawnbroker's door. She rang the bell and thumped the door simultaneously.

"I know you're in there," she shouted. "I must speak to you."

A wobbly female voice answered. "What do you want?"

Kendal gripped the ammonite in her pocket.

"I need to retrieve some important jewellery. I have the money." No answer.

"I'm very sorry about the robbery, but I must get my friend's ring. It's vital." She heard sniffing. "Is Mr Field all right?"

"How do you know about the assault? Who are you?"

"My name is Kendal Tudge. I'm a client of Mr Field. I read about it in the *Echo*."

"My husband is in hospital. We're not open. You're going to have to wait."

"Was anything stolen, Mrs Field?"

"Fortunately, not. My husband put up a fight."

"Do you have access to his safe, Mrs Field? I'm going – um – overseas for a new job. I can't go unless I return this ring to my friend." Hard to break the lying habit, but Pam's great-grandson was friendly, and Gull Island was surrounded by sea.

"I do, but I don't know if my husband would be happy if …"

"Look, it's a blue sapphire with diamonds, I have the receipt, and Mr Field will know who I am. I'm… a colleague. He's contracted me to do some freelance work."

"My William doesn't use contractors. He works alone."

"Mrs Field, you sound like someone who has experienced a lot of life. Do you have time to hear my story?"

"You've got five minutes," said the wife. "And then I'm calling the police."

Kendal took a deep breath and stroked the fossil's grooves. "Well, I live in a retirement home, even though I am not old enough, and I have a lot of debts…."

It was weird telling the truth. Especially to a door. She couldn't see how it was being received. But telling the truth meant freedom from constantly thinking ahead to before she spoke. It was a relief to confess her mistake to a stranger. Perhaps she should become a Catholic instead of a lightweight Quaker.

Mrs Field said nothing. She might be calling the police.

"Which is why I have to get the ring back," concluded Kendal. "I can't make it all right for poor Pam, but I can return it to her great-grandson and disappear with a clear conscience. Sort of."

"William sometimes shares the reasons people pawn precious possessions. Sad stories mostly. But yours is one of the oddest."

Kendal squeezed the ammonite. Would telling the truth work?

"I'll check with William this afternoon. When'd you want to come?"

"I'm booked on a ferry on Monday. So, any time before then."

"I'll do my best."

Result! Kendal kissed the ammonite.

Rosie from the book group was thrilled to rent Flat 4 from Kendal.

"Perfect timing," she said when Kendal rang. "The school holidays start soon, and my dreadful family are about to descend on Grandma for their annual free holiday. If I move into your flat they can make as much noise and mess as they like in my house, eating takeaways and covering the carpets in sand. I'll simply sit in the sun on your patio, have all my meals cooked for me and occasionally grace them with a visit. Wonderful!"

Kendal explained she hadn't decided if she would eventually sell the flat or whether Gary would insist on installing a permanent tenant. Rosie wasn't concerned.

"It's the ideal way for me to find out if I like living in sheltered accommodation," she said. "Name your price."

Kendal didn't know how much Jurassic Court's renting residents paid but since she had nothing to pay until January, anything Rosie gave was a bonus. She still owed two thousand on her credit card.

"What about five hundred a month?"

"That's chicken feed!" said Rosie. "Full board and activities, in peak season? Let's say a thousand. In cash. I'll bring it round."

Kendal opened her notebook and amended her list:

Tudge Exit Strategy
Find a job✓
Get the ring back ✓ (almost)
Sell or rent Flat 4✓
Punish Gary

The start of the school holidays had transformed Bloscombe as the resident boomers shared space with holidaymakers clutching children and bags-for-life instead of shopping trolleys.

The Carry On Camping assistant welcomed Kendal like an old friend and was delighted to put together a weather-proof kit for a tiny island in the Bristol Channel. She folded an array of waterproof and moisture-wicking clothes into a red frame backpack.

"The DFLs only want crocs and fleecies," she said. "It's great to sell proper gear. As Wainwright said, there's no such thing as bad weather, only unsuitable clothing. You'll survive anything the elements can throw at you with this lot."

Kendal spotted a box of skiing hats on the top shelf. It would be nice to have something to protect her highlights.

"Out of season, so they're BOGOFF," said the sales assistant.

Buy-one-get-one-for-free was a familiar acronym, but what was DFL? No need to pretend to know anymore. She could simply ask. Be honest.

"What's DFL, and who is Wainwright?"

The sales assistant pointed at a braying couple trying on sun hats.

"Down From London," she whispered. "The people who make it impossible to rent here. Wainwright is the greatest writer about walks." She pointed at the walking snacks and selected a bar of Kendal Mint Cake. Kendal braced herself. "He lived in Kendal, where he wrote all those guides to the Lake District. They named a shopping centre after him."

Acronyms were handy, and Kendal was a cool name.

The independent shops which had appeared so pointless when she first arrived made total sense now Kendal had cash and friends to buy presents for. She filled her new rucksack with fudge, ammonite-shaped coasters and Baileys Miniatures. She bought a Margaret Thatcher corkscrew for Jennifer in Mines-a-Double off-licence and sorted Clare's present at Peninsular-Pets who had a 2-4-1 deal on catnip books for cats.

Kendal was buying wrapping paper and cards when her phone buzzed. It was the pawnbrokers. Kendal wished she had the lucky ammonite to hand.

Mrs Field's voice was louder than before. "I've talked to my husband. He's happy for you to collect the ring as long as you bring cash, and he says take your paintings and medals too. Does that make sense?"

Kendal beamed. "Yep, thanks. I'm on my way."

The road to Bournemouth was rammed with camper vans and caravans but Kendal channelled a Quaker vibe and avoided shouting, swearing or dangerous overtaking and reached the pawnbrokers calm and relaxed. She handed Mrs Field the money, and the pawnbroker's wife relinquished the ring, maritime paintings, and medals in return. Kendal offered the stack of advertising leaflets.

"I didn't distribute these once I heard about the burglary. But you could use them later."

"No need," smiled Mrs Field. "William has decided to sell the business. He wants a stress-free, safer career. He's going to staff a school crossing. Not well paid but something to get him up in the morning."

Kendal nodded. Lollipop man! Perfect for the creepy pawnbroker and cheaper than Viagra.

Kendal placed the paintings on the back seat and clipped the seat belts around the frames. She zipped the medals and the precious ring into her backpack and turned on the radio. Crazy, squeaky jazz but she didn't care. All music was fantastic, now she'd got the ring.

The dodgy strawberry seller was in the lay-by again. With a different sign: Lowcal Cherreees

Kendal parked to buy a box. Bad spelling didn't irritate anymore.

The ground was covered in cherry stones.

"You know he has pips, yeh?" leered the seller.

Kendal nodded. "Stones. Yes, of course."

Cherry-man smiled. His teeth were stained with juice. "Come back next year they'll be cherry trees here."

It wasn't true. But Kendal didn't care about other people's lies. Or mess. Lies and mess. A title for her life once. But not anymore.

Carla and Emma were preparing supper when Kendal returned from Bournemouth.

"Heh, ladies. Can I ask a favour?"

"Anything for you, doll," said Carla.

"Can I borrow some cleaning stuff, to make my flat nice for my tenant?"

"You don't need to clean it, love," said Emma. "Might be tricky to get into the corners. We'll get the staff to do it for you."

Kendal laughed. "Remember, I'm not old. I actually can bend properly."

Emma grinned and handed Kendal a bucket of bottles. Carla passed the broom.

"Enjoy yourself, Mrs Mop."

Kendal's flat looked better with the shelves cleared of knick-knacks and the maritime paintings covering the faded patches. It really was the perfect space for one person to live in. People don't need great big homes. Just somewhere to sit, wash, sleep, cook and read. Kendal opened the French windows. The air outside was still warm and she could smell the sea. She washed the cherries and placed them close to the Boston fern and the ammonite. She perched the ring on the top cherry.

"I'm truly sorry I took you," she whispered. The fern trembled.

Kendal popped a cherry into her mouth. Deliciously sweet. She ran her tongue over the hard stone, pursed her lips and propelled it across the room. It rolled under the bed. Kendal bent to retrieve it, squeezing herself under the bed and shining her torch to see through the cobwebs and dust. Emma was correct, it was tricky to clean under the heavy bed and it was obvious no one had for a long time. She chuckled as she found the cherry stone, now covered in hair and dust. This was the answer! The perfect spot for Pam's ring to be re-found.

Kendal ran into the bathroom and opened her make-up bag. The mascara she no longer wore was sticky and lumpy. She dabbed it onto the ring then transferred the cherry stone's dust onto the gloopy mess. She stared into the bathroom mirror, widening her eyes and aping shock. Her last bit of acting.

"Girls, girls! Look what I've found!"

Carla slammed the fridge door. "All right, Kenny girl. What's occurring?"

"I'm deep cleaning my flat. I pulled the bed right out and found this."

Kendal held the ring out. "Blue, with diamonds is what Pam said, isn't it?"

Carla whistled.

"Lemme see," squealed Emma.

Kendal passed the ring. "Be careful, it's mucky. Filthy under my bed."

Carla started to cry. "Poor Pam. She hadn't gone doolally, after all."

"Poor you, Carla, as well," said Emma. "I bet a few of the residents believed her accusations about you and the cleaners in cahoots." She handed Carla a glass of cooking sherry. "Drink this, my lovely. You've had a shock."

Carla pushed the drink away. "How did it get in your flat ?"

Telling the truth might get tricky here. Kendal spoke carefully.

"No one cleans under beds. Pam came into my flat for a Digital Drop-in, but she didn't lie down. Anyway, she had already lost it." All true statements.

"It must have happened when Clem was there," said Carla.

"Unless he took it from her room," said Emma. "Or hid it for someone else."

Kendal frowned. "Uncle Clem was an honourable man. He wouldn't have."

"She was sweet on him," interrupted a voice through the serving hatch. Prue's head came into view. "Clem was quite a catch. Single, intelligent, relatively fit."

Carla and Emma smiled. Kendal nodded. This was going well.

"She was disappointed when he made it clear he wanted to stay a bachelor," continued Prue. "We all were. But we accepted it. Happy to be good friends and neighbours instead. That's the power of Jurassic Court. Living with other people, but also alone."

Emma nodded. "We're always on hand, Prue. Us or Gary."

"Never mind that. How did the ring get under his bed?" insisted Carla.

"I'm no detective but there are any number of possible reasons," said Prue. "She could have put it there herself. To have a reason to keep visiting. She was always knocking on his door. Clem was such a gent. He didn't like to be rude."

Kendal could hug Prue. This was excellent help. No need for lies. If she had more time, she would accompany Prue on the longest, dullest fossil hunt.

"We will never know why Pam lost or hid her ring in Clem's flat," said Prue. "But we must thank Saint Anthony for finding it. The saint of lost things."

Emma was cleaning the ring with silver polish. She held it into the light. The diamonds glinted. "So, what you going to do with it, Kenny girl?"

This was easy. "Give it to whoever inherited Pam's estate. Obviously."

"Best it go to Gary then," said Emma. "The boss will know what to do."

Kendal frowned. "I'm trying to keep out of Gary's way. Could one of you take it to him?"

"You trust us then, Kenny?" said Carla.

"Of course, I do," said Kendal. "I never believed you were involved."

Carla started crying again. Emma re-filled her glass.

"Don't forget it's my choice for Movie Night this evening," said Prue. "You young women might learn something. Julia Roberts escaping a messy life to find happiness abroad."

Eat, Pray, Love was relatable (though a stretch to match Gull Island with Italy, India, or Bali) and Prue's introduction would've been enjoyably bonkers, but Kendal couldn't be near Gary.

"Apologies Prue, but I have to pack. I'm leaving on Monday."

Kendal didn't need an influencer tell her how to cull her wardrobe. It was simple. She would only pack the new gear from Carry On Camping, Clem's jumpers, her jeans, shorts, T-shirts and bikini, and everything else could be dumped. When she returned from Gull Island to go travelling, or move elsewhere, she would buy new clothes. Cool, stylish but age appropriate.

Everything must fit into the new rucksack and her old backpack. The laptop made the team, but the Kindle didn't and, having double checked she'd packed the correct chargers, Kendal sacrificed one vibrator. She removed the photo of her parents from the heavy frame and slipped it carefully between her jeans and waterproof trousers.

The lawn and garden were deserted. Everyone was at Movie Night. Kendal opened *The Tudge Transformation Toolkit* notebook and scanned the material she'd handwritten before the laptop arrived. The fake CV was no longer needed, nor Boomer Banter, and the Ageing Insights pages were nonsense. The only useful section was Nature Notes. She folded those pages into the new rucksack, carried the metal waste-bin onto the patio, and began to burn the rest. The residents knew she'd been a fake, but nobody should read her crib notes with their offensive observations and opinions. She'd got so much wrong. Bloscombe wasn't boring and older people were not to be lumped into one, amorphous demographic. She wouldn't call anyone a boomer again. Or a millennial.

Kendal packed the second vibrator, medals, and Kindle into her old pull-along suitcase, alongside the orthopaedic shoes and Clem's collection of hats. She lifted the case onto the top of the wardrobe. Something to open in the future when, or if, she had more room. Her legacy. Though she had no one to leave it to.

The next day was Kendal's last at Jurassic Court. She couldn't face Gutless-Gary so she missed breakfast and asked Audrey to send her apologies to the Quaker Meeting.

"I understand, sweetheart," said Audrey. "I'll say a silent prayer for you."

The last task in the Tudge Exit Strategy was Punish Gary but it no longer seemed necessary. Only one more day at Jurassic Court and she'd never have to see him. They'd have to communicate about the flat but face to face contact was over. Kendal was moving on and Gary was history.

Carla's Sunday roasts were the best, but she couldn't risk seeing the person-whose-name-she-would-no-longer-say. Kendal slipped into trainers, sprang over the patio wall, and jogged to the beach. The Albatross offered a roast lunch too. Vegan, overpriced, and served on silly sharing plates, but the sea view was superb, and the waitress knew her gin.

Afterwards, Kendal strolled along the prom. The sea was the most crowded she'd seen it. Weekenders in wet suits, locals without. It was her last time on Bloscombe beach for a while. Kendal decided to collect her costume and towel and give the sea a try. It was warm and safe. She must seize the moment.

On Sunday afternoon, Jurassic Court's benches were normally overflowing with snoozing, well-fed residents but, today, the gardens were deserted as Kendal walked up the drive. There was no one in the foyer and the dining room, already set for supper, was empty too. Someone was giggling somewhere.

Probably Carla and Emma smoking outside the kitchen. She glanced into the day room.

"Surprise!" A noisy cheer greeted Kendal from the circle of chairs and sofas. A home-made banner dangled over the movie screen:

BON VOYAGE KENDAL

Kendal gasped. They were all there: the residents, Carla and Emma, Joe and Linda, the gardeners. No warden. Audrey hurried to the door. "Gary sends his apologies, Kendal. He has something urgent to do somewhere. But he sends his best wishes."

"Really?" said Kendal.

"Well, no," answered Audrey. "He's too proud because he has a title."

"The warden has a title? Like Sir or Lord?"

Philip steered Kendal into the room. "She means entitled," he whispered. "As a straight white male." Philip was talking like someone from THRUm. Philip winked. "Your Digital Drop-in teaching has opened me up to so much, Kendal. I'm thinking of coming out."

There was no time to respond to this as Kendal was propelled to a reclining chair. Carla thrust a glass of Prosecco into Kendal's hand and Emma pushed a packet of Kit Kats onto her lap.

"We're going to miss you, my lovely," said Emma. "Though we won't have to buy so many of these now."

"Did you know I was taking them?"

"Course we did, my luvver. You only had to ask."

Jennifer clinked her glass. "I can't condone what you did, Kendal, but I can't condemn you either. Jurassic Court is Shangri-La, and it is plausible one might step over the mark in order to remain here. But, as the great Margaret Thatcher, used to say…"

Prue interrupted, "Or, as the Sufi mystic said, if you never know forgiveness, you'll never know the blessings God gives."

Albert waved his stick, "Or, as the Wurzels sing, 'I've got a brand-new combine harvester and I'll give you the key'." Kendal felt her eyes prick as the residents joined in. "Come on now, let's get together in perfect harmony."

Brian switched on his music system. Madonna's *Express Yourself* reverberated around the day room. "I've downloaded an eighties selection," he shouted. "To remind you of your real teenage years."

"Ta, da!" shouted Audrey, dragging a curtain off a large lump on the floor to reveal a mini-trampoline, complete with safety rail and bottle of hand sanitiser. "It's for us to rebound on. You can have the first go, Kendal."

Kendal grabbed the rail with one hand and held her glass in the other. The trampoline was extremely springy and she was grateful for pelvic floor exercises but regretted not wearing a sports bra.

"Let's get this party started," whooped Audrey.

"Wait for me!" shrieked a familiar voice. Clare stood in the doorway clutching two bottles of Prosecco. "What on earth are you doing, Kendal?"

Kendal waved. "I'm on the rebound!"

There was something exhilarating about the trampoline. When Kendal wasn't bouncing, she was supporting a resident. The fear of falling, which spoiled so many physical activities for older people, was removed as they gripped the handrail and the staff moved close. Carla placed a mop and bucket nearby.

When the residents had bounced enough, Emma brought in tea and cake. Kendal collected her bag of presents and sat on the sofa with Clare.

"You all set then?" said Clare. "I'm going to miss you."

"I'll have my laptop. We can probably Facetime or at least email," answered Kendal. She handed Clare her present. "A little thank you for the boys."

"Books for cats!" squealed Clare. "Who would've thought such a thing exists. You are such an original, Kendal Tudge." Kendal beamed.

All the residents were thrilled with their gifts. Jennifer insisted on finding a bottle with a cork to use her Margaret Thatcher corkscrew. As Albert manfully twisted it around a bottle of vintage claret, she started to giggle.

"Our great leader astride a red. Extraordinary!"

One by one the residents shuffled over to hug Kendal and whisper messages of support. It was like Clem's funeral, except this time it was Clare next to Kendal, and the accolades were for Kendal not her uncle.

"I'll think of you every time I mount the Rascal," said Brian.

"I'll remember you with each paper straw," said Prue.

"I've ordered a new wig," said Wendy. "So, I can look like you."

Everyone thanked Kendal for helping with the new technology, the Residents' Association, the activities, and the important role she played in rescuing Albert from hospital. No one was upset about her pretend age. Kendal suspected Wendy and Shirley hadn't even understood it.

Kendal had never felt so liked. It was almost overwhelming. Kendal didn't want things getting messy so she sipped instead of glugged the Prosecco, avoided the claret and refused a mini-Baileys. It was enough to sit next to Clare and be herself, amongst good friends. When Brian began to pack up the disco, and Emma and Carla put on aprons, Kendal realised she hadn't thought about Gutless-Gary all afternoon. Well, not much.

A few residents enquired where Kendal was moving to and she was able to be both truthful and vague. "Overseas to see a bit of the world."

Only Audrey insisted on specific details. "So, I can write to you. Keep you informed about the Anti-Grave Raves and let you know if your tenant is behaving anti-socially."

"You've mastered email, Audrey," said Kendal. "We could communicate online. It's quicker and no cost. You can send attachments too."

"Brian's too big and I can't spare him."

Kendal laughed. Audrey-banter was the best in the world. She owed it to Audrey to tell the truth. "I've got a job and accommodation on Gull Island, an island off Cornwall, but don't tell anyone. I don't want Gary to find out."

"Cross my heart, I'll not tell." Audrey mimed zipping her lips together. "And if I do by accident then don't worry. The old biddies here remember nothing for long."

Kendal shook her head. "Don't make assumptions about older people, Audrey. It's ageist and inaccurate. Believe me, I know."

Audrey and Clare hugged Kendal. Tears threatened. Kendal extricated herself from their embrace.

"Got packing to finish," she mumbled and sprinted to her flat; the first time she'd run inside Jurassic Court.

At her door, she unpinned the Busy-Available sign. Could be useful on Gull Island. With pub, shop, coastguard, or fire-fighting work she was going to be busy. With no Gary, she might possibly be available. Kendal slipped the ammonite into the last space in her backpack, double checked the route to the ferry terminal, closed the blinds on the French windows and lay down. Her last night in Flat 4.

Leaving Jurassic Court and her friends hurt like hell.

32

Most of the ferry's passengers were vomiting but Kendal felt fine. Better than fine. If she was a millennial, she'd have said awesome. If she was a boomer, tickety-boo or on cloud nine. But Kendal didn't need another generation's colloquialisms anymore. As a forty-four-year-old, solvent woman, embarking on an adventure, Kendal felt fucking brilliant.

"What can I get you, love?" said the barman. "We've got ginger tea if you're queasy."

Kendal surveyed the bottles mounted behind his head. "Rum, please. Double."

The barman grinned. "Proper pirate, aren't you?"

"And have one yourself," said Kendal.

"Don't drink on Mondays, but thanks. Any ice?"

Kendal shook her head. "Best to avoid it on a boat."

"Don't get you."

Maybe sailors never watched *Titanic*. Kendal shrugged. Her stomach warmed to the rich sweet rum. She turned to the spray-covered window. "I'm going outside."

"Right, make sure you're upwind of the others."

The waves were heading in a different direction to the boat making it pitch considerably. Kendal manoeuvred past passengers bent over sick bags or trying to sleep. At last, she found an empty bench at the front of the boat. She pulled her hood tight to stop her hair flapping. The other passengers were lightweights. They should read Hornblower.

"Watch the gap, sweetheart," shouted a giant deckhand at Gull Island's tiny jetty. "Big bag for a little girl. You staying a while?"

The boat was rocking, and the gangplank was wet. Not the

moment to get irritated by sexist remarks. Kendal took the sailor's hand and inched forward.

"I'm taking a job here, actually."

"You've come at the right time. Summer's great." He pointed to a Jeep parked on the quay. "There's the boss. Introduce yourself, then you won't have to carry your stuff up the path. It's steep."

Cai Evans sat inside the rusty vehicle, rolling a cigarette. He wore a khaki beanie, a green T-shirt, and shorts with metal clips hanging from the waistband. Red faced, unshaven, overweight.

Kendal knocked on the window. "Hello. I'm Kendal."

The manager pumped her hand. "Welcome to Gull Island. Paradise for mavericks and nature lovers. Now, where's your stuff, Kendal Tudge?"

Kendal pointed at her rucksack in the pile of luggage on the quay. Cai grasped the bag with one hand, grabbed a sack of post with the other, and tossed both into the back of the jeep. They edged along the narrow road passing passengers scanning the cliffs with binoculars. Kendal kept her eyes on Cai as he talked her through the demands of the job and the joys of the island. This man was her new boss and she'd never seemed to get on with authority figures. She needed to put some effort in. Kendal observed her new manager and made a mental list.

Cai Clues
Didn't joke about her name
Used the word 'maverick' intriguingly
Did not use jargon or acronyms (yet)
Been pleased to see her and impressed she hadn't been seasick
No distracting sexy vibes.

Cai drove over a bumpy cattle grid and parked in the centre of a stone yard.

"To the south are the staff cottages, behind you is the store, and to the north is the beating heart of Gull Island, the Mermaid Tavern."

"Where shall I start?" asked Kendal, keen to appear hard-working. "Pub or shop?" Ferry passengers were already forming a line outside the pub and the shop door pinged constantly as visitors hurried to buy food, drink and souvenirs. "Looks like you need extra hands in both."

"Get your quarters sorted first," smiled her new manager. "Doesn't matter about queues. All part of the visitor experience. The island is only five miles long but day trippers rarely move further than here." He threw the post bag into a small office next to the pub and carried Kendal's bag to a stone terrace of tiny cottages.

"These are our staff cabins. They're all different. Take your pick. I'll see you later."

"Shall I phone you when I'm sorted?"

"No point, signal is rubbish. Internet too. Come and find me, love."

"In the office?"

"In the pub. Where everything happens."

A choice of home, a pub as an office, and a manager who wasn't controlling. Life on Gull Island looked good.

Some of the cabins had double beds, fires, and small gardens, but Kendal chose Cabin 3, the only one with a private bathroom. Simply furnished but better than most bedsits, it had a wooden table and chair providing enough room to eat or write, and a tiny kitchen galley. Kendal unpacked her bags and placed the ammonite on the shelf below the bathroom mirror. The reflection of the spiral was pleasing. A non-Gary reminder of her old life at Jurassic Court.

It was almost four months since she'd last been employed. Important to make a good impression. Kendal cleaned her teeth (not good to smell of rum on the first day) and applied fresh lip. She wasn't pretending to be older, younger, better qualified or any other fake version of Kendal, but she still wasn't sure what to wear. She slipped on a green T-shirt and stood for a moment holding the key. Was she a Londoner who locked doors or a local who didn't? She left the key in the lock. She owned nothing of monetary value and it would be a good start to the new job to trust her colleagues.

A light breeze ruffled Kendal's hair as she crossed the courtyard to the Mermaid Tavern whose dining area was packed with visitors sprawled over tables and benches. An hour before they were chucking up breakfast yet now they munched chips and pasties and swigged pints of beer. Every available surface was covered with dirty glasses and plates. A red-faced woman behind the serving bar distributed a constant stream of pasties and sausage rolls. Through the hatch, two men in aprons and chef trousers stirred and chopped.

Kendal squeezed past piles of fleecies and backpacks to the bar.

"The fish will be fed well this evening," said a voice at Kendal's shoulder. It was the giant who'd helped her ashore. He took a long swig of beer and grinned. "They'll be throwing it up again when the ferry goes back." He held out his hand. "I'm Taks, pleased to meet you. Welcome to Gull Island. Beer or wine?"

Kendal surveyed the room. "I'm looking for Mr Evans. He's going to do an induction to my role. I mean, roles."

"Get a pint down you, love. Wine or beer? Cai, won't care."

"Lime and soda, please."

Cai Evans burst into the bar. He slapped the giant deckhand's back. "Haven't you something useful to do, mate? Bugger off and let me show our new member of staff around."

Kendal followed Cai as he explained how the bar and kitchen operated. Then they crossed the courtyard to the shop, and he described the shelf stacking systems and the postal service. Finally, he took Kendal into the office and showed her where the staff rotas were displayed and how to understand the weather forecasts.

"Help yourself to a staff hoodie, apron and T-shirt and feel free to eat anything in the shop past the sell-by date. Left over meals in the Mermaid are yours if you want them as well. If a visitor offers you a drink, mark the gratuity-book, and have it when you're off duty. Any questions?"

There was a lot to do but the tasks were rational and there was no mention of targets or performance indicators. Cai had introduced her to ten Gull Island staff. Two looked younger than Kendal and three appeared older, but the rest looked forty-something. Her age. All were friendly, happy, and welcoming and Kendal was pleased to notice no one triggered her lust muscle, despite an impressive display of abs and glutes. She slipped on the fresh T-shirt and tied the apron.

"Ready for action, Cai."

Gull Island life was busy but fulfilling. The shifts were long with no time for introspection or brooding. The ferry brought a hundred visitors a day and each week the self-catering properties were freshly inhabited with excited renters who had waited years to book a stay on the tiny island. Kendal buzzed between pub and shop: pulling pints, stacking shelves, buttering rolls, counting stamps, and answering the same questions.

Yes, there is 4G but it's not working today. Yes, the meat in the pasties is local. Made with Island-bred lamb. Yes, puffins/seals/dolphins/pygmy shrews have been spotted. No, I wasn't born here.

The public were always happy; day trippers delighted to be off the boat, renting guests thrilled with their quirky accommodation, and campers obsessed with wildlife or beer. No one complained about anything as long as pints and puffins kept appearing.

Between shifts Kendal explored the island, walking from end to end, getting to know the ponies, goats and sheep and relishing the dramatic sea views. Cai lent her a pair of binoculars and soon Kendal was as excited as everyone else about each day's reported wildlife sightings.

Most weeks, someone organised a party for the staff who lived on the island, usually involving fancy dress improvised from soft furnishings or random items left behind by visitors. Cai built a barbeque on the tiny beach and Australian-Amber, the red-faced, kitchen manager, taught Kendal how to cook fresh fish and mussels. Taks, the giant deckhand, took Kendal fishing and lent her a rod to use from the beach. Kendal couldn't stop grinning as she distributed grilled mackerel she caught and cooked herself.

"Mate, you've done ace on the barbie," said Amber. She started to undress. "Come on let's go for a nikky swim and then watch bush telly. Jupiter is rising."

Kendal, aware how little attention she'd given to muff tidiness, searched for an excuse. "My mother said you should never swim after eating."

"Don't be a whinger, Tudgy. No one's looking at your map of Tasmania."

Kendal slipped modestly into the dark water. The pebbles bit into her feet but the sea felt soft and almost warm. Mid July and she was living on an island. Not the Caribbean, but still, somehow exotic.

"I feel so alive," she shouted.

Afterwards they sat round the fire toasting marshmallows. Bush-telly turned out to mean watching the fire and the stars.

Spotting her first seal Kendal imagined sharing the experience with Gary. He would have loved to hear about the whiskered face and blubber-clad creature that looked so like Albert. It would have been fun to impress him by naming the many colourful lichen and flowers clinging to the trees and rocks. But Gary was no more and she had to train her brain to blot him out. The best obliteration method was exercise.

Kendal was surprised and delighted to realise she'd become genuinely outdoorsy. Running, swimming, fishing, birdwatching, and foraging. Always on the move. When she wasn't outdoors, or working, Kendal relaxed in her cosy cabin. Not drinking, eating, or scrolling. Simply sleeping. Deep, long, intense sessions with complicated, but not frightening, dreams from which she woke refreshed, ready to open the windows and examine the sky. Gull Islanders were obsessed with weather and soon Kendal was too. It changed so quickly; you could see clouds arriving and count the seconds till rain dropped.

Apart from daily applications of Factor 50 and a weekly leg shave Kendal didn't think about how she looked, dressing mostly in shorts and T-shirts, with Gull Island branded hoodies and jeans on windier days. Despite the ready availability of alcohol and cake she ate and drank sparingly. Occasionally, Kendal turned her door sign from Available to Busy and unpacked her vibrator, but mostly a fast jog to the lighthouse or a thrilling session bouldering across a cliff scratched the same itch and pushed Gary-fantasies from her head.

Thinking about the warden was a total waste of time. It made her sad, mad, and bad. Sad because she missed him, angry because he'd overreacted, and bad because it made her want to break stuff and there was nothing to break, or steal, on Gull Island.

Gary Vaughan must stay as Gone-Gary even though there were so many brilliant bits of nature on the island he would have adored. Seals, puffins, strange goats, huge flocks of different gulls (hence the island's name) and fascinating rare fungi, lichen and wild orchids.

Not thinking about Gary was made easier by a curious lack of communications from Jurassic Court. Even allowing for the terrible internet and telephone signal it was odd how few emails or texts Kendal received. In the first week away, she'd got four supportive texts from Clare, three pocket-dials from Audrey, and an email from Philip detailing his new online dating experiences. Prue sent a postcard of a yellow mandala which Kendal placed on the bathroom shelf next to the ammonite. The pattern was pleasing but Prue's spidery writing made the message unreadable. Something about Jurassic Cautions and Wendy's Big Guns. The second week saw a lengthy text from Clare about how happy Book-group-Rosie was in Jurassic Court and a WhatsApp photo from Brian of the Rascal's punctured tyre.

Then nothing more.

Australian-Amber was unpacking the post bag in the office when Kendal popped in to check her work schedule.

"Sorry, mate. Nothing for you." Amber frowned. "Hope you're not disappointed?"

Kendal shrugged, "It's OK, Not many people know where I am."

Kendal didn't miss the soft food at Jurassic Court, or the revolting conversations about feet and earwax, but she mourned the daft miscommunications and misunderstandings, and the wisdom, honesty, and interesting back stories of her old neighbours. The Gull Island teammates were enthusiastic, energetic, and friendly but they rarely expressed vulnerability or gave much away about their pasts. Like Kendal, they probably had reasons why they'd elected to live on an island. She was still in a closed community but, this time, the residents were fit, active and undemanding. The visitors were easy too. She was simply a nice barmaid or efficient shop assistant. Interacting was uncomplicated.

There was one high spot by the church where the internet worked. Sometimes Kendal visited between shifts but found no emails or messages. It was like the last days of a job or school when people say let's keep in touch, but no one does. Old people, of course, were well-used to companions disappearing. Audrey, Brian, Prue, and the rest of her friends at Jurassic Court lived in the moment and, as she was out of sight, she was therefore out of their minds. It was nothing personal. Annoying to realise Gone-Gary was correct, however. The residents were institutionalised.

More upsetting was how quickly Clare had stopped communicating. Clare was supposed to be her friend but then Clare had a lot of concerns; tricky councillors, dodgy staff, book clubs, children, and grandchildren to support. Not forgetting the poetic cats and, to be fair, Kendal hadn't communicated with Clare either. Maybe Kendal had become institutionalised on Gull Island?

On a hot Sunday in July, when she knew Clare would not be working, Kendal walked to the high spot and held her mobile in the air. At last, a bar of signal appeared, and she started to type:

Clare, apologies for radio silence.
Been incredibly busy and the signal is rubbish.
Hope all is going well with job, family, book club, cats.
Have one for me at the Albatross or Lazy Seagull.
I'm all about bird spotting now!

Kendal imagined the text flying over the sea, dropping into Dorset, and landing in Clare's comfortable living room. Clare would put down whatever book she was clasping and read the text. She would grin, stroke Shelley (or Keats) and reply with something amusing but authentic. Tell Kendal how much she was missed (and maybe how unhappy Gary was?).

But she didn't.

33

Gull Island properties were furnished with paintings, photographs, and books appropriate to their age and original purpose. Instead of televisions, knick-knacks, or endless cushions, they had soft sofas, and jigsaws. A bit like the Ammonite room, minus the computer and puppets.

Friday was changeover day but Iris and Lola, the cleaners, had drunk a bottle of port the night before and were struggling to clean the rental properties before the ferry with the new guests was due. Kendal, familiar with dessert-wine-hangovers, offered to help.

"Thanks Kendal, it shouldn't be too gross," groaned Iris. "The rental visitors never make too much mess because they won't be allowed to stay again if they do. These nerds love puffins more than parties."

"You can take first pickings of anything you find," added Lola. "Clothes, books, and jewellery go to the office lost property box, but drinkable or edible stuff is ours."

"Although anything majorly past the sell-by date we have to give to Henry," said Iris. Kendal frowned. She'd been on Gull Island a month and not met Henry. Perhaps he was a recluse?

"Where does Henry hang out?"

"In the pigsty!" laughed Iris. "He'll be sausages by December."

The last property on the cleaning rota was the old lighthouse. Its guests had left behind two pairs of trousers and a pile of paperbacks.

"Can you do the lantern room, Kendal?" whined Lola. "I'm not up to those stairs."

Kendal was interested in experiencing the view from the top. She reached for their cleaning caddy. "Yes, happy to do it."

"Got to get some carbs down me," said Iris. "See you tonight. We owe you big time."

The lighthouse steps curved like the spiral of the ammonite, a physical reminder of climbing Bowerman's Nose in Dartmoor, before everything went pear-shaped. She reached the top and gasped. No clouds or contrails. The whole island was visible, surrounded by sparkling sea. In the distance she could see the Cornish coast. Gone-Gary would've adored it.

The lantern room had two striped reclining deckchairs and an old-fashioned clock. The visitors had left a large packet of crisps, three cans of tonic water and a half-finished bottle of gin. Kendal sat in the blue striped chair and watched Iris and Lola sway back to the office. They were having a fun summer before going to university. She hoped they stick it out longer than she had. Get themselves a proper education and career jobs. Nice partners. Mortgages, babies, pensions.

She kicked off her trainers, opened the crisps, emptied two cans of tonic into the bottle and rested her feet on the other deckchair. Sun bounced off the metal railings lining the room. Kendal closed her eyes and remembered climbing Portland Bill lighthouse as a child with her parents. They'd laughed at the name because Dad had said the ticket was expensive like a bill.

Kendal remembered how exciting it had been watching the light swing round. She'd held her parents tightly and they'd kept her safe. Lighthouses kept sailors safe. Handsome, heroic, gentlemen like Hornblower. Like Gary...

The G and T was gin heavy. Kendal opened the last can of tonic and added it to the bottle. She wished she had ice but there was no way she was going down those stairs to battle with a frozen icebox. Or fetch a glass. They'd been no daytime-drinking since she left Dorset. It was Kendal's first day off in a month and visitors were not allowed into the rental properties until five. Plenty of time to chill. The heat in the lantern room was delicious. The canvas chair relaxing. She was cocooned in a hot, safe space. Kendal placed the bottle on the floor and closed her eyes. Changeovers were tiring. The ticking clock was hypnotic.

"I hope I'm not disturbing you? Didn't see you there." A husky voice reverberated around the lantern room. The sun was in her eyes and it was difficult to locate the source of the sound. She tried to stand but the low deckchair held her tight.

"I was given to understand no one would be here. Please forgive me. I'll come another time. Enjoy your stay." The voice trailed away as its owner stepped down the staircase. She stuffed the empty crisp packet, cans and gin bottle into her cleaning caddy, gave the deckchair a hasty sweep and hurried down the steps.

A slim, dark man in pink linen shirt and button jeans crouched by the bookcase, pulling books off the shelves and flicking through their pages. His hair was thick and sharply cut and he wore a vintage wristwatch and tortoiseshell glasses. He turned and smiled at Kendal.

"Do you mind if I finish checking the collection? I won't be long. The lighthouse is the last on my list and I got distracted by the logbook." He pointed at the leather-clad journal where visitors wrote their thoughts and recommendations.

"The last guests have created an outstanding record of their stay. Head office will love this."

Kendal thought the comments in the visitors' logbooks were snobby and smug. Observations about wall colour, alongside wordy descriptions of the weather and boasts about swift completion of the jigsaws. The best bits were by children who were not so enamoured of the digital detox and limited retail experiences at Gull Island.

"I'm sorry the property wasn't empty," she said, clamping a duster over the gin. "The changeover took longer than I anticipated."

"I'm not a guest." The man stood and held out his hand. "Anaish Anand. Call me Nish. Who are you?"

"Kendal Tudge, I'm working on the island. Sorry I fell asleep. I don't normally do the cleaning. It's knackering. The Tavern and the shop are my jobs. Great pasties, amazing stamps." She was babbling.

"Kendal? From the old Norse word keld?"

"Um, maybe. What is keld?" It better be something pleasant.

"A spring, as in a fountain or a well, not the season."

Kendal smiled.

"Sounds cool, thanks. If you're not a guest, why are you here?" The only visitors who weren't guests were sailors. He didn't look like a yachtie type. She pointed at a painting of a shipwreck and grinned. "Are you a pirate?"

Nish frowned. Was mentioning pirates a racial slur? Kendal clasped the duster and wiped the painting.

"A-ha, me hearties. Pieces of eight, pieces of eight." Nish was attempting pirate talk so presumably wasn't offended.

"You'll be no good on September 19th," said Kendal.

"William Golding's birthday?" said Nish. "Do the visitors run amok and fight each other?"

"It's International-talk-like-a-pirate-day. A big thing here, apparently. Highlighted on the staff rotas."

Nish laughed. "Well, sadly, I'm only here for a couple of days."

"Where are you staying? All the staff cabins are taken."

"I've got to wait and see if any guests fail to arrive. Otherwise, it's the bed in the church vestry. I'm not tough enough for camping."

"So, what is your work?" asked Kendal. Nish brushed his hand over the bookshelf. He had very white nails and soft, smooth skin.

"The best job in the world. I visit all the historic properties the trust owns across Britain and curate their bookshelves. Check what's missing and restock. Spend my life in beautiful buildings and second-hand book shops. I try to avoid buying online. I like to feel the pages, assess the condition."

"Pretty niche, Nish!" She'd made fun of his name. Making her a hypocrite as well as a possible racist.

"It is. Each bookshelf is different. So, in Gull Island each house will have copies of *Birds of Gull Island*, alongside publications specific to the property's original use. The Old Schoolhouse has *Tom Browne's School Days*, for example and here, in the lighthouse, there should be a copy of Virginia Woolf's you-know-what."

Kendal didn't. Someone to research, alongside William Golding and Tom Browne "So you get paid for filling other people's bookshelves?"

"I have a senior librarian role at Oxford. This is more of a hobby. I like the curatorial aspect. It's creative as well as geeky. Us librarians are a weird bunch."

Kendal could go with this. "I have a friend who is a librarian. In Dorset. Does all kinds of extra stuff. Book groups, silver surfing classes, campaigns. She's amazing."

Nish grinned. "Good to hear. There are some awful stereotypes about us. I'm glad you've got a wider view." He pulled a phone out of his pocket.

"No signal here."

"I know, I've been before," said Nish. He began to photograph the bookshelves. "I'm speed-auditing. Be finished quicker this way and then we could walk back to the Tavern together. It's almost Friday night, you know."

Nish-the-librarian was interesting like Clare, neither too old or young, possibly single and he had beautiful eyes. He was the best-looking bloke she'd seen since arriving at Gull Island and she could tell he was keen. The walk to the pub was over too quickly.

The Mermaid was buzzing. As well as the guests who'd arrived on the ferry there was an influx of yachties who'd decided to moor for the night.

"All hands on deck, Kendal," shouted Cai from the back of the bar. "Sorry, but your day off is off. Bar or kitchen?"

"Get her pulling pints!" shouted a yachtsman. "She's got to be faster than you, mate."

"Pasty making, please," begged Australian-Amber, wiping sweat out of her eyes.

"Table clearing is surely the priority," said Nish.

Kendal surveyed the crush at the bar, the queue at the food counter, and the tables covered in dirty plates and glasses. A strategy was needed.

"Drinks first, carbs later. Get enough alcohol in this lot and they won't notice the tables."

She slipped under the bar flap, dipped her hands under a tap, and turned to smile at the nearest impatient yachtie. "What's your poison, sir?"

The next two hours passed in a rush of pint pulling and bar banter. Occasionally Kendal glimpsed the librarian clearing tables and collecting rubbish. Australian-Amber squeezed under the counter to grab some bottles for the exhausted kitchen team.

"Seen the new busboy, Kendal?" she whispered. "Wouldn't mind him wiping me down!"

At last, the campers, yachties and guests began to slip away to their beds. Kendal drank her first beer and opened a packet of crisps. No sign of Nish.

"Thanks a million, Kendal," said Cai. "You saved the day. Take some time off this week when you can. No need to follow the rota too closely. I trust you. You're a great worker."

Kendal walked to her cabin enjoying the stars and the light breeze. Some of the campers were singing and she could hear yachtsmen laughing as they stumbled to the harbour. Bats swooped past towards the church spire. There was a light in the back of the church. Must be Nish in the vestry. He'd stopped her thinking about Gary for six hours. Interesting to visit Nish in the church and block the bastard out for longer, but she'd worked crazy hours; hard, physical standing-up, full-on labour. She was hungry, sober and every limb ached. Time for bed. Her one.

Kendal lay under her duvet with a tray of toast and herbal tea and reflected how she had changed since she left London. She'd turned into a mature woman, not a party-girl who jumped blokes the minute she met them. Especially on an uncomfortable camp bed in a church. She wished she had someone to acknowledge how she'd developed. Her parents? Maxine? Clare? Audrey? No, not Gary. Have to share it with herself.

The next morning Kendal raided the lost property box and selected a pair of linen palazzo trousers, striped sailing shirt and a spotty Alice band (with no hairs). The trousers were big, but she cinched the waist with a knotted rope. The white linen enhanced her tan and the grey roots of her bleached blonde hair were held at bay by the band. The whole ensemble worked. Coastal-grandmother meets soft-girl-grunge.

Nish was on his knees sorting the bookshelves in the Mermaid Tavern when Kendal arrived for the morning shift. He had a perfect nape undercut which would be gorgeous to stroke. She pushed her hands into the large trouser pockets. "Got any Hornblower editions in there?" she asked.

He turned and smiled. Perfect teeth. It was nice having Nish on his knees below. She knew she looked good.

"I'd love to include them, but he didn't get to sail round here. Are you a fan?"

Kendal nodded. "Almost my specialist subject."

Nish raised his eyebrows. "Unusual choice for a woman, if you don't mind me saying."

"I'm an unusual woman," responded Kendal. Yes, she could still flirt.

Nish placed a battered paperback into a bin bag. "I've got an hour's work left and then I'm done. When are you off duty?"

"She's got today off," shouted a voice from the bar.

"Take her away," added another from the kitchen.

Kendal swivelled. Cai and Amber made shooing gestures.

"Seems like I'm free."

"Great, meet you outside the church at twelve. Bring a packed lunch. I've got the map."

Kendal jiggled the knot on her rope belt. "You can't get lost on a tiny island."

"I could," said Nish. "I can navigate the Dewey Decimal System with my eyes closed but can't find my way home sometimes."

London-Kendal regularly couldn't find her way home but Gull-Island-Kendal chose not to share. Too much information on a first date.

Salad boxes and flasks filled with soup were the daily virtue signals of the annoying drones at THRUm but whenever Kendal made a packed lunch she'd eaten it before she'd left the tube. London-Kendal bought unhealthy meals in the canteen or, if desperate, nicked sandwiches from Pret.

The Gull Island shop's sin box was full of past-the-sell-by-date cheese, salami, and sausage rolls. Nish looked like a possible vegan, so she added a tube of vegetable paste, two Bakewell tarts and a packet of crisps.

Iris was sorting postcards by the cash desk. "Thanks so much for helping us yesterday," she said. "You are a great teamie."

Kendal had never been called a team player before. She smiled. "No problem, I had a little snooze afterwards and woke to find a tall, dark stranger in the lighthouse and now we're going on a picnic."

Iris winked. "Awesome. The stuff of dreams. Enjoy yourself." She opened a box of postcards. "These new ones show the view from the lighthouse. Do you want some?"

In quiet moments during her shifts in the shop, Kendal had cast an eye over the postcards the visitors handed over to be sent to the mainland. With their special Gull Island franking mark, they were a relic from another age when it was enough to share a picture of a place and not include yourself. Postcards were like tiny presents. It would be cool to send old-style greetings to Jurassic Court.

"Thanks Iris. Give me a couple of packs and some stamps please."

She would write personal messages appreciating aspects of each resident and they would have fun comparing postcards at breakfast. Instead of Digital Drop-ins she'd provide Analogue Attachments for all her friends at Jurassic Court. Except Gone-Gary. That idiot who couldn't paste links onto his phone probably adored old-school postcards. Too bad. His loss. She wouldn't send him anything. Ever.

Two hours till the kind-of-date. Kendal found a felt pen with italic nib in the lost property box and settled in a deckchair outside her cabin. Not much space on a postcard, especially as she knew to use large letters for elderly eyes. The residents might show their postcards to each other which meant she must write something personal and different to each resident. She'd write them in room order. Starting with Flat 15.

Dear Jennifer,
Greetings from Gull Island where I'm surrounded by sea and wildlife.
No proper roads. Bad for buggies.
I hope you are dancing as much as you can.

Dear Shirley,
Greetings from Gull Island where I am working.
It has two superb lighthouses and delicious pasties.
The fresh air makes me sleep a lot. You'd love it.

Dear Wendy,
Plenty of JOY on Gull Island.
Everyone is eco. No plastic straws.
It's sunny and windy – tricky for hair.
I hope Adele and all your family are well.

Dear Prue,
Greetings from the ammonite and me.
The pub here is busy but I'm abstaining.
I'm visiting a church today too.
Thanks for your postcard. Write again if you can.

Hello DJ Brian,
Your Rascal would hate the roads here.
Hope you are looking after the old girl?
And the mobility buggy too – boom boom!
Keep raving.

Hello Philip,
Hope the dating is going well and you're meeting some nice chaps.
Lots of friendly folk on Gull Island but terrible internet.
Missing you all.

Dearest Albert,
I'm learning about farming on Gull Island. Over 100 sheep here.
Healthy lifestyle, lots of exercise and the work is fun.
Please keep healthy too.

Dear Jim,
Gull Island is wild.
The pig is called Henry and eats everything.
He will be made into sausages apparently.
There are four horses too. But they won't!

Dear Jacob,
Gull Island is like an outdoor gym.
Loads of stiles and steps to climb.
I'm almost as fit as you.

Hello Sam,
Over 300 different species of plants on Gull Island.
The Gull Island cabbage is beautiful.
Perhaps you could grow one in Gardening Club?

Boomer banter was harder to write than speak. With postcards you couldn't edit or delete the message and none of the cards seemed quite right; she shouldn't have mentioned blowy hair to wig-wearing Wendy, she'd lied about abandoning alcohol, Philip might groan at his gay status being discussed in public, Sam could get confused by the cabbage, and Brian's Rascal joke didn't work. She was supposed to be meeting Nish and she hadn't written to Audrey and Book-Club-Rosie.

Dear Audrey,
You'd love it here.
Lots of parties and sing-a-longs.
Hope Rosie is keeping my flat clean!

Book-Club Rosie would have to do without. Besides she wasn't a friend, she was a tenant, and no landlord had ever sent Kendal a friendly postcard. Kendal wished she could write more to Audrey but then postcards were supposed to be short and breezy. Like texts, before voice messaging and emoji overload. She sighed, stuck on the stamps, and grabbed her bag. No point overthinking.

The sky was perfect, she had a day off, loads of food, and a sort-of-date with a guy who was nothing like Gary even though the sort-of-date was sort of like the sort-of-date they'd shared on Dartmoor before it all kicked off.

34

"I've not met a woman into Hornblower before," said Nish, as they descended the steps to the coastal path. "Are you a keen reader?"

Kendal executed a rapid mental decision tree. If she answered yes, and was pressed to discuss recent readings, she could blather about the book group book, but if he asked further reading-related questions she would be exposed. She should be honest.

"Not really, it's just I inherited my uncle's flat in a retirement complex. He loved nautical books and stuff and I read them just because they were there."

"Was it weird living in an old peoples' home?"

There was a flash of orange over the sea. Kendal lifted her binoculars. She focused on a puffin swooping onto the water and tried to decide how to answer.

"Weird sometimes," she said. "But also, fun." Still telling the truth.

Nish raised his binoculars, and they tracked the bird as it landed on the cliff with a fish in its beak.

"My grandmother is in a home. I hate going there. As Shakespeare said, 'when the age is in, the wit is out' and it's true. The old dears at gran's are zombies."

Nish was nice but prejudiced. He'd be hopeless at THRUm.

"Actually, the residents at Jurassic Court are bright, independent and very funny. I enjoyed their company and learned masses from them." Kendal's eyes misted. She pressed the binoculars into them. "It's awful how society stereotypes older people and the places they live. There are huge differences between lifestyles and generations. Nursing homes, for example, are worlds away from sheltered housing or assisted living. Lumping them together is as bad as thinking people with Asian heritage are all the same."

Kendal strode to an abandoned quarry, selected a spot out of the wind, and opened the packed lunch. The librarian followed.

"I'm sorry, Kendal. You're absolutely correct. Please forgive me."

Kendal grunted and peeled a Babybel. Nish opened his backpack.

"Can I offer a chilled white Rioja with a bumper sour cream and jalapeño snack pack as an apology gift?"

The sun was directly above, the only sound the waves and a few gulls, and they were surrounded by yellow gorse with its sweet coconut scent. Pointless to be cross in such a perfect place. Kendal reached for a glass with one hand and passed the crackers and tube of vegetable paste to Nish.

"This looks gross but tastes super umami," she said. "My accepting-apology gift."

Butterflies flicked over the gorse. Kendal didn't know what breed they were and didn't want to guess. Fritillary, and her show-off nature knowledge, could stay on Dartmoor. She wasn't trying to pretend anymore. The wine was delicious. A perfect match for Babybel and sausage rolls.

"It's so peaceful here," she murmured. "But at the same time, exciting."

Nish nodded. "It is enchanting. Nowhere else in the world like Gull Island."

Kendal closed her eyes. "I'm glad I came here. I'd got into a toxic situation in Dorset."

"Poisoning the pensioners?" Nish giggled. "Sorry, am I being insensitive again? I'm not used to drinking in the day."

Kendal shook her head. "No, you're fine, Nish. It's me. I made a terrible mistake. Committed fraud. Pretended to be someone I wasn't. Dyed my hair, wore disgusting make-up and stupid clothes."

"Painted Lady," said Nish.

"No, the opposite. I made myself insipid and dull which I wrongly thought was how a sixty-year-old looked."

Nish giggled again. "The butterflies. They're Painted Ladies, migrants from Africa."

Kendal shook her head. She knew that! Gary Vaughan had told her. It didn't matter, she wasn't trying to build rapport inauthentically anymore. If she forgot a nature fact, or didn't know it in the first place, it didn't matter one jot.

Nish refilled their glasses. "I'm probably pushing my luck here, Ms Tudge, but why on earth did you pretend to be older than you are? Was it for the bus pass or something?" He batted his hands over his glasses. "Sorry, I'm being silly. It's the wine. Seriously, what made you pretend to be older? Must have been a stretch. You're nowhere near sixty."

Kendal gazed at the horizon. "I'm forty-four, jobless, single, possibly perimenopausal. I've no qualifications, no family and hardly any friends. Until recently, I owed money left, right and centre and, if I am being totally truthful, I had an unhealthy relationship with drink, drugs, and sex."

Nish's eyes widened. He screwed the bottle cap tight. "Right. But why?"

It all came out. The inheritance. The lost job. House prices in London in relation to retirement flats in Dorset. How it was all paid for in advance by Uncle Clem. The loveliness of Audrey, Prue, Brian, Philip, Albert, Carla, and Emma. Swimming in the sea, making friends with Clare, getting fit, learning about gardening, Movie Night, the auction. Kendal divulged every detail of her life at Jurassic Court. Apart from the lost ring and the broken heart. At last, she stopped.

"You're a great listener. Are you shocked at my fraud?"

"No, it's intriguing." Nish rested his glass on a flat rock and edged closer to Kendal. "I'm always pretending to be someone I'm not. Adapting my accent, or adopting certain behaviours to fit in. It's human to act differently depending on who you are with."

Kendal covered her face. "Not to the extent I did."

Nish removed Kendal's hands. "Means to an end, Ms Tudge." He wove his fingers into her hair. "You're intriguing. This place is intriguing. We can be ourselves." Kendal's scalp tingled. Cheryl, at Hair By Barry, was good but this took head massage to another level.

Nish's fingers moved to Kendal's shoulders, tracing the collar of the linen shirt. Her breasts woke, her pulse raced. He kissed her forehead. His lips were soft, like a woman's. She closed her eyes and let him push her gently onto the soft turf. He untied her rope belt and stroked her stomach. His touch was as light as a butterfly. She didn't care which type.

The scent of Nish was delicious, his hands were extraordinary, and his tongue, when he finally slipped it into her mouth, was magical.

"I looked up the meaning of your name," murmured Nish. "I was wrong about Keld being the word for Kendal. It's a combination of the river Kent combined with the Norse word dair for valley."

Valley, spring whatever. Kendal was gushing. Positively torrential.

Nish moved alongside Kendal. They fitted together perfectly. She moved her hands to his groin.

Kendal groaned. Nish groaned back. His moans grew louder. Perhaps he'd not been touched by anyone (other than a hairdresser) for a while too?

"Wow, you're so uninhibited, Kendal. I've never heard a woman make so much noise. This is so intense."

The moaning was deafening, yet Nish was talking. Kendal must be making the sex sounds herself.

"I think I'm having an out of body experience," she whimpered, hoping it didn't indicate a repeat of the trans global amnesia episode. There was no hospital on Gull Island and she didn't want her first helicopter flight to be something she couldn't remember afterwards.

The piercing moans were climaxing. Which she and the librarian were not. They sat up, buttoning shirts and brushing off grass.

"Someone's having a pretty intense time," said Nish.

"Leave them be," said Kendal. "They'll finish soon."

The moans continued. Kendal scanned the gorse. Nish took her hand and they tip-toed to the edge of the cliff path. The sound was coming from the beach below.

"Maybe someone is injured. Fallen off the cliff?" said Kendal. "The shore is impossible to reach here without climbing gear."

Nish lay flat on the path and shifted carefully towards the cliff edge.

"Oh God, please be careful, Nish. The cliffs are unstable. Full of cracks."

A tragedy to lose the leading candidate for nicest-bloke-of-the-decade.

Nish's shoulders began to heave. Perhaps he had vertigo. Kendal lay beside him. He was laughing. He pointed at the sea.

"It's a baby seal. Crying. How can a small creature make so much noise?"

Kendal followed his finger down the sheer drop to the narrow beach. A pale grey pup lifted its head out of the shallows and howled. The cry bounced against the cliffs and roared over the path.

"Is it hurt?"

"Only emotionally! It's lonely. Probably looking for its mum." Nish reached for his binoculars. "I can see the parents further out to sea, by the headland. Neglectful parenting, or tough love? Who knows?"

Kendal lifted her binoculars. The wailing was unbearable. "Poor creature," she whispered. "Stranded on a beach alone."

"He'll find some mates soon," said Nish. "And they can run amok. Like in *Lord of the Flies*."

Kendal frowned. "What do you mean?"

Nish brushed gravel off his trousers. "I thought you said you knew William Golding's classic?"

It had been a huge relief to confess her fraud earlier. Lies were unnecessary now. She flicked a twig off the palazzo trousers. "To be honest, I don't.

"It's about some boys who survive an airplane crash on an island and, with no adults around, start behaving badly. An allegory for the conflict between civilisation and savagery."

"Right. Well, I don't know much about any books. I pretended I did to build rapport. Another disguise. Like these clothes, which aren't mine, but I put them on because I thought you might like the coastal grandmother look."

Nish took her hand. "I've no idea what, or who, a coastal grandmother is. I never notice what people wear and I get more than enough literary talk at work. Don't be hard on yourself. I like you as you are. I don't care how old or young you are or what you do for work. Now shall we walk and look for a secluded spot where any odd sounds are made by us?"

With all the properties rented out, a full camp site, and a ferry-load of day visitors the island teemed with bird spotters, artists, rock climbers and outdoor yoga enthusiasts. Nish and Kendal explored every nook and cranny but each time they began exploring each other's nooks and crannies, a visitor would appear.

"The world and his friend are outdoors so we should go inside," announced Nish, as they sidestepped a group of volunteers rebuilding a dry-stone wall. "My space in the church is quite cosy. No one will be in there on a beautiful day like this."

Kendal'd done the sex in an airplane toilet thing but never tried it in a church. Touch of late-Eighties Madonna vibe. Irresistible.

They held hands and walked back to the village. Nish delivered a concise history of the church while Kendal ran a mental list of how sex-ready she was. Her skin and body were the best they'd been for years, and her feet were freshly pedicured by one of the kitchen girls who was training to be a beautician. Despite not shaving for months, her beaver was more Isle of Wight than Map of Tasmania. Maybe she was perimenopausal and her body hair growth was slowing? There'd been a few grey hairs, but Kendal had been assiduous in tweezering them into oblivion. However, it wouldn't be dark for a while and Kendal was wearing her worst knickers. Also, she couldn't assume Nish had condoms.

"I've got to pop into the shop," she said. "I'll meet you in the church in ten minutes."

Nish hugged Kendal and whispered in her ear. "Don't be long. I'm raring to hear you make abandoned seal sounds."

"Taks worn you down?" said Australian-Amber in the shop, winking at the packet of condoms. "He's a persistent bloody hulk, isn't he?"

Kendal laughed. "I'd have to be desperate to spend money on Taks. It's not him."

Amber tore open a sweet packet and thrust a finger of fudge at Kendal. "Oh, Lord. You've not picked a day visitor, have you? Bound to be married. Or diseased."

Kendal pushed the fudge into her mouth. "It's not Taks, or a day visitor, it's mwha ish." Telling the truth, with a mouth full of chocolate.

"Who?"

"Sorry Amber, gotta go."

The matching underwear set lay clean and lonely at the bottom of Kendal's wardrobe. She splashed on cologne (left by guests on a writers' retreat), retied her rope belt with a slip knot, brushed her teeth and applied subtle lip. She'd forgotten how uncomfortable a push-up bra and lacy thong were. Still, she wouldn't be wearing them for long.

Kendal picked up the ammonite and gave it a polish. Would Prue ever wear a thong? What would Wendy say about sex in a church? At least Albert would approve of eating a finger of fudge in one mouthful.

Kendal walked to the post-box. The cards made a satisfying thud as they landed. She'd get some more and send to Carla and Emma. Maybe Mad-Maxine and PoshJosh too. She might even post to Dogbreath-Deirdre and her ex-colleagues at THRUm. Let them know she was still alive and kicking. She had nothing to hide now. She shouldn't call them rude names anymore. Just Maxine, Josh and Deirdre.

The church was chilly after the heat outside. The smell of candles and wood polish mingled pleasantly with her cologne. Kendal walked past the empty pews to a carved door in the back of the church. A cork popped as she pushed it open.

"Kendal Tudge, I do declare. Welcome to my humble abode."

The single camp bed looked uncomfortable, but the hideaway was secluded, smelled exotic, and the limited light was flattering. Nish sat on an embroidered hassock holding two glasses of fizzy, wearing nothing but white boxers. A dark happy trail travelled up his stomach. It had been almost four months since Kendal had had sex with anyone other than herself. Her longest dry season. Kendal was primed. She looked good, felt good, she was – horrible, but accurate, phrase – gagging for it.

She kicked the door closed and held out her hand. Nish downed a glass, stuffed his tongue into Kendal's mouth and expertly unwrapped a condom (his own) without a word. Kendal didn't need talk; the stop-start hot afternoon had been excellent foreplay and now the darkness and heavy religious setting demanded a fast and furious coupling. She wedged herself below an iron coat rack. A black and red priest's robe fell across her face. It was a standing-room-only sex situation, with urgent fingers and insistent tongues. She couldn't see Nish, but she could feel his mouth against her thigh, tugging at the rope belt.

"Doesn't need untying," she whispered. "It's a slip knot."

Nish grunted and the palazzo trousers fell to the floor.

Kendal pulled her stomach in. He shoved the thong aside, dragged his boxers down and pushed his cock in.

"You are a gushing spring, Kendal," he sighed. "I'm going to make you moan like a seal."

He needed to stop talking. All distractions must be blocked.

Kendal shifted her back against the wall. After pulling so many pints and humping crates her arms were strong. She gripped the metal hooks above her and swung her legs firmly around Nish's waist. The angle was perfect.

"Christ, you're fit!" he panted. Kendal grinned.

"You better be too," she gasped.

DONG, DONG, DONG! The vestry exploded as a bell chimed above their heads. The noise bounced off the roof and into the tiny room. Other bells began to peal. A cacophony of horrible sounds. Kendal's body tensed. Every part of her contracted.

Nish howled. "You're too tight. Stop clenching."

Kendal shook her head. She couldn't.

"What's going on? It's not Sunday."

"Bloody bell ringers," groaned Nish. "Since the trust had them restored the bells have become hugely popular with visiting groups of ringers." He shifted his legs. "Try to relax."

Kendal had always been proud of her pelvic floor. Now it was a liability. Far too tight. Her arms ached. She lowered her legs and the librarian slipped out.

"They don't know we're here," said Nish. "Let's try lying down."

Kendal shook her head. "I'm not feeling it, Nish."

Nish giggled. "Doesn't appeal then?"

Kendal frowned. "Sorry?"

"Appeal, like peal of bells. The ten bells here make a rare peal. It's why the church is so popular with campanology groups." He tugged his boxers and patted the camp bed. "They'll be at it for hours. We could be too."

Kendal tightened the rope belt. The camp bed looked unstable and puns were not appropriate during sex. Especially bad sex.

"Moment's gone, Nish. And so am I."

35

Kendal tried to keep aroused long enough to get home, find her vibrator, and finish what Nish had started. She listed the good stuff:

Nish's legs, stomach, and happy trail
Nice fizz, passable boxers

It was disappointingly short. Nish should have known about the bellringers. Checked with the office or something. Or maybe she should have? She was nit-picking. It wasn't only the bells putting her off.

Kendal passed the Mermaid Tavern. Noise poured out of the windows. She ought to muck in and help. Might take her mind off the bad sex list:

Standing up sex is better in the movies
Nish rubbish at dirty talk
Nish nice – but ...not

Kendal yanked the cabin door, grabbed her vibrator with one hand, switched the kettle on with the other. By the time the kettle clicked, so had Kendal.

Sex with herself wasn't satisfying though. She felt restless and irritated. Perhaps a walk or run might restore her sense of well-being, but the athletic bracing in the church had made her legs ache. She might as well help out at the Mermaid.

Kendal showered, dressed in jeans, a Gull Island hoodie, and puffin baseball cap and threw the balled-up thong, cologne, and packet of condoms in the bin. The pain in her legs was worsening. She grabbed a packet of paracetamol off the bathroom shelf. The ammonite wobbled. Some kind of critical message from spooky Prue? Kendal stuffed it in her back pocket.

The bar was wall-to-wall with bearded yachties wearing Helly Hansen, Musto, and rubber boots. Cai hugged Kendal as she slipped under the bar flap.

"Life saver, girl. It's mayhem here and the bellringers will be arriving any moment. Even thirstier than the yachties."

"Why are there so many here?" shouted Kendal.

"It's the annual Round-Gull-Island race. Big storm on the way, so they're taking shelter and will go back tomorrow."

Two hours passed in a non-stop whirl of pulling pints and stonewalling. Cai was correct about bellringers and alcohol but, at least, they saved their banter for each other. The plummy sailing types shared theirs with the Mermaid staff and, as the pain killers wore off, Kendal found it difficult to remain polite.

"Cai, I'm taking a breather to grab something to eat," she gasped after a retired rear admiral grabbed her baseball cap for the fifth time.

"Take as long as you need," shouted Cai. "Help yourself to anything."

Kendal slipped into the kitchen and opened the fridge. Nothing but coleslaw, pasties, and cheese. It had been a long day and the kitchen lights were too bright. She poured a glass of milk and opened a packet of crisps. Australian-Amber bustled in carrying a crate of tomatoes.

"Wotcha, mate. How'd did the date go? That gorgeous bloke was desperate to find you. Did you find him? You'll be needing another packet of condoms I expect."

"Can I have some tomatoes?" asked Kendal. "Can't face the beige food."

"That bad, eh?" said Amber. She began dicing salad. "He said he'd been trying to contact you for days, so I explained about the signal."

"He knows about the signal. He's worked here before." Kendal frowned. "And I only met him yesterday."

Amber placed a fluffy bap stuffed with tomatoes, avocado,

and salami in front of Kendal. "Weird! He said he used to work with you."

The sandwich was delicious. "He works with both of us. He's the part-time librarian, goes round all the trust's properties checking books and stuff."

"No, that's Nice Nish. He comes every summer. Bit posh for me, but definitely easy on the eye." Amber handed Kendal a strawberry ice cream carton. "It's not him. This bloke's tall, middle-aged, but in good nick. Lovely eyes. Nice voice."

Kendal tried to remember the blokes she'd worked with at THRUm. They were much younger that her and none of them had lovely eyes.

"Probably one of the sailing twats. They've been a pain in the arse all evening. Thanks Amber, I feel much better now. I ought to go back and help the guys in the bar. See you tomorrow for outdoor yoga?"

Amber laughed. "You'll be lucky. It'll be pissing down tomorrow. Big storm on the way."

Kendal opened the dishwasher. The pain in her legs had got worse and now her feet felt horribly tender too. Probably the onset of the infamous plantar fasciitis experienced by middle-aged people. She wished she hadn't left the charity shop orthopaedic shoes at Jurassic Court. Kendal caught her reflection in the shiny door. She looked exhausted with bags under her eyes, disappearing lips and pale, almost non-existent brows and lashes. She didn't care. She was done with looking attractive. Such a waste of energy. She padded back into the bar.

"Cai, I'm knackered. Can I go home now?"

The manager squeezed her arm. "Ah, there you are. There's a bloke here desperate to see you. He's been looking for you all evening. I told him you wouldn't be long."

Kendal sighed. "Not the rear-admiral, Cai? He's a pest."

Cai scanned the packed room. "No, not one of those pillocks. Nice bloke. He said his name. Now what was it?" Cai tapped his head. "Oh God, best ever Welsh manager, isn't it?"

Kendal yawned. "I don't know, Cai and, frankly, I don't care. I'm going home now."

Cai nodded. "It'll come to me. Sweet dreams pet. Hope the storm doesn't keep you from your beauty sleep. No offence, but you look like you need it."

Light rain fell as Kendal hobbled home. The stars were hidden behind cloud, but she knew all the potholes and bumps. The pain had spread into her back. If a storm was on its way, then there would be no boat on Sunday and the island would be emptier. Tomorrow was the last day of July. A month since she'd arrived on Gull Island. She hadn't had a period since the disastrous Dartmoor trip. Of course, she had PMT.

The rain was getting heavier. She forced her feet to hurry, glad she didn't have to fuss with keys and could walk straight inside her cabin. She needed more painkillers and a herbal tea. Choosing drinks used to be red or white? Now it was Sleepy Time or Soul Purpose? She'd choose Soul Purpose; its red colour was more attractive than the piss green of Sleepy Time. Each teabag tag had a message or mantra. The slogans were ridiculous, but she still read them.

There was a light on in her cabin which was strange since it hadn't been dark when she'd left. Kendal tried to remember if she had told Nish where she lived. Bit cheeky turning up this late, especially after the ding-dong in the church. Maybe it wasn't him? Gull Island was the safest place in the world but some of those yachties were appallingly drunk and they could have found out where she lived. With no keys, phone or hairbrush, the ammonite in her pocket was her only weapon. She squeezed it between her knuckles and opened the door.

"Hello Kendal." A tall figure sat at the table. Her heart stopped.

Gary! Sipping tea with a red tag.

Soul Purpose.

Kendal dropped the fossil and it rolled across the floor. Gary stopped it with his foot. He wore no shoes or boots.

"Is this the ammonite you found with Prue? From Almonds Chine?"

Kendal nodded.

"You took it with you?"

Kendal nodded again.

"Sweet. Prue will be pleased."

The wind was gathering strength and rain had begun to hammer on the cabin roof. Kendal's legs were buckling. She needed to sit down, but Gary had the chair. She squeezed past the table to her bed. Kendal longed to collapse onto the duvet, but she propped herself against the wall.

"Are you OK, Kendal?" said Gary, rising. "Do you want a glass of water? Or a tea? I hope you don't mind I helped myself?"

Kendal's mouth was dry. She watched Gary at the kitchen galley. His head almost touched the ceiling. She recognised her favourite shorts, but the clinging baby-blue shirt looked new. His back was wide and square. Impossible to wrap legs around.

"Where are your shoes?" she whispered.

Gary turned. "Outside, by your bin. They stank. I've walked around the island three times." He handed her a cup. Kendal didn't trust her hands.

"Put it on the floor."

Gary poured fresh water onto his tea bag. Lightning flashed. "Storm coming."

"I know. What are you doing here, Gary?" Her voice was weak, and now her face ached as well as her legs, back and feet.

Gary straightened a sock. "Looking for you, Kendal." He stared at the other sock. "To apologise. To tell you, in person, how sorry I am." His face was red, his mouth trembled. Tears glistened in the corner of his eyes.

Kendal twisted her tea bag to read the tag.

Life is the flow of love; you're invited.

The pauses between flashes were shortening and Kendal reached for the blind cord. Gary jumped to help and their hands touched as another bolt of lightning lit the sky. Kendal gasped. Gary pulled the blind shut and fell to his knees. She could smell his hair. Woody, citrus and something sweet.

"Please forgive me, Kendal. I've been an idiot. It's been madness since you went away. Overwhelming. The residents, the staff miss you. They're all desperate to hear you're OK."

Kendal snorted. "Nobody has been in touch for weeks. They weren't supposed to tell you where I am either."

Gary covered his face. "It's been so difficult, Kendal. I'm so glad you're all right. At least, I hope you are."

Kendal stood. "I love it here. Good job, nice people, loads of fun and nobody gets angry or pompous." She'd found her voice. "Tell Rosie she can have Flat 4 for as long as she likes. I'll take whatever she offers."

"Everyone's been trying to contact you. You never answer phone calls or emails.

Kendal sighed. "I don't care. I don't need to. No point looking back is there? Jurassic Court is ancient history. And so are you, Gary. You're Gone-Gary!"

The warden's face was as pale as his knuckles. They both jumped as thunder crashed outside the door.

"You're going to get wet in the campsite, Mister Tough guy."

"I haven't bought a tent," said Gary. "I missed the boat, looking for you all day. Could I bunk on the floor? I'm so sorry, I'm such an idiot."

The crashing outside the door was getting louder. The wind seemed to be shouting her name.

"Ken----dal, Ken----dal," it whined.

"There's someone outside," said Gary. "Are you expecting a visitor?"

"No," said Kendal. "I want to go to sleep."

"Shall I answer it?"

"Yeah, on your way out."

Gary opened the door, and the wind blew it wide. A soaking wet Nish swayed in the doorway holding a pair of walking boots. "What big feet you have Kendal Tudge," he slurred, and beamed at Gary. "Oh hello, there. And who are you?"

"I'm Gary Vaughan, Kendal's friend and those are mine." He grabbed the boots. "Who are you?"

The librarian tried to offer his hand but couldn't let go of the door handle. He swung into the room and held on to the edge of the table. "Anaish Anand. Pleased to me you. Meet you, I mean. And I am…"

"Very drunk," said Kendal. "Go back to the church Nish. The storm is getting dangerous."

"I am, I am…" Nish rolled his eyes and attempted to stand straight. "I am Kendal Tudge's boyfriend. And she is my girlfriend." He crashed onto the table.

Gary, who was trying to find space to put his boots, stared at Kendal.

"Is he?"

"It's none of your business, but no. I don't have a boyfriend, or a girlfriend, or a dog, or a cat, or…" Nish began to groan. The cabin was far too small for three people. Especially one who might chuck. Nish smelled disgusting. He probably had already.

Kendal folded her arms and forced herself to stand. "Gary, I want you to go now and take Nish with you. He's staying in the church and you can stay with him. There'll be some bell ringers camping out there too. Maybe some sailors as well. There's cushions and rugs there and you can borrow my torch. Leave it at the tavern tomorrow."

Gary tried to speak but Kendal had climbed into the bed and pulled the duvet over her head. She heard him pull Nish towards the door.

"Come on, mate. Let's get you home."

The door slammed. Kendal waited till the footsteps

321

disappeared and slunk out of bed. She locked the door and carried the mugs to the sink. She couldn't resist reading Gary's tea bag tag.

Be kind to yourself and let the right one in.

Kendal shook her head and hurled the tea bags into the bin. The condom packet peeked out from below the balled-up thong.

"Kendal, you idiot," she murmured. "Plastics go in the non-combustible bin."

She had never felt so exhausted. Or old.

Tomorrow, she'd sort it.

And the bin.

36

Sleepy Time lied. Kendal was awake all night. It wasn't the storm; it was the aches and pains sweeping through her body, and the crazy mess in her mind. What was Gone-Gary doing? Why had he come to Gull Island with clinging clothes and a clean smell? What did he mean by madness at Jurassic Court since she'd gone?

Kendal listed Jurassic Court's possible snitchers. Prue had sent a postcard so she knew the address, Audrey wouldn't be but she might have told Brian and he was always gossiping. Philip was a possible, Clare could have mentioned it. Pointless guessing. More important to devise a strategy for the next day. Meanwhile her stomach had bloated horribly. The extended lump made her look pregnant. The deluge of blood in the toilet bowl made it clear she wasn't.

Kendal dragged the duvet over her head and stuffed tampons in her ears. At seven the storm stopped. She lifted the blind and surveyed the puddle-covered fields. There'd be no day trippers with this going on. She could afford a lie-in. At eight fifteen, the bells began to peal. Irritating, but not as loud to her as they must be to Gary and Nish in the church (unless they'd got into a fight and fallen off a cliff.) Kendal grinned. Men were ridiculous!

Kendal cooked eggs, made a pot of strong coffee and had a long shower. Her stomach had deflated, and the period pain subsided. She dug deep in her rucksack and found a tube of foundation, a mascara wand and an eyebrow pencil. With food inside and subtle make-up outside, she felt almost normal.

Gary claimed the residents had been trying to communicate with her but Kendal couldn't find out unless she visited the Wi-Fi router in the church which would mean risking a meeting with Nish or Gary. Cai had a booster in the office which he let staff access if they needed to get online for something critical. She'd not asked to use it before but finding out who at Jurassic Court had sent messages was critical. She missed her friends and desperately wanted to discover if Gary's assertion was true.

Kendal pulled on her hoodie, turned the sign on her door to Unavailable, and crossed the empty yard to Cai's office. The manager sat hunched in front of the weather charts.

"Morning Cai, can I use your hotspot please?"

"When you ask like that, sweetheart, how can I refuse? Plug it in there."

Cai swivelled his chair towards Kendal. "Glad to see you're looking lovely again. I was concerned yesterday. Now, look at this weather. This low-pressure front on the way means no boat for at least two days so the helicopter will be coming. This will be your first one, isn't it?"

"Looking forward to it, Cai. Being ground crew, yeh? Another string to my bow."

"Get used to it, girl. If you're planning to stay till winter there'll be plenty of helicopter days."

Kendal's phone erupted with beeps and alerts. Emails, texts, and messages poured in.

Cai patted her arm. "You're popular. Hope it doesn't mean you'll be off. Hard to get good staff like you."

Kendal blinked. She'd never had good feedback from a manager before. She waited for a but, followed by the rest of the shit sandwich. Nothing. He meant it.

"Um, I don't know what my plans are," she mumbled.

"Something to do with the persistent bugger who arrived yesterday, is it?" said Cai.

"It was you who told him where I was?"

"Sorry, Kendal. He said it was a matter of life and death. Shall I get Taks and the boys to chase him away?

Kendal was examining her phone. "Mmm, no, yes. I don't know. Sorry Cai I need to concentrate on my messages."

"Go ahead, girl. But shout if you need help. No man is an island, as the bard said."

Kendal began scrolling. Gary had told the truth; forty-three emails from Jurassic Court; ten texts from Clare, fifteen WhatsApp messages from Carla and Emma and three voicemails from an unknown number.

She hurried to her cabin and made another pot of coffee. She'd start with Clare because her silence had been the most upsetting. Yet Clare's texts were mystifying, full of confusing comments about cautions, trustee pronouncements and Dominic's direct action. No mention of cats, family or the library. She'd re-examine later.

Kendal turned to Carla and Emma's WhatsApp stream which was called The Cautions and featured hazy photos of crowds around the gates of Jurassic Court. Dominic from the library appeared to be standing on a pillar and, in a blurry video clip, he threw flowers at a blonde woman with a clipboard. The clearest images featured the Boston fern Prue had given Kendal. Different residents carried it in various locations: Brian astride the Rascal, Wendy across the day room sofa, Jennifer atop the mini trampoline. Albert held it by his face and seemed to be feeding it crisps. Kendal smiled seeing the residents. They looked like they were having fun and she was pleased to see Albert hadn't been pushed out. Nice of Carla and Emma to send so many pictures but it would have been helpful if they had typed a few captions. Their final post was a link to *Spotlight*, the local television news, followed by eight emoticons of champagne bottles. Without a signal Kendal couldn't connect.

She opened a packet of crisps and pressed play for the voicemails from an unknown number.

"Hiya Kendal, Arlo here. Pam's great-grandson. Phoning to thank you for her ring. Poor old thing was so confused. It was great to hear you'd found it. Thanks for all the help you gave her, especially getting her online. All the best to Jurassic Court. You're a great gang."

The next message was a week later. Why was he phoning again? Perhaps he had changed his mind, had started to query how Kendal had found the ring, or why it took so long to be found after Pam declared it lost? Kendal's stomach lurched. She had done wrong, and here was the punishment.

"Hello Kendal. I've talked to my family, and we want to sell the ring and give the money to the warden to improve digital provision at Jurassic Court. My company is going to match whatever we make in the sale. It'll be over fifteen thousand, at least. Get in touch and we can discuss what you need."

Kendal's eyes filled. This was amazing. She didn't deserve it.

The final message was from two days earlier.

"The warden's told me about your situation. What a mess! He wouldn't tell me where you are but, if you're still working with older people, get in touch. Maybe my company could fund you to deliver digital workshops elsewhere? Equipment is no use without skilled facilitators. By, the way, I never believed you were a resident. Too gorgeous by far if it isn't an inappropriate comment."

Kendal wished she could Google Arlo. He hadn't look impressive at Pam's funeral, but was clearly successful if his company could donate large gifts to retirement homes. If he was entrepreneurial, he might understand deficit financing and be sympathetic to explanations about pawning Pam's ring to solve a cash flow problem. The Derbyfield fiasco was the only wrongdoing she'd still not shared. She longed to be absolved.

So far, only Arlo's voicemails made sense. Kendal yawned, poured more coffee and opened the newest email from Audrey who still hadn't mastered predictive text.

"Subject: Victory is sweet.
Dearest Kendal, Jurassic Cautions have desiccated council flunkeys and the Thrusts have catapulted and say J.C. welcomes multi generation living.
So you can come back with tail held hi.

PS – Rosta next door is buying Pam's flat so Doom, our amazing activist is sofa surging in your flat. PPS - Philip's special friend is moving in too.
PLEASE get in touch. We all mess you. Xxxxxyxxxx"

Kendal frowned. Audrey was adorable but barking.

There was a soft knocking at her door. She opened it reluctantly. Gone-Gary and Nish. Both damp and unshaven, but no bruises or broken noses.

"Can we come in, Kendal?" said Gary, hanging his head.

"Only if you can explain what the hell is going on."

Nish opened his mouth.

"Not you, Nish, him!"

The men shuffled into the tiny space and stood sheepishly by the bed. Kendal took the chair and sipped her coffee.

"Well, speak then."

Nish stared at the coffee pot and tried to reach the crisp bag. Gary stared at the floor.

"After you left, the residents were very unsettled and, er, they made their feelings clear." Gary picked a nail tag. "There was a dirty protest."

Kendal flinched. "Ugh! How?"

"Covered the fidget blankets in potting compost."

Kendal smiled.

"Spread Prue's lip balm sticks over the windows."

Kendal shuddered.

"And threw crocus bulbs in the pond."

Kendal nodded. The gifts from charities had found a use, at last. Dear crazy Audrey and Prue. Always thinking creatively. Never wasting anything.

"What did they do with the key rings?"

"How do you know about those?" exclaimed Gary.

"I'm asking the questions here!" growled Kendal.

Gary stared at his feet. "They linked them together to make a chain and locked the gates."

"Genius," said Kendal. "Audrey's been trying to get rid of those freebies for years."

"Actually, it was Wendy's idea," said Gary. "She organised passive blockades at Greenham Common."

He lifted his head and looked directly at Kendal. She forced herself not to smile. It felt both strange and familiar to be talking about the residents.

"Are these students?" asked Nish. "They wrecked one of our libraries at Oxford because we stocked Rudyard Kipling."

"No, Nish," said Gary. "These are mature people who care about society. And particularly care for a very special person who unfortunately I misjudged."

"Then what happened?" snapped Kendal.

"Clare and Dominic brought the placards from their library campaign and Prue painted new messages on the back. Dominic chained himself to the gates and Clare got the television crew over. It snowballed. The council and the trustees were inundated with complaints and on Wednesday the constitution was changed at an emergency residents' meeting. Now the complex is multi-generational and anyone of any age can live there, providing the committee approve. No one can be forced out, whatever their age, medical condition, or sexuality."

Kendal forced herself not to clap. She channelled Tudge Trudge and kept her face in neutral. "So why are you here Gary? Why didn't they ring the office and tell me?"

Gary reddened. "I told them not to. I wanted to see you in person and explain how I'd overreacted. I was angry, confused and I should have been kinder. I wanted to be the one to convince you to return to Jurassic Court and I'm here to ask for forgiveness and to beg you to come home."

Nish clapped. "This is so dramatic. Better than an abandoned seal." He prodded Kendal. "What you going to do, Ms Tudge?"

Kendal stood and opened her door. "Get some space. Go away and leave me alone."

Nish grabbed the crisp bag and strode outside. Kendal turned to Gary.

"Both of you!" she yelled.

37

The pub was packed with excited guests waiting for the helicopter to take them home. No one cared about the extra cost or the long delay, they were simply thrilled at the prospect of a six-minute flight instead of a two-hour vomiting boat trip. Everyone was happy except Gone-Gary who sat hunched in a corner seat, staring as Kendal rushed between bar and kitchen.

"Go to the staff room, girl," ordered Cai. "Get the hi-vis kit on. Remember to keep your head down and your spirits up. And don't take the ear defenders off."

The landing field was on the island's highest spot. Kendal could feel the phone in her pocket vibrating as it found the signal and more messages came through. Being ground crew for the helicopter was full-on and Kendal had to concentrate. No time to check messages or think about the warden and Jurassic Court.

Only six passengers at a time could fly in the tiny helicopter. The pilot kept the engine running while arrivals climbed out and leavers climbed in. The noise and the downdraft were all-consuming. Just a few minutes between waving off the departing passengers and corralling the next six into the correct waiting spot. Her fellow crew were old hands, practised at holding back over-eager passengers and supporting the anxious ones.

After six trips, the pilot switched off the engine to take a break. Kendal slipped into the Mermaid Tavern to grab a coffee and a snack. She tried to avoid Gary, but he spotted her and darted past the piles of luggage to grab her arm.

"Kendal, please give me a chance. We need to talk."

"Let go! I'm busy. A hundred passengers to get onto the helicopter today, plus a waiting list."

"I have to get back. Emma and Carla are working their socks off."

"So am I."

Kendal strode through the Staff Only swing door to the kitchen where Australian-Amber was sliding pasties out of the oven. She slapped one on a plate and handed Kendal a mug of coffee.

"Take off your hi-vis or you'll cook in here."

Kendal began to eat and remembered the vibrating phone. Two texts from Clare had downloaded.

> Hi K, hope you having a wild time in Gull Island.
> Sorry my messages are confusing.
> That's chemo brain for you. Only four more sessions.
> It's rubbish but it's worth it.

The pasty was impossible to swallow. Kendal dropped her mug and pushed the plate away. Clare was having chemotherapy! She opened the second text.

> Read back my texts. I realise I didn't tell you.
> Sorry, hope it is not a shock. Try not to worry.
> It's breast cancer, but the prognosis is good. They got it early."

Images of her parents in the hospice raced through Kendal's mind. Not another person she loved getting cancer. Especially after she'd given all those clothes and ornaments to the cancer research shop. It wasn't fair!

Kendal rushed to the staff toilet and collapsed on the floor. Iris and Lola were cleaning the washbasins.

"You, OK, Kendal?"

Kendal vomited noisily. She limped to a sink. Iris offered hand sanitiser. Lola passed paper towels.

"My friend back in Dorset, the best friend I've ever had, has got breast cancer. She didn't tell me, I didn't know." Tears poured down her face.

"You better go, hon," said Iris.

"Take the helicopter. Staff are allowed to in family emergencies," added Lola.

Kendal trembled. "She's not family. I don't have any." She sobbed loudly. "I can't let Cai down."

Lola hugged Kendal. "Tell him it's your mother."

"We'll cover for you," said Iris. "I'd rather be ground crew than cleaning."

Kendal washed her hands and surveyed herself in the toilet mirror. The bright light accentuated every line and freckle and her hair was like straw from the wind and salt. Her pale lips, faded eyebrows and chin needed attention. She'd stopped making an effort.

"I can't lie anymore."

Cai handed Kendal a small brandy and led her into the office. "We'll get you on the last flight, girl. No charge. I've had a bell ringer begging for a job. She won't be as good as you, obviously and I suppose she'll be constantly ringing the bloody things, but she'll squeeze into Cabin 3 and be grateful for it. I'll be able to exploit her mercilessly." He hugged Kendal. "Give us a shout anytime if you want to come back. We'll always have room for you, Kendal Tudge."

Kendal gulped the brandy. "You're the best boss I've ever had, Cai. The first not to sack me too."

Cai looked over her shoulder. "That bloke is outside the office. Do you want me to deal with him?"

"I can fight my own battles. You get back to the bar and tell the pilot to hurry. There are loads of passengers to get off the island." Kendal grinned at Cai. "Including me now."

Kendal handed her hi-vis jacket to an excited Iris. The rain was pouring again. She jogged to her cabin and slammed the door behind her. Nish was lying on the bed reading a book. Mercifully, fully dressed.

"Ah, there you are my favourite gushing spring," he drawled.

Kendal balanced her rucksack on the chair and began to pull clothes out of her cupboard. "I'm not a gushing spring. Keld has nothing to do with my name."

"Oh, apologies, Ms Tudge. Why don't you sit down with me?"

"I haven't time. I'm leaving Gull Island today."

"Gary's persuaded you, then? I'm honoured to lose you to such a worthy opponent. He is a terrific chap and so devoted. Coming all this way to plight his troth."

Kendal wrapped the ammonite in a pair of pants and stuffed it into a side pocket.

Nish folded his book. "I do hope you and Gary might visit me one day in Oxford. I'd love to show you around."

Kendal pulled the Busy-Available sign off her door and handed it to Nish. "Hang this in the church to warn the bell ringers next time you're seducing someone."

Nish grinned "There won't be a next time. The church is sacred to your memory."

"Nish, can you go now? Been great to know you but I need to retrieve stuff from under the bed."

Nish moved in for a kiss, but Kendal brandished her vibrator at him. "And, incidentally, you have not lost me to Gary. I am leaving because my friend is ill, and I'm going to see her."

"Ah, right. Sorry to hear that. See you around."

Nish turned the sign to Available, hung it round his neck, and sauntered into the rain. Kendal checked the back of the wardrobe and found Uncle Clem's tweed hat. It still looked good. She would wear it to contain her hair in the helicopter downdraft. She was bending to clear the food cupboard when the door slammed again.

"Nish, I have not got time. Piss off." Two Kit Kats lurked at the back. Long past their sell-by date.

"It's not Nish, it's me."

The low slow burr.

Kendal felt faint. She could hear the helicopter engine roaring.

She stood too quickly. Cabin 3 was whirling too.

Gary caught Kendal. He pulled her close. Sandalwood with top notes of spearmint.

"I love this hat," he murmured. "Ever since I first saw you in it."

The door rattled and rain splashed against the roof. Kendal couldn't tell if the beating sound was her, Gary, or the helicopter. They stayed entangled as the noise disappeared. She closed her eyes. His lips brushed over her forehead, and he tucked a tendril of hair behind her ear.

"I've wanted to touch your hair for so long," he whispered.

Kendal grinned. "The blonde, the grey, or the in-between I've got now?" Her voice disappeared into his T-shirt. The yellow one he wore to feed the birds.

"I love every hair, whatever colour or style," said Gary. He stepped back to look into her eyes. "And I love you, Kendal. So much."

Kendal said nothing. She kept her eyes shut. Being held by Gary reminded her of something. Or somewhere. She should reply to Gary's declaration, but she had to hang on to the sensation.

The roar of the returning helicopter broke the spell.

"I've got to finish packing."

"Me too. I'll see you in the queue."

News of Kendal's departure spread, and when Gary and Kendal approached the helicopter field all the staff were waiting. One by one they hugged and fist thumped Kendal. Very different from the way she'd left THRUm.

As soon as she tracked a signal Kendal sent a text to Clare.

Coming back to Bloscombe.
Can't wait to see you.
We'll get through this.

Amber had created a goodbye card featuring Kendal's head on a puffin's body, Lola had liberated a puffer gilet from lost property, and Nish had bought a musical snow globe of the Gull Island church and its bells. Kendal stuffed the gifts into the front pocket of her rucksack. She held her hat with one hand and grabbed Gary's arm as they ran, heads low, to the helicopter door. Lola and Iris snapped the seat belts tight and blew kisses whilst running backwards from the deafening aircraft.

The wind and rain showed no sign of easing. The helicopter felt more precarious now Kendal was a passenger instead of ground crew and the noise was much scarier without ear defenders. Gary clenched his teeth. Kendal squeezed his hand.

"The flight's only six minutes, Gary," she shouted into his ear. "Quicker than getting the residents to the gate on a Well-being Walk."

Rain dripped down Gary's orange cagoule. His huge legs pressed against her thighs. He held out his hand. A Kit Kat nestled in his palm. Kendal laughed and opened the wrapper.

The helicopter ascended from the field and they stared through the tiny window watching the ground crew waving. It swooped across the field and within seconds they were above the lighthouse, the harbour, and then the heaving sea.

Kendal split the chocolate bar and handed half to Gary. He sucked the chocolate off the end and winked. She felt the rush.

Four more minutes till they landed. If the rotor blades failed, or Gary ran amok and opened the door, she had to confront the one thing spoiling her happiness. No amount of Sleepy Time could absolve her. She had to confess. She pushed her mouth against his soft ear lobe.

"Gary, I didn't find Pam's ring in my room. I found it in hers."

The warden frowned. His hand touched the emergency door handle.

Kendal gulped.

He smiled.

"I know. I worked it out. Don't worry, I know you had your reasons."

Kendal bit her lip. How did he know? He moved his hand from the handle and held hers tight.

They'd reached the mainland and seconds later they were hovering over a field of sheep unperturbed at sharing their space with a thunderous machine.

The ground crew unlocked the door, and Gary climbed out. He held out his hand for Kendal and they followed a yellow line across the grass to a hut that doubled as a luggage terminal. Gary picked up her rucksack and swung it over his cagoule. It was still raining.

Gary unzipped his thick waterproof and pulled Kendal towards him. The helicopter was preparing to leave. She needed to be sure.

"How did you know? Can you forgive me?"

Gary squeezed her tight. She could feel his heartbeat above the helicopter roar.

"Flat 4 was deep cleaned when Clem died. It would have been found then if it was there. I checked the room myself before you moved in." He kissed Kendal's nose. "I wanted it to be perfect for the princess who didn't do voicemails and had a thing about weird smells, acronyms and puns."

"You knew?"

"I worked it out and of course I forgive you. None of us are perfect."

He was right. Kendal released her breath. She was forgiven.

They waved as the helicopter took off with six new passengers.

"Are you sure you're happy to leave?" shouted Gary.

"I can't wait to be at Jurassic Court," she said. "Back home in the Home."

They followed the pavement-less lane towards the car park, passing a small campsite. Kendal counted the tents. Two large green, one small orange. Horrible weather for camping.

Gary squeezed Kendal's hand. "Everyone's going to be so happy to see you. My job will be a thousand times better with you back. You could work too. Pam's great-grandson wants to fund activities. You could be the activities coordinator, if you wanted."

Kendal nodded. Everything was possible.

"Any rules about inappropriate staff relationships?" she asked. "THRUm was obsessed with those kinds of things."

Gary laughed. "Well, it's never happened before. But no, there will be no rules to stop me and you doing what we should have started months ago."

A black electric BMW hummed past. Kendal flinched. Gary squeezed her against the hedge, encasing her with his heavy waterproof. She could smell blackberries, mown grass and bacon. Perhaps the campers were having a good time, after all.

Like she did, long ago, with her parents in their orange tent.

Orange. Like Gary's waterproof.

Gary's embrace reminded her of how it felt in the tent. Snugly tucked between mum and dad, listening to the rain and staring at the canvas roof. She'd been safe, protected and loved. Like now.

Acknowledgements

My father provided inspiration and my protagonist's name. William Kendal Fry (1927 to 2021) lived in a residential home on the Jurassic Coast. When my life felt exhausting I fantasised about moving in.

Thanks to readers Vesna Goldsworthy, Wendy O'Shea-Meddour, Carla Jenkins, Kate Wilson, Emma Hillier, Susanne von Englelhardt, Ashley Pharoah, Amber Husain, Sarah Scally, Sally Hounsham and Siobhan Harrison.

Huge love to the wonderful Huxleys in my life Dom, Matt and Chris. Cheers 'en.

9 781068 518829